the accidental life of greg millar

ALSO BY AIMEE ALEXANDER

Pause to Rewind

All We Have Lost

the accidental life of greg millar

Aimee Alexander

This is a work of fiction. Names, characters, organizations, places, events, and incidents are either products of the author's imagination or are used fictitiously.

This book was first published by Penguin Ireland as *Love Comes Tumbling.*

Published by Lake Union Publishing, Seattle
www.apub.com

ISBN-13: 9781503934184
ISBN-10: 1503934187

Cover design by Lisa Horton

Printed in the United States of America

To the girl
who can carry off the name Aimée Serendipity.
You make me proud.

1.

A bird has just flown into my car – a moving car, a moving bird, heading in different directions yet somehow magically intersecting. I thought, at first, that it had simply flown close to my open window, passing by on its way somewhere else, but a manic flapping behind my head proves otherwise.

'It's a blackbird,' says Fint, beside me.

'I don't care what it is, just get it out before I crash the bloody car!' If he hadn't been smoking, we wouldn't be in this mess.

I put on my hazard lights and swerve onto the hard shoulder. We hop out, Fint leaving his door wide open. He runs to the back and bangs at the window. The bird flies up front and out. In a blur, it's free.

'Now that's what I call spooky,' he says.

'I know. Weird.'

We stand looking at each other.

'An omen,' says Fint, eyes wide in an effort to look menacing.

I smile. Fint is about as menacing as a sandwich.

We get back in.

Fint looks over his seat. 'By the way, he shat on your upholstery.'

'Thanks.'

He smiles, pulls out his laptop and opens it up.

~

The diversion has made us late for a meeting with our biggest client, a publishing company that we design book covers for. When you run your own business, punctuality is something you respect. I'm keeping just below the speed limit in the fast lane when I realise we've company. At my bumper is a black Mercedes Sports Convertible. I'm wondering what kind of idiot drives with the top down on a cold March morning when said idiot swerves to overtake me on the inside.

'Unbelievable,' I say.

'What?' asks Fint, looking up from the laptop.

'People like that cause accidents.'

'People like what?'

'That guy just passed on the inside.'

'Oh,' he says and goes back to work.

'"*Oh?*" He could kill someone the way he's driving.'

Fint looks at me, eyes suddenly knowing.

'Stop looking at me like that.'

'Like what?'

'Like you think I'm overreacting because of . . . Oh, forget it.'

'Because of what?'

'You *know* what.'

There's a silence.

'It would have been his birthday today,' he says.

'Don't you think I *know* that?'

He turns to look out of his window.

I loosen my grip on the wheel and inhale deeply. 'I'm sorry.'

He looks back at me. 'I miss him too, Luce. But it's been eighteen months. Maybe it's time to move on.'

'You are the *only* person I'd let away with a comment like that,' I say. Ever since we met at art college, we've shared everything – friendship, career, secrets . . . And now, it seems, painful truths. Only it's not the truth. 'Move on. What does that even mean?'

Up ahead, the lights turn red. I slow to a stop, glance to my left. 'Didn't get far, did he, for all his rushing?'

Fint looks across.

'Here, roll down the window,' I say.

'What? Why?'

'Someone should tell people like him . . .'

'Lucy, you're not a vigilante. You don't *know* him. This is how road rage incidents start.'

I lower the window. Stretch over. 'Excuse me?'

He glances across. Good-looking guy, around forty, tight haircut. He turns down his radio.

'Are you planning on killing someone today?'

He smiles. 'It's not on my agenda, no.' He pauses, then adds, 'Wine gum?'

'*What?*'

He holds out a packet of sweets.

'So it *never* occurred to you that driving like that could cause an accident?'

His smile only widens. 'I'm touched by your concern.'

'Continue to drive like you are and you'll be touched by something with a lot more impact.'

'Lucy,' Fint whispers.

'Has anyone ever told you you look lovely when you're angry?' he calls across, as though nothing has ever rocked his world.

I return to the wheel, roll up the window and glance straight ahead. 'Gobshite.'

'Cute gobshite.'

'Fintan, do you *have* to look on every man as a potential conquest?'

'*Potential?* My dear, you underestimate me.'

I smile. The lights go green and I pull away. Fast.

The Merc stays level with us.

'Ignore him,' I say. 'Fintan, *stop* looking over. You'll just encourage him.'

'If anyone's encouraging him, it's you. Slow down. Jesus.'

The Merc catches us, but has to slow behind a tangerine Nissan Micra doing, I don't know, thirty?

I slap the steering wheel. 'Ha! Got him!'

I check the rear-view mirror. He's passed the Micra and is whipping into the inside lane. I accelerate. As does he. Neck and neck, I peer across. He's like an ad for tooth whitener. I raise an eyebrow, turn back to the road.

'You're taking on a Mercedes, Lucy. Do you think that's wise?'

Almost by way of an answer, it eases ahead of us.

We round a bend and I smile. He's stuck behind a slow car in the fast lane. I join the line of traffic on the inside, which is moving faster. I keep my eyes on the road as we overtake him.

'You absolute hypocrite!' says Fint.

That's when reality hits. I slow down and let the traffic go ahead as guilt crushes down on me, worse than ever, guilt that I can go on without Brendan, live, breathe, function . . . even forget how he died.

~

I indicate and turn off for the industrial estate where our client, Copperplate Press, one of Dublin's leading publishers and wholesalers, is based. A black Mercedes Sports Convertible is parked in front of the building, its top coming up.

Fint closes his laptop and looks up. 'Hey, isn't that . . . ?'

'Don't. Look. Over. Wait till he goes in.'

Fint hops out.

They meet in front of the Merc, say a few words, then look my way.

I pretend I've dropped something.

When I finally surface, I see that they're coming over. Right, well, I'm not staying here. I step out of the car, chin high.

'Ready, Fintan? Or are you just going to stand around chatting all day?'

'Hello,' Racer Boy says with that smile of his.

I nod and walk past them.

He rushes ahead of me and holds the door.

'Exhilarating,' he says, following me into the lobby.

I stop and turn. 'I'm sorry?'

'The race. Exhilarating!'

I raise an eyebrow. 'I'd have described it as dangerous.'

'Why do it, then? If it was so *dangerous*?'

Grinning, Fint passes us, heading for reception.

I walk over to the black leather couch.

Racer Boy follows. He sits at the other end. Unfortunately, it's a two-seater.

I pick up a newspaper. 'Better tell them you're here,' I say, nodding to the desk.

'Time enough,' he replies, not budging. 'Look, I'm sorry if my driving offended or annoyed you, or whatever the problem is.'

'There's no problem,' I say, without looking up from the paper.

'It's just, the way you took off back there; I thought you were challenging me. No. To tell you the truth, I thought you were flirting.'

I stare at him. 'Well, you were wrong. I was definitely *not* flirting.'

'My mistake. It's the car; people are always trying to race—'

'Not me.'

'You know,' he says, leaning towards me. 'You have a remarkable face.'

'Look. That might work for—'

I'm interrupted by Matt O'Hagan, MD of Copperplate Press, who's practically sprinting across reception, shouting, 'Greg! Greg!' at the top of his already loud voice. Matt: small man with the presence of a low-flying aircraft.

Racer Boy stands. Matt, reaching him, extends a hand. They shake. It strikes me then, as Matt gushes over him, that he didn't have to announce his presence for Matt to know he'd arrived. If you knew Matt, you'd appreciate how unusual that is.

'You found us easy enough? We'd have sent a car . . .' I've never known Matt to send a car anywhere for anyone.

'Actually, I enjoyed the drive.' This is directed at me. 'I was just introducing myself to . . .'

Matt finally realises I'm not a mannequin. 'Oh, Lucy, Lucy, hello, hello.'

'Hello, Matt.' I stand, smile, shake his meaty hand. 'We're here for a meeting with Orla. There's Fintan behind you.'

'I see, I see,' he says without turning. 'So, you've met Greg Millar, then?'

Whoa. Back up. Greg Millar? The writer? I call to mind the publicity shot on the jacket of his latest bestseller and give it a haircut. It *is* him. Knowing my luck, Copperplate has just signed him.

'Lucy, here,' Matt blares, 'designs our book jackets. Does a bloody good job, too, don't you, Luce?'

He has never, until now, called me Luce.

I produce a smile from somewhere. 'Nice to meet you . . .' I've a problem saying his name.

'Greg.' He holds out a hand.

'Greg,' I confirm, shaking it and trying to ignore the look of amusement that's spreading across his face.

Fintan, like the cavalry, arrives to let me know that Orla's ready for us. Best news I've had today.

2.

Next day, I'm at my desk, working on a corporate logo for a financial institution and trying not to nod off, when Matt rings. I move the receiver an inch from my ear and wonder what he wants. Matt never gets involved in day-to-day business.

'I want to set up a brainstorming session. We've signed Greg Millar! I want all heads together for the marketing campaign of his new title. Greg himself will be sitting in, so I want a good show. You and Fintan from Get Smart.'

Just demand the managing partners. I try to sound enthusiastic. 'When were you thinking?'

'Monday. Give Glenda a call to firm up a time. I've asked her to get a copy of the manuscript over to you. Remind her when you're talking to her, would you? Oh, and it might be wise to get cracking on some ideas before the meeting.' He hangs up.

This is the first time I've heard of an author sitting in on a Copperplate Press brainstorm. But then, Greg Millar is not just any author. His books hit Number One all over the world before they even go on sale, such are the pre-orders. Matt's been in the business long enough to know that authors like Millar don't walk in off the street every day, and when they do, you bring out the dancing girls.

~

Five days later, I follow Fintan into the boardroom of Copperplate Press, which has undergone quite a transformation. On the walls are posters of Millar's published titles. Running up the centre of the table are hardback and paperback editions, with media folders forming a mini skyline at the end. On the sideboard, refreshments have been laid out: pains au chocolat, coffee, croissants. I'm sure Millar has seen all this before. And yet he looks enthusiastic, standing up and beaming at us as he shakes our hands.

There are only two seats left: one beside Millar, which Fintan takes, and one opposite. I feel his eyes on me as I sit. I busy myself unloading my briefcase, wishing Matt would hurry up and get started.

At last, the MD clears his throat. I look up to find Millar studying me. There's something innocent about his smile. It seems to say, 'Great to see you again.' No more. My return smile is professional. Then I turn my attention to Matt, who's standing now and looking around the table.

'Thank you all for coming. Before we start, I'd like to share what a great personal thrill it is for me to have an author of Greg Millar's calibre join our list here at Copperplate Press.' He turns to the novelist. 'Congratulations, Greg, on your decision to move to an indigenous publisher in your home market. Inspired! *Inspired!* Let me take this opportunity to personally guarantee that you'll receive every support available here at Copperplate Press.'

'Thank you, Matt,' Millar says with an appreciative nod.

Matt's eyes sweep the table. 'You'll all, by now, have read the manuscript. So, Lucy, any thoughts on covers?'

He *always* does this, lulls you into thinking he'll waffle on forever, then boom! He springs. I look at my spiky-haired, dark-suited partner, who has agreed to do the talking.

'You can stay sitting, if you like, Lucy,' says Matt.

Fintan nods for me to go ahead as it's clear that's what Matt wants.

'Thanks, Matt,' I say, glued to my chair. I switch to pitch mode. 'Well, firstly, I'd like to say that I really enjoyed *A River Too Wide.*' I feel Millar's eyes on me. 'Fintan and I' – I look at my partner, hoping that everyone else will, too – 'had our own brainstorm back at the office. We feel that, while the jacket should complement the traditional look of . . .' – *What should I call him?* – 'Greg's' – *Cringe* – 'previous titles, we think that, this time around, the cover could focus more on the main character than the plot. Cooper is such a great protagonist—'

'Great idea!' Millar interrupts. 'Why hasn't anyone thought of that before?'

'I imagine that it made sense, in the beginning, to have the jackets primarily indicate the genre because you were establishing your reader base,' I say. 'We feel that the covers should continue to do that, just shift the focus to Cooper. He has such a loyal following. He's another Morse, really, isn't he?' I stop. I'm coming off as a fan. Which I actually am. I just don't want Millar to know it.

'Do you have anything for us to look at, Lucy?' asks Matt, pushing it as usual.

'Only roughs. I need to source some images before showing you anything.'

'Hmm.' He looks at Millar.

'I'd love to see your roughs, Lucy,' the author says, with what seems like genuine enthusiasm rather than the double entendre I initially suspected.

Matt's nodding furiously. I decide, there and then, to bill him extra for the job. I pull my work from a folder and hand it across to Millar.

'They're just concepts, at this stage,' I explain.

He takes a moment. Then: 'Wow! These are incredible.' He passes them to Matt.

'*Yes!*' he enthuses – most likely because Millar's just done the same.

It's decided that Get Smart should go ahead and develop the discussed concepts. The brainstorm moves to other areas of marketing – in-store display, author tours, signings, talks, PR, advertising, social media. Orla, in marketing, is a natural performer. Jim, the sales manager, is equally enthusiastic. The PR woman, Debbie, suggests a list of possible angles. The only person who doesn't say much is Emma, the managing editor. And I get that. How much editing is an author of Greg Millar's calibre likely to need?

As we're leaving the boardroom, Copperplate's hottest new property suggests that we celebrate. Matt names a local pub. I open my mouth to make my excuses, but get a look from my client. It's settled. I'm going.

~

We get to the pub just before the post-work rush. Matt spots that the snug is free and makes a dash for it. Fint remembers an urgent call and excuses himself, leaving Millar next to me. I look at my disappearing partner and realise that there *is* no urgent call. My self-appointed Cupid is popping out to refill his quiver.

We're packed tight. Matt dominates the conversation, but knows how to keep it lively and sharp. Everyone chips in, except me. At first, I'm happy listening, but I soon become aware that Millar has gone equally quiet, speaking only when asked a direct question. I feel he wants to turn to me and say something. I avoid looking at him, yet notice his every movement, word, breath. Our legs are touching. I move mine away by crossing them. It does nothing to stop the tension that is building between us. *What the hell is wrong with me? I don't even* like *this guy.* My face is burning. I have to get out. Cool down. Get a grip.

I stand and excuse myself.

People have to file out to let me pass.

The cool air in the toilets is a relief. Piped music, something light from the charts, makes everything seem more normal. I look around. Nothing like porcelain lavatories to bring you back to earth. I read the graffiti – 'Beware Limbo Dancers'. Arrows point to the bottom of the door. On the other side of it, high heels make quick, uneven steps. Their owner slams the door next to me and takes a long, noisy leak. She sighs with the simple, uncomplicated pleasure of relief. I remember why I'm here and begin to tense. Maybe I could slip away. Would anyone notice? I think of Matt, then a solution. I'll just sit in a different place. It'll be fine.

I wash my hands, hum to the music, and look in the mirror. One last deep breath. I walk out.

Wham. I crash straight into him.

'Oh, God, sorry,' I say, stepping back.

He steadies me. 'You OK?'

'Yeah, yeah, fine.'

Three seconds of silence, then, 'Have dinner with me, Lucy.'

I wait for his smile, but it doesn't come, leaving nothing to hide behind. 'I can't . . . I'm sorry.'

'Why not?' he asks with childlike simplicity.

'I'm . . . with someone . . . Sorry. But thanks. Really.' Brendan is private.

'Is it serious?'

'Sorry?'

'Your relationship . . . Is it serious?'

'Yes, it is.'

'Well, that's no good.' His smile is back. 'Whatever happened to fun?'

It died.

'Come out with me, Lucy. And forget about serious . . .'

'I can't.' I hear the finality in my voice.

So, apparently, does he. 'I'm sorry. Of course you can't.' He shakes his head as if he was stupid to ask.

'I'd better get back,' I say.

'Of course.'

It's a while before he rejoins the group. Not long after that, he leaves.

~

At work, next day, I pick up the phone to his voice.

'Lucy, hi. Greg Millar here. I was wondering if we might discuss some ideas for the cover of *A River Too Wide*.'

'Ah, OK, sure.' But not really. No author has ever contacted me directly. 'What were you thinking?'

'Oh. I was hoping we could meet to discuss it.'

I wonder if this really is business.

'You know, Greg, publishers don't really like their authors to deal directly with the designers they use. They like to control the design themselves, you know?'

'It was Matt who gave me your number. How about lunch?'

'I'm sorry, but I'm busy for lunch all week,' I lie. 'It would have to be at our offices.'

'Fine. How about tomorrow?'

Better to get it over with. 'Ten?'

'Ten.'

~

Tomorrow comes. And with it the deadline for the bank logo. By ten, I've already put in four hours. I'm manipulating a computer-generated design, on screen, when Sebastian, one of our trainee designers who doubles as a receptionist, struts into my office wearing a flamboyant mix of pastels – pink, lemon and white, reminding me of Neapolitan ice cream. Behind him is Millar, who has once again managed to elicit special treatment; Sebastian never shows visitors in, just buzzes us when they arrive at 'reception' (his desk). And yet here he is, offering to make tea and coffee, something that he is always too busy to do. Millar declines. With nothing more to offer, Sebastian reluctantly leaves.

I come from behind the desk to shake the author's hand. He beams, making my planned gesture too formal. I cancel it, leaving myself at a loss – *What am I supposed to do out here between him and the desk?*

'So,' he says, checking a chunky diving watch. 'How much time do we have?'

'An hour should do it, I think.'

'Great. Grab your coat; we're going out.'

My eyes widen. 'I'm sorry. I can't . . . I . . .'

'Oh, come on. Nice spring walk on St Stephen's Green. We'll talk business, get some air, feed the ducks. Think how creative we'll be.'

I look at my desk, then back at him. I think of Matt, our biggest client. 'All right, but I have to be back here at eleven.' I tap my watch to make a point. Because evidence is mounting that Greg Millar doesn't take no for an answer.

~

We do talk business. Then we just talk – not difficult when you share a passion for books. It's strange how unsure he is about his work. He wants to know what he could have done better, which characters could have been improved. As if a) I'd know and b) I'd tell him. I do say what I liked, what worked for me.

'Wow. You'd make a great editor,' he says.

I laugh.

'I'm serious. I should hire you on a freelance basis.'

'You wouldn't be able to afford me,' I joke, with such ease it frightens me.

At twelve – *Is it really twelve?* – he has to go. To collect his children from school. Greg Millar is a dad. It changes my view of him – to someone safer, more human, somehow. We walk to his car. He unlocks it, but doesn't get in.

'So,' he says, smiling. 'Now you know. I'm just a regular guy, not a jumped-up prat in a fast car.'

I look down, embarrassed that he has seen through me.

'Have dinner with me, Lucy.'

Oh God. I think of Brendan. Visualise his face.

'It's just food,' he says.

'I know. It's just that . . .'

'Nothing serious. I swear.' He criss-crosses his heart.

I haven't seen that done since I was a child. It makes me smile.

'Tomorrow,' he says. 'I'll pick you up from work.'

I've enjoyed his company. He lifted my spirits. He's a good guy. I wonder if we could just be friends.

'I'll take your stunned silence as a yes.' He smiles. 'I'll call you in the morning.'

'Well, you can *call* . . .'

Before I get the 'but' out, he says, 'Great!'

I laugh. Because you've got to admire his persistence.

'Can I drop you back to the office?'

I picture my desk covered in pink Post-it notes from Sebastian. I visualise the unfinished logo. 'No, thanks. I feel like a walk.'

That night, in bed, I face reality. Seeing Greg Millar, even for one meal, would be a mistake.

The following day, when he calls, I try to tell him. It proves impossible. He talks like it's a given. He's booked the restaurant. Sounds so enthusiastic. 'No' just won't come out. Oh, God, we're going.

By six, I've adopted a philosophical approach. It's only dinner. I'll keep it superficial. Impersonal. Work-focused. I'll enjoy getting out of the apartment. And I'll leave at eleven. Ten thirty.

He wanted to pick me up at six. I opted for seven thirty. At that exact time, I get a call from security to say that he's downstairs in the lobby. I delay going down, not wanting him to think there's anything special in my having dinner with him. In the bathroom mirror, I make myself look more businesslike than usual.

I take the stairs, like I always do. Rounding the last corner, I see him; perched at the edge of the red leather two-seater in the lobby we share with an architectural firm and PR agency. He's leaning forward, forearms resting on legs, absorbed in *The Irish Times*, frowning. It's the first time I've seen him without him seeing me. He looks freshly showered, cleanly shaved. Crisp white shirt. Denim discarded in favour of linen. That he has made an effort softens something in me. He glances up. Catches me – *Oh, God* – smiling. *Why am I smiling?* He beams, stands and folds the paper. He lands it down on the glass-topped table and starts towards me and I swear it's in slow motion. I laugh. Don't know why.

Closer. He's had a shaving accident. A tiny nick near his ear makes him vulnerable. Human. Borderline adorable. *What is* wrong *with me?* Reaching me, he stoops to kiss my cheek. Then the other. A scent of aftershave fills the intimate space between us. I stop breathing. Avoid his eyes. Remind myself of Brendan.

He takes my hand and we walk, in sync, out into the crisp air. He's humming a song I've always liked. When he gets to the 'knock me over stone cold sober' bit, he sings the words. I look at his profile. And I know I should have said no.

3.

The restaurant is a two-star Michelin off Merrion Square. I've brought some of our bigger clients here for lunch occasionally, but I have never splurged on dinner in my time off. The maître d' greets me like a regular, but Greg like a personal friend. He stays with us for a complimentary pre-dinner drink, then shows us to our table – one of the finest. A reverse snob by nature, I've never been able to fault this place. The art is the real thing – Louis le Brocquy, Roderic O'Conor – the ceiling high, the space open, the walls white to highlight the paintings. Dining tonight are three prominent businessmen, a celebrity dancer and her husband, and a TV anchorwoman. Those I don't recognise have an air of confident, anonymous wealth.

I'm true to the promise I made myself and keep things superficial. This works until we're waiting for our main courses to arrive, when a lull settles.

'Lucy, there's something I've been meaning to tell you. It's a little awkward. Well, I'll just say it.' He pauses. 'Fintan told me about your fiancé.'

'He *what*?'

He puts his hands up. 'No details, just that he died. And that you're . . . vulnerable.'

'*Vulnerable?* I'll give *him* vulnerable.'

'He was just looking out for you. He saw us together in the pub and didn't want you hurt.'

'Didn't want me hurt! Jesus! When did this conversation take place?'

'You make it sound subversive. It wasn't. After you and I . . . spoke, I went out for a smoke. Fintan came out to set me straight. That's it.'

I shake my head. 'Unbelievable.'

We're quiet. I imagine he's regretting his honesty.

'I'm glad he told me,' he surprises me by saying. 'When you said there was someone else, I was going to leave it.'

'You should have.'

His eyes widen.

'I shouldn't be out – with anyone,' I try to explain.

He seems to consider that, holding his chin, running a thumb along his lower lip. When he finally speaks, his voice is gentle. 'I felt like that for a long time – after my wife died.' I want him to go on, but instead he says, 'Listen, we don't have to talk about this. It just didn't feel right, me knowing and you not knowing I knew . . . God, there's English for you!'

I smile.

'Look, all I want to say is that I understand. That's it.'

'What was your wife's name?'

'Catherine.' He looks past me. 'Hard to believe it's been five years,' he says as if to himself.

I make circles on the table with my dessertspoon. Eventually, I look up. 'Does it get any easier?'

His mouth smiles, but not his eyes. 'A bit.'

'Only a bit?'

'For a long time, I didn't want it to; it would have meant forgetting.'

'That's how I feel!' I've never told anyone that; didn't think they'd understand.

We're silent as the meal arrives and the waiters lift the silver lids from our dishes in one fluid, synchronised motion.

I pick at my food, appetite gone. 'How did Catherine die? If you don't mind me asking.'

He shakes his head. But his voice is hoarse when he says one word, 'Childbirth.'

I didn't expect that, not with modern medicine. 'You don't have to tell me . . .'

Rotating the salt cellar, he begins. 'We'd been warned not to have another baby. The first had been very difficult for Catherine. She developed pre-eclampsia, which could happen again. She wanted to risk it. I didn't. When our daughter was four, it came to a head. Catherine was heading for forty and wanted a brother or sister for Rachel before it was too late. Cathy had been an only child herself and didn't want that for Rachel.'

'So you agreed to go ahead.'

'No. Cathy stopped taking precautions. She only told me after she became pregnant.'

'Must have been hell going through that pregnancy.'

His eyes meet mine. 'I was nervous, angry, but I never thought . . . I'd lose her.' The last three words are a whisper.

I reach across and hold his hand. And then, I'm telling him. 'I used to have this thing for Ben & Jerry's ice cream – Phish Food. I'd always have a tub in the freezer. But this one night, we ran out. Brendan grabbed his coat. "Back in a sec," he said. He was smiling when he walked out of the door. He never came back.' I look at Greg. 'I killed him,' I whisper.

'You did *not* kill him.'

'No. I know. The dangerous driver, the wet surface . . . But if I hadn't wanted that *bloody* ice cream . . . he'd be alive.' The pain tugs at my heart. The empty hollowed-out feeling expands inside me. The anger flares. 'We just *assume* when someone walks out through that door, they'll be back. Back in a sec. We were two weeks away from our wedding. Had so many plans.' I smile. 'He used to threaten me with ginger children. I told him I *wanted* ginger children. Lots of ginger children. But really just two children. I thought two would be enough.' And then the first tear falls. 'I'm sorry. I should "let him go", "move on", take all the advice, but I can't.' I bow my head. 'I don't want to.'

He steals his hand back and enfolds mine in both of his. 'Screw the advice.'

I wipe a tear. 'Was she your soulmate?'

He smiles and nods. And his eyes well suddenly, surprisingly. He laughs. 'The state of us. Here.' He passes me his serviette.

I dab my eyes with it.

'I gave it to you for your nose.'

I laugh. 'Are you *kidding*? People will have to clean it.'

'True enough.' He roots in his pocket. 'Used hankie?' he asks doubtfully.

'Better,' I say. 'As long as it's dry.'

He smiles. 'It's dry.'

I put my hand out for it. Then blow my nose.

'OK, I need it back now.'

I laugh as he uses it – in all its freshly soggy glory.

'We're like blood brothers now,' he says, putting it back in his pocket.

'Bonded by snot.'

'And loss,' he says, suddenly serious.

I look into his eyes as the truth hits. 'Did you even get time to grieve? With a baby and a little girl?'

He shrugs. 'At first, it was hard. Rachel was only five and for a long time she blamed her baby brother for taking her mum away. There were times – like four in the morning when he woke up hungry – that I found myself resenting him, too, and Cathy, and myself.' He smiles. 'But he's a gorgeous kid who won us over without even trying. We got through it. As you do.'

It's been so hard without Brendan, but I've never imagined how much harder it would have been if I had two little people relying on me to keep their world spinning.

'How did you manage?'

'I got help.'

'A psychologist?'

He laughs. 'A nanny, someone to look after Toby while I tried to cope with Rachel.'

'What about your family? Didn't they help?'

'Well, there's only my mother and my younger brother, Rob. It's not in me to rely on them – or anyone, really.' He smiles. 'Rob was pretty stubborn, though, insisting on taking Rachel out; it got her away from the warzone for a while.'

'How are they now, your children?'

'Great, thankfully. Hilary – the nanny I hired – is still with us. She loves them as if they were her own.'

'You were lucky to find her.'

'Don't know what we'd have done without her.'

'Still hard, though.'

'If it wasn't for my writing and the kids themselves, I don't know . . .' His voice trails off.

'I don't have kids, obviously, but I've never been more productive at work,' I say. 'It's become my life. I don't want another one – not without him.'

'I saw that pain in your eyes, the day we met. It was what made you remarkable.'

I've never in my life changed my mind so dramatically about a person. 'And your driving . . . You understand now why it drove me crazy?'

He nods. 'Brendan. I'm sorry.'

'The wine gum was a nice touch, though.'

'I thought so.'

We share a smile.

The tables around us have emptied. There's so much left to say, though. It little matters where, but my apartment is close and neither of us feels like being in anonymous company in some noisy, packed venue.

It isn't as if we fall into each other's arms the minute we get through the door. We're just talking. Some small memory makes me cry. He wipes away my tears. When I look up, his face is incredibly close, his eyes, lips. Then I'm kissing him as much as he is me. The attraction I felt in the pub erupts, stronger now. Comfort, passion and understanding consume the past. Our shared melancholy ignites us as we rush to fill the void in each other's lives, to patch each other up, to end a pain that haunts us. This is different to anything I have known. And afterwards, when Greg starts making five-year plans that include me, I laugh, though I know he is serious.

4.

Quickly, we become inseparable, or at least as inseparable as work and his children allow. We speak over the phone enough times a day for Sebastian to start calling him Lover Boy. We meet for brunch whenever we can and go out most evenings. It feels like an orange disc of effervescent Vitamin C has been dropped into the still water that was my life.

On any given night, I never know where we'll end up: bowling, shopping, art gallery openings. Bars, bingo, clubs. The airport. Church. He's up for anything as long as there's adventure and fun to be had. In fact, he's making me realise that adventure and fun are to be had pretty much anywhere. He seems to know everyone. And if he doesn't, he gets to. He lives life like it might be snatched from him at any moment.

Today, he has persuaded me to 'work from home'.

'This is *not* work!' I call over the sound of the wind.

'Don't worry! We'll work,' he shouts from where he's sitting beside me on the floor of a plane. I say plane with great generosity. This thing is so tiny that when I first saw it, I did an about-turn. But Greg turned me back. Now that I'm inside and at four thousand metres, it feels like a death box with a basic lack of doors, and wings that seem too small to keep anything in the air.

'OK, let's go,' my skydiving buddy says into my ear – this stranger I'm entrusting my life to.

We scooch across the floor, tied together.

I glare at Greg. 'I can't believe you talked me into this.'

He blows me a kiss.

And now my legs are dangling out of the plane and I'm trying to concentrate on the instructions my 'buddy' is calling into my ear, when he eases my head back onto his shoulder then tips me forward – *Oh, Christ* – out into the sky. And we're falling, plummeting through clouds on our stomachs with the wind roaring in our ears and the earth rising up to meet us. He pulls my arms out and reminds me to bend my legs. I think of all those people you see on TV who seem to be falling *slowly*. A silent scream rises inside me.

A sudden jolt up and a gigantic wedgie inform me that the chute has opened. The instant floaty silence makes me realise that my scream was not, in fact, silent.

'You OK?' my buddy asks.

'Fine,' I say, dying – my scream was peppered with rapid-fire 'fucks'.

But now it's all lovely and peaceful like the world is on pause. And I wonder if this is what it's like being in the womb – only with air, and not wet, obviously. I could stay like this forever. We spiral down like a leaf. I even take the controls for a while.

Too soon, and with surprising ease, we land.

'So, will you do it again?' my buddy asks.

I nod enthusiastically and then look up. Here he comes, his orange chute open – the guy who is not killing me after all, but bringing me back to life.

~

We *do* work. In my apartment, he pulls a chair up beside me at the table. I look at him and laugh.

'You're like a teenager in a library who fancies a girl studying there.'

He points at me. 'That's *exactly* what I'm like.'

I kiss him, then open my laptop and start to work, but today it doesn't feel like work. The ideas come pouring out. I look at Greg tapping away on his keyboard.

'Is *this* how you're such a great writer? You *live*?'

He raises his eyebrows. 'Oh, so I'm a great writer, am I? You kept *that* quiet.'

I smile. 'Wouldn't want you getting too cocky,' I joke.

'Too late, I'm in love with myself now.'

'Actually, you know what? Crap writer. Really crap. Abysmal.'

'Still cocky.' He presses my nose. 'Have we done enough work now?' he asks like a child who's tired of homework.

I smile and close my computer. 'We've done enough work.' I've never been so productive.

'Great, because I have evil plans for you.' He lifts me up and carries me to bed. Where his evil plans send me into orbit.

~

Afterwards, in the shower, he washes me – not in a romantic, sensual Hollywood manner – he scrubs me with a soapy facecloth like I'm a kid. He even lifts my arms up to clean under them. I can't stop laughing.

'You're *filthy*,' he says.

'*You're* filthy,' I counter, referring, with a warm glow, to his bedroom antics.

I raise my chin as he scrubs under my neck, my body shaking with contained laughter. Behind my ears is particularly funny.

'Haven't I *told* you not to play in mud?' he continues.

'Admittedly, you have,' I say, laughing again.

'You've been a naughty girl, Lucy Arigho.' He slaps me lightly on the ass with the cloth.

'I *have* been naughty. No more playing in mud for me.'

He narrows his eyes like he's considering that in all seriousness. 'On second thoughts, I *do* like cleaning you.'

'Weirdo.' *Who'd have thought I needed a weirdo in my life?*

'Flattery will get you everywhere.'

Sometimes I wonder if we're seeing too much of each other. But then, when Greg's not with me, everything is flatter, buzzless, slower. At weekends, when he's with his children, I see friends, shop, visit art galleries. But whatever I do without him seems like filling time. Not that I expect to be included in his family life. I've seen enough TV to know that lone parents are careful about introducing new partners to their children; I respect that.

I haven't told anyone. Fint knows, of course. And Sebastian, sleuth that he is. Apart from that, no one. I don't want to jinx it, just live it. But then Greg asks me to the book launch of a friend and we get snapped together for a social column. I imagine my dad opening his Saturday newspaper and seeing his daughter smiling out, a stranger's arm around her. He wouldn't say anything, but I know he'd be hurt that I hadn't told him. We're supposed to be a team, Dad and I. I've always been good enough for my father, the person who encouraged my quirky sketches and convinced my mother I could make a career out of my talent. And so, I need to talk to him before Saturday. Unfortunately, my mother is Information Control. She'll want – no, *expect* the news first. And I've learned to avoid upsetting her whenever I can.

Always one for the practical gift, my mother, so I arrive armed with smoked salmon. I'm smuggling in a giant bar of Fruit & Nut for

Dad who is, as usual, on strict rations. Mum answers the door in her Alpen apron, wearing a navy pullover and a tweed calf-length skirt. No jewellery. Sensible shoes.

We've never been easy with each other, Mum and I. A cup of tea gives us something to do. She does the kettle bit. Me, the cups and saucers. Always saucers in our house. We make the usual small talk – my sister, Grace, and her children feature strongly. When Mum offers the recipe for the apple tart she has heating in the oven, I know we're running out of topics.

So I come out with it. 'I'm seeing Greg Millar.'

'Who?' she asks, setting her cup back at the centre of its saucer.

'Greg Millar.'

'From college?' The oven timer pings. She ignores it.

'No, Mum, there was no Greg Millar in college. He's an author.'

'Oh.' She thinks for a second. Squints. 'Have I heard of him?'

I shrug.

She puts a finger to her mouth, looks up for a few seconds, then back at me. 'No, doesn't ring a bell. What kind of books does he write?'

'Crime novels. He's pretty popular.'

'I'm sure he is, dear. So. How long have you been' – she roots around for the appropriate phrase – 'seeing him?'

'A few weeks.' Thinking of him makes me smile.

'Early days, then,' she says, bursting my bubble.

'It's not serious. It's just, I thought you should know, in case . . . I don't know . . . you hear it from someone else, or something.'

'Sure, who would we hear it from?' She looks over at Dad as if to say, 'We never go out.'

He doesn't see her, sitting, as he is, in his armchair, behind the paper. His favourite spot.

'Do you want me to get the tart?' I ask.

'Oh. Yes, Lucy, please. And cut a slice for yourself and your father.'

'Did someone say apple tart?' His head pops up.

I smile at him.

He gets up, drops the newspaper onto the chair, stretches and makes his way to the table. He's quiet until I hand him his slice. Then he looks at me.

'So, it's not serious, is it?'

I *knew* he'd be listening. 'Nah,' I say, smiling again.

'This looks good, Mum,' he says, scooping up two quick dessertspoons of whipped cream and landing them onto the tart, then flattening the heap with the back of the spoon.

Watching him, she frowns.

'D'you know, Lucy,' he says, 'that people have a habit of saying that things aren't serious when that's exactly what they are?'

I lift my eyebrows innocently. 'Well, it's not, Dad.'

'Don't ever commit a crime, love; you'd never get away with it.'

I make a face at him.

'How did you meet him?' asks my mother.

'Work.'

'I'm not surprised. You do little else.'

I've had a lifetime of learning when not to reply to her. This is what I do now.

'Is he good to you?' she asks.

'Yes. He is.'

'Does he make you laugh?' asks Dad.

I start to smile, thinking of the way Greg mimics Matt. He squats down, comes right up to me, then looks up and asks me to dance. He gets the voice, the mannerisms just right.

'Oh dear,' says Dad. 'I think we've lost her.'

'I hardly know him.'

'I believe you,' he says, looking like he doesn't. 'So, how often do you see each other?'

'A good bit.'

'Every day?'

'Pretty much.' He has a way of getting information out of me; the good cop approach.

'Ah,' he says, in a case-dismissed tone.

We're silent. The ticking of the kitchen clock reminds me of afternoons spent at this table trying to interest myself in the life cycle of the earthworm.

Suddenly, he points his fork at me. 'Didn't he write *A Time to Die*?'

I sit up. Beam at him. 'Yes, yes, he did.' *Good man, Dad.*

'Is *that* him?' asks my mother. 'His books are filthy. He's divorced. Or separated or something. Oh, Lucy.'

'His wife died, Mum. Hardly his fault.'

'Yes, well, just be careful. Men like that are complicated . . .'

'OK, look, I'm going.' I stand, trying to stay calm, keeping my voice upbeat. 'Thanks for the tea, Mum.' I kiss her cheek, grab my bag.

'There's no need to go . . .' she starts to say.

'I'm late, Mum.' My standard excuse.

Dad follows me into the hall. 'She didn't mean it, love. She's just worried about you.'

I say nothing.

'She means well, Lucy.'

'Sure.'

'It's like the apple tart.'

'*What?*'

'Did you see how I got that cross look of hers when I loaded on the cream?'

'You noticed?'

'Of course I noticed. Anyway, why do you think she made the tart, if she didn't want me to have any?'

'Beats me.'

'She thinks that by fussing she shows that she cares.'

'Oh, come on, Dad.' This is what happens when your father retires early to take up psychology.

'And d'you know why she's like that?'

'Enlighten me.'

'Her mother was the opposite – airy-fairy, never around, no discipline whatsoever, let them run wild. That's why Mum has always come down hard on you. Both of you. She thinks that's what good mothers do. Trust me, Lucy. She only wants what's best . . .'

'That's the problem. Nothing else is good enough. Nothing ever will be. I knew she'd have a problem with Greg. She had to. I don't know why I came.'

'She's just a worrier, Lucy. Wait till I go back in there. She'll be all upset. Guarantee you.'

I sigh.

'How's the work going?'

'Fine.'

'Good. Look, the main thing is that you're happy. And you are, aren't you?'

'For the first time . . . in a long time.'

He smiles. 'That *is* good news. Listen, when it comes to your mother, let it all wash over you. Like I do.'

5.

It's our second month anniversary. Not that I've told him. I just asked him over. I'm cooking vegetarian curry. Curry, because it's Greg's favourite. Vegetarian, because I am one. I've gone all out, frying each of the spices from scratch. I'm way behind and hassled when he arrives. I haven't even changed. He kisses me, lands a bottle of Bollinger down on the counter.

'Happy anniversary, darling,' he jokes.

I laugh. 'Happy anniversary, cupcakes.' I kiss him and turn back to the cooker.

'Isn't the *guy* supposed to call the *girl* cupcakes?'

I wink. 'I live dangerously.'

'Want to read the acknowledgements for *A River Too Wide*?' He pulls them from the back pocket of his jeans and hands them to me.

'Oh, great!' I put them aside. 'Let me just get this under control first.'

'Here, I'll do that.' He takes the wooden spoon from me and starts to stir the sauce. 'There's another page when you're finished with that,' he says.

'OK.'

'You know what? Just skip to the second page.'

'Why?'

He winks. 'Humour me, Luce.'

There's something about the way he says it. I hold my breath as I turn the page. Could one of my favourite authors of all time have dedicated a book to me?

On the page are three words. Marry me, Lucy.

I freeze.

He turns and presses into my hand a small, navy velvet box. I keep my eyes fixed on the box – so I don't have to meet his.

'Open it,' he says softly.

I'm stuck. If I do as he asks, he'll assume it's a yes. If I don't, I'll have to tell him it's a no. He's waiting. I have to do something. So I lift the tiny, resistant lid. Inside is a solitaire in the shape of a triangle. So simple. So special. It couldn't be more perfect. That he went out on his own and selected this for me and got it so instinctively right breaks my heart, considering what I'm about to do. I look up at him. I don't want to hurt him. I love him, I realise.

'What is it?' he asks.

'Nothing,' I croak.

Silence. I can smell the curry starting to burn.

'You don't want to,' he says quietly.

I look down at the ring to avoid answering, but watch in horror as a tear falls, landing splat on the diamond. I worry that the shop won't take it back.

'You don't love me.'

I look into his eyes. 'I do, Greg. I do love you. But I can't marry you.' It's what I planned with Brendan. It would be like slotting someone else into his place. And I can't do that. Not now. Maybe not ever. 'Marriage is such a big step.'

He puts his hands on my shoulders and looks into my eyes. 'It's Brendan, isn't it?'

I nod. 'I'm sorry.' I close the box, place it on the counter and push it towards him, hating myself for hurting him. That I'm crying doesn't make it any better. He takes my hands in his, kisses my forehead then pulls me into a hug.

'It's OK,' he says, rubbing my back. Then, with a 'Shit, the dinner,' he lets me go, turns, lifts the pan and carries it to the sink. He opens the window and wafts the air. At last, he turns back to me and smiles. 'So much for that.'

A wave of love swells inside me. 'Greg. I'm sorry.'

He shakes his head. 'No worries.' He looks down, shoving his hands into his pockets, leaning against the sink. 'I was wrong to ask so soon.' He looks up. 'I just wanted you to know how committed I am to you.'

I go to him and wrap my arms around his waist. 'And I'm committed to you. But we don't need grand gestures . . .'

'It wasn't a gesture. And it's not a whim. I've thought this through. It would make so much sense. As it is, I live two separate lives – you and my family. I don't want you to feel separate.'

'I don't want to either. I'd like to meet Rachel and Toby. I'd like to share the rest of your life. Just not as your wife.'

He nods. 'You're right. I have to stop rushing things for fear they'll end.'

I press myself into his chest. 'This won't end.' But I, of all people, know that it can, in an instant.

He pulls back. 'Let's pretend I never asked. OK? Let's forget the whole thing.'

I try to think of ways I might have said no without hurting him.

He reaches for a roll of kitchen paper. 'Here,' he says, ripping a sheet off and putting it to my nose. 'Blow.'

I half laugh.

'Come on. Blow.'

I do.

He squeezes it over my nose. 'You love me. That's a start.'

~

I spend the night awake. Saying yes would have been wrong. But saying no feels equally so. I'll never forget his face. Ever.

~

First thing next morning, I make my way to Fint's office, bleary-eyed. He's at his desk, juggling, something he does when trying to come up with ideas. I turn to leave.

'Where are you going?' he asks, letting the balls flop, one by one, into his hands.

'You're busy.'

'Nah, nothing coming.' He returns the colourful juggling balls to their shiny metal box. 'So, how are things?'

'I'll just close the door.'

He raises an eyebrow.

With the world shut out, I slump into the chair opposite him, reach forward and help myself to one of his juggling balls. I drop it from hand to hand.

'Well?'

I look up. Everything has shifted. Normally, Fint seeks my advice on his (complicated) relationships and I try to avoid his interference in mine. 'Greg's asked me to marry him.'

He eyes me carefully. 'You don't seem too happy.'

I shrug. 'I can't do it to Brendan.'

He gets up and comes around. Taking the ball from me, he sits on the desk. 'Brendan's dead, Lucy.'

'But he's not gone! He sees everything I do. I know he does; I feel it. I can't just marry someone else. I can't do it to him.'

He eyeballs me. 'So say no.'

'I did.'

'Well, then. What's the problem?'

'I love him.'

'That *is* allowed, Lucy.'

I sigh deeply. 'I *do* want to be with him. I want to be part of his life. I want to wake up to his face every morning. I mean, what if something happens to him and we never— '

'Hang on. Whoa. Slow down. Nothing's going to happen to Greg.'

'How do you know?'

'Because lightning doesn't strike twice.'

'Not true. A park ranger was struck by lightning seven times in the States. It's in the *Guinness Book of World Records*.'

He smiles. 'Remind me to include you in the next pub quiz.'

'I'm serious, Fint. If Brendan and I knew what little time we had, we wouldn't have hung around for all the practical things to be in place – apartment, furniture, whatever. We'd have married straight away. We'd have had a child. And I'd have a part of him to hold to me now. I don't want that to happen again . . .'

'Lucy, it won't.'

'I couldn't bear it. He makes me so happy. I love him so much.' I'm a mess.

'Come here.' He gives me a Fintan Special – a great big bear hug. And lets me cry. When I've moved to the intermittent sobbing stage, he pulls back. 'OK. Here's what Uncle Fint thinks. One: You love Greg. Two: I don't blame you; he's a great guy. Three: You're lucky to get another chance. And four: You should enjoy it. That's it.'

'And Brendan?'

'You know how close I was to Brendan. I miss him, too. And I miss him for you. I miss you being together. But do you *think*, for one *second*, he'd want you to be miserable for the rest of your life because of him? Really, do you? Because you know the way he loved you. And he wouldn't want that. He'd want this – happiness, a future. I know he would. I feel it, Lucy.'

I want to believe him. So badly.

'When you met Greg, you were in pretty shitty form, weren't you?'

I remember back. 'Yeah.'

'Why?'

'You know why. It was Brendan's birthday.'

'Well, have you ever thought that Greg might have been Brendan's present to you?'

I squint at him. 'Come on.'

'Were you supposed to be at that meeting with Orla?'

'No.' One of our designers, Jake, had rung in sick.

'And what a coincidence, you and Greg meeting like that – in traffic, on your way to the same place.'

'Life is full of coincidences.'

'Why did you even talk to him in the first place?'

'You know why. He was driving like a maniac.'

'Which upset you because of Brendan. So, really, it was fate, something set in motion in another world.'

'You don't believe that. You, of all people.' The world's greatest cynic.

'So, how did I think of it, then?'

~

I can't work. I leave the office and walk. Before long, I find myself lighting candle after candle in the Pepper Canister church. I try to talk to Brendan, but find I'm talking to myself. Not even the tiniest flicker of a candle flame in response. Nothing. I leave the church, and walk back to my car. Half an hour later, I pull up outside my sister's house. If I'm not going to hear a spiritual voice, at least I'll get a sensible one.

6.

I don't make a habit of asking Grace's advice. It's not easy to listen to someone who never makes mistakes. But now I've asked and am waiting for an answer, watching her carefully from the other side of the ironing board. She is ironing and beautiful. Like an ad for it: You, too, could look like this, if you had an iron. Hard to believe we're from the same gene pool. Why have I come? Do I really need the Voice of Reason?

'They're not easy, you know, children,' says an amazing mum. Grace gave up her career as a doctor to stay at home with her kids.

'But Shane and Jason are adorable,' I say.

'Not twenty-four hours a day, they're not. What we're having here is a rare moment of peace.' Jason's asleep and Shane's at Montessori.

'I know it's hard, but they're young. They get easier. Don't they?'

'They'd better,' she laughs, lifting the iron. Jets of steam shoot out and up into her honey-blonde hair. It won't frizz. 'Look, Luce, you're my little sis, so I'm going to be straight – as long as you don't tell Mum . . .'

I look at her as if she's just insulted me; I never tell Mum anything I don't think she'll find out.

'Parenting is the hardest, most thankless thing I've ever done. I'm not complaining; it was our decision. They're our kids and we love them. But his wouldn't be yours. You'd get all the hassle – probably more – but none of the good things that come with a child being a tiny piece of you. Have you thought that they mightn't accept you?'

'Maybe not at first. But in time . . .'

'They might drive you apart. It happened to Colette.' Her best friend, who fell in love with a divorced father of two.

'She had to put up with manipulative teenagers; that's different.'

'All children manipulate their parents. They develop it into an art form. Trust me, even babies manipulate their parents.'

Jason's up a lot during the night. Grace is tired; that's all this is.

'What about discipline?' she continues, lifting the iron and drawing her head back to avoid the steam. 'If you got married, who'd discipline them? Have you thought of that?'

In a word, no. I've been so focused on the dead, I forgot the living. 'Greg will.' I presume.

'Well, he should – if Colette's experience is anything to go by. And when he's not there?'

'I don't know. I'd have to, I suppose.'

'And what if they turn around and say, "You're not my mother"?'

'They've a nanny!' I suddenly remember. 'Hilary. She'd do the disciplining.' Thank God. 'And I'm good with kids, Grace. You know how good I am with Shane and Jase.'

'You spoil them. And that's fine. An aunt should. But a parent can't afford to. They'd turn into tyrants. Another thing: Parents can't switch off. You hand them back to me at the end of the day, and off you go to your peaceful apartment. Parenting is full-time. They don't go away. Just think about it, Luce, OK? It wouldn't be easy, that's all I'm saying.' She places a folded pillowcase on a pile and takes a shirt from another with a sigh. 'God, I hate ironing.' She looks up at me. 'I take it they know, the children?'

'I haven't said yes.'

'But they know you're seeing each other?'

'I don't know. I don't think so.'

'Haven't you met them?'

'Not yet.'

She throws me a look that says, 'Don't you think that would be a good idea?'

'There's no point unless I'm going to be in their lives, is there?'

She switches off the iron and comes to sit with me at the kitchen island. Her voice is gentle when she says, 'Lucy, I just mentioned children to make you appreciate the practicalities of this. I know you've been through a tough time. More than anyone, you deserve happiness, but do you really need to say yes now?' I'm about to say 'No,' but then she adds, 'I mean, how well can you know someone after eight weeks?'

I rush to defend what we have together. 'I know Greg.'

'But how? How can you know it's love after just eight weeks?'

'I feel it.' I'm touching my heart. 'I died with Brendan. Greg has brought me back to life, given me a reason to live.'

She says nothing.

'He understands, Grace . . . He lost his wife.'

'Ah.'

'It's not just that. I love him. He's made me happy again. I never thought I could be.'

'I just wish you wouldn't rush.' I want to say 'I'm not,' but she ploughs ahead with, 'There are so many hurdles – his fame . . .'

And I'm defending him again. 'He's a writer, not a movie star; people either don't recognise him or don't care.'

'The age gap.'

'Eleven years is nothing. And age doesn't matter anyway when you're with the right person. Greg's so young in his outlook, Grace. Sometimes I feel I'm the older one.'

'You've got the rest of your lives to be together.'

I look at her. 'I will never' – pause – 'make the mistake of assuming that again.'

She stops. She rests a hand on mine. Her eyes well.

But I don't want her pity. I want her approval. I want her to say 'Do it.' Because, suddenly, I want to. The more obstacles she puts in my way, the more I want to jump them. Every one. I don't want anything to stop us. I love Greg and I want to be with him, be part of his life, his family. And out of nowhere, I have the strongest feeling that Brendan wants this for me, too.

'It's right, Grace. I know it is.'

She takes my hands in hers. 'Then don't listen to me. Always the cynic, always looking beyond what people say, never trusting. And still, I didn't know the man I married until after I'd married him. Don't listen to me.' She smiles. 'Sure, you never do anyway, do you?'

'No.' I smile back. It's been hard to listen to the person I've been compared to and fallen short of all my life, the person who got a degree that pleased our mother, the person who got married young to a guy with no complications – not too old, not widowed, not a father and not famous. Kevin, Grace's husband, shares the top percentile with her in looks, intelligence and in all that matters to society. They are a Mary Poppins couple: practically perfect in every way. There have been times I've caught Kevin looking at me as though thinking, 'Thank God, I got the good sister.' Which makes me glad he did. I can't imagine being married to someone so judgemental. Not that it's a problem for my sister. The only thing that keeps Grace and me on the same side is our mother. Even the perfect daughter isn't quite good enough for her.

~

I sit on my bed in Brendan's rugby jersey. I take his photo from its frame and press it to my cheek. It feels cold and one-dimensional.

Because it is. A cheap imitation. But it's all I have. I look into the eyes that once swept me off my feet – and kept me off them – for two magical years – right till the end. I run my finger over his mouth. And I'm crying.

'I'll never stop loving you. You know that. I'll never forget.'

And maybe it's my imagination, but I hear his voice – so clearly – in my head, a voice that says, 'Be happy.'

It's what he would say.

7.

Greg slips the ring onto my finger and sweeps me up into his arms, kissing me over and over until I'm laughing.

'So, when can we do this?' he asks.

I pull back. 'When Rachel and Toby are ready, Greg. I don't want to descend on them. They have their own lives.'

'They'll love you.'

I smile nervously. 'I hope so.'

'You'll have to meet them!' He thinks for a second. 'I know, we'll have a barbecue, and invite Rob.' I wait for him to suggest the only other member of his family – his mother – but he doesn't. 'So, how about Saturday?'

'Saturday?' Only two days away. After all that Grace has said, I panic.

'My place,' he says.

I look at him. This is my future now; I can't run from it. 'All right, then,' I say with false jollity.

Greg starts planning vegetarian options while I try to remember everything my sister said about stepchildren.

~

Greg comes to take me to his home, which will become my home, to meet his children, who will become my stepchildren. If I hadn't spoken to Grace, would I be as nervous? I feel as if I'm going for an audition. If I arrive with presents, will they think I'm trying to win them over? If not, will they think me mean? Greg has told me not to worry about gifts. Did he check with the children, though? And what should I wear? I don't want to look too young and highlight the age difference. Nor do I want to look as if I'm dressing like I'm trying to be their mother. Though Greg has already told me a lot about Rachel and Toby, all the way there I bombard him with questions.

'Stop worrying, you'll be fine.'

We're driving along one of the most beautiful coastal roads in Dublin when Greg indicates and swings into a driveway. Up ahead looms something more than a house. It's the kind of place that might be chosen for celebrity weddings. It has turrets. And grounds. It doesn't just overlook the sea, it's right on it. A blue, blue sea with little white caps.

'My God, Greg!'

He dismisses it as 'bricks and mortar'.

'A lot of bricks and mortar.'

'Could all be gone in the morning; nothing's certain in life.'

One thing's certain to me: Greg's home has to be worth millions. This is life on a different scale. While I'm trying to digest this, he jumps from the car, comes round and opens my door. He takes my hand and we crunch gravel till we get to the steps. He slips a key into the lock. But there is no grand tour.

'They were out the back when I left. Let's go see.'

I catch a fleeting glimpse of old and new – original features combined with stripped wooden floors and architectural furniture. I want to stop and admire the art – all modern, all wonderful. Oh, and there's a library! He drags me on.

We reach the patio. On a newly cut lawn, bordered by swings, a climbing frame, trampoline and basketball hoop, two children are playing football with two adults. They are so absorbed, they don't see us. It's not a challenge to work out who's who. The slight, dark-haired boy with the khaki combats and light blue top featuring multi-coloured skulls looks about five: Toby. The equally dark and slender, but much taller girl in three-quarter-length denims and a cerise top has to be Rachel. I try to remember what I was like at ten, what I thought about, liked, disliked. Wish I knew more about older kids. Greg's brother, Rob, has the trademark family colouring and build, though his face is more boyish than Greg's. You can tell there's six years between them. Only Hilary, the nanny, stands out as different – fair and sturdy, her hair pulled back into a tight ponytail. She is wearing a loose, long-sleeved T-shirt over stretch denims.

Rachel tackles Rob.

Hilary shouts, 'Go, Rachel.'

Toby calls to his uncle, 'Over here, I'm open.'

I smile.

Rachel gets the ball. Rob retreats to the goal. He dives as she kicks hard. Toby groans and holds his head while Hilary and Rachel cheer and high-five each other.

'Guys,' Greg calls. 'Come meet Lucy.'

Four heads turn in our direction. Rob's smile is immediate and wide. He starts towards us. Hilary has to say something to the children to get them to move. I feel guilty for interrupting their game.

'Welcome to the family,' Rob says, his handshake firm.

It feels premature, but I smile. 'Thank you.'

'I see he hasn't offered you a drink.' He tut-tuts at his brother. 'Can I get you a beer?'

'That'd be great, thanks.'

Hilary arrives with the children. She looks younger, close up. More my age. A year or two older, maybe. The heaviness of her body in the distance must have added years.

Greg introduces us all.

'Hello,' I say, smiling from one to the other.

'Hi,' says Toby, yanking up his trousers.

Hilary says, 'Nice top.'

'Oh, thanks.' I look down to remind myself what I'm wearing. 'Oh, BT2. Greg got it for me.'

As Rachel's face clouds over, I realise my mistake. How *stupid* to say Greg got it.

'Rachel, say hello to Lucy,' prompts Greg.

'Hello,' she mumbles, looking at the ground.

'That was a good goal,' I say.

She shrugs without looking up.

'I'm a good kicker,' declares Toby. 'Did you see me?'

'Yes, I did. You were great out there on the pitch.'

He looks to where they were playing, then back at me as if I have visual problems. 'It's just the garden.'

'True enough,' I say, feeling like a fool.

'Can we have our Coke now?' Rachel asks Hilary, as if that was the bribe for coming over.

The nanny looks at Greg.

'Sure,' he says.

She takes the children inside.

'Back in a sec,' Greg says, and goes in after them.

Rob hands me a Corona. 'Cheers,' he says, raising his bottle.

'Cheers.' I clink mine to his.

The beer calms me. I remind myself that this is never easy. For anyone.

Then Greg is back, clapping his hands and heading for the barbecue. 'OK, let's get this show on the road.'

'Want a hand?' I offer.

'Nah. You're grand. Get to know your future brother-in-law. There's a knack to this thing.'

Rob and I sit at the long, wooden patio table.

'So, how did you two meet?' Rob asks, as if I'm a novelty.

I tell him. Briefly.

He laughs. 'Greg Millar flirting in traffic! Wonders will never cease. As for getting engaged after two months . . . I don't know what you've done to him.'

'What I've done! It's completely the other way around. It's what he's done to me.'

'Now, now. Don't get smutty.'

I laugh. 'He has such a great philosophy, though . . .'

'Greg? A philosophy?' He looks dubious.

'Yeah,' I say, surprised. 'Live for the moment. Embrace life.'

'Greg?'

'Yes, Greg.' *What's his problem?*

'Well, I don't know what your secret is, but I've never seen him so . . . so *zesty*.'

We look over at him. He's singing and acting out an Eartha Kitt song, in between flipping burgers.

'But he's always like that,' I say.

'Maybe with you.'

'Not just with me, with everyone. He's so . . . well, as you say, zesty.'

He raises his eyebrows. 'Must be love.'

'What are you two talking about over there?' Greg calls.

'You,' I say. And, as I get up and go to him, I rationalise. Lots of people are different with their families: more responsible, serious. *I* am, with my mother.

Hilary and the children come out onto the patio.

Automatically, I take a step back from Greg.

Rachel's carrying a fishing rod; Toby, a pair of binoculars; and Hilary, a picnic basket.

'Where are you all off to?' asks Rob.

'Down to the sea for picnic!' calls Toby excitedly. 'Wanna come?'

'No, thanks, buddy; *someone* has to eat the barbecue.'

They head for a gate at the end of the garden.

'Why aren't they eating with us?' I ask Greg.

He looks awkward. 'I wouldn't worry, Luce. These things take time.'

Which basically means they didn't want to eat with me. *That's OK,* I tell myself. *It's not personal. They're just not ready for a stepmother. Any stepmother. And 'These things take time' is a lot more realistic than 'They'll love you'. How he ever thought they'd just automatically love me I don't know. At least he didn't force them to eat with us. They'd have really hated me then.*

~

Later that evening, Greg's upstairs reading Toby a bedtime story. Rachel and Hilary are in another room watching a movie that Rachel has, apparently, been dying to see. And Rob's telling me something I didn't know.

'Yeah, Greg basically brought me up.'

'He *did*?'

'Didn't he tell you? Our father died when I was four. Greg was ten.'

I'm stunned. 'I knew your dad had died; I just assumed it was relatively recently.'

He shakes his head. 'I have two memories of my father. One is him wrapping me up in a warm towel after a bath. The other is him letting me blow my nose into his hand when we didn't have a hankie. That's it, apart from a few photos.'

'You said Greg brought you up – what about your mum? Didn't she look after you?'

'She had to go out to work. Two jobs, both paying shite: a supermarket and a dive that called itself a hotel. She was always gone. Greg did everything. Got me to school, fed me, helped with homework, put me to bed. Never complained. Every night he read to me: Sinbad, Biggles, Superman, Spiderman, the Hobbit . . . Our heroes came from the library.'

'I can't imagine how hard it must have been, becoming a father at ten.'

'You know, he never made me feel it was a chore, never treated me like some stupid kid he was stuck with. He spoke to me man to man. I fucking worshipped the guy. Trailed around after him. Copied everything he did. Wanted to be just like him. He wasn't like a father. And he was better than a brother. He was my hero, you know?'

I wonder why Greg has never told me. I imagine them, Little and Large, side by side, but not holding hands. Large looking out for Little.

'I was tough work, though,' Rob continues. 'Always first to put up the fists. I'd lose it, like that.' He snaps his fingers. 'Greg was the one who stopped me hanging out with troublemakers. He taught me to fight through hard work, getting somewhere, not lashing out. He kept my eye on the ball, until I learned to do it for myself. He put me through teacher training college while he worked, in printers first, then bookshops, until his own books started to get published. I was so fucking proud of him when they did. If there was one person who deserved it, it was Greg.'

'Wow.'

'I can't believe he didn't tell you. If I was him, I'd be shouting it from the rooftops.'

Much later, it's just me and Greg sitting in front of the fire, waiting for a taxi to take me home.

'Rachel and Toby are so well-behaved, and seriously beautiful,' I say.

'It's the genes.' He smiles.

'I'm glad they went off on the picnic. I don't want them to feel like they *have* to like me, you know? I'm hoping it will happen by itself – in time.'

He kisses my cheek. 'They'll love you.'

How can he be so sure? What if they never do? And what if he can't love me if they don't? I need to stop thinking.

'You and Rob seemed to hit it off,' Greg says, playing with my hair.

I turn to him and smile. 'He's lovely. Almost as nice as you.' I look at him. 'I can't believe you never told me you pretty much brought him up on your own. That's a big deal, Greg.'

'He's exaggerating.'

And he's *being modest.* 'I bet you were such a cute kid. I can just imagine you. Curly hair, shorts, long socks, a cut on your knee . . .'

He smiles. 'Sounds a bit Little Lord Fauntleroy to me. We were more like the scruffy kids in a *Beano* comic.'

'I wish I'd lived next door.'

'So do I. Think what we could have got up to.' He smiles suggestively.

'Not with my mother around.'

'Dead right, too. Look how lovely and innocent she's kept you.'

'Though I do occasionally get "filthy" and need a good cleaning.'

He laughs.

'Must have been so hard, though, growing up without your dad.'

He shrugs. 'It was no big deal. We were fine.'

'Rob said it was a heart attack.'

He looks at his watch. 'This taxi's taking ages. I think I'll give them a shout.' He pulls out his phone and makes the call. 'It's on its way,' he says. Like I don't know that.

'Greg, if your dad died so young from a heart attack, you should have, like, a cardiac check-up or something.'

'Yeah, probably,' he says vaguely.

'Definitely.'

'You know what, Lucy? I'm tired. Let's talk about this another time.'

'Sure.' It's not just modesty. It must have been so hard, he doesn't want to go back there.

8.

Greg and my dad have just returned from the customary game of golf that takes place any time there's a *hint* of a boyfriend becoming serious. It's a family joke by now – Dad's the least judgemental person I know. He ends up loving everyone. Weird thing is, he hasn't given me the usual, surreptitious thumbs-up. Has he just forgotten? Not that it would make a difference to me; I don't need anyone's approval. The whole golf thing is just Dad being funny, anyway. Still . . . weird.

At least the tough nut of the family is melting under Greg's charm. Why? Because it's genuine. He simply spots Mum's patchwork, neatly cast aside in the kitchen, and becomes obsessed. How did she choose the colours? Did she ever think of depicting a narrative on a quilt? Does she know any men who do patchwork? Maybe she could teach him? Or maybe he could come up with a story for one of her wall hangings? None of us appreciates Mum's patchwork. She has her sewing buddies who recognise the painstaking hours of effort that go into her work, but we just don't get it. Boyfriends have always complimented her cooking; never her patchwork. Big mistake, I realise now.

I wonder if I should try the same approach with Greg's mother, Phyllis, a few days later as we're on our way to visit her for the first time.

'What hobbies does your mum have?' I ask Greg.

'Hobbies?' He frowns. Finally, he comes up with, 'She's pretty religious, I guess.'

I'll have nothing in common with her, nothing to talk about! Just as well I've dressed conservatively and urged Greg to be on time.

Five minutes early, we drive through two imposing pillars, into the grounds of a beautiful old building that looks more like a sanctuary for war veterans than a nursing home.

I am not *having a conversation about God. I'd just fail.*

But, in a bright, leafy reception area, we're informed that Phyllis isn't feeling up to two visitors today and will see only her son.

'I hope she's OK,' I say.

'Just tired,' the receptionist explains, but she looks a little awkward.

'You go ahead,' I say to Greg.

'You sure?'

'Yeah. I'll go for a walk.'

'I won't be long.'

'Take your time.'

The lawns are beautifully manicured, the shrubs trimmed, the flower beds weed-free. I stroll around, trying not to worry that she doesn't want to see me. After twenty minutes, my mobile rings. Greg's on his way out.

We meet at the door and walk to the car.

'Was she OK?'

'Fine. Just tired.'

'Not ill, though?'

'Nah. She's a tough old bird,' he says with love in his voice.

'Why is she in a home, Greg?'

He smiles. 'Thought you might ask.' He shrugs. 'It was her choice. She won't come to live with us. She's very independent.'

'But being in a home isn't being independent, is it?'

'Here, it is. You should see the set-up. There's a section for active residents. She lives in a suite. It's like a top-class, one-bedroom apartment. She comes and goes as she pleases. She has a few good friends she likes to fuss over. She has the chapel and her flat-screen TV. She has every modern convenience without having to cook or wash for herself. Rob takes her out shopping once a week. And she visits us for lunch every Sunday – on her own terms; she takes a taxi there and back.'

'She sounds like a character.'

He smiles. 'She's that all right.'

As we drive through the gates, I turn to him. 'OK, so this is going to sound paranoid, but do you think she just didn't want to see me?'

'No, Lucy. She was tired, that's all.' But he doesn't look at me.

And I know, instinctively, that here is another person who doesn't want someone new in Greg's life.

I meet Colette, Grace's friend, in a coffee shop. We settle down in a quiet corner, me with a coffee, Colette, peppermint tea. She waves away my thanks for her time. Then I fill her in.

'So, how many times have you met Rachel and Toby now?' she asks.

'Three. Once for a barbecue, then a movie, then we took them to a playground.'

'And how did you get on?'

'They're very quiet. Polite. Like I'm a total stranger. Which I am. They stick with Hilary – the nanny – mostly.'

She nods like a doctor listening to symptoms. 'And how are you with them?'

'Terrified. I'm parachuting into their little lives. Sometimes I feel like apologising.'

She smiles. 'Well, you're lucky in one sense; they're still young. Teenagers are so set in their ways. If they take a dislike to you, that's pretty much it. But,' she says brightly, 'every situation is different, every *child* is different. You just have to feel your way. Have you bought any step-parenting books?'

'Three.'

She laughs. 'Only three?'

I smile.

'And how are you with Greg around the children?'

I have to think about that. 'Well, I avoid public displays of affection like the plague – obviously.'

'Recipe for disaster, right there,' she agrees.

'I try not to feel like he's judging how I am with them. Because he's not. He's not like that. He knows it'll take time.'

'Good. And, listen, if you learn nothing more from me than this, always remember you're in this for Greg. That's the most important relationship here. There'll be tough times, challenging times, when you feel like you can't go on. That's when you'll need to remind yourself why you're doing this.' I swallow. 'But I really believe that, if you're patient and sensitive to the children's needs, if you give them space, carefully build a relationship and *never* try to replace their mother, then, *eventually*, you might all fit together.'

The word 'might' has never sounded so huge.

I make Colette repeat everything she's just said so I can take notes.

The following day, Greg and I drive to meet Ben and Ruth, his in-laws, Catherine's parents.

'Seeing as you're going to be their grandchildren's stepmum, I think it'd be good to meet them, at this stage. I think they'd appreciate it.'

I nod. Nervous, of course.

As we turn into the five-star hotel, he says, 'I should warn you: you might find them a little cold.'

'Oh?'

'It's nothing to do with you, you understand?'

'What, then?' I'm sceptical after the Phyllis incident.

'It's to do with me.'

'In what way?'

'It's no big deal. I'm just not their favourite person. I'm not worried about it. You shouldn't be. They adore the kids, who are their last link to Catherine. They're polite to me. I'm just telling you because I don't want you to think their chilliness has anything to do with you. OK?'

'OK.'

We pull up in front of the hotel. A valet opens my door, giving me no time to dwell on what Greg's just said. The hotel doors are opened for us. The flower arrangement in the lobby is bigger than I am. A piano tinkles in the background.

'There they are,' Greg says.

They stand when they see us, their smiles reserved. Ben is tall and noticeably lean, with an air of success. His wife, by contrast, looks timid, slightly plump and almost six inches shorter.

Greg introduces us. We shake hands and sit. Ben does the talking, or, rather, questioning. I'm the subject of his attention. When he asks how Greg and I met, I know not to mention cars racing on a motorway.

'Work,' I say. 'I design Greg's book covers.'

'So, you're a graphic designer? Who do you work for?'

'I'm a partner at Get Smart.' I wonder if he knows it.

He nods. 'And will you continue to work after you're married?'

I've never considered an alternative. 'Yes,' I say, wondering suddenly if Catherine did.

I spend an hour under the spotlight. It feels like an eternity. An eternity on the defensive. It's as though they've already decided that I'll fall short of their daughter.

~

'Sorry about that,' Greg grimaces as we sit in the car. 'I thought if we met on neutral territory Ben would behave himself.'

'I need a drink.'

He smiles. 'It was good we did it, though. They're driven by worry. At least, *now*, they know you're not a Mrs Doubtfire.'

'I *love* Mrs Doubtfire.'

'Trust me, Mrs Doubtfire would not be their cup of tea.'

I look at him. 'Did Catherine work?'

'Yes, Catherine worked. Lucy, do *not* compare yourself to Catherine. Do *not* feel intimidated by them.'

'What did she do?'

'She was an architect. Lucy, we've done our duty. Forget about them now.'

'What's their problem with you, anyway?'

'Ah!'

'Ah, what?' I look at him.

He sighs, long and loud. 'That goes way back.'

'Do you see me rushing anywhere?'

He smiles. 'All right. I was never exactly what they'd planned for their only daughter. Didn't go to the right schools. Wasn't from the right part of town. Wouldn't know an old boys' network if it came up and bit me on the arse.'

'He's a snob, basically,' I say, guessing that Ruth just follows his lead.

'Ben thinks writing books should be a hobby.'

I roll my eyes.

He shrugs. 'Doesn't bother me. It's his problem.'

'Well, I think you're great,' I say, squeezing his thigh. 'Although, I don't know . . .' I take my hand away. 'What school did you say you went to, again?'

He makes a face at me.

9.

'Remember that day we spent working from home?' Greg asks one evening when we're out for dinner.

I smile. 'We'll have to do it again; I'm feeling filthy.'

He reaches across the table, takes my hand and runs his thumb across my knuckles.

'I've a better plan. Why don't we work from the South of France for the summer?'

I laugh.

'I'm serious. I always spend the summer there with the kids. I've a villa—'

'Greg, much as I'd like to, I'm a partner in a business. I have responsibilities.'

'Doesn't that make you *more* flexible?' asks the man who never sees obstacles.

'Not really.'

'The villa's set up with everything – Internet, Wi-Fi . . . And we could buy anything else you need. Think of the work environment: sun, sea, sand . . . and showers.' He raises his eyebrows suggestively.

'My clients, Greg. They need to see me.'

'You could pop back for meetings. I'm sure Fint would be open.'

'I don't know. It'd be asking a lot. Maybe I could take a three-week holiday and after that pop over for weekends.' The idea of a holiday at all is a novelty.

'Why not run the idea by him, at least?'

'Greg, even if he was happy with me working from there and my clients were OK with it, and everything was fine on the work front, what about the children?'

'What about them?'

'Would they really want me there?'

'Lucy, this would give you a chance to spend more time with them, for you all to get to know each other better.'

I see the merit in that. As it is, every time we meet it's around some specific activity, which makes everything seem formal and stilted. Maybe if we were all on holiday . . .

Then again, 'Where would I stay? I couldn't stay with you; imagine how they'd feel. Me suddenly moving in.'

He reflects – for a split second. 'You could stay nearby; it wouldn't be a problem. I could look into it . . .'

I run it by Fint, still not convinced it's what I want. When I see his face, I realise that this is the first time that his joint roles as Cupid and business partner have come into conflict. He tries to hide his surprise, then asks a series of logistical questions, the replies to which inform him that the villa is fully equipped, that I can be on a plane and home in two hours for brainstorms, meetings et cetera, and that Greg will cover the cost of flights.

'It'd just be for the summer, right?' he confirms.

'I won't stay that long.'

He sucks a thumbnail. 'It *is* our quietest time.' He mulls it over. Then his face brightens. 'You know, it's not a bad idea for one of us to cover base while the other takes a decent break. Maybe next year I could finally organise that trip to South Africa I've always dreamed about. Stay a decent amount of time . . .'

'Of course. But, Fint, I'm not sure I want to spend the whole summer there. I was thinking of just playing it by ear for two or three weeks – you know, work while I'm there, see how it goes. If it's not working out, I'll just come home,' I say to myself as much as to him. 'And I'll be over and back all the time.'

'Let's try it, then. See how it goes.'

~

Before heading to France, we organise a night out so that Greg can meet Grace and Kevin. We keep it simple, opting for a popular Italian restaurant in town.

'So, who *inspires* you?' Kevin asks Greg. It's the fifth in a series of literary questions. 'Who's your *muse*?'

Greg looks across at me as if to say, 'Help!'

'Lucy! Of course!' Kevin misinterprets.

'I hope I don't inspire scenes of murder and destruction,' I say.

'You *know* you do.' Greg smiles.

Kevin's sudden bark of laughter sounds false.

Leaving the restaurant, Greg turns to us. 'Let's check out that casino in Merrion Square.'

Grace's face lights up.

But Kevin grimaces. 'I think we should call it a night, hon.' He looks at Greg apologetically. 'I'm the medical director of a pharmaceutical start-up. Crazy busy, as you can imagine. Shouldn't even be out tonight.' He turns to his wife. 'Grace?'

'Yeah. I'm going to the casino.'

Go, Grace.

'But Jason wakes at six.'

'Have I ever not woken up to feed our children?' Grace snaps. 'I'll see you back at the house, Kevin.'

~

From outside, the casino looks like any other three-storey, Georgian redbrick on the square. Inside, it's like a gentlemen's club. Grace and I are slow to part with our chips, expecting to lose. And that's exactly what we do. Greg piles his chips high and barely looks as the wheel spins. And yet he wins. Consistently. He starts to give away chips – for luck.

Grace and I retire to the bar.

'Is Greg OK?' she asks.

'Yeah, fine. Why?'

'Oh, nothing. I was just wondering – is he always so energetic?'

I laugh. 'Always.'

'He never seems to stop, though. Does he?'

'He's just one of those people who's always on the go.'

'Must be exhausting.'

I eye her. What's she getting at?

'Dad was shattered after playing golf with him.'

'Wait! Did Dad talk to you about Greg?' It feels like a deception, somehow.

'He just mentioned the game, that's all. Greg wanted to go for another eighteen holes.'

'He was probably joking, Grace. He *does* have a sense of humour.' I can't believe they were talking about Greg behind my back. 'Grace, are you trying to tell me something here?'

'I'm just wondering why he's so highly charged . . .'

'Greg lives life. He experiences it. And d'you know why? Because he knows it could be snatched from him at any moment.

Maybe if you'd lost someone you love you'd be "highly charged". Greg's alive, Grace. And he's making the most of it.'

She bites her lip. 'Sorry.'

'Forget it.'

'No. You're right. More of us should live like that.'

I'm sorry, then, for snapping. 'The boys are young. And Kevin's snowed under. Start-ups are always like that. Remember when Fint and I set up Get Smart? I don't think anybody saw us from one end of the day to the next – unless, of course, they were working for us. It'll get better, Grace.'

'Might help if he'd a sense of humour.'

'Who? Kevin?'

'Who else?'

Where has this come from? OK, he was a bit annoying in the restaurant, but I've never heard Grace complain about Kevin – ever.

'He's so serious,' she continues, moving her swizzle stick around the glass. 'He . . . never . . . laughs.'

'He was laughing tonight.'

She gives me a look that cuts right through me. 'That wasn't laughter. That was him trying to be the alpha male. He was competing with Greg; didn't you see that?'

'I thought he was just in good form.' And, OK, a bit of an idiot.

She shakes her head sadly. 'Competing.'

'Men do that, though, right?'

'*Some* men.'

'Kevin has other qualities,' I say optimistically.

'Name one.'

Jesus. This is the guy who looks down his nose at me. 'He works hard?' I try.

She scoffs.

Then it hits me. 'He's stressed! You know when your mind's on something – like, say, your new business – you probably try too hard to be social because you're not feeling social at all!' I'm a psychological wizard.

She shrugs miserably.

'Grace! This is Kevin we're talking about. You're crazy about Kevin. You're the perfect couple.'

Her 'Yeah' sounds tired. She reaches for her bag and stands. 'Come on. Let's go.'

We find Greg behind a skyline of chips, looking perky and adorable.

'Hey, Greg, let's go,' I say.

He looks up as though lost in the world of risk. 'Oh, hey! You out of chips? Here, have some of mine.'

'No. Let's actually go.'

'OK, sure.' He stands immediately.

'Sir, your win!' says the croupier.

'Oh, OK, great. Thanks.'

I shake my head in disbelief as more chips are pushed his way.

Greg collects our coats and holds them up for us as we put them on. 'How about a club?'

Grace looks at me. 'You go. I'll catch a cab.'

'Absolutely not,' Greg says. 'We'll all go.'

We flag down a taxi and drop Grace home. Then it's back into town to a club. Because we could all be dead tomorrow.

10.

Greg, Hilary and the children go ahead to France while I finish up a job at the office. A week later, Greg collects me at Nice Airport. Looking tanned and fit, he lifts me up and twirls me round. I laugh. It's only been a week, but I've missed him so much.

He grabs my case and takes off. I have to run to keep up.

Outside, his Range Rover is parked illegally. He throws my case in the back and makes for the front. I think he's opening my door for me, like he always does, but when he jumps inside, I realise my mistake. Left-hand drive.

I go around.

The engine's already running when I climb in. The car's an oven. 'Gordon Is a Moron', a punk favourite of Greg's, is blaring. Two months ago, I'd never heard of it. And, though it's hilarious, I turn it down and the air conditioning up.

We follow a sign for Marseilles, Cannes, Antibes. The grey and green of Ireland have been replaced by hazy blue and faded olive. We hit a motorway. Sea on our left; mountains on our distant right. We really are on the Côte d'Azur.

Greg's hitting a hundred and fifty kilometres an hour. The limit's a hundred and thirty. Even that seems high.

'Could you slow down a bit, Greg?'

'Christ, sorry,' he says when he sees the speedometer.

Soon, we turn off the motorway for Antibes and make our way through the outskirts.

'Nearly there,' he says, resting a hand on my leg.

At a roundabout, we take a smaller road. Then a smaller one again. We begin to climb.

'There it is,' he says, pointing up the hill. I catch a glimpse of a large, two-storey villa, surrounded by pine and eucalyptus trees. It has a terracotta roof and walls of a lighter shade, hidden in places by bright purple bougainvillea. Its shutters are a friendly light blue.

'It's beautiful.'

'I've found an apartment for you, about a kilometre up the road.'

'Great, can we dump my stuff there first?'

'Ah, come say hi to the kids first.'

Tired after the early morning flight, I was hoping to rest for a bit. Still, I shrug. 'OK.'

As we pull up outside the villa, he gives my hand a squeeze.

He swings open the heavy wooden door. Inside, it's darker, but only a little cooler. Overhead, fans slowly rotate. Terracotta tiles flag the floor. The walls are a warm yellow. Floor-to-ceiling pillars remind me of ancient Rome. In the living room, a fireplace dominates. It's in the shape of the sun's face, its wide-open mouth housing the hearth. Around it, three couches are strewn with children's clothes, sunscreen tubes, books, a bottle of Evian and an inflatable, bright green turtle. A large, mahogany chest acts as a coffee table. On it is a pottery vase filled with eucalyptus and bougainvillea. A woman's touch. Hilary, no doubt. I stop at an entire wall of books, wanting to explore.

'There'll be time later,' he says, taking my hand.

From outside comes an echoey distant scream, followed by a splash.

'Come on, they're in the pool,' he says.

We walk out to blinding white light. Everything seems over-exposed. I lower my sunglasses. To my left, beyond a low, stone wall, the view down to the bay is spectacular. Straight ahead, a wooden table is charming in its simplicity. Multi-coloured towels hide the chairs that surround it. On the ground are flip-flops and sandals, scattered as though abandoned in a hurry. Wet patches have small footprints leading to and from a large rectangle of blue in the near distance.

There they are: Toby being hurled into the air by Hilary, and Rachel swimming towards them. Toby reminds me of Mowgli from *The Jungle Book*: slight and sallow, with longish, dark hair and a little red triangle of swimming togs. His goggles are huge compared to the size of his face, making him look half alien, half fighter pilot. Rachel is a streak of dark hair and splashing arms and legs. Hilary, looking robust in a black one-piece, spins Toby around in the water.

'Hi, guys,' calls Greg as we approach the pool.

They turn.

'Dad!' shouts Toby. 'Did you see that?'

'You should be in the circus, Tobes.'

'I know. Yeah.'

I smile.

'Do you want us to come out?' asks Hilary.

'No, Hilary, we're coming in.'

I look at Greg. My bikini's packed at the bottom of my case. I'm visualising it when he grabs my hand and jumps, taking me with him.

'Whee!' he calls.

The sudden drop in temperature adds to the shock. I find myself underwater, face up, legs higher than the rest of me. His hand is gone. I can't see him. I turn over in the water then kick and swim to the surface, breaking through into dazzling light, gasping for air and coughing. I make it to the side of the pool, where I cling, head down, trying to restore normal breathing. At last, I look up. He's already out of the pool, shaking himself like a dog. I open my mouth to say 'You big eejit,' but close it again, remembering the children. Then I hear them. Laughing. I turn around. Clearly, I'm the entertainment. I smile to show I'm a good sport then press my palms on the hot slabs lining the pool and push myself up and out.

Greg comes to me with a towel.

'That's mine,' says Rachel, who has stopped laughing.

'It's an emergency,' says Greg, handing it to me.

'It's *mine!* I don't want her to have it.'

Mortified, I hand it back to him.

'I'll get you another,' he says, disappearing into the villa.

I stand alone, feeling conspicuous, stupid and wet.

'Your legs are bleeding,' Toby calls.

I look down. The dye from my red leather sandals is running in little streams down my feet. It looks like a scene from the Old Testament. I want to disappear, vanish. I make for the villa, dripping red.

'Here you go,' Greg says when I get inside. He wraps a large white towel around me.

I stare at him. 'Why did you do that, Greg?'

He stops, as if considering that for the first time. 'I don't know. Fun?'

'I'm trying *so hard* to make an impression with Rachel and Toby . . .'

'But they thought it was hilarious.'

'No, Greg. They thought *I* was hilarious. I want them to like me, not think I'm a joke. I felt like such a fool out there.'

'I'm sorry. I didn't think.'

'How can they respect me if you don't?'

He looks hurt. 'I do.'

'Well, that's not how it seemed. It was such a stupid thing to do.'

'I'm sorry, Luce. I was just trying to break the ice. Everyone's so nervous. But you're right, it was stupid. I'm sorry.'

~

We drive in silence to the apartment.

It's in a small, upmarket block. On the second floor, Greg opens the door, then hands me one of two keys. My first impression is of a bright, airy space. Very modern, with clean lines and white walls. Most importantly, it's air conditioned.

'Where's the shower?' is all I say.

It's a relief to be alone, warm water pounding down on me. I close my eyes and breathe deeply. I wash my hair and start to calm down. Red dye swirls down the plughole, taking my anger with it.

Finally, I reach for a white towelling bathrobe. It still has its sales tag on. That he has thought to go out and buy this for me reminds me of what's important – Greg's a good guy who meant well. Normally, I love his childlike approach to life. Normally, it's refreshing. Maybe if I hadn't been so tense, so eager to make a good impression on his children . . . I don't know. I wrap my hair in a towel and go in search of him.

He's sitting on the bed, looking guilty.

And suddenly I wish it was just the two of us – no children, no complications, no one to impress or win over. I shake free my hair from the towel and the thoughts from my head. I sit beside him, wrap my arms around him.

'I'm sorry,' he says. 'I should have given it more thought.'

'Forget it.' I smile when I say, 'It cooled me down.'

He kisses me then gets up. 'Come see the view from the balcony.'

Outside, the air is hot and dry and carries the fragrance of . . . I'm not sure, herbs? The cicadas sound as if they're in overdrive. Off in the distance, a glittering sea merges with a clear, blue sky. Pine trees in the near distance are heavy with cones, like eco-friendly Christmas decorations. Closer still, almost within touching distance, is a eucalyptus, its drooping silver-green leaves looking cool and unruffled in the heat. Its bark is peeling off in thin strips, like flesh-coloured stockings, revealing smooth white skin underneath. I turn to tell Greg how magical it all is and how happy I am to be here with him, only to discover that he's gone back inside. I find him sitting up in bed, bare-chested and beaming, clothes abandoned on the floor. He has draped a leg over the sheet in fake seductiveness. He raises and lowers his eyebrows. I laugh, let my robe drop and join him. And soon, I've forgotten everything, except how much I adore him.

When we eventually return to the villa, Hilary has made dinner – a tuna pasta dish, and the children's favourite, apparently. Greg must have forgotten to mention that I'm vegetarian. I can't afford to be more different than I already am. So I tuck in with what I hope looks like enthusiasm. At least it's not steak.

I wear a friendly face, say little and listen, hoping to learn as much as I can about this pre-prepared family I've promised to become part of. Toby chats about sharks; in particular the fact that they have to keep moving to stay alive, which means they have to swim in their sleep.

'Imagine that!' he concludes.

That he seems oblivious to me is reassuring. Maybe I'm not such a big deal to him. Rachel, on the other hand, I frequently catch peeping out at me from behind a curtain of hair she's let fall between us. When I smile, she looks away.

When dinner's over, I start to collect the dishes. Hilary stands quickly, taking the plates from me.

'It's fine,' she says. 'I'll do it.'

'No, no. I'd like to help, Hilary.' I certainly don't expect to be waited on.

'It's OK,' she says, looking down at the plates in her hand. 'I know where everything goes.'

'At least let me carry things to the kitchen.'

'I'm fine. Honestly. Thanks,' she says firmly.

She disappears into the kitchen.

I look at Greg, wondering how I'm ever going to feel part of this family.

He smiles reassuringly.

'Do you want coffee?' I try.

'That would be lovely, thanks, Lucy,' he says like he understands.

The kitchen is beautiful, with an old-fashioned sink and simple wooden cupboards painted pale green. The work surfaces are oak, as is the chunky, basic furniture. Really, really pretty. I wonder if Catherine designed it, or whether she and Greg did it together, or if it was like this when they bought the villa. That they shared so much reminds me of what little history Greg and I have. I bring myself back to the present – coffee. I start to search the obvious places.

'What are you looking for?' Hilary asks.

Instinctively, I feel I've walked into her territory. 'Coffee?'

'I'll do it.'

'Hilary, look, I don't want you to feel that you have to do anything for me. I'm going to be around a bit and I'd like to pull my weight.' Her face is blank; I can't read it. 'It would be great, though, if you could show me where the coffee is.'

Without a word, she goes to various cupboards and pulls out an original steel coffee percolator (so romantic!) and the paraphernalia that goes with it.

'Thanks,' I say, and set to work.

'Sorry, but could you move, please?' she says after two seconds. 'I have to use the dishwasher.'

'Sorry.' I shift along, thinking that maybe I should stay out of the kitchen for a while. I do *not* want to make an enemy of Hilary.

~

'Hilary, aren't you joining us for coffee?' asks Greg, surprised.

'No, thanks. I have to get Toby ready for bed.'

'We're on holiday; there's no rush.'

'I'd prefer to stick to routine, Greg, if that's OK?'

'Sure. Whatever you think.'

She coaxes Toby away from the DVD he's watching. Rachel gets up.

'Going up already, Rache?' Greg asks.

'I'm tired,' she says, looking directly at me.

Greg doesn't see it. 'OK,' he says. 'Say goodnight to Lucy.'

''Night, Lucy,' says Toby.

''Night, Toby.' I smile at him.

'Rachel?' Greg prompts.

She looks at me, eyes dark, then turns to go.

'Rachel,' says her father in a warning tone.

'It doesn't matter, Greg,' I say, not wanting him to make a big deal of it. I smile at her. She glares back.

'Rachel doesn't like Lucy,' offers Toby, matter-of-factly.

I blush.

'She doesn't want her to be on holidays with us. She doesn't want her to be in our family. She hates her, ackshilly.'

For the second time in one day, I want to disappear.

'Enough, Toby,' says Greg. 'Rachel, I told you to say goodnight to Lucy; now say it.'

I don't want him to force her. 'Greg, please, it doesn't matter. Really.'

'Goodnight,' she says, as if the word means 'I hate you'. She races to the stairs and thunders up. Hilary follows, looking calm and unruffled.

'You can't force her to like me, Greg,' I say quietly.

'No, but I do expect manners.'

'I have manners,' says Toby.

'And a big mouth,' retorts his father, picking him up and turning him over so that his bare feet are against Greg's face. 'Bristle attack,' he says, grabbing his feet and rubbing them against his evening stubble. Toby screams. And they both laugh.

I have never felt like such an outsider.

Hilary comes back downstairs. Though she returns my smile, it's without any great warmth.

'Is she all right?' Greg asks her.

'She's a bit upset. The change, an' all,' she says, lifting Toby from Greg's lap. 'Maybe you could have a word with her when you go up. Come on, squirt,' she says to the boy who is to become my stepson, a transition that seems monumental.

'Do I have to?'

'Yes. You have to.'

Off they go, Toby twisting her hair in his fingers.

Greg winks at me. 'Let's go for a beer on the terrace.'

That's where we are when Hilary returns with Toby, squeaky clean and dressed for bed. Hilary kisses the top of his head and says goodnight to him, then to us.

'My God,' Greg exclaims. 'It's a mass exodus tonight.'

'Tired,' she says.

Greg takes Toby upstairs for a story. Watching them all disappear, the enormity of what I'm taking on finally hits. I'm marrying one man, two children and a nanny. Theoretical children are so much easier than real ones who come with personalities, opinions, objections. Can Rachel really hate me? Already? She doesn't even know me. Then again, that's the problem. Rachel doesn't know that I'm on her side, that I want what's best for her, that I want the two of us to get on. If only I could make her see that. Not that she'd listen to me. She probably wouldn't listen to Greg either; he's the one who brought me here. She'd listen to Hilary, though. It's so obvious that Rachel loves her. But would Hilary help?

'Let's go,' I say, when Greg arrives back.

'Where?'

'To the apartment.'

'Why?'

'So we can be alone for a while.'

'We're alone now.'

'I know, but really alone. Just the two of us.'

He looks hurt. 'This is home. The apartment is for appearances, for you to sleep in, that's all.'

I have to get out of the villa. I go to him, kiss him softly on the mouth and whisper, 'It could be for other things, too.'

He smiles. 'I know somewhere closer.' He takes my hand and leads me to his bedroom. 'See? Much quicker.' He beams, tugging at my clothes.

I tell myself that it doesn't matter that we're in the villa. In here, we're alone. I close my eyes and try to think of nothing but what's happening in this room. It's getting easier and easier, but then the bed begins to groan with a telling rhythm. And I tense.

'Greg, stop,' I whisper.

'What?' he whispers back.

'Someone will hear.'

'Have you seen how thick the walls are?'

'Hilary's next door.'

'Hilary doesn't have bionic hearing. Now, wait till I show you this little trick.'

His little trick shatters my resistance.

~

Afterwards, we lie in silence, a film of sweat covering our bodies; the air so heavy, it's hard to breathe.

'Greg, you need to get air conditioning.'

'What do you think I am, a philistine? When in Rome, live like the Romans.'

'I'm sure plenty of the "Romans" have air conditioning.'

He turns to face me. 'This villa's designed for the heat. And the Millars are a tough breed. Don't want us becoming soft.'

'How about a few electric fans, then?'

'Wimp.' He smiles. 'We'll get some tomorrow.'

'Greg?'

'Mm-hmm?'

'Do you think Rachel will come around – eventually?'

He raises himself onto an elbow and tucks a stray strand of my hair behind my ear. 'Of course. Once she gets to know you. Right now, it's the idea of sharing her life with you she doesn't like; not you personally.'

I sit up. 'I thought that maybe Hilary might put in a good word for me with her. But I think I annoyed her today. You know, got in her way or something.'

'No. It's a good idea. If Rachel listens to anyone, it's Hilary.'

'Might be unfair to ask, though; I'm not sure she likes me.'

'Hilary? Of course she does. She's just focused on the kids. She'd do anything for this family. Want me to ask her?'

'Ah. No, not for the moment. Just let me get to know her a bit better first, OK?'

'OK.'

We're quiet for a while. 'Greg?'

'Uh-huh?'

'Could you drop me at the airport, tomorrow?'

'Leaving already?' He smiles.

'I want to rent a car.'

'A car? Why?'

'Just to get around.'

'Sure, I'll take you wherever you want to go.'

I smile. 'I know. And thanks. But you've the kids. What if I have to go back to Dublin for work and you need to take them somewhere?'

'I'll figure something out.'

'I don't want you to have to. My being here is putting you all out already.' I pause. 'And, Greg, I really think that, for the moment, we should try to remain a bit separate, you know?'

'How do you mean?'

'Well, I don't think it's a good idea for me to be a constant presence at the villa.'

He scratches his head. 'I know what Rachel said to Toby sounds bad, but I think it would be a mistake to overreact, here. The children need to get used to you being around.'

'I know, Greg, but slowly.'

I feel his disappointment.

We say no more on the subject until he's dropping me off at the apartment.

'We'll get that car tomorrow, then,' he concedes.

I smile. 'Thanks, Greg. It's the right thing.'

'And I'll pick you up for breakfast at the villa in the morning?'

I wonder if I got through to him at all.

11.

Next morning, I wake early and walk to the villa, taking in the scenery and getting some exercise. It seemed like a great idea, until I arrive at the front door and can't decide what to do. I have a key, but if I use it, it might seem pushy. If I don't, it'll just seem stupid. Everyone knows I have it. Oh, what the hell. I slip it in.

I'm heading for the living room when, from inside, I hear Rachel say, 'She talks to us like babies. Is she some kind of dork or something?'

I stop; my stomach twists.

'She's probably just not used to kids,' Hilary says.

'I don't want her to get used to us. I want her to get lost.'

'Rache, remember when I came first? You didn't like me either.'

'I did so.'

'No, Rachel, you didn't. It took a long time. But you did in the end. Lucy seems nice. Maybe you should give her a chance.'

'Why? I don't want a stepmother. Did anyone ask me? No. He never asked, Hilary. He never checked. He always checks big decisions with us. Always.' She breaks down.

Oh, God. I feel so guilty.

I close the front door quietly. I race back up the hill. We've done everything wrong. We should have been more measured in the way Greg introduced me. I should have been his 'friend' first. We could have got to know each other as individuals before bringing the whole stepmother thing into the equation. But that would have been deceitful. If only things had happened more slowly. If only Greg hadn't parachuted me into their lives. Hilary was so sweet, standing up for me like that. I've been wrong about her, too. She mustn't resent me being here, after all.

I'm not long back at the apartment when Greg arrives – with croissants and pains au chocolat. 'You want to be a bit separate. So. Here I am.' He smiles.

I hug him.

We make coffee and go out onto the balcony.

Then I tell him what happened.

He grimaces. 'You OK?'

'Yeah. It's Rachel I'm worried about.'

'I need to sit down with her and have a chat. She needs to let off a bit of steam with me.' He pulls out a pack of cigars and holds it up as if to say, 'Do you mind?'

'Have you started smoking?'

He smiles. 'Let's just say, I've stopped stopping.' He cups his hand over a cigar and lights it slowly, ritualistically.

I look out over the trees, remembering the conversation. 'It was nice of Hilary to say what she did.'

He places the lighter on the table. 'Told you she was like that.'

I realise I know nothing about her. 'What did she do before coming to work for you?'

'Worked in a crèche for a while.'

'Why did she leave?'

'She wanted to work more one to one with kids. Her own marriage had just broken up because they couldn't have children.'

'That's terrible.' I try to imagine the sense of loss she must have felt as someone who so clearly loves kids.

'They were married five years, trying for children most of that time. In the end, the whole IVF thing wore them down. It had become their sole focus. When they finally gave up, there didn't seem anything left to salvage from their relationship.'

'That's so tough. When did she tell you all this?' It doesn't strike me as the kind of thing a nanny would unburden herself of easily to a male boss.

He stubs out the cigar, stands and goes to the balcony rail, placing his hands wide apart on it and leaning forward. After a few moments, he turns and looks me in the eye. 'Actually, Lucy, there's something I need to tell you.' My stomach lurches. 'I wasn't sure how to bring it up before because I didn't want to make it any bigger than it is . . .'

I want to tell him to stop. At the same time, I need to know – every detail.

He shoves his hands into his pockets and takes a deep breath. 'OK.' He comes over and sits down. 'Way back, at the beginning, not long after she started, when I was pretty low' – he pauses – 'something happened between Hilary and me . . .'

There it is, absolute confirmation. *Jesus.*

'Once. Only once. I was so down after Catherine died. For the first few months, I drank a bit. One night, Hilary was there, saying the right things, doing the right things. And . . .' his voice trails off. 'Afterwards, I was so ashamed; I was her boss, for Christ's sake. I apologised profusely, told her that if she wanted to leave I'd understand, that maybe it would be better if she did. I was straight with her, explained that it had happened as a result of grief, nothing more. She understood. Said she was grieving too, for the family she couldn't have. It was all about loss – on both our parts. We agreed to forget that it ever happened. Never spoke of it again. Hilary does her job. And does it well. Life has carried on. It's ancient history. I just thought you should know. I want to be straight with you, Luce.'

I nod. Can't trust myself to speak. That they've shared this makes the foundations between us a little less steady. But then he *has* told me. And it was just once. And a mistake. Still, I'd feel a whole lot better if they didn't have that history, ancient or otherwise.

We manage to finish breakfast. We even have sex and shower together. Greg's more affectionate, gentle and loving than ever, and I want to be fine about this. But when he asks if I'm coming to the villa to work from his office with him, I find myself explaining that I'd make more progress here, that I like to work alone, that the villa's too warm and that the children need a break from me. He looks disappointed, but says nothing, just that he'll collect me at twelve thirty for a swim and lunch. That would be lunch prepared by a woman he's had sex with, eaten in the company of a girl who hates me.

~

When Greg's gone, I open up my computer, but concentration escapes me. I pick up the phone, needing to hear a familiar voice.

'Bonjour!' I say when Fint answers.

'Bonjour, yourself! How's life in heaven?'

'Oh, you know, just hoovered my cloud.'

He laughs.

'Any news?'

'Yeah, I'm single again.'

'Aw, Fint.' There was always one issue in his relationship with Simon. 'He wouldn't "come out", would he?'

'Nope. And that's not as simple as it sounds.'

'I know. I'm sorry.'

'I'm past all that angst, Lucy. He needs to deal with this himself; I'm not a shrink. So, how are you?'

'Fine. Good. Great.'

'What's wrong?'

'Nothing.'

'Come on, this is Uncle Fint you're talking to here.'

I share the reality of life on my cloud, ending with the Hilary newsflash.

'OK,' he says. 'I'm going to ask you one question. Do you trust Greg?'

If it wasn't Fint, I'd be indignant. 'Of course. Absolutely.'

'Well then, you've nothing to worry about, have you?'

He always was a clear thinker. 'No. I suppose not.'

'What are you going to do about Rachel?'

'I don't know. Be patient. Try not to take it personally. Get out a bit more with Greg, just the two of us. I was hoping to try to get to know Hilary a bit better, but I don't know. After what Greg's said . . .'

'Forget about that now. Greg's marrying you, isn't he? If he'd wanted Hilary, he'd have asked her a long time ago.'

He has a point. 'Thanks, Fint. I needed that. What are *you* going to do?'

'Work.'

I laugh. We're so alike, Fint and I.

Greg collects me for our swim. As we're heading for the pool, his phone rings. It's his agent. He goes inside to take the call, leaving me standing on the terrace, watching Toby, Hilary and Rachel play together in the pool. I take a deep breath and stick to the plan. I dive in and swim the full length, underwater, in complete and blissful silence. I pop up at the shallow end, suck in air and flick back my hair.

'Deadly,' says a voice beside me.

In the time it has taken me to swim the length, Toby has extricated himself from the others and is bobbing in the water beside me. The whites of his eyes seem so clear against the brown; his lashes are clumped together by water. I smile.

'You're a great diver,' he says.

'Thanks, Toby. And you must be a great swimmer to get over here so fast.'

'Yeah. I am. But I can't dive.' He has a dimple on one cheek.

'It's very easy. All you have to do is relax.'

'I can relax.' He lowers his goggles, then lies on his back, sticks his tummy in the air and tilts his head so far back that if it weren't for the goggles, his eyes would be flooded.

'That was very good relaxing, all right,' I say.

He stands up, just managing to keep his chin above water. 'Can you learn me to dive?'

'I don't know. Maybe we should ask your dad if it's OK with him.'

'He wouldn't mind.'

I'm sure he wouldn't. But Toby isn't my child. I'm trying to decide what to do.

'Want me to ask him?'

'Not now, he's on the phone.'

But Toby's already gone, slipping up out of the pool like a frisky otter and darting towards the villa.

Hilary calls, 'Toby. Walk. Don't run.' He looks at her and slows to a walk. 'Good man.'

He comes racing back out with a thumb in the air. When he reaches me he asks, 'Can we do it now?'

I smile. 'Sure.'

'Hey, Rach-el. I'm going to learn to dive before you.'

Oh, dear.

'I can dive already.'

'Nah. You're crap.'

'Ah, ah' is out before I can stop it.

He looks at me and stops.

I feel like laughing; I've disciplined by accident. And the world is still spinning.

~

I teach Toby to dive from a sitting position first. He does as I say, no fear, head down, arms straight, and fingertips pointing at the pool. I wait in the water and catch him every time he surfaces.

'You're brilliant!' I exclaim in admiration.

He beams.

Soon, he's diving standing up. I'm stunned by his progress.

He's so proud of himself. He can dive. But, more importantly, his sister can't. Not really. Not as well. I recognise that feeling. I experienced it the first time my father realised I could draw.

The children grow hungry and Hilary takes them inside. Still waiting for Greg, I swim a few lengths before coming out. As I cut through the water, I wonder if the best way forward is to concentrate on Toby. Maybe, then, Rachel will see that I'm actually an OK person.

After another half-hour, I give up waiting. I shower by the pool, dress and go looking for Greg.

In the living room, Hilary's on one of the couches with Toby, rubbing sunscreen onto his legs.

'That was fun,' I call to him.

'Oh, Jesus,' says Hilary. A worm of white sunscreen shoots from the tube she's holding and lands on the couch. 'You gave me a fright.'

'I'm sorry. I'll get a cloth.'

'Don't worry about it,' she says. 'Greg won't mind.'

I rub at it with my towel anyway. 'Did you enjoy that, Toby?'

'*Yeah!*'

'Yes, thank you,' corrects Hilary.

'Yes, thank you.'

I smile.

'Guess what? Hil's bringing us to Aqua-Splash after lunch.'

'What's that?'

'This cool place with lots of pools and slides and stuff. Wanna come?'

Greg and I had planned to get that rent-a-car. But it can wait.

'Lucy has work to do, Toby,' says Hilary.

'Actually, I'm not that busy today. I'd like to go with you, if it's not a hassle for you.'

She colours. Quietly, she says, 'It's just that I'm not sure Rachel is ready for you to come on trips with us yet.'

'Of course.' I tussle Toby's hair. 'Another time, Toby, OK?'

'OK.'

I find Greg in the office, on the computer.

'What happened to you?' I ask.

'What?'

'We were supposed to be going for a swim.'

'God, sorry. I got distracted by the phone call, then had some ideas for the book.'

'No worries.' I've made progress with Toby. And it feels amazing.

12.

Talking to Toby is proving a bigger challenge than I thought. Hilary is always there, and always joins in. Because she knows him so well, the conversation takes off without me. She knows how to interest him, how to make him laugh. By the time the conversation ends, usually with Hilary taking him off somewhere, I'm on the perimeter again. As for getting to know Rachel? She exits rooms whenever I enter.

It's hard to imagine ever becoming stepmother to children who already have a mother in Hilary. She makes the meals, cuts up Toby's food, is naturally physical with them. She hugs and touches them in such a casual, easy way. She carries Toby when he's tired. They snuggle into her when watching DVDs. They run to her when hurt. Hilary can call Toby 'runt' or Rachel 'idiot' and make it sound loving. I can only imagine what would happen if I used those terms with them.

In desperation, I hit on an idea and suggest to Greg that we take the children off for the day, just the two of us.

'I don't know,' he says. 'In France, Hilary usually comes everywhere with us.' He's searching his desk for a reference book and is flinging everything aside into a messy heap. He looks up. 'I wouldn't want her to feel left out.'

'I understand that, Greg. It's just that I don't feel I'm getting to know Rachel and Toby at all.'

He stops what he's doing, his eyes registering. 'OK. Let's do it.' He gets up, there and then.

But when he proposes the idea to the children, there's a problem: Rachel won't go without Hilary.

So we plan a communal trip.

But as I get ready, I develop a headache. I also start to wonder what's the point? With Hilary there, I'll still be the outsider. With my head thumping like this, I'd be better off lying down.

Greg seems annoyed that I'm not coming, but honours his promise to the children and takes them. I return to the apartment in the Clio I've rented, pop two Nurofen and lie down. I wake an hour later, headache-free and glad to be alone.

After pottering around for a while, I feel like a swim. I drive down to the villa and let myself in, revelling in its emptiness. I dive into crystal blue, feeling at peace in my soundproof, underwater world. I come up for air and dive back under again.

I sit at the side, legs dangling in the water, while the sun beats down on my back, drying it in minutes. I lie in the shade with a book. Greg's caretaker arrives in a sarong and bare feet to clean the pool.

I go inside and ring Fint. His voice reminds me what I miss about him. Everything, basically. The blotchy way he applies fake tan. The dapper way he dresses (the dark purple rugby shirt with lace collar and cuffs, the cream shoes, his black, rectangular glasses). The way he bursts out with 'Ooh, he's a ride' at the sight of any reasonably attractive man. I even miss the way he hears about someone's sudden illness and worries that he has it, too.

'I'm thinking of coming over,' I say, on impulse.

'When?'

'Whenever you like.'

'Great. Just give me a day's notice.' He talks of new jobs that have come in and I volunteer immediately for two – to design the cover of a quiz book and the template of a newsletter for a breakfast cereal company. Neither is a particularly exciting project. Each will, however, provide a distraction and a reminder that I'm good at *something.*

~

My anti-family mood begins to wear off. At six, I decide to cook a meal so that Hilary won't have to. I prepare vegetables for a stir-fry. Soon, everything's ready to be thrown into the wok. I ring Greg's mobile to see where they are. It goes to voicemail. I put off cooking until I'm so hungry I have to eat. I take a little of everything and make a portion. As light begins to leak from the sky, I start to worry. I keep trying his phone, without success.

By eleven, I'm pacing the kitchen, imagining all sorts of scenarios, when I hear the car outside. I open the door to sleeping children being carried by a couple. They look like a happy family arriving back after a long, enjoyable day out. Except for one thing. Hilary doesn't look mumsy. Her flouncy, white skirt is pretty damn short and her top is clingy and low cut. It doesn't put me in the best of moods.

'What happened to you?' I ask Greg when he comes downstairs from putting Rachel to bed.

'Nothing.'

'Why were you so late?'

'I didn't realise there was a curfew.'

'There wasn't. I was just worried. You weren't answering your phone.'

'If you'd come, you'd have known we were fine.'

'I had a headache.'

'You could have taken something. I was writing, Lucy. I stopped because you wanted to go out. Then you changed your mind, and

I carried on to keep the kids happy. Now you're angry I wasn't home sooner. What do you want from me?'

'Nothing.' I put my hand to my forehead. 'I just want us to get on. All of us. I want to build a relationship with your children, but something always gets in the way. I'm trying so hard to fit into your life and get to know everyone . . .'

'So, why didn't you come with us?'

'I didn't feel well. And I was tired. This is hard, you know? How can you get people to like you when they don't even want you there?' I break down.

He takes me in his arms, says nothing, and just rubs my back over and over. When he speaks, it's to apologise. 'I'm sorry, Lucy. I know you're trying. I should have come back sooner. I was annoyed with you for staying here. I was being a dick. I'm sorry, OK?' He's smoothing back my hair, clearing away my tears.

'I want it to work, Greg. I don't want to upset Rachel or Toby. And I already have by just being here. I don't know, maybe I should go home for a while.'

'You're going nowhere.' He kisses me softly, again and again, until I kiss him back. We make it to the bedroom and I find comfort where I always have been able to with Greg.

~

Later, I try to sound casual when I ask, 'How soon after her marriage ended did Hilary start working for you?'

'Months.'

'Must have been good for her to have a distraction.'

He smiles. 'I'd call us more of a challenge than a distraction; we were such a mess. But you're right. I think that did help Hilary.'

'What age is she?'

'Thirty-two, thirty-three. Why?'

'I don't know. I guess I'm just surprised that she's still happy to live in, especially having been married. I mean, I'm twenty-nine and I'd want my own place.'

He frowns. 'I never thought of that; Hilary's been with us for so long. When she started, I needed her, round the clock. It seemed to suit her, then. Of course, she's probably changed. God, she must have. I never thought about that. Of course, you're right. She should be out there, getting on with her life. Not stuck with us twenty-four hours a day. Especially after we're married. I'll talk to her.'

I don't want to go back to the apartment tonight. I want to fall asleep in Greg's arms. I set the alarm for six thirty and snuggle into him.

~

I wake at three in the morning to find Greg sitting up in bed, furiously writing.

'Greg?'

He looks over. Beams. 'Behold! Athena awaketh!'

'What?'

'Athena. The Greek goddess of wisdom and victory. Fierce, fearless and righteous.'

'What are you doing?'

'Can't sleep. My mind's buzzing. I keep getting these amazing ideas. If I don't write them down, they'll be gone in the morning.'

I close my eyes to the light, the energy. *Are all writers like this?*

'Oh, and sorry about the book,' he says.

'Hmm?' I lift heavy lids.

He's holding up what looks like the novel I was reading. 'I'll buy you another.'

'It's yours. I got it from the living room.'

'Phew! I've written all over it. Couldn't find anything else.'

'It's three o'clock.'

'Already?'

I squint at him. 'Are you like this every night?'

He smiles and ruffles my hair. 'Go back to sleep, my little Greek goddess.'

I yawn. 'OK, 'night.' I turn over and put a pillow over my head.

~

Daylight wakes me before the alarm. My watch says six. Greg's already up and gone. I pull back the sheet. Already, the air's hot. I dress quickly and check to make sure I've left no evidence of myself. I find Greg in his office, at the computer, wearing nothing but boxers, staring at the screen, his fingers racing across the keyboard. I smile. No wonder he's so good at what he does. He's obsessed. I yawn, kiss the top of his head and tell him I'm heading back to the apartment. He glances up, his unshaven face and spiky hair giving him an almost wild look that makes me smile wider. He winks, then is back to the computer, flying. I rub my eyes and decide that, actually, it's too early to be up.

~

A few days later, after a morning's work, I call down to Greg, hoping that he'll join me for a swim then lunch out, just us two. When I get there, he's on a roll at the computer. He suggests I go ahead to the pool; he'll be right out.

Hilary and Rachel are finishing up their swim. Toby's getting up from the towel he's been sunbathing on – it's funny to see such a young sun-worshipper. The pool is settling back to calm, the inflatable turtle, Paddy Power, still bobbing up and down. Goggles and flippers lie abandoned by the steps.

I call a friendly hello to the group headed my way. The only person who answers is Toby. The others just walk past. Rachel's behaviour I understand. Not Hilary's. She's never had a problem with me before. I tell myself not to worry. I carry on, slip out of my flip-flops, lower my goggles and dive in. I spend a good half-hour swimming, mostly underwater.

Hungry now, I shower and go to retrieve my towel, which I've left hanging on an airing rail on the terrace. I find it thrown to the ground, replaced by Rachel's togs. Hilary's coming back out. She holds my gaze. It's as if she wants me to know that she did this. I say nothing. Just pick up the towel, shake it and wrap it around me.

'So, you're trying to get rid of me?' Hilary says.

I squint at her. 'Sorry?'

'Greg told me.'

'Told you what?'

'Your plan to get me out of the way.'

'What are you talking about?'

'Have me live out first, then it's only a matter of time.'

I colour. 'Hilary, it wasn't like that at all. I just said to Greg that you might *like* to live out.'

She folds her arms, leans her weight on one leg and points the other out in front of her. 'Yeah, well, all he can seem to go on about now is how I need a life of my own.'

'Look, Hilary, I'm sure Greg would be delighted for you to stay living in, if that's what you want. We just thought you might like to have a choice, that's all. We were thinking of you.'

'Oh, I'm sure *Greg* was.'

'As was I.'

'If you think I believe that, you're dumber than you look.'

'Excuse me?'

She advances, hands on hips, head extended. 'You come barging into this family. No warning. Against my better judgement,

I decide to give you a break. I tell the children not to worry, that they just need to give it time. I tell Rachel you're probably a really nice person. And there you are, all along, going behind my back, trying to get me out of the picture.' She shakes her head. 'Unbelievable.'

'It wasn't like that. Trust me.'

'Trust you? Why should I trust you? You've every reason to want me gone. You've already started trying.'

'Hilary . . .'

'Look. Spare me the wide-eyed innocent routine, OK? I came out here to tell you something. And here it is: I'm not going anywhere. I love this family. So, you can give up trying to be cute. I've been here a lot longer than you, and I know this family a lot better. If you want to take me on, then do. But know one thing: I'll win.' With that, she turns and pounds back to the villa.

I stand rooted, heart pounding, face burning, amazed by her anger and devastated that I've just made an enemy of someone I'd hoped might become an ally.

13.

I lean against the door of Greg's office, which I've just closed behind me.

'I've just had a major run-in with Hilary.'

He looks up from his computer, removing the pen that he had gripped between his teeth.

'She thinks I want to get rid of her,' I say, walking towards him.

He frowns. 'Why?'

I sit on the desk, facing him. 'You told her it was my idea she might like to live out. Now she thinks I don't want her here at all. What did you say to her?'

He pushes back his swivel chair. 'I didn't say it was anyone's idea. But obviously I didn't make myself clear . . .'

'Can you remember what you said?'

He frowns. 'Not exactly. Something along the lines of time moving on, her priorities changing and that I was sorry for not realising sooner. I told her if she wanted to move out when we got back to Ireland, that'd be fine.'

'But you didn't explain that it was just a suggestion; that she didn't have to if she didn't want to?'

'I thought she'd assume that.'

'She thinks I asked you to have her move out.'

He pumps the top of the pen with his thumb. 'OK. No worries. It's a simple misunderstanding. Let me have a word with her. See if I can clear it up. After all, we *were* thinking about her; we were trying to make her life easier.'

'I know, but she doesn't see it that way. And she seems to have made up her mind. You should have seen her; she was fuming.'

'She's a good person, Lucy. Honestly. Let me talk to her. We'll probably all be laughing about this in a few days.'

'Yeah,' I say without conviction. I stand up. 'Let's go out for lunch, Greg. I need to get away from here for a while.'

He smiles. 'You're not the only one.'

∾

That night, I phone Grace. Tell her everything.

'God, she sounds uptight. What's her problem?'

'She thinks I'm trying to get rid of her.'

'I know, but why? All you were doing was giving her the option of more freedom.'

'I know. I know. But what if she's right? What if, subconsciously, I suggested it because I want her gone? She makes me feel so inadequate. And I can never get near the kids with her always around. I can't even have sex without worrying that she'll hear. How weird is that?'

'What's weird is the way she's reacting. At her age, she should be delighted at the prospect of having a social life, not attacking you for suggesting it. I'd watch out there, Lucy. She seems over-attached.'

'She and Greg had sex once.'

'*What?*'

'Way back. Only once. When he was upset. He told me about it. It meant nothing to him . . .'

'But what if it meant something to her? I'd get her out of the house.'

'Grace, I can't do that. I can't ask him to fire her; she's been with them so long. She's part of the family. The children love her.'

'All the more reason to get rid of her. She's too close. I mean, come on, Lucy, she *fucked* him.'

'Once. Five years ago. I can't ask Greg to get rid of her. I can't. This is a very difficult time for the children. They need routine, stability now' – I've been reading my step-parenting books – 'not to have one of the people they love most in the world sent away.'

'You're taking a gamble.'

'Grace, even if I asked him to, he'd talk me out of it. I know he would. He thinks the world of her. He's going to talk to her. It'll be all right.'

'OK. But you know what I think.'

'How's Kevin?'

'Kevin? Do I *know* a Kevin? Because the name rings a faint bell.'

I smile. 'Still working hard as ever?'

'I'm jealous of his office chair. It sees more of his arse than I do.'

I laugh, scratching a mosquito bite near my ankle.

'How's work going?' she asks.

'Fine. I think I'll pop over soon. I miss it.'

'Good. I'm glad. I was worried you might quit.'

'Why?'

'A lot of stepmums do . . . To compensate, you know, for the "step" bit.'

'But lots of biological mums work.'

'It's a guilt thing. Don't fall for it. Whatever else happens, don't give up work. Biggest mistake I ever made.'

'But you wanted to . . .'

'Yeah, I wanted to be the perfect mother.'

'But you *are*.'

'Lucy, there's no such thing.'

'You could go back to work.'

'Are you kidding me? The kids would never see either of us. Everything would come crumbling down.'

'You could get a nanny.'

'After what you've told me? Forget it.'

~

Greg has spoken to Hilary. He says everything's fine. It was just a misunderstanding. Still, I'm cautious, unable to forget her rage. I'm putting my swimsuit and towel into the washing machine at the villa when she appears. I risk extending an olive branch.

'Hilary, I'm doing a coloured wash. Would you like to put anything in?'

'No, thanks.'

'The machine's practically empty. Why don't I save you a job?'

She sighs loudly, walks from the kitchen, returns with the laundry basket and drops it on the floor beside me.

Okaay. I sort the clothes and fill the machine. Then I'm stuck. I don't know which cycle to select. I don't want to ask Hilary, but squatting in front of the unfamiliar, French machine, I don't have a choice.

'What cycle do coloureds go in on, Hilary?'

She doesn't answer. I turn around to see if she's heard. She's slicing tomatoes at great speed. I'm about to ask again when she looks up.

'B,' she says.

~

One cycle later, I'm pulling clothes from the machine, my face burning. Disaster. Rachel's pale pink top: blue-grey. Greg's yellow polo shirt: pea-soup green. Toby's Bart Simpson T-shirt: blue-grey with patches of green. I've ruined at least one item belonging to everyone.

'What did you *do*?' Hilary asks, coming up behind me.

'Nothing. I put them in on B, like you said . . .'

'Not B. *D.* I said D.'

I'm stunned, sure she said B. I look at her. But her face is blank. Innocent. I don't know what to think. She *wouldn't* have done this on purpose, would she? She wouldn't deliberately upset everyone just to get at me?

'Never liked it anyway,' Greg says about his top.

Toby bursts into tears. 'Bart Simpson *can't* be green. He just can't. The Hulk is green. *Not* Bart Simpson.

Oh Jesus. 'I'm sorry, Toby. Next time I'm in Dublin, I'll buy you another, OK? I'll buy you two.' I'll look in France, but as he got it in Dublin, I'd better not make promises.

And Rachel? Ah, Rachel.

'Are you *stupid* or something?' she spits when she sees her ruined top.

I'm speechless. My face flashes red.

Greg walks into the kitchen. 'Rachel, what's going on? I could hear you from my office. How dare you speak to Lucy like that?'

'She ruined my good top.'

'And that gives you the right to be rude? Lucy's a guest here. Apologise this minute.'

'Sorry,' she mumbles.

'I didn't hear you,' he says.

I'm cringing.

'Sorry, OK?'

'You're getting very cheeky, young lady. You'd better change your attitude. D'you hear me?'

'Yes, Dad.' More subdued.

'Go to your room, immediately.'

She does. Not before giving me daggers.

Part of me wishes Greg had let me handle this; another knows I wouldn't have known how.

'Come on, let's get out of here,' says Greg.

~

We drive to Cannes. It's like nowhere I've ever been. Everything seems lazy and slow. In the hazy distance, pale lilac mountains could be a mirage. Yachts and powerboats cut through the water, creating lines of white through blue. The sea sparkles like diamonds. Nowhere in the world would they be more appropriate. Lamborghinis, Porsches, Ferraris pull up outside five-star hotels. A line of upmarket boutiques – Dior, Chanel, Bvlgari – faces sun and sea, the elegant mannequins bizarrely dressed for winter, many draped in fur.

It's too hot to walk along the seafront. We sit under an umbrella in the ultra-glam Martinez. I press my ice-filled glass to my face, then scoop out a cube and run it along my arms, legs and the back of my neck until it melts. I take another and slip it between my foot and flip-flop. I look up to find him gazing at me as if I'm a creature of great amusement.

'Don't you feel the heat?' I ask.

'No. But I'm glad you do.'

Two Japanese tourists sit down at the table next to us.

'Ohayo gozaimasu,' Greg says to them with a mini bow. Greg has recently taken up three languages – none of them French.

They nod, smile shyly and reply.

'Ressun sono ichi,' he says then.

They look at each other, then at him. They smile.

'Ah, lesson number one,' one translates.

We laugh.

Getting out alone with Greg always returns my sense of perspective – our relationship is what's important; the rest will just take time.

We get back to the apartment that evening and sit on the balcony as the light leaves the sky, watching swallows swoop and dive through the branches of the eucalyptus, like fighter pilots on manoeuvres.

~

The following morning, there's an email from Fint. Get Smart is up for a big pitch. Four agencies, three of them international, are in the running for an account to design the corporate identity for a retail giant planning a shopping mall in a busy suburb of Dublin. Fint wants me home next week to meet the managing director and take the brief.

I ring him straight away. He's as excited as I am. This is an opportunity to move us up a notch, to become one of the big guys.

I go down to the villa to tell Greg. But he's not there. According to a sour-looking Hilary, he has taken the children off on his own. I'm surprised he didn't tell me. Still, he must need time alone with them, especially Rachel, so I just text him to have fun.

I return to the apartment to try to finish the projects I'm working on so I can be free next week to tackle that pitch.

At dinnertime, I return to the villa, assuming they'll be back. They aren't. I ring Greg. They're in Cannes – at the kiddies' bumper cars. He'd forgotten the time, but says they'll grab a pizza rather than come home yet.

On my way out, I notice that Hilary has started to prepare dinner.

I let her know that they won't be back.

She slams down a knife. 'He could have told me.'

'I think he lost track of time.'

'What am I supposed to do with this?' She looks at the half-prepared food.

'I'm sure it'll keep till tomorrow.'

'That's not the point,' she says, moodily.

I leave her to it.

At ten, Greg calls to say they're on their way; he'll meet me at the villa. I arrive before them and keep out of Hilary's way, reading a book on the terrace. I get up when I hear the car outside. Greg bounds through the front door, an inflatable swimming ring around his neck, roller-blades in one hand, a giant, blow-up toothpaste tube under an arm, keys in his mouth, eyes incredibly bright. I stop laughing when I see the children, sunburnt and laden down with shopping bags and exhaustion. Rachel closes the door with her heel. Toby lets his bags spill onto the floor and slumps down beside them.

'I'm thirsty,' he says.

'Anyone for a swim?' Greg asks, heading for the pool.

Hilary's face is thunderous. 'Can't he see they're exhausted?'

I say nothing; just go to get two glasses of water. When I return to the hall, she's lifting Toby up, muttering about how children need their sleep.

I follow them upstairs. When she settles Toby, I give him his drink and say goodnight.

Rachel refuses hers. I leave it by her bed, anyway.

I go back downstairs and out to the pool. Greg's churning through the water like a human propeller. I stand and watch. Up, down, up, down. Not stopping, not resting. Where is he getting the energy? Is this what happens when he hits a creative burst? He overworks, then has to blow off steam? Is that what this is, some sort of stress? Looking at him is making *me* stressed. I call out that I'm going back to the apartment. He doesn't seem to hear.

14.

The following day, I go down to the villa to see if he has recovered. Hilary tells me he 'popped out' three hours ago to buy screwdrivers and hasn't returned. I go into his office to call him.

'Where are you?'

'In Nice.'

'Did you get the screwdrivers?'

'Screwdrivers?'

'You left three hours ago to get screwdrivers.'

'Oh. Yeah. Screwdrivers. God, I'd forgotten. Why did I need them again?'

'No idea, Greg.'

'OK. It probably wasn't urgent.'

'What are you doing now?' I ask.

'Oh, I've just met some people. We're having a beer. Anyway, listen, I've just booked a super restaurant for us tonight. I'll pick you up from the apartment at seven.'

'Aren't you going to be back before then?'

'I've one or two things to do. Just be ready at seven, OK?'

'OK.' I hang up.

I'm walking out of his office when Hilary appears.

'Not coming back, is he?'

'He'll be back around seven,' I say, so she can let the children know.

'You know, I wouldn't be so smug if I were you.'

Smug? What's she talking about?

'There's a pattern, you see, with Greg. First, he starts to disappear, and before you know it, there's a new woman on the scene.'

I laugh. 'Thanks for the tip, Hilary.'

'Well, here's another: Be very careful what you say to your boyfriend, because it all comes back to me. We had a great laugh about how you thought I'd put in a good word with Rachel. Don't look so surprised. Greg tells me everything.'

I can't believe he told her when I specifically asked him not to. *Were* they laughing at me? No. Greg wouldn't do that. She's lying. But he must have told her. I can't believe he did that. What else has he said? And who are these people he's having a beer with?

~

Back at the apartment, I put an emergency call through to Grace.

'You know what I think?' she says when I finally pause for breath.

'What?'

'Greg thought he was doing you a favour, asking Hilary to have a chat with Rachel. And she's twisted it to cause tension between you. Face it: she's trouble, Lucy. I mean, can you really imagine Greg and Hilary in some corner somewhere giggling together at your expense? Come on!'

'No. I suppose not.'

'And so what if he's staying out for a few hours? He's been writing non-stop. Hasn't he?'

'Yeah.'

'She's obviously manipulative.'

'D'you think she made up that stuff about other women?' I ask.

'Do you?'

'Greg's said there's been no one since Catherine.'

'Except Hilary.'

'He doesn't count Hilary,' I say, as much to myself as to Grace.

'Do you believe him?'

'I don't see why he'd lie. I mean, what's wrong with having relationships as long as they're one at a time?'

'You need to talk to him, Lucy. Tell him what she's been saying. Because if she's saying things like that to you, who knows what she's saying to him?'

'God.' I never thought of that.

'Always beware the jealous woman.'

A wave of self-pity hits. 'What has she to be jealous about? She's the one the children love.'

'Come off it, Lucy. Of course she's jealous. You're going to be part of the family, a stepmother. She'll still be a hired employee. She was the mother figure until you arrived. You've taken that from her.'

'No, I haven't. She's still like their mother.'

'But you'll be their stepmother.'

'That's just a title.'

'A title she'd probably like. Think about it. From what you say, she doesn't have much of a life outside work. No phone calls. No mention of friends, boyfriends. This family is her life. The closer you get to the children, the more she'll be pushed out of the way.'

'I'm not sure I'll ever get close to them.'

'She probably still fancies Greg. I mean, she fucked him, didn't she?'

I wish she wouldn't keep bringing that up.

'He's an attractive man. She loves his kids. Maybe you're the cuckoo in her nest.'

'Jesus, Grace. Stop.'

'Learning that she was infertile would have been extremely traumatic. It's not beyond the bounds of possibility that she subconsciously substituted the family she couldn't have with Greg's.'

'Grace, you're scaring me.' I watch a swallow zip by, its life free and easy.

'All I'm saying is watch out. Your relationship is young. This is just another complication you don't need. Nip it firmly in the bud, Luce. Talk to him. Tell him what's going on, what she's been saying. Get him on his own. Out of that claustrophobic villa. You need to sort this out. Now. Dress up. Take him out for dinner. Take control. Enough is enough.'

'He's not going to get rid of her.'

'Let him decide.'

'If I ask him to, it would be like a showdown – what's good for me versus what's good for his family. I know who'd lose.'

'Then don't ask. Just tell him what's happening. And keep working. Don't let all this interfere with your career. Don't let it swamp you. You've something you're good at, something you enjoy. Don't let that slip.'

There suddenly seems an awful lot at stake.

~

I spend much of the afternoon trying to work out what I'm going to say to Greg and how I'm going to bring it up. I will, though, as soon as he arrives.

But he arrives a different man.

'Your hair!'

'What d'you think?' he asks, turning full circle.

'It's . . . It's certainly different.' It's white. Not blond. White. And short.

'I was just so bored with it,' he says, sounding like Fint.

Then I notice his ear. There's a diamond in it. 'Did you get your ear pierced?'

'Cool, eh?' Now he sounds like Toby.

I stare at him. His shirt is red silk. His tie, black leather. He looks like a pimp.

'Here. I got you something too.' He produces a designer carrier bag and stands over me while I take out the glossy box within. I slide off the lid. I lift the crispy, white paper to reveal more red silk. Slowly, I lift it out. It's a dress, though there's not much of it. So, this is what he was doing.

'It's lovely,' I say.

'Try it on.'

'Now?'

'Now.'

I pretend to be fine about wearing something so daring. I strip to my thong and slip into the silk sheath. I stand in front of the mirror. And frighten myself. It's a fabulous dress – if you're a supermodel. If you have that confidence, posture and poise. If you don't mind your nipples showing through the fabric. If you're comfortable with the fact that most of your breasts and legs are on display. If you want every curve of your body highlighted. I'd die if I had to wear it in public.

'Wow,' he says.

I nod. 'Very nice. Thanks. Great. Lovely.' I start to take it off.

'What are you doing? Aren't you wearing it?'

'I thought I'd keep it for a special occasion.'

'This is a special occasion.'

I think of Hilary, Rachel and Toby. What would they think if they saw me in this? What would anyone think, especially given how Greg's dressed?

'You know, Greg. I don't think it's me.'

'Of course it's you. You look fantastic. So fantastic you'd better not move.'

His hands are on my breasts, his mouth on mine. We need to talk, not fuck. He cups my arse in his hands, caresses it through the silk. It's my weakness and he knows it. I'm putty. He slips the straps off my shoulders and explores my breasts with his tongue. He takes a nipple in his mouth. I groan at him to stop. He knows I mean the opposite. He lifts me and flings me onto the bed. There's something so masterful about the way he does it that I'm turned on. That he looks different becomes suddenly exciting. I look down and run my hands over his white stubble. With every kiss, he whispers that I'm sexy, with every caress that I'm hot. Which makes me feel it. He doesn't remove the dress. Just my inhibitions.

When I see my reflection in the mirror again, I'm a different woman. Proud, confident, sexy. Able for such a dress. No problem. I'm a woman. Should I be afraid to show it?

~

In the car, I have to tell him to slow down. He slips a CD into the player and the car fills with a Japanese language lesson. I smile as he tries to repeat what he's heard. It's impossible. Doesn't stop him trying again after the next burst.

By the time we arrive in Cannes, we're sore from laughing. Parking, always at a premium, seems non-existent. The traffic is backed up. We crawl past the art deco Martinez, then the more traditional Carlton, lit up in all its glory. We inch past Christian Lacroix et al. Still no parking. Greg's getting jittery.

Finally, he zips into an underground car park and is lucky enough to find a Jeep pulling out. He parks, hops out and opens my door. The heat takes my breath away.

By the time we're at street level, I feel like I've been in a sauna. I wipe moisture from my upper lip and turn my face to the sea in the hope of a breeze. There isn't a puff. The back of Greg's shirt is beginning to stick to him, but he doesn't seem to notice. People who pass us are flagging – children being carried, looking flushed and tired, a man wiping the top of his head with a folded handkerchief, a woman fanning herself with a street map. The only person who appears to have any energy is Greg, walking briskly and talking non-stop.

I'm relieved when we get to the restaurant, a chic spot with cream parasols, crisp white tablecloths and a clientele of glitterati.

Greg seems to know the maître d', slapping him on the back with an 'Ah, bon soir, Philippe'. Under his breath, to me, he adds, 'Hope he's feeling energetic tonight.'

We're led to a quiet table in a corner.

'Ah, mais non, Philippe,' says Greg, gesturing to a table we passed on the way in. It's positioned between two others. 'That one would be much more sociable.'

My heart sinks. 'Greg, this a much better table.'

'Aw, Lucy, let's be sociable tonight.'

I'm about to tell him we need to talk when he turns and makes for the 'sociable' option. Philippe, looking surprised but accommodating, follows. Reluctantly, I do, too.

Once seated, Greg whips his serviette in the air to open it, almost hitting the woman at the next table.

'Pardon, madame,' he bows, flamboyantly.

She shakes her head. 'Ce n'est pas grave.'

The sommelier hands a wine list to Greg who, after a quick glance, snaps it shut and orders three bottles of champagne.

'Three?' I ask.

'We have neighbours,' he says, glancing from one table to the other.

'We don't know these people,' I say in an urgent whisper.

He shrugs. 'It's a gesture of goodwill.'

Greg's not a showy person, what's he doing?

The dewy metal buckets arrive, as, shortly after, do surprised but enthusiastic thanks – 'Merci beaucoup' from the couple on our left, and a mix of 'Thank you very much', 'Most kind', 'You shouldn't have' and 'Fantastic' from the two English couples at the table to our right. They ask if we're celebrating something.

'Life,' Greg says, then, 'Salut!' raising his glass high.

'Salut,' everyone joins in, glasses clinking.

'Ladies,' he says to the women, 'you're both looking ravishing tonight.'

Ravishing? Is he kidding?

But the 'ladies' seem charmed. I wait for Greg to return his attention to our table, so I can raise the subject of Hilary. He doesn't. Instead, he seems intent on involving as many people as he can in lively debate. The French couple concentrate hard for a while, but soon bow out. Still, Greg has a captive audience in Tony, Felicity, James and Janet. He guides the conversation like a conductor, his finger acting as baton. Hopping from one random topic to the next, he whips up laughter, a little heated discussion, and tops it off with argument – seeming to disagree with any arbitrary point for the sake of debate. Once he's got everyone worked up about something, he changes the subject with a jokey, 'Well, I'm glad we all agree on that.' Interrupting is pointless. He is on a roll. And while he can be downright funny, I may as well not be here. After my first glass of champagne, I stop drinking, realising that Greg doesn't intend to and someone has to drive back. For me, the evening and my plans for discussion have been ruined. All I can do is sit it out.

'You know what you look like?' Greg asks Tony.

Tony looks bemused, awaiting the punchline.

'An Anglican parson.'

I try not to choke, remembering an Eddie Izzard comedy sketch about Anglican parsons having no arm muscles. I glance at Tony. He doesn't seem offended, joking as he is about Felicity being the one who does the preaching in their house. It's all very funny as long as people keep laughing. But what if they stop?

Greg's remarks are becoming more and more risqué. It's as if he's testing the fine line between funny and insulting. Does he want to see how far he can push it with these people? Is that it, some bizarre social experiment? Well, if he's not careful, he *will* cross that line. And the fun will end. Someone will stand up to him and make him stop. Why am I the only one to see this? Is it because I'm not drinking? Or is it because this is the man I love, not an amusing stranger I'll never see again. I *care* what's happening here. Because something *is* happening. It's not drink; I've seen Greg drunk. This is something else. Something serious.

The restaurant begins to empty, our French neighbours leaving with a polite but unamused goodbye.

Felicity and Janet disappear to the Ladies, leaving me with the three men.

'Guys,' says Greg, 'what do you think of Lucy's dress?'

'Smashing,' says Tony.

'Stunning.' James is not far off leering.

'Would you believe Lucy didn't want to wear it tonight?'

'But you look so good in it, love,' says James.

'D'you know what I had to do to convince Lucy to wear this dress?'

'Greg!'

'Ah, come on, Luce, let's tell them.'

'Greg, if you say one more word, I'm leaving.' And, by God, I mean it.

The men are quiet, the atmosphere changing.

'Let's get another,' says Greg, jovially holding up an empty champagne bottle.

Janet and Felicity return.

'Is he always so entertaining?' Janet asks me.

'And cheeky,' adds Felicity, eyelashes on full-bat.

I can't trust myself to answer without unleashing the rage I feel. He's been encouraging them all night. Flirting with them. The men, too, I'd think, if I didn't know better. Unable to sit through any more without exploding, I excuse myself.

In the Ladies, I catch my reflection in a mirror. It's not who I am. I look at the dress. Why did he get it? To turn me into someone else? Was Hilary right? Is this the beginning of the end?

When I finally come out, the restaurant is empty. I think that they've left without me. But then I see them, all five, at the top of the restaurant, Greg teaching his new pals what seem to be *Riverdance* steps. I glance at the waiters, expecting exasperation. In fact, they're sitting at a table chatting together, sharing a bottle of champagne. I know who's paying. Suddenly, I wish myself back at my apartment in Dublin, in my own bed, alone with a quiet, dependable book. Thank God, my meeting with Fint is in the morning; thank God, I'm going home. That thought propels me forward.

I walk up to Greg and remind him of my early start. He looks surprised as if suddenly noticing my rage. He excuses himself from the happy group and goes to settle the bill.

Once outside the restaurant, he looks sheepish, as if expecting me to explode. I will. But in private. I make straight for the car, in the unusual position of being in front. Reaching it, I turn and speak for the first time. It's brief.

'Give me the keys. I'm driving.'

As soon as we're inside, I turn on the engine for the air conditioning, but don't pull out. Instead, I demand, 'What was all that about?'

'What?' he asks innocently.

'That display, back there.'

'The dancing?'

'No, Greg, the general behaviour. What is *up* with you?'

'I don't know what you're talking about.'

'Are you *on* something?'

'On something?'

'Greg, you're high as a kite.'

'I'm in good form and you think I'm *high*? Get a life, Lucy.'

'You insulted those people.'

'I did not.'

'You don't think that telling a man he looks like a parson is insulting?'

'No.'

'You were lucky they hadn't seen Eddie Izzard. And you were lucky they were in such good form.'

'And who put them in good form? Me, that's who.'

'You humiliated me.'

'I *humiliated* you? Just how, exactly, did I do that?'

'Don't pretend you don't know. You were going to talk about our sex life – in public.'

'So?'

'*So? Is he serious?* 'That was completely out of line.'

'I don't see why. Everyone has sex. I was just being open about it, that's all.'

'It didn't cross your mind, *at all*, that *I* mightn't feel like being as "open"?'

'Not until you got all prissy about it, no.'

'Prissy! Jesus! You were flirting with those women.'

'I was being friendly.'

'Friendly? What is *wrong* with you? What is it – speed? Ecstasy?'

He laughs. 'You think I'm on drugs?'

'You're high, Greg. Don't sit there and tell me you're not high.'

'OK. Maybe I *am* high – on life.'

'Oh, come off it.'

But no matter what I say, he won't admit to anything.

I speed back, drop him at the villa and drive on. He can have the car back in the morning.

Inside the apartment, I can't sit still. Out on the balcony, the whole evening replays in my mind. How dare he treat me like that? And he *was* flirting. I remember Hilary's warning. That we never got to discuss that makes me feel like putting my fist through a wall.

15.

On the flight home, all I can think about is Greg. He's on something, no question. But what? And when did he start? He's always been energetic. But then I remember Rob saying how he'd changed. Could he have started taking something back then? Even Grace commented on his energy. What if she saw something I didn't? I need to talk to her . . .

As soon as I get to Dublin, I change my return flight to allow an overnight. In a taxi to the office, I ring Grace and ask to stay. She's delighted; Kevin's off at a medical conference in Barcelona for the week and she thinks she might be reverting to the mental age of two.

I arrive at the office two hours before the meeting. I hug Fint tighter than usual and try not to cry. Then it's into the boardroom and down to business.

'I emailed you the newsletter template yesterday,' I say. 'Did you get it?'

'Yeah, I'd a quick look.'

'It's not the final final, but it's nearly there.'

'It's good. Do you want to take the jacket for Copperplate's latest chick lit author, Clodagh Hughes?'

'Sure.' In fairness to Copperplate, they let us be creative with their women's fiction. They don't insist on a picture of a smiling woman every time.

Fint hands me the brief.

Moving on, he tells me he wants to give Sebastian more responsibility, maybe send him on a course. I think it's a good idea. We discuss various projects for current clients and what we're doing to attract new business. Then Fint briefs me about the retail giant we're about to meet and we go through our new business presentation, which has been modified to highlight the work we've done on corporate identities, particularly for fast-moving consumer goods companies. We run out of time for lunch.

~

The meeting goes well. The MD seems a pleasant enough man. He speaks about the project, then his marketing director gives us the brief. It will be a major job if we get it – just the kind of account we need to stretch us as a firm.

Afterwards, Fint and I go for a late lunch. It takes a while to comfortably bring up the question that I've been wanting to ask since I got to the office.

'Remember that guy in college, what was his name, again, River?'

'That nutter?'

'Was he on something?'

'Ye-ah.'

'What?'

'Dunno, some sort of speed. Why d'you ask?'

'No reason. I was just thinking about him today, that's all.'

'Not getting enough excitement in your life?'

I smile. 'Whatever happened to him?'

'Couldn't tell you. Probably fried what little brain he had.'

'Ah, come on, Fint. Some of his work was really creative . . .'

'Yeah, but what a cop-out, having to get high to get creative.'

My heart stops as it all starts to make sickening sense.

~

It's four by the time we finish up. I pop into the St Stephen's Green Shopping Centre and buy pyjamas and fresh underwear. I'm thrilled to find Bart Simpson T-shirts. I get two, as promised. Rachel is trickier. In the end, I opt for a black top with a square of fabric sewn on the front, featuring a black and white shot of two cuddly kittens, framed with a red velvet trim. It's either that or a similar one in grey with puppies, or a completely different stripy one. Even if I've made the right choice, it'll be the wrong one for Rachel. I buy wine for Grace and toys for the boys. Then catch a cab there.

She's unloading shopping from the car when I arrive and, though casually dressed in a grey T-shirt and skinny jeans, looks stunning, as usual. She could be Norwegian. I can see why Dad used to call us Snow White and Rose Red. Always so different.

I start to help. The boys are both asleep in their car seats. They look so cute – flushed and soft-skinned. Two angels. I can't help remarking on it.

'You wouldn't say that if you saw them in the supermarket. Jesus, they had me driven demented.'

We take the shopping inside and, while I start to unload it, Grace goes out to the car to get Jason. She sets him down in the portable car seat on the kitchen floor. I offer to get Shane, but she doubts that I'll manoeuvre him out of his seat and upstairs to bed without him waking. I doubt it, too.

'I think he's coming down with something,' she says when she returns to the kitchen. 'He normally wakes when the car stops. And he was so cranky. He only gets that bad when he's sick, poor little guy.'

'Poor you,' I say, about to put lettuce into the crisper.

'Forget the lettuce. Get the wine open.'

I laugh and do as instructed.

'Right then. We'll have a stir-fry – when we've had a glass or two. Come on, let's go into the sitting room.' She carries Jason. I carry the wine.

The place is in chaos. Toys everywhere. Children's feeders. Baby bottles. A heap of clothes that Grace must have taken out of the dryer and abandoned before sorting. This is *not* Grace. She catches me looking at her.

'Excuse the mess,' she says, not looking at all bothered. 'When the cat's away . . .'

'I thought you were the cat.'

'Lucy. One cat in any home is enough. Anyway . . .' She shakes her head as though clearing the thought. 'How are tricks?'

I look down at the glass I'm twisting around by the stem. 'Pretty crap, actually.'

'Hilary?'

'No. Greg.' I look up at her. 'There's something wrong, Grace.'

She sits forward.

'Remember when you asked me if he was all right and I told you he was fine?'

'Yeah?'

'Well, I thought he was. But now he's not. Definitely not. You said he was energetic, then. You should see him now – he's high, Grace.'

She nods quickly, as if to say, 'Go on.'

I talk through the events of the night before.

'Wow,' she says, putting her glass down. 'That's pretty extreme.'

'It has to be drugs, right?'

She pulls her legs up beside her. 'I wouldn't be sure without seeing him, Lucy.'

'I know, but you must have *some* idea.'

'He's never mentioned a tendency to get high?'

'No. Sure, he doesn't even think he *is* high.'

'Or low?'

'No. He's always in great form. Just not *this* great.'

'OK.' She thinks for a moment. 'What about his family? Have any of them commented on his behaviour?'

'Rob, his brother, mentioned how "zesty" he was, and how much he'd changed since he met me.'

'But he didn't seem worried?'

'No. He thought it was great. He thinks it's love.' What a ridiculous concept that seems now.

'OK,' she says again.

'He's taking something, isn't he?' I whisper.

She takes a long breath. 'It's a possibility, Lucy, though, without seeing him, I'd be slow to pin it down to any one thing.'

'What kind of drugs?'

'Let's not jump to conclusions . . .'

'OK, if it *were* drugs, which ones?'

'*If*, then most likely amphetamines. Speed. But he'd want to be taking a hell of a lot . . .'

'Are they addictive?'

'Yeah.'

'But not dangerous?'

'Well, not at low doses. But someone taking high doses over a long period . . .'

'What could happen?'

'Lucy, it may not be drugs.'

'What could happen?'

'Well, there would be a risk of paranoia and stuff, but I think we're getting ahead of ourselves. You have to talk to him, first, Lucy. Get him to admit there's a problem. Because something's definitely up.'

'But that's exactly it. He doesn't think there is.'

'Well, then you have to show him how his behaviour's affecting other people.'

'I tried, last night. He thinks the problem's with me. He called me prissy.'

'Well, show him what this is doing to the children.'

'I don't think it's actually affecting them.'

'Trust me, Lucy, if it's affecting you, it's affecting them.'

'No. They enjoy his energy. He can be great fun. Very adventurous. OK, they get tired sometimes . . .'

'He's not irritable, at all?'

'Only last night, when I cornered him. Otherwise, no.'

'Something, at least. Still, Lucy, you've got to act. He's unlikely to do so himself. Highs are addictive. Once you're up, you want to stay there.'

'Maybe I should join him. Must be a hell of a lot better than reality.'

She smiles. 'I know what you mean. Just keep at him, though, until he admits there's a problem. Then get him to a doctor, preferably at home. You know I'll help in any way I can.'

It sounds so easy. I know it'll be anything but. Still, at least I have a goal, a sense of direction. And I have something else: the feeling that I'm not alone. I hope I can hold on to that when I'm back in France.

16.

The plane touches down at three. Cardigan off. Sunglasses on. Riviera Radio keeps me company in the car as do Grace's words. I get to the villa, fired up and ready for positive action. But there's no sign of Greg, and I sense that something's wrong. Rachel has a face on her like a brewing storm. So does Toby.

'What is it?'

'Dad didn't come back,' he says.

'From where?'

He shrugs.

'Where's Hilary?'

'Kitchen.'

They follow me in.

Incredibly, Hilary is tearing at a French stick with her mouth.

'Where's Greg?' I ask.

She drops the bread, including the bit she had between her teeth. She brushes crumbs from her chest and turns. 'Ever think of knocking?'

'The door was open, Hilary. Now, what's going on?'

She straightens up, chin high. 'He promised to take us to Antibes for ice cream. I got the children out of the pool, helped Toby get dressed. When we were ready, he'd gone.'

'Where?'

'I don't know, do I? I'm just the hired help.'

'Did you try his mobile?'

'No,' she says with pride.

'OK. Well, I'm sure there's a reasonable explanation.' Somehow, I suspect that may not be the case. I ring his mobile, looking confident, until I hear it, somewhere in the villa. 'How long's he been gone?'

'An hour.'

'Well, why don't I take you?' I say to the children.

'Forget it,' says Rachel gloomily.

Toby is quiet. His face is flushed and he looks languid. Hilary has all the windows and doors open to create a breeze, but the villa is stifling. This boy needs to cool down.

'Toby, would you like to see my apartment? It's nice and cool, and I've Magnums in the fridge.'

He looks up. 'OK.'

'Rachel, would you like to come?'

She eyes me as if I've just offered to pull a tooth. 'As if,' she says, summing up our relationship in two words.

Toby holds my hand as we leave the villa. Hilary looks murderous.

~

Toby scans the apartment. 'You're right, it's nice and cool.'

'Would you like a drink?'

'Yes, please.'

'Sit down there, and I'll get it.'

'Ooh. The seat's cold, too.'

'It's leather,' I call from the kitchen.

'I like leather.'

I find myself smiling.

I return with two glasses of orange juice and hand him one. 'Cheers,' I say and hold my glass out.

'Cheers, big ears,' he says, cheerfully clinking his glass against mine. 'It's really quiet here,' he says, looking around. It strikes me as an odd thing for a child to appreciate. 'Is that a balcony?'

'Yep.'

'Can we go on it?'

'Sure.'

Once out, he doesn't stay long. 'Nifty,' he says, and goes back inside. He sits in the exact spot he was in earlier. 'I like it here.'

'Me too.'

'Can I stay with you?' He looks at me with big brown St Bernard eyes, the puppy I always wanted as a child.

'Why would you want to stay with me?'

He shrugs.

'Is it a bit hot at the villa?'

He nods. 'And really noisy. Even at night-time. I can't sleep. Dad never goes to bed. He shouts on the phone and his music's really loud. I hate that song.'

'What song?'

'A little more satisfaction, baby. I hate it.' He puts his hands over his ears.

I wait until he takes them down again. 'Why don't you ask him to turn it down?'

'I do. But when I get back into bed he turns it up again. So I don't ask him any more. Can I stay with you? Please?'

'I don't know, Toby. I think your dad would prefer you to stay with him.'

'Just for one night? Please? I'd be very good.'

I get up, go over and sit beside him. 'Would you like to go for a little sleep now? You look a bit tired.' He looks exhausted.

''K.'

'I'll be out here, working, OK? Sleep as long as you like. And when you get up, we'll have a Magnum.'

''K.'

I hold his hand and lead him to the bedroom. When he's settled, I cover him with a sheet and sit on the edge of the bed until he sleeps. It takes less than a minute. His little face looks so vulnerable.

I go back outside and try to work, but can't. What's Greg up to? If Toby's being kept awake, Rachel is too. She's older; she *must* know something's up. Because something *is* up. And we really, really need to talk. If only I could just get him to focus, stop for one second. Sit still. Stop talking. Stop moving. Just listen for five minutes without interrupting me or himself.

~

When Toby wakes, I invite him to stay for the rest of the day.

'*Yes!*'

I call the villa.

Hilary answers.

'Is Greg back?'

'No.'

'Right, well, just to let you know, Toby's staying with me for a while.'

A brief pause before she says, 'Yeah, well, just make sure he's back for dinner.'

It's like *Upstairs, Downstairs*. The staff's running the place.

I teach Toby to play draughts and am amused by how competitive he is. We eat the Magnums. I show him how to play Spider Solitaire on my laptop.

'Are you a child prodigy?' I ask because he's so bloody quick.

'What's that?'

Phew.

He's such good company, I could keep him forever.

I ring Hilary again. 'Greg back yet?'

'No.'

'Right, well, when he does get back, you might tell him I've taken Toby out for pizza.'

'You can't!'

'Why not?'

'He's not your child.'

I almost laugh. 'He's not yours either. His father's not home. He's hungry. I'm taking him out for a meal. If you've a problem with that, I suggest you talk to Greg.'

She slams the phone down.

~

We drive to Antibes and find an outdoor table at a restaurant overlooking Place Général de Gaulle. We share the same side of the table, looking out. A woman walks by, carrying a Yorkshire terrier. A central parting divides its back into two glossy curtains of hair. Behind the woman skips a pair of twins, encircled by a hula hoop. But it's the fountains that interest Toby. Dotted around the square, they have water shooting straight out from the ground, alternating between wide, light sprays and single slender jets. They disappear in a pattern, leaving only wet ground and the uncertainty that they were ever there. Then they reappear again just when you thought they were gone for good. Toby creates a game of second-guessing the display, at which I lose miserably.

At last, our food arrives – spaghetti for him, as they don't do pizza. Listening to this dark little boy chat about bumper cars, piranhas and self-flush loos makes me realise how special he must be to Greg. Where is he, then? What's he doing, disappearing off without telling anyone?

'Are you cross with Dad?' he asks, catching me off guard.

'No. Why?'

'Hilary's cross. Dad always tells us where he's going and when he'll be back.'

'There's probably a good reason why he had to hurry away. Maybe he remembered something he had to do. He'll be back later and we can ask him then, OK? But we're having a nice time now, aren't we?'

'Yeah. When are you and Dad splitting up?'

That stalls me. 'What do you mean?'

'Hilary said you'd be splitting up soon.'

'I see. Well . . . We've no plans at the moment. I think Hilary might be a bit confused.' *And an interfering cow.*

~

We don't rush back. I take Toby for a ride on a tourist 'train' that drives through the narrow, winding streets of the town. We buy ice creams, then fake tattoos that we place on our arms, reminding me of when I was a kid.

Eventually, it's time to go. On the way home, Toby needs a pee. Like, now. No, he can't hold on. He has to *go*. With no other option, I pull in to the side of the road, worried about the possible existence of some obscure French public exposure law.

But it's fine. He's climbing back into the Clio and we haven't been arrested.

'Mission accomplished,' he says, and I know where he learned that one.

I smile sadly and tussle his hair.

As soon as we arrive back at the villa, Hilary snatches him from me.

'Look at the state of you,' she says to him. 'You need a bath, young man.'

The spaghetti and ice cream have given his T-shirt a whole new look. But so what? He's five. It'll wash out.

She's holding out his hands, examining the tattoos.

I wink at him. And he winks back.

She starts to herd him towards the stairs.

'Goodnight, Toby,' I say. 'You were great company.'

He smiles. 'Thanks for the basketti.'

Red is the colour of Hilary's – entire – face.

~

Back at the apartment, to distract myself, I check my emails and have a more detailed look at the brief we've been given by the retail company. Before I know it, though, I'm Googling amphetamines. I visit site after site and read list after list of the effects of speed. Alertness, increased energy and confidence, rapid movement, talkativeness, excitability – one by one, I tick them off. To suffer insomnia, though, Greg would need to have been taking speed for a long time and in high doses. The sites don't give any advice on how to come off the drug, but warn that doing so can lead to tiredness, depression and emotional exhaustion. Seems like a small price to pay. I'd welcome a bit of exhaustion.

At eight, I ring Greg's mobile. He's back. I go down to the villa. Straight to the office. He's frantically rummaging through a drawer. What's he looking for, his next fix?

'What happened earlier?' I ask.

He looks up. 'When?'

'When you disappeared.'

'What?'

'You were supposed to take the children for ice cream, but you went off and never came back.'

'Oh, right, that. I must have forgotten.'

'Where did you go?'

'To see a man about a dog.'

'What man? And what dog?'

'It's an expression, Lucy.'

'People hide behind expressions.'

'I'm hiding behind nothing.'

'So, where were you? And who were you with?'

He gives me a look that says 'What have you turned into?' But he does answer. 'I was in Monte Carlo.'

'Monte Carlo?'

'A little principality beyond Nice.'

'I know where it is, Greg. Not why you had to suddenly drop everything to go there.'

'No reason.'

'There must have been a reason.'

'Well, if there was, I forget it.'

'Just like you forgot the kids. You know, Greg, they dropped everything for you. And then you dropped them.'

He starts back at the drawer, mumbling, 'I'll make it up to them, OK?'

'How?'

He pops his head up. 'I don't know. I'll spend time with them.'

'When?'

'Now. If it'll make you happy.'

'It's almost Toby's bedtime.'

'So? He can sleep in.'

'He can't sleep *at all* with the racket you make.'

'What racket?'

'Loud telephone conversations, music blaring . . .'

'He's imagining things.'

'He asked to come and stay with me, today. He's not imagining things.'

'OK, OK.' He gets up suddenly. 'Stop nagging. I'll keep the music down, OK?' I open my mouth to speak, but he cuts me off with, 'And I'll go play with the children right now, if that's what you want.'

'Don't you need to find whatever you're looking for, first?'

He scratches his head. 'I can't remember what I was looking for.'

Let me help. 'Speed, amphetamines . . .'

'What?'

'Drugs, Greg. I know you're taking them.'

He laughs. 'Well, you know more than I do.'

'Admit it, Greg.'

His face changes. 'What is your *obsession* with drugs? What is *wrong* with you?'

I feel like snapping the same back at him. But I don't want to fight. I want to sort this out. I try to keep calm, focus on my mission.

'Look, Greg, you've a problem. We both know it. If you could just admit it, we could do something about it . . .'

'The only problem I have is you, Lucy,' he says, turning and walking from the room.

He leaves me standing, winded. Hurt stops me from reacting immediately. Anger propels me forward. I go after him, ready to ask, 'What do you mean I'm a problem? If I'm such a problem maybe I should leave?' But I walk straight into a happy family scene. Toby, dressed for bed, is running to get paints, while Rachel is heading to the office for paper. I slow down, try to lift the expression on my face. That's when I see Hilary, looking like she's ready to start fitting.

'Right,' she snaps. 'Forget routine. Fine. I'm going to my room. And I won't be back down.' She pounds up the stairs.

'What's wrong with her?' he asks.

I keep walking; amazed he has the nerve to talk to me.

'Where are you going?' he asks cheerily, as if the argument between us never happened.

'Bed,' I answer only because the children are watching.

'Don't go. You're great fun.'

I feel like clocking him.

They're sitting down to paint as I walk out of the door. And I wonder how long it will be before Greg has to go somewhere, do something, or be with someone other than us.

17.

A good night's sleep helps my perspective. I love Greg. Or, at least, the Greg I met. He brought me back to life, gave me another future. I don't want to throw that away. I didn't get another chance with Brendan, but I have one with Greg. Whatever the problem is, he reacted the way he did because I was backing him into a corner. I should have tried to stay calm, support him more. If I'd been smart about it, I wouldn't have mentioned drugs at all. I'd have told him I was behind him. Whatever the problem, we'd get help together.

Out on the balcony, watching the sun on the sea, I try to work out how to bring the whole thing up again, this time with tact. It won't happen down at the villa. If he comes here and is in good form . . .

I spend the day working. It helps to steady me.

Late afternoon, I hear his key in the door. I turn. He breezes in, bright and cheery.

'The kids are in the car. Are you coming up the mountains with us?'

I hesitate. We won't be able to talk with the kids there. And we can't talk now because they're sitting out in the car.

'Come on, it'll be great,' he says, taking my hand.

And I think that, maybe, if we could just get on today, then later I could risk broaching the subject again.

Hilary's in the back of the Range Rover with the children. Toby seems to be developing some kind of heat rash. I turn up the air conditioning.

Greg drives to Grasse and, from there, up into the Alps. As we climb, the temperature outside begins to drop from thirty-six degrees to thirty-two. The scenery is breathtaking. Sheer-drop cliffs, mountain streams, gorges, waterfalls. Tiny hillside villages perch precariously, prettily.

Higher and higher we go. We're almost at the top, when over the precipice float paragliders slowly descending in smooth arcs, like skiers down a slope, leaning to the left then right and finally landing in a field beside the road. Without a word, Greg pulls over and hops out. We watch him approach the small group folding their wings like sails. When he returns, he has signed up for lessons.

We make it to Gourdon, a tiny fairy-tale village with postcard views. In the car park we're ambushed by a very cute and amateur sales force – little, blonde, Alpine children selling home-made bundles of lavender. We buy one for a euro and make their day. We wander through tiny streets, while Greg tears on ahead, stopping every so often to examine an item for sale or to strike up conversation with strangers.

Through open windows float the sounds of voices and crockery as families prepare for their evening meal. Rachel and Toby are hungry. We find a restaurant.

Greg is talking, on and on, at high speed, about French politics. Another day, another monologue. The rest of us eat in silence, Hilary moving her Coke to avoid grains of rice that fly, every so often, from Greg's mouth. Then something happens to drag us from our now practised inertia. Greg stops making sense. One minute he's talking about politics, then about going somewhere in the car. Then the car turns into a boat, as happens in dreams.

I'm afraid he'll worry the children, so I try to jolt him back to reality before he gets any worse. 'Greg, we've never been on a boat together.'

He doesn't seem to hear. Just carries on. 'The boat went twenty knots an hour, shower, power, flour.' Gibberish.

My God!

'What's wrong with Dad?' asks Toby. 'He's talking funny.'

Greg snaps at him. 'Nothing's wrong with me. What's wrong with you?'

After that, no one talks. No one eats – apart from Greg who finishes his meal in minutes and reaches over to help himself to mine. I give him my plate. Toby's head is bowed, his shoulders raised. He doesn't make a sound, but I know he's crying. I want to tell him everything will be all right, put my arm around him. But Hilary gets there first, with hers. He looks exhausted, his little face flushed, his hair damp with sweat. I ask for the bill and am told, by my fiancé, that I'm no fun. Once out of the restaurant, he bounds ahead back to the jeep. We follow behind, a quiet group. Somehow, I end up carrying Toby.

'What's wrong with Dad?' whispers Rachel.

And while Hilary struggles for an answer, I say, 'It's hot, Rachel. He's been working very hard. Doing too much. He just needs sleep.'

Hilary raises an eyebrow at me.

'I need sleep, too,' says Toby.

'I know,' I say. 'Just close your eyes and rest on my shoulder. Everything'll be fine.'

By the time we get to the jeep, Toby's asleep, his face damp against my T-shirt. I feel a wave of responsibility for him. Even for Rachel.

Greg has the engine revving.

I ease Toby onto his booster seat and strap him in.

I open Greg's door. 'I'll drive,' I say.

'What do you mean, you'll drive? I'm already driving.'

'Greg, please don't make a scene. Just let me drive.' I say it quietly.

'Is there something wrong with my driving? Is that what you're saying?'

'No. I just think I should drive. You've had a beer.'

'One beer. Below the limit. I'm driving.' That's that. Adamant.

I climb in the front passenger seat, in silence.

Darkness is falling on the way back down the mountain. Greg insists on returning by a different route from the one we came, despite my telling him that it looks like a very minor road on the map. It is, we discover, wide enough for one car only. He is tearing down it, making childish 'vroom vroom' noises and 'weees' on hairpin bends. He takes the corners so fast I imagine us going over the edge. I hold the door handle, close my eyes and pray. My heart's pounding. My foot keeps hitting an imaginary brake. Just inches away from the wheels, the ground falls away into a gorge. A beautiful gorge that tourists snap on a daily basis. A gorge that will become world famous if Greg Millar's Range Rover ends up smashed at the bottom.

'Greg, slow down.'

He ignores me.

'Dad, please slow down,' says Rachel, sounding terrified.

It's as if he hasn't heard her.

'Greg,' I say, quietly so they can't hear at the back. 'If another car comes around that corner, we're over the edge.'

'Where's your sense of adventure?'

'Greg, please. You're going too fast.'

'I'm not going too fast,' he snaps.

Silence now. But he does slow. I turn around to check the children. Toby's still asleep, which shows just how exhausted he is. Rachel's face is burrowed into the side of Hilary's formidable chest. She's sucking her thumb, something I've never seen her do. My eyes meet Hilary's. Slowly, she shakes her head. I sit back and close my eyes.

No more.

Somehow, we make it back to the villa. I carry Toby up to bed while Hilary puts her arm around a shaken and visibly upset Rachel. Together they go into her room, Hilary whispering reassurances. The door closes behind them.

I find Greg in the kitchen, knocking back a glass of water.

I'm much too angry to be supportive. 'What's wrong with you, Greg?'

'Why do you keep asking what's wrong with me? Nothing's wrong with me. What's wrong with you?'

'Why were you like that?'

'Like what?'

'Oh, come on, don't tell me you don't know. You were driving like a madman. You could have killed us all.'

'Rubbish.' He slams down the empty glass. 'I was totally in control.'

'Is that right? So, what would you have done if another car had come round the bend? Where would you have pulled in? How would you have stopped in time?'

'You're such a panic-merchant. I'd have handled it.'

'In that case, you're deluded. There would have been no way out. If you can't see that, you have a serious problem.'

He laughs. 'Lucy, it's not me who has the problem, it's you.'

'Don't twist this, Greg. What's going on?'

'If you bring up drugs again, God help me, I'll lose it.'

'You're high, Greg. Don't stand there and tell me you're not high. And, whatever the cause, it has to stop. It's got to a point where it's dangerous. You could have killed us up there. You could have killed your own children. Do you hear me, Greg?'

'Lucy, love, you really should see a doctor.'

I explode. 'There's nothing wrong with me. You're the one with the problem. Tearing around, awake all night, snapping at the children, living in your own fast-paced world, becoming so detached from me and yet expecting sex like it's your God-given right. It's you who needs a doctor. You!'

I've given him too much rope. And he's hanging me with it. Holding in a scream, I storm from the villa.

Tears distort the lights of the oncoming cars.

I'm having no impact. It makes no difference to him whether I'm here or not. I have to get away. Put distance between us. Maybe then I can think, work out what to do, find a way forward, if there is a way forward. For now, I have to go.

Back at the apartment, I write Greg a letter, explaining. I won't drop it off at the villa. Better for him to find me gone, to experience the shock of that, to read from start to finish what he never allows me to explain to his face. Better to have him react. I book the first available flight home. It leaves tomorrow afternoon, return open.

18.

Sitting in the departure lounge at Nice Airport, I'm hoping the children will be OK. They have Hilary, who will stay with them through anything. But Hilary hasn't exactly been coping. I wish I'd thought to leave her the key to the apartment. But then, could I trust her with the letter I left Greg? I'm distracted by a woman coming through Passport Control. Weird how thinking about a person can make you see them in others. She looks just like Hilary. She even has the same denim jacket. Hair. Posture. I stare as she turns. It *is* Hilary, arriving in the departure lounge pulling her case behind her. What the hell is she doing here?

'Hilary?' I call, starting towards her.

She looks in my direction. There's a moment of connection. Then she looks straight ahead, about to walk past.

'Hilary. Stop. Wait. What are you doing?' Up close, I see that her eyes are rimmed red, her face puffy. 'What happened?'

'Ask your boyfriend,' she spits and starts to take off.

'Hilary. Stop. Please. Tell me what happened. How could you have left the children alone with him after last night?'

'How could *you*?'

Instant guilt. 'I have to go home for a while. I knew you'd be there. I was relying on you.'

'It's hard to mind children you no longer work for.'

'You *resigned*?'

She squints at me. 'You always were a bit slow, weren't you?' This time, she does walk off.

They pick *that* moment to call my flight.

I have to get on that plane. But I see Toby's tired little face in my mind. *Shit.*

I call the villa. The phone rings and rings. What if Greg has left them alone and they're afraid to answer? I call again. And again. I'm getting desperate when Rachel, finally, picks up.

'Hello?' She sounds so young, so scared.

'Rachel? It's Lucy. Is everything OK?'

The line dies.

Oh, God. He has *left them alone.*

I dial again. *How have I allowed myself get into this situation?* I look up. People are lining up for the flight. I can't go. I can't believe it. But I can't go. I want to kill Greg – if he hasn't already driven off a road somewhere. I want to kill the immature, irresponsible gobshite he's become.

I leave Departures in a state and have problems explaining why I can't get on the flight. Major fuss. For security reasons, they need to get my bag off the plane. The flight will have to be delayed. But security is security. And these guys mean business. They won't let me go until I've the bag firmly in my possession. I tell them I don't care about the bag. They can dump it, blow it up for all I care. I just have to get somewhere. It's an emergency.

Red tape first, emergencies second, mademoiselle.

~

I burst through the door of the villa to find Greg absorbed in a mural he's started on the living room wall. It's all over the place. He's covered in paint, as is the floor.

'Where are the children?' I demand.

'Upstairs.'

'Are they all right?'

'Of course they're all right, why wouldn't they be?'

'I met Hilary.'

'Where?'

'At the airport. What happened, Greg?'

He stops painting and looks at me. 'What were you doing at the airport?'

'It's not important. What happened with Hilary?'

Leonardo abandons his fresco in favour of a whiskey. 'Want one?'

'No, Greg. I don't *drink* whiskey, as you know. What happened?'

He sighs dramatically. 'Hilary, Hilary, what's the fascination with Hilary?'

'Greg!'

'All right, if you're so concerned – I let her go.'

'Why?'

'I was sick of looking at her. Moody cow.'

'And that's a good enough reason to fire her?'

He doesn't answer, drains his whiskey and returns to the wall.

'Rachel and Toby love Hilary. They need her. Especially now.'

He twists around. 'What do you mean, especially now?'

'Nothing.'

'They'll get over it.'

'Will they?' I squint. 'Are you sure?'

He looks straight at me. 'There was nothing great about Hilary.'

'She's been with you since Catherine died. She helped you through that—'

'I helped myself through. If you think I can't survive without Hilary, you're mistaken. I'm perfectly capable of looking after—'

'Did something happen?'

'No,' he says, too quickly, too loudly.

'Then why?'

'I had enough of her, OK?'

'When did this happen, when did you fire her? It must have been last night if she managed to get a flight today.'

He ignores me, daubing buttercup yellow on the wall.

'Did you even take her to the airport?'

No answer.

'She was your responsibility, Greg. Did you even check to see if she'd enough money to get home?'

'If you met her at the airport, she obviously did.'

'What is the matter with you? You used to be thoughtful. You used to appreciate people.' I pull out my mobile, look up her number and dial. Her phone goes to voicemail. I leave a message asking her to call me. I tell her that the children miss her (which is a given) and that Greg's sorry.

'I'm not fucking sorry,' he says before I can hang up. 'I don't want her back here. And you'd better not ask her again if she rings back.'

'So, what are you going to do? Who's going to mind the children while you write? Who's going to keep the place tidy? Who's going to cook the meals?' *And who's going to be here when you do your disappearing stunts?*

'I'll hire someone else.'

'Just like that? An English-speaking nanny the children will love as much as they did Hilary. You'd better start looking in the sky, Greg, because I hear Mary Poppins is good.'

He ignores that.

I can't believe I'm saying it, but . . . 'You need Hilary. She's been with you five years. If she calls, then I'm inviting her back.'

'She won't come back. Trust me.'

What has he done? What has he said? He isn't telling me everything, that much I know. Something must have happened. Something definitely happened.

I go upstairs, check Toby's room. Empty. I go to Rachel's. The door is closed. All's quiet, but I sense they're inside. I knock gently.

No answer.

'Can I come in?'

Still nothing.

I open the door a fraction, peep around. Rachel's sitting on the bed, Toby's head in her lap. She's smoothing his hair, over and over.

'Hi,' I say.

Rachel doesn't budge. Toby sits up, but says nothing. He's been crying. I smile at him and go sit on the edge of the bed.

'Get off my bed,' Rachel says, with hate in her eyes.

I stand. 'Sorry.'

I squat down and talk to Toby. 'Are you OK?'

Nothing.

'Are you sad about Hilary?'

'Yeah,' he says.

'Toby,' says Rachel.

'Sorry, Lucy,' he says, 'but I can't talk to you.'

'I'm so sorry about Hilary. It's hard when someone goes away . . .'

'Goes away?' Rachel's chin is jutting out. 'You mean is sent away, fired. You got Dad to fire Hilary.'

'Sorry?'

'You heard me.'

'I heard you, but you're wrong. I had nothing to do with this.'

'Yes, you did. You were jealous because we love her, not you . . .'

'Rachel, I wasn't even here.'

'You told Dad to fire Hilary before you left. Hilary told me and she doesn't lie. You're the liar. You're the one who spoils everything. You.'

'I'm sorry you think that, Rachel.'

'No, you're not. You're happy because Hilary's gone. You think we'll like you now. But we won't. We won't even talk to you. And we won't cooperate.' She folds her arms.

'Well, I'll be downstairs if you need me.'

'Don't worry, we won't.'

~

I go back downstairs, furious with everyone: with Hilary for lying, with Rachel for being impossible and with Greg for creating this whole bloody mess. I prepare dinner because I know that he won't have thought of food all day.

My efforts are wasted. Greg has gone to get turpentine for the mural and hasn't returned. Toby has a sick tummy. And Rachel? Well, Rachel's response to what I put in front of her is, 'I'm not eating *that*.'

All of a sudden, I need to hear Dad's voice. I go outside and call home.

Mum answers. 'I thought you'd forgotten about us.'

'Sorry. It's been a bit hectic – workwise.'

'Oh, I'm glad, Lucy. I wouldn't want you to fall down on your job just because you're engaged. I was a bit worried when you said you were spending the summer in France.'

'Is Dad there?'

'Always look after yourself, Lucy – in any relationship.'

'Yeah, OK. Is Dad around?'

'He's here beside me. I'll hand him over in a sec.'

'Mum, I'm ringing from France.'

'Of course, sorry. Here he is now.' I hear her warn him not to be long. I feel guilty then.

As soon as Dad gets on the phone, I sit down.

'Hi, pet. How're you doing?'

I smile at the sound of his voice. 'Good. You?'

'Never better. How's Greg?'

'Fine.'

'And the kiddies?'

'They're all right.'

'These things take time.'

'Yeah.' Suddenly, I'm close to tears. I shouldn't have called.

'How're you coping with the heatwave? It's all over the news. People have died in Paris. Others are leaving the country.'

'We're managing.'

'No doubt Greg has the place air conditioned.'

I could wail – honestly, wail.

'Better let you go,' he says. 'This must be costing you a fortune.'

'No. No. It's fine.' My voice starts to crack, my eyes to smart.

'You all right, love?'

'Yeah, yeah, fine,' I say, a little too high. 'Actually, I think I'll go. I haven't talked to Grace in ages.'

'Good idea, love. Ring your sister.'

'Bye, Dad. Love you.'

'You too.'

I can't ring Grace. I can't do anything. Except cry.

It's eleven and there's no sign of him. What if I walked out, behaved as irresponsibly? Would he cop on then? No, probably not. I punch his number into my phone. And seethe as it goes unanswered. Where the hell is he? In a nightclub, music pumping? With these 'other women' Hilary enjoyed mentioning? Or speeding along the motorway, radio blaring? Or maybe he's looking at his phone right now, seeing it's me and ignoring it. Or he's on his way home, hearing the phone, reaching for it, going over a ravine, car sailing through the air in slow motion and ending up overturned, wheels spinning? Stop, Lucy. Stop it. He'll walk through the door any second, without a scratch. And what good will all the worrying have done? None. Get some sheets, make up a bed. Sleep. Don't think.

I carry bed linen to one of the guest rooms, make the bed and go find a fan. I. Am. Not. Going. To. Worry. I look at my mobile. *He's fine.* I get under the sheet. Pull it back, again. Check my watch. *Where is he?* I close my eyes. Open them. Get out of bed. Check on the children. Return to bed.

When the phone in the villa rings at three, I know without looking what time it is. I run to it.

'Hello?'

Silence.

'Bonjour? Bonsoir? Hello?'

There's someone there; I sense it.

'Greg?'

The line goes dead. I wait by the phone in case it rings again. After five minutes, I go back to bed, relieved that it wasn't the French police. Relief changes to rage when I think of what he's putting me through. Next time I see him, he's getting two words from me. I'm leaving. He'll have to cop on then, he'll have to remember his responsibilities. This is his problem, not mine.

Somehow, at some stage, I fall asleep.

At nine, I wake to the sound of hushed conversation and light footsteps on the stairs. Rachel and Toby are up. I throw back the sheet and go to Greg's room to check if he's there, though I already sense that he's not.

I'm right.

I dress, then give the children a comfortable few minutes before heading down. I find them in the kitchen. Toby's sitting at the table, legs dangling. He's looking down at his bowl, into which Rachel's pouring Coco Pops. There's a protectiveness about the way she's standing over him. She looks like a very vulnerable mini-mum. I get a sudden urge to save them.

Rachel turns. I'm graced with a scowl. Then it's back to the business at hand. I'm not here.

'Good morning,' I say, brightly.

No answer.

'Would anyone like some toast?'

No eye contact.

I busy myself making coffee, then sit at the table. Expecting continued silence, I'm surprised when Rachel speaks.

'Did you stay here last night?'

'Yes.'

'Why?'

'Because your dad was out and I didn't want to leave you on your own.'

'Oh.'

Her eyes narrow again. 'Where did you sleep?'

'In one of the guest rooms. Why?'

'No reason.'

Silence returns.

'Where's Dad?' asks Toby, chocolate staining the edges of his mouth.

'Gone again, as usual,' Rachel says, with the exasperation and bitterness of a long-suffering wife. I know how she feels.

I sip my coffee, hoping they don't work out that he's been gone all night. 'So, what would you like to do today?'

Toby glances at his sister. She frowns a silent warning. He looks down into his bowl.

'How about Aqua-Splash?' I ask.

His head pops up. 'Yeah,' he says. Then, 'Ow,' as his sister kicks him. He looks down again, gives a quick nod as if telling himself to be quiet.

'We're not going,' she confirms for both of them.

He closes his eyes.

'Look,' I say, 'are we going to get on with life, or are we going to mope around?'

'Mope around,' says Rachel, victoriously.

'OK,' I say. 'Suit yourself. I've plenty of work to do. I was just trying to make your day more enjoyable. But if you want to hang around here, fine.'

Toby looks pleadingly at his sister. But she won't budge.

Despite my attempts at blasé, I keep an eye on them, dragging my laptop around wherever they go. If they're in Rachel's room, I'm in mine. If they're downstairs, I am, too. I'm trying to be subtle about it, but, when they go for a swim, this becomes impossible. I appear in the water two minutes after they do. Rachel glares at me then turns to her brother.

'Come on, Toby, let's go,' she says, without taking her eyes off me.

'But we just got in,' he whines.

'Come. *On.*'

'No.'

'Fine,' she says, furious at having to leave her accomplice behind.

I wink at him.

He smiles. It's the one thing we share. We're the youngest and we don't always like it.

He has his mini-rebellion then goes back to his sister. They spend the rest of the morning in her room, door closed. When they emerge, she's fussing over him, getting drinks and food, or putting him in the bath to keep him cool. She even trims his fingernails. She's becoming a little Hilary, with Hilary expressions and mannerisms. And just like Hilary, she doesn't want me there. Let's face it: I can think of a lot of places I'd rather be. I could kill Greg, out there in his own colourful, interesting, loud galaxy, while I'm stuck here, struggling with his children.

19.

Late morning, Fint calls. He wants me back in Dublin to brainstorm for the big pitch. There's no way I can commit to that. Not with Greg gone and no idea of when he'll return, not when I can't trust him with the children if he *does* return, and not when there's the possibility of him leaving them alone again if I do go.

'What do you mean you can't come? We have to brainstorm on this. It's a major opportunity.'

'I know, Fint. I'm sorry, I just can't come over immediately. The children's nanny has walked out.'

'So? Whose children are they, Lucy?'

'Greg isn't well.'

'What's wrong with him?'

'I . . . I don't know.'

'I see,' he says, sounding like he doesn't.

'Look, let me see if I can find someone, a new nanny. There must be agencies over here. Give me a week, OK? Just give me a week to find someone, then I'll be over.'

'A week? Are you kidding? Have you seen our deadline?'

'I'm really sorry, Fint, but I can't come yet. Not till I sort this out.'

'Can't? Or won't?'

'Can't.'

'Lucy, I really think you need to look at your priorities. Your personal life is taking over. I can't keep making concessions. You made a commitment to come home for meetings. Well, this isn't just any meeting. This is huge. This is an opportunity to bag the biggest, most prestigious account we've ever had, and you're prepared to blow it. We're supposed to be a team.'

'I know, and I'm sorry.'

'So come.'

My stomach is knotted so tightly I could throw up. 'I'll try. I'll find a nanny agency . . .'

'I'm carrying this partnership,' Fint continues, his voice telling me he's barely holding his anger together. 'You know, Lucy, if you can't keep up your business commitments, well, I don't know, maybe it's time to start talking about—'

'Fintan, you know that if I could come right this minute, I would. I'm sorry. But I can't help it. I can't leave these kids.'

'You're putting babysitting before Get Smart. This is a partnership, Lucy. The effort is supposed to be fifty-fifty.'

'If you want me to quit, I'll quit. OK? I can't take this. I've had enough. I'll ring you tomorrow, and we can sort this out.'

'Right, that's really mature. First you back out of your commitments, then you quit . . .'

I hang up. *What's the point? What's the fucking point?*

~

I ring Grace. My relationship, my career . . . my *life* is falling apart.

'I'm coming over,' she says.

'What d'you mean you're coming over? You've the kids . . .'

'I'm bringing them.'

'There's a heatwave . . .'

'Have you air conditioning?'

'In the apartment.'

'Fine.'

'You don't need to do this. There must be nanny agencies over here.'

'So. You find an agency, what then? Is your French good enough to wade through CV after CV, conduct interview after interview in a foreign language? Even if you manage to get someone, will they last? I mean, who'd want to work for a person in Greg's condition?'

I feel like wailing.

'Look. I may as well be over there as here for all I see of Kevin. I'm bored out of my tree, stuck in the house for the last week because of the rain. It's not as if my diary's full of prior engagements. It's not as if I have a bloody diary. Lucy, I need a challenge. And let's face it: you could do with a hand.'

I say nothing; I need her to come, but it's too much to ask.

'I am *not* going to let you give up your career,' she says. 'One in the family is enough. Let me talk to Kevin. But, in the mood I'm in, fuck Kevin and the horse he rode into town on.'

'Grace, I warn you; it's a circus over here.'

'Lucy, I think I've a fair idea.'

Mid-afternoon, Grace calls to confirm that she's coming. I feel my body deflate in relief. In under a week, they'll be here. I call Fint before he leaves the office.

'It's me,' I say.

'I thought you'd quit?'

'Don't you watch the movies? You weren't supposed to accept my resignation. You were supposed to shower me with compliments and beg me to stay.'

'Are you kidding? I was furious with you, Lucy.' He stops. 'But it's OK. I've calmed down now.' He pauses. 'What's happening?'

'Grace is coming over to give me a hand.'

'Grace?' He sounds surprised, as if there really might be a problem after all. 'Is everything all right?'

'Yeah.'

'Greg OK?'

'Yeah. No. Look, I'm sorry about earlier. The last thing I want to do is let you down. You've been great, really great.' I'm starting to get upset.

'Forget it, Lucy, I'd a brainstorm with the guys. Sebastian sat in. He was amazing.'

'Really?'

'Yeah. Incredibly creative. We'd a very productive meeting.'

'That's good,' I say, beginning to feel left out.

'Look, if things are so difficult over there right now, we may be able to manage without you. We've some really good ideas to go on now.'

'No, no. It's fine. I'll be over. How's a week today?'

He checks his diary. 'Fine.'

'OK. I'll let you know when I've booked a flight.'

~

Within minutes of hanging up, I get a call from Matt. He wants to know where Greg's overdue edits are. He can't get Greg, so he's using his clout as one of my biggest clients to see what I can do, to 'hurry things along'.

I check Greg's desk. It's chaotic, cluttered with mounds of paper, books, half-eaten food, three overflowing ashtrays, CDs, newspapers, *Asterix* comics. The mess spills onto the floor and along it like a creeping virus. Handwritten notes and computer printouts are covered in doodles, diagrams and cartoon sketches, all outlining ideas. He's written on everything from paper to receipts, napkins, bags, even toilet paper. Instead of his usual loose scrawl are tiny letters and words, jammed together, as if he's trying to condense an epic onto a postcard.

I go to turn on his computer and realise it's already on, screen blank from not being used. When I move the mouse, what he's been working on comes up. It seems to be a novel. But the sentences don't follow on from each other normally. They're unlinked in thought, connected only by words, either words that rhyme or the actual same word at the beginning and end of two adjacent sentences. Is it some sort of experiment? One thing's for sure: no publisher is going to accept it. No publisher is going to *understand* it. Better to show Matt nothing, than this.

I save and close the file, then search for the completed edits. Without success. What will I tell Matt? A wave of hopelessness crashes down on me. I realise that, whatever's wrong with Greg, it's much too big for me. Maybe even for Grace. I rest my forehead against the cool mahogany of the desk and close my eyes.

There's a rumble of distant thunder. I open my eyes and see how dark it's become. I go to the window. Angry storm clouds, the colour of charcoal, are gathering on the horizon like soldiers preparing for battle. The air's heavy. I swing open all the shutters. Out on the terrace, I gather in bone-dry clothes, towels and togs. A weak flash of lightning. Then the sound of a bowling ball running along a wooden floor. Faites attention! Nous venons! I stand on the terrace, arms folded, and wait.

The rain, when it comes, is torrential, blotting out all other sound. The children come to the doorway and watch. And there we stand, transfixed by the storm, my only thoughts how much trouble we are in.

The storm rages all evening until it loses its novelty value for the children. At nine, Rachel decides it's time for bed. When Toby starts to protest, as he always does, she promises to read him *Captain Underpants*. As they climb the stairs, I hear her telling him that they should brush their teeth first, to get it over with.

I call, 'Goodnight.'

Only Toby turns. He gives me a little smile, then carries on up the stairs, his sister holding his hand.

Apart from intermittent lightning flashes, it is fully dark when the sound of a loud and unfamiliar engine outside alerts me. I go to the window. Headlights dazzle, then die, leaving darkness. Someone's coming to the door. I switch on the outside light and peer out. Sitting in the drive is a beautiful silver sports car, top down in the middle of a thunderstorm. I open the window and stick my head out to see who's at the door.

Greg.

He's soaked through, white hair glistening under the light, as he fumbles with his keys.

I open the door.

'Oh. Hello!' he says, surprised.

'Whose is that?' I ask.

'The car?' He turns to admire it. 'What do you think? Porsche Boxster. Cool, eh?'

'Yeah. But whose is it?'

'Mine.' His chest expands.

'You bought it?'

'Yup. Nought to a hundred in six seconds. Put that in your drum and bang it.'

'Where's the jeep?'

He runs a hand through spiky, albino hair. 'I traded it in.'

'Where's all the stuff that was in the boot?'

He bites his lip.

'Where will the children sit? How will we fit anything into that little boot?'

He drags two distressed fingers across his forehead. He looks down at his open-toe sandals and tanned, sandy feet. Then he lifts his head, throws his arms in the air in a 'Who cares?' gesture, as if the process of thinking is just too much.

'And you remembered to change your insurance, right?'

He looks like he's about to blow, an android suffering a circuit overload.

'Greg. We need to talk. This has gone on too long. You need to stop, OK? You need help.'

'I buy the coolest car and I need help.' He rolls his eyes, then turns a hundred and eighty degrees.

'Where you going?'

'For a run.'

'We're in the middle of a thunderstorm,' I call after him.

He legs it down the drive, his shirt clinging to his back.

I slam the door. Kick it. An angry crack of thunder causes the windows to vibrate. The car alarm goes off. Lightning illuminates the entire room. Immediate thunder sounds like a plank of wood cracking. Blue light invades the room. Flash, waver, flash. Smack. The rain is heavier than ever.

I check on the children and find them in a deep sleep on Rachel's bed, back to skinny back. I cover them with a sheet, turn off the fan. I gaze at them and sigh. They don't deserve this. Nobody does. How can such a great father just lose interest in his family? Can drugs really do that to a person?

I go to my room, sit on the bed and wrap my arms around my knees. I never thought I'd say it, but if only I'd never met him. My world was safe. *I* controlled it. Why did I have to go and expose myself to this? Wasn't it enough to lose one man? Because I'm losing Greg. He's living his own life now, separate from me. To him, I'm a bore. So, why not offer me the drugs? Maybe he did, the night of the red dress and the restaurant. If so, he got his answer when I told him I didn't want to be treated like that. And I don't. I want to live in the real world. And I want the man I love to want the same. Is that too much to ask? Apparently so. Which leaves me with only one option – to end this, to leave the man I love because he has chosen a meaningless, hurtful and destructive path. That I've made that decision breaks my heart.

~

I wake early and immediately sense change. I feel Greg's presence. I can't see him, but I know he's near. I hear his breathing. I sit up. And there he is, asleep, finally asleep on the floor beside the bed, still in the clothes he was wearing during the storm. He looks like someone who needs rescuing. I slip my pillow under his head and cover him with the sheet. That he came and found me and lay beside me softens something in me.

It's daylight, but dark. The rain has eased, but thunder continues to rumble and lightning flickers, pale pink against a dark grey sky. I check on Rachel and Toby. They're at their bedroom window, looking out. I stand in silence beside them. Toby starts a stream of questions about forked lightning, sheet lightning and people getting electrocuted. Rachel just wants to know if her dad's home.

'Yes,' I say. 'And he's asleep.'

There's hope in her eyes when she looks at me. For the first time, we've something in common.

20.

At twelve, Greg's still asleep. I'm sitting in the kitchen, nursing a coffee, when, on the table next to the keys to his Porsche, his iPhone begins to vibrate. Hilary's name comes up on the screen. *Finally*, I think, and pick up.

'Hello, Hilary.'

She kills the line. I should have known she would. I sigh and am about to put back the phone when I notice that Greg has missed calls. Hilary's been ringing him non-stop for days, at all hours. For goodness' sake, if she's so desperate for her job back, all she had to do was call me. Why is Greg being so pig-headed? He must have heard *some* of the calls. And why didn't she try the villa? That's when I finally figure out the source of that silent calls – Hilary, ringing for Greg, and hanging up when I answered. This is more than wanting her job back. This is crazy.

It's lunchtime when Greg surfaces. Dark circles ring sunken eyes. A long, red line runs down his cheek where he's slept on a crease. He's changed out of his wet clothes, but still looks shabby and unshaven. His T-shirt and trousers hang off him, making me realise how much weight he's lost. He looks burned out, as if the last two weeks of sleepless nights have finally caught up with him.

'Hi,' I say.

'Hi.' He half smiles, half looks at me, dragging out a chair and slumping onto it.

I plug in the kettle, then turn, folding my arms and leaning against the worktop. Neither of us speaks; we just watch the rain through the open doors.

'Hilary's been ringing your mobile – constantly.'

'Oh?' He doesn't look at me.

'What does she want?'

'Dunno.' He gets up, goes to the fridge, pulls out a carton of juice and drinks directly from it.

'She called here, too, and hung up when I answered. What's going on?'

He shakes his head. Shrugs.

'Surely, she got through to you at some point?'

'She said something about wanting her job back. I told her it was out of the question.'

'Why?'

'I don't want her back, that's all. Where are the kids?' He looks to the door.

'Upstairs.'

'What are they doing?' He puts the carton back. Yawns. Scratches the side of his face.

'Avoiding me.'

'Both of them?'

'They think I told you to fire Hilary.'

'Why?'

'Because she told them I did.'

'Jesus. Why?'

'Who knows? Revenge. A parting shot.' I look at him. 'Greg, can you sit down for a sec?'

His eyes register that something's up. But he doesn't argue.

'We're in trouble,' I say.

I see him swallow.

'I can't go on. Not like this. You snap at me and the children. Sack Hilary. Then disappear whenever you want for hours, nights at a time, without any explanation. I don't know where you are, who you're with, what you're doing. You won't talk to me. You don't care. Just leave me here, minding your children as if I'm some kind of idiot. They're your responsibility, not mine. At this stage, the only reason I'm still here is so that nothing happens to them. I can't trust you to mind your own children, Greg. You've lost all sense of responsibility. You have a family, a successful career, a fiancée, commitments, but you just don't seem to care. It's as if all you want is to be out having a good time, getting high, to hell with the people who love you. Did you know I've had Matt hounding me for the edits to *A River Too Wide*?' He opens his mouth to say something, but I don't let him. 'I've had enough, Greg.'

'I'm sorry, Lucy. I . . . I haven't been myself. So restless. Always something else to do . . .'

'You used to be a great father. I admired you for it.'

'I don't know what's got into me. I'm sorry. You're right. I'll change. I won't go out . . .'

'What is it, Greg? Are you bored with us?'

'No.'

'Isn't life exciting enough for you?'

'Of course it is.'

'Is there someone else?'

'No. No.'

'Please, Greg. Just tell me what it is – I want to know what ended our relationship.'

He gets up, comes to me and takes my hands in his. 'There's no one else, Lucy. Just you. I love you. I won't go out. I'll stay in. I'm sorry. I just don't know how I've let things get this out of hand.

I don't understand it myself.' He sniffs. 'I promise I'll stick around, be here for you, for the kids.' He rubs his bristly chin.

'How do I know I can trust you, Greg? You say you'll do all these things and then you don't. I'm tired. So tired. I need to go home, now. Get Rob over here to help you with the children. They're not my responsibility. I've tried to make this work. I've tried so hard. But I can't do this any more. I just can't.' I look down at the beautiful triangular solitaire that reminds me of another time, another man. I close my eyes and begin to remove it.

'No, Lucy. Please. I promise you, there's nowhere else I want to be, just with you and the kids.'

'Then, why aren't you?' I manage to prise the ring off a finger swollen from the heat. I hold it out to him. 'Take it. Please take it.'

He looks desperate. 'I love you, Lucy, I swear. Give me a chance to prove it, Luce, please. Give me a week. You'll see.'

Can I believe him? Can I trust him?

'One week,' he says.

I enclose the ring in my fist. For once, we are talking. He is actually listening. Promising to try. All he wants is a week. And, much as I want to, I can't deny him that. 'One week, Greg. That's it. One week.'

He hugs then kisses me. 'Thank you, Lucy. Thank you. You won't be sorry, I swear.'

Neither of us moves. He hasn't held me in a simple hug like this for what feels like a very long time. Eventually, I ask him to call the children for lunch – they might come for him.

They look wary, not sure what to expect.

'Hi, guys,' Greg says.

Toby looks at me.

I smile reassurance.

'Hi,' he says quietly, taking his place at the table.

'Hi, Dad,' says Rachel, eyeing her father carefully.

We sit down to eat. For a long while, no one speaks. The children look like they're on full alert, as though expecting an outburst or a sudden ingenious idea that spells disaster.

'Maybe, when the rain's stopped, we could go for a swim?' he suggests in a voice that sounds very calm – for him.

Toby looks at Rachel, unsure.

She seems to mull it over. 'Can Lucy come too?' she asks without looking at me.

Though I know why she's asking, I'm still surprised.

'Of course,' Greg says.

~

After lunch, the children go upstairs to change into their swimming togs. Greg helps me clear the table.

'They hardly said anything over lunch,' he says.

'They didn't want to upset you.'

He stops halfway between the table and the sink, glasses in hand. 'Why would they upset me?'

'Greg, everything upsets you lately. Especially the people who love you.'

He looks bemused.

He needs his next hit. Any minute now, he'll go.

But he doesn't. There's no next hit, no more high. Instead, over the next few days, he glides slowly back to earth, to us, his boundless energy fading like a dying wind, his restlessness with it. He seems content with our company again, no longer desperate to befriend the world. Gradually, he resumes the simple acts of living that I once took for granted – eating, sleeping, listening. At times, I wonder if I imagined it all. But then, there's a silver sports car outside, an unfinished mural on the wall, an office that looks like a hurricane struck, a diamond earring, white hair and a red dress.

And there are worried children.

'Dad, what was wrong with you before?' asks Toby one night, sitting on his father's lap having his toenails cut.

Greg doesn't take his eyes off Toby's feet. 'When?'

'Before. When I didn't know what you were saying.'

Now he looks at Toby, confused and worried. 'You didn't know what I was saying?'

'No.' Toby's eyes search mine for confirmation.

'None of us did,' I say.

Greg seems stuck. 'I don't know,' he says, finally. 'Must have been the heat. Yes, that was it. The heat.'

No way. Not just heat.

'But it's still hot, Dad,' insists Toby.

'Not *so* hot, though. It's cooled down a good bit, hasn't it? And you can understand me now, can't you?' He smiles and ruffles his son's hair.

'Yeah.'

'Well, then. That's what matters, isn't it? Everything back to normal.'

Is it, though? I'm still waiting for the next disappearing act. Despite how wonderful he's been over the last few days – staying at the villa, cooking the meals, swimming with the kids, listening – I can't allow myself to believe that this is over. After all that's happened, for Greg to stop, just like that, seems too good to be true. Still, I ring Grace to let her know. No point in her embarking on a wasted journey. She's relieved that Greg's feeling better, but, as she has the flights booked and could do with a change of scene, she's going to stick to her plan.

I was hoping she might.

~

The following day, when they come through Arrivals, I feel almost teary to see them. My own, personal cavalry. In one hand, Grace is pushing the trolley. In the other, she's carrying a heavy-looking Jason. Shane's sitting on the cases like he's king of the castle. I wave like mad. Grace has to stop the trolley as Shane decides to suddenly disembark. I squat down and he runs to me. I squeeze him tight and stand with him in my arms. I plant a raspberry on his cheek. When Grace reaches us, I pop Shane down and take Jason from her. It's good to feel his podgy little arms around my neck, though it reminds me of the gulf between Greg's children and me.

21.

Arriving back at the villa from settling Grace and the boys into the apartment, I walk in on a phone call.

'You have to stop ringing here, Hilary,' Greg says, the back of his head visible over the top of the chair.

I can't move.

'No,' he says. 'That's impossible. No. This is for the best . . . There's nothing here for you . . . I'm sorry. I love Lucy. You need to start a new life, for your own sake. I'm sorry about what happened. Really, I am . . . But there's no future for you here.'

Why did he have to say he loves me? What happened?

I reverse out of there.

On the terrace, I try to think. Then, I get a call myself.

'Lucy, hi. It's Hilary.'

'Hello, Hilary.' My voice is cold, flat.

'I was just wondering . . . You know when I left and you offered me my job back?'

I say nothing.

'Well, I'd like to take it.'

'I'd have to talk to Greg about that.'

'Why? Why would you need to talk to Greg?'

'Because Rachel and Toby are his children.' *Obviously.*

'Oh, forget it.' She hangs up.

~

I wait until evening, when the children are in bed. We're out on the terrace, smoke from Greg's cigar floating on the balmy air. Down in the bay, the sea is flat and glassy. Lights along the coast look warm and cheerful.

'Hilary rang me today,' I say, interrupting the peace.

'What did she want?' he asks, his casual tone sounding fake. He starts to roll his cigar between his fingers.

'Her job back.'

'What did you say?'

'That I'd have to check with you.'

'Good.' There's relief in his voice.

'What's going on, Greg? Why's she so anxious for her job back?'

He reaches for his bottle of Kronenbourg. 'I don't know. I guess she's very attached to the family.'

'The family? Or you?'

'The family,' he says firmly, but, instead of meeting my eyes, he rubs condensation from the beer bottle. 'She's been looking after Rachel and Toby for so long. And you know her history; you know she can never have kids of her own.'

'Then, why did you fire her? And why won't you take her back?'

'She needs a life away from us. For her own sake.'

'I know that. But why are you suddenly so adamant about it? There was no need to fire her. Couldn't she have just lived out?'

'She needed a clean break.'

'Did something happen between you?'

'No.' He stubs out the cigar.

'She's in love with you, isn't she?'

'Don't be ridiculous.' He stands suddenly, his back to me.

'Am I? Am I being ridiculous? Or are you hiding something?'

He walks away, hand on the back of his neck. Then he stops, turns. And finally meets my eyes. 'OK. All right. Maybe she does have . . . feelings for me. What can I do about it? Nothing, except keep her away.'

'Is that what all this is about?'

He doesn't blink when he says, 'Yes.'

'So, something *did* happen the other night, the night you fired her?'

He nods slowly.

'What?'

He sits back down, takes a moment. 'She came on to me . . .'

'Jesus.'

'Nothing happened, Lucy, I promise you that.'

'Then, why didn't you tell me?'

'I just wanted to get rid of the problem. Deal with it. Fast. I thought that if she wasn't around, that would be the end of it.'

'But it's not, is it?'

'She'll get tired of ringing.'

Silence falls between us. I look out at the pine trees, silhouetted black against a colourless sky. That's when I tell him.

'She told me you were seeing other women when you started disappearing.'

His head swivels in my direction. '*What?*'

'She said it happens every time you get bored with the person you're with. You take off and bingo! There's another woman on the scene.'

He looks stunned. 'She's making it up. She wasn't even around when I was married to Catherine. And there's been no one since . . .'

'Except Hilary.'

He looks hurt. 'I told you about that. I explained.'

'I know,' I concede.

'I can't believe she said that. You didn't *believe* her, did you?'

'No, Greg. I didn't. But then you kept disappearing, no explanation. And I kept remembering that time at the restaurant when you were flirting with those women. And I didn't know what to believe . . .'

'What women?'

'Those "ravishing" English women.'

'Jesus, I don't even remember their names. I was out for the night, in good form. I wasn't flirting.'

I'm quiet.

'Lucy, you know I'd never cheat. Not on you. Or on Catherine. Why didn't you talk to me about this?'

'You haven't exactly been the easiest person to talk to.'

He looks away. Quietly, he asks himself, 'What the fuck was I up to?' He leans forward, placing his elbows on his legs and his hands in prayer position in front of his mouth. He stays like that for a long time. Then he turns to me.

'I'm sorry, Lucy. For everything. For being so hyper, always on the go, for taking off and not being here for you.' He stops, looks up, straight into my eyes. 'But I have never been unfaithful to you. Not once.' His eyes look sad that I might have doubted that.

The pressure of the last few weeks suddenly hits. My throat burns, my eyes fill. 'She told Toby that we were going to split up.' The first tear falls. 'She said you both laughed together about me wanting her to talk to Rachel.'

'*What?*'

I glare at him, anger erupting like a flare. 'I asked you not to tell her, Greg. Why did you?'

He runs his fingers up and down his forehead. 'All I did was ask her to have a word with Rachel. I thought I was doing you a favour. Of course I didn't laugh at you. Why would I do that?'

I shrug. Then a sob hits.

'Christ. This is a nightmare. I can't believe Hilary said all those things.'

'I'm not making this up.'

'I know. I know you're not. It's just hard to take in, that she's capable of this kind of manipulation. I'm just . . . I don't know, I'm just stunned.'

'Weren't you stunned when she came on to you?'

He looks hurt by the knife in my voice. 'Yes. Of course I was. But that was impulse. What you're talking about is calculated manipulation and downright lies.' He stops. Then, quieter, he says, 'I trusted Hilary. I trusted her with my family. And I exposed you to her. I don't know what to say, Luce, except that I'm so sorry.'

~

When Greg arrives down the following morning, he no longer has white hair. All that's left is dark shadow. He makes two calls: the first to his caretaker who he asks to come paint over the mural, the second to the garage where he bought the Porsche. The salesman who sold it to him will indeed have a look at the car with a view to taking it back.

The garage buys back the Porsche for a considerably lower price, rain having damaged the interior. The old, reliable Range Rover is returned, contents untouched as it was still waiting to be serviced. Never has a full boot seemed such a sane and normal thing.

On our return journey, Greg calls in at the jewellery shop where he bought the diamond earring and asks for the precious stone to be set into a pendant for 'mademoiselle'.

That afternoon, Greg arranges to get air conditioning installed in the villa. It's true, I realise, what they say about actions and words.

~

'So?' was Rachel's reaction when I told her my sister and her kids were coming over. Toby wanted to know if they were bringing toys. Greg wondered why they weren't staying at the villa. Now, I drive to the apartment to collect them for dinner. Grace comes to the door laden with the usual paraphernalia that goes with small children. I help her get everything, including the boys, into the car and apologise in advance for the meal – a basic pasta dish. She tells me it's a treat not to have to cook. My nephews' noisy exuberance makes me realise just how quiet Rachel and Toby have become. Shane marches up to them with presents – water guns almost larger than him. They look surprised.

'Cool,' says Toby, checking his out.

'Thanks,' says Rachel, squatting down to him and smiling. 'How does it work?'

As Shane demonstrates, Rachel gives her dad 'Isn't he cute?' looks. Grace asks her to help screw the portable baby seat onto the table. Rachel enjoys the challenge, and offers to put Jason in. She lifts him with such care, then makes sure to secure the straps.

We sit down to eat. Shane's lively, innocent banter is a relief. Everything has been so tense here. So brittle.

Grace picks up pieces of penne that Jason has scattered over his tray and places them back on his plastic plate. 'Food's for eating, Sonny Jim.'

Shane finishes first. Grace reaches into a giant patchwork bag and pulls out crayons and paper. Everyone concentrates on the masterpiece. It's such a relief to have someone other than Greg to focus on. I pick up a crayon that has fallen to the ground and put it back beside my busy nephew.

'Like my picture, Rachel?' he asks with the confidence of someone who knows she's going to say yes.

'Yeah, it's brill,' she says. 'What is it?'

'Poo,' he says proudly.

She laughs.

'A word of advice, Rachel,' says Grace, smiling. 'Never ask Shane what he's drawing.'

'I was thinking that,' she says, and smiles at him.

After dinner, out by the pool, Rachel, Toby and Shane have a water fight, the boys teaming up against the only girl. Shane, though only three, is pretty handy with a weapon.

'I will experminate you,' he shouts, running after a laughing Rachel.

After the war, they cool down in the pool, Grace and I joining them with the baby, who is decked out in a sunproof costume that covers most of his body. Under his little hat is a smiley face. Jason loves the water. Rachel asks to play with him. And so, while the boys mess around together, she finds a shaded part of the pool and starts a game, pushing the baby away in his bright yellow float, then pulling him back towards her, talking in a high-pitched voice and making expressive faces. He is gurgling and chuckling.

It's official: Grace and the boys are a hit.

That night, when Greg comes to my room, he's as gentle and caring as he used to be before a whirlwind overtook his body. After, when he holds me close and tells me he loves me, I do believe him. And when he tells me that there's never been anyone else, I believe him, too. In the morning, the one week I promised him is up.

I'm not going anywhere.

When the phone rings around eleven, I half expect the line to die.

It doesn't.

'Hello,' says an older male voice I recognise but can't pinpoint immediately. 'Might I speak to Greg, please?'

'I'm afraid Greg's not available right now. Can I help?'

'Is this Lucy?'

'Yes.' It's Ben, I realise.

'This is Ben Franklin. We met—'

'Oh, yes, of course, Ben. How are you?'

'Well, thank you. I was hoping to have a word with Greg.'

'Actually, he's in bed. I'll just run up and see if he's awake.' I do. He isn't. I run back down. 'He's out cold. Will I get him to give you a call when he gets up?'

'When do you think that will be?'

'I'm not sure.'

'Actually, Lucy, perhaps you could pass on a message. If you could just tell him that Ruth and I are popping over to Antibes for a few days and we were hoping to meet up with him. Perhaps we could take you both out to dinner tomorrow night?'

'Oh,' I say, surprised, knowing how things are between them. 'That sounds lovely. I'm sure it would be fine. When Greg gets up I'll ask him to give you a call.'

'How is everything?'

'Fine, thank you.'

'How are the children?'

'They're well. Would you like to speak to them? They're just upstairs . . .'

'No, no, I won't disturb them. I'll see them tomorrow, or the day after. Well, I'd better go.'

'Thanks for the call. And the invite.'

'Odd,' Greg says, when I tell him. 'Ben hates the South of France. You should have heard him when we bought the villa. In all the years we've had it, they've never been out.' His eyes narrow. 'I wonder what's on his agenda.'

'Does he have to have an agenda?'

'Ben Franklin always has an agenda. I just wish I knew what it was.'

22.

On the Cap d'Antibes, we drive through the pillared entrance of the exclusive Hôtel du Cap-Eden-Roc. Never has a name seemed more appropriate; it's like arriving in Eden. Tall pines tower over us as we wind our way down to a crystal blue sea. The car is valet-parked, but we're early, and Greg suggests a stroll up to the bar at the main hotel, explaining that we've arrived at the restaurant, a separate building, on the water's edge.

We walk through paradise. The people we pass are immaculately dressed and beautiful. Almost unreal. At the terrace bar, we find more of the same. Men in blazers and crisp open-necked shirts, hair slicked back. Slender, tanned women with long, straight hair wearing designer dresses and high strappy sandals. A man at the next table has just come off a boat and is telling his fan club about a party he has been invited to, hosted by a Hollywood star's ex-wife. Greg rolls his eyes.

We have a quiet drink together, then, at eight thirty, we stroll back down to the restaurant. The view is incredible. The sea is no longer the Mediterranean, but a private lake belonging to the hotel, or so it seems. The sky is a wash of pale blue and pink. Lamps have been lit around the perimeter of the restaurant and candles glow on every table. A pale yellow moon and sidekick star hover overhead, the sky the ultimate ceiling. It is magical.

Breaking the spell, the maître d' informs us that our hosts are at the table. We follow him. They stand when they see us. Ben's greeting is a businesslike handshake. Ruth follows his lead.

We have our linen napkins opened for us by waiters and menus slipped into our hands.

Ben steers the conversation. It is formal and stilted. There are polite questions about the children, France and the weather. As usual, I feel we're being judged.

As we're finishing coffee, Ben says, 'We've had a visit from Hilary.'

My heart thuds.

'She seems worried. Is everything all right, Greg?'

'Everything's fine. Couldn't be better, Ben,' he says, flashing a wide smile. 'I'm not sure what Hilary's worried about.'

'She's concerned about the welfare of our grandchildren.'

Jesus.

'The children are fine,' Greg says, without faltering. 'You can see for yourself tomorrow.'

'Yes, yes. And how are you feeling?'

'Never better.'

'And the driving? No problems there?'

'None.'

'Good. Good. Getting plenty of rest?'

'What is this, Ben?'

'Nothing. Nothing. Just making sure you're all right. Not getting too much sun, that sort of thing.' He's fiddling with his tie.

'Well, thank you for your concern,' Greg says through gritted teeth. 'But, as you can see, I'm a big boy. Quite able to look after myself. And my children.' His coffee cup clangs against its saucer as he lands it down. 'You know what? Let me get this, Ben.'

'No, no. I wouldn't dream—'

'I insist.' He calls the waiter, pulling out his wallet. He pays without looking at the bill.

Nothing more is said, apart from curt goodbyes.

~

Greg doesn't speak until we're pulling away. 'Well, that was humiliating.'

I look at him. 'You were right about something being up.'

He yanks at his seatbelt; it jams. 'Who does Hilary think she is, upsetting them like that?'

'She must have really freaked them out, to have them hopping on a plane to France.'

'Of all the people to freak out.' He pulls away, fast.

'The tension at that table. He really has a problem with you, Greg. It's more than him just being a snob, isn't it?'

He doesn't answer, just races past tiny beaches, families still swimming and picnicking in the moonlight. Finally, he says, 'He blames me for Catherine's death.'

'What? *Why?*'

'They both do.'

'They said it was your fault?'

'No. They'd never do that.' He pulls in behind a parked car to let another through on the narrow road. 'I just knew. Sensed it. They couldn't look me in the eye. Not then. And not since.'

'But how can they blame you? Catherine died in childbirth.'

He pulls out again. 'Who got her pregnant?'

'Oh, come on.'

He shrugs.

The traffic slows as we reach throbbing Juan-les-Pins. We stop at lights. He looks across at me.

'They knew we'd been warned against having another child. When Catherine got pregnant, she told them it had been her idea. They still looked at me as if I was a complete idiot for allowing it to happen. I was as worried as they were. When she died, they couldn't face me. And, to be honest, I couldn't face myself – or them. Hilary used to take the children over to see them. It was easier for everyone.'

'So, that's how she knows them well enough to do this.'

'Oh, they love Hilary. She looked after their grandchildren while the oaf tried to pick up the pieces.'

The car in front moves forward and we're driving again.

'Weird the way he said "our grandchildren", – so possessively. As if they're actually his kids,' I say.

'They're his last link to Catherine. They couldn't be more precious to him. And, though at times he drives me crazy, I suppose he does love them.'

~

Next day, we drop the children off at the Hôtel du Cap for an afternoon by the pool with their grandparents. There's no way Greg will stay. And, to be honest, I get the impression we're not welcome.

We return to the villa, where Greg starts to clear out his office. How, he wonders, did he let it get into such a state? He starts at the edges and works his way in. One by one, black bags appear outside the door, reassuring me that things are on the mend.

After two hours, I go in to drag him out. He's sitting at his desk, head in his hands.

'You OK?'

'No.'

'What is it?'

He looks up. 'It's rubbish. Everything I've been writing is rubbish. It just doesn't make sense.' He picks up page after page and shoves them at me. 'Look. Look at this. Does any of this make sense to you? Because it sure as hell doesn't make sense to me. And I wrote it. Apparently.'

I pretend to read it for the first time.

'See? See?'

'Well, it's . . . It's just very, very creative.'

'Did I write that? Did I really write that shit? I must be losing my mind.'

How can he not know what he's written? 'Come on, take a break.'

'Did you know I was writing this?'

'No,' I lie. 'Come on. Come away from it. Start again later.'

'What if I produce the same crap?'

'You won't. Just do the edits for *A River Too Wide*. That will get you into the swing of things.'

'I don't know.'

'Go out to the pool, have a swim, clear your head. I'll tidy your desk. I won't throw anything out. I'll just file it—'

'Dump it. Dump the whole bloody lot of it.'

'OK. I'll dump it. Now go.'

I shred what he's written so he never has to face it again. I clear away books, magazines, DVDs, returning them to their cases. Any real rubbish, I bin. All that remains, apart from his computer, are the edits for *A River Too Wide*.

~

Later, we collect the children.

'How did that go?' asks Greg, twisting round in the front passenger seat.

'All right,' says Rachel.

'Just all right?'

'Boring,' says Toby.

'Yeah. They wouldn't let us do anything. They wouldn't let me go on the rope ladder even though I'm ten.'

'They wouldn't let us dive.'

'They kept putting sunscreen all over us,' says Rachel. 'Even though we had some on and I can do it myself.'

'Oh,' says Greg.

'They wouldn't let us have Coke,' says Toby. 'Even though I said you let us.'

'Or chips. And they kept asking us if we're happy.'

'I hope you pretended to be,' says Greg.

'No. Not with them. With you.'

I stall the car. Behind, a horn blows.

'With me?' Greg asks.

'Yeah. They kept asking questions about you.'

'What kind of questions?'

'Were you cross with us? Were you talking funny? Were you driving funny?'

'And what did you say?' he asks quickly.

'I lied,' says Rachel. 'I said you were fine.'

Greg and I exchange a glance. He looks so guilty. He turns back.

'Well, thanks for sticking up for me, Rache,' he says, his voice gentle. 'And I'm sorry, guys, if I've been a bit, you know, snappy. It won't happen again. I promise you that.'

''S'OK, Dad,' says Toby. 'At least you let us have Coke *and* chips.'

Just the reassurance he needs.

Next morning, I fly back to Dublin for the brainstorm. Last time I was in the office, I never got a chance to sit at my desk and take a few moments. Now, I swivel around in my chair. Flick on my computer. Slide open my drawers and peek inside. I pick up a chain of coloured paper clips I probably made during some brainstorm or other. When the screensaver comes on, it's a picture of Greg and me, grinning at the camera. It seems so long ago since I put it up, but it's still only weeks. We look so happy, vibrant, together. I run my finger over his face and my eyes fill with tears. We've been through so much in so little time. I make a wish that it's all over, then I take a deep breath and get to work.

Half an hour later, we're in the boardroom. Fint's looking great – tanned and relaxed. Sebastian, too, is the picture of health.

'So, what did you think of my proposal?' I ask Fint.

'Good.'

'Only good?' In the Dictionary of Fint, good means . . . well, bad.

'No, no. It was good . . . Sebastian had some ideas too. Do you want to present them, Sebastian?'

A presentation? I thought this was a brainstorm.

Sebastian looks awkward, for Sebastian. He takes us through a PowerPoint presentation, his confidence building as he goes. I'm stunned by the freshness of his ideas, so innovative they show mine up as jaded. Which, I realise, they are. I look across at him as if seeing him for the first time. Whatever happened to my enthusiasm? How have I lost it? I had it before I left. I've never been the kind of person to applaud after presentations. But I do after Sebastian's.

'Sebastian, that was amazing.'

He beams. 'Thanks, Lucy.'

'And to think that if you hadn't gone to France, we'd never have discovered this Natural Born Designer,' Fint says.

I feel a stab of something – regret, maybe? A touch of envy? It isn't that I resent him his talent – far from it; I just wish I knew where mine has gone. It's not good, being away from the office. Too much is happening without me. I'm losing my handle on things. I should be at the centre of this project, not the perimeter. I need to come home more often. No, I need to be home, full stop.

~

I touch down in Nice, an hour late. With no baggage, I'm one of the first out. I look for Greg, but no one's here to lift me up and swing me around. I check my watch. My mind takes off. Could something have happened? Has he reverted to his old ways? I'm about to pull out my phone when I catch sight of a blonde beauty rushing in the door, carrying a baby. Grace, as usual, is oblivious to the heads she's turning.

'Sorry I'm late,' she says, out of breath. 'I knew the flight was delayed, so I wasn't rushing. Somehow, I ended up late.'

'No worries.' We hug. 'Hey there, handsome.' I kiss Jason. 'I was just going to get a taxi.'

'You should have known one of us would be here.'

We walk out into the sun.

'Is Greg OK?'

'Yeah. Fine. Though he seems a bit drained. Didn't feel up to coming. He should probably take a tonic. He looks as if he might be coming down with something.'

'He's probably run-down. If we stop at a pharmacy on the way back, would you be able to pick out something?'

'Assuming my French holds up.'

We get to the car and strap Jason in the back. Grace hops into the driving seat. I sit in beside her.

'How'd your meeting go?' she asks.

'All right.' I sigh. 'Some bright young spark showed me up.'

'Lucy, you're not exactly old and dull,' she says, before reversing out of the space.

'Oh, yeah?' It's exactly how I do feel.

'Is everything OK?' She squints.

'Yeah. I just should be back there more often.'

'Maybe you should go over more regularly. Once or twice a week, say.'

'Hmm. Maybe . . . Where's Shane?'

'At the villa. Rachel's making up games for him and Toby. They're in their element. She's very good with them, isn't she?'

'Yeah,' I say, still surprised at this fun side to her.

'God, the way Shane trails around after her. It's so cute. It reminds me of how you used to follow me around when we were kids, remember?' She looks over.

'All I remember is how you wouldn't let me play with your friends.' I smile.

'You know, I still feel guilty about that. Let me take this moment to officially apologise.'

'It's OK, Grace.' I laugh. 'I think I recovered without major psychological scars.'

'You were great, though. Remember when you were five? That was it: no more being my personal slave. You'd had enough.'

I smile, remembering. We stop at lights. I glance at the car next to us. A guy in a baseball cap is nodding his head to music.

'You never really liked me, though, did you?' she says.

'*What?* Are you mad? Of course I liked you.'

'You called me Little Miss Perfect.'

'Not to your face.'

'Which was even worse.' She pulls away from the lights.

'We were kids, Grace. Just because I called you a dumb name doesn't mean I didn't *like* you.'

She looks at me. 'So, why did you do it?'

'I don't know,' I say, irritable at being cornered. 'Because you were perfect. And everyone loved you. And you did everything right. And I didn't . . . OK, I admit it, maybe I *was* a bit jealous.' I can't believe I'm admitting to her something I've never admitted to myself.

'Well, you needn't have been. I wasn't Little Miss Perfect. I was Little Miss Wanna Be Perfect. And that's how I've spent my life – trying. Trying to impress a mother who can't be impressed, followed by a husband who can't be impressed. Which is a bloody big waste of a life, I can tell you.' Her voice breaks.

I reach across and put my hand on hers.

'I've wasted my life, Lucy. I married someone because my mother liked him. How stupid is that? What about what I liked? Why didn't I think of that? *She* doesn't have to live with him. *She* doesn't have to listen to him.'

'Do you want me to drive?'

She shakes her head.

'You sure?'

She nods.

I rummage in my bag for a hankie and hand it to her. 'I'll hold the wheel.'

She nods again. And blows. Then drops the hankie in her lap. 'I'm fine. Fine.' She sniffles. 'I just needed to blow off steam. Tell someone.'

I rub her arm. 'Well, I'm glad it was me. And I may only be your sister, but I think you're perfect. You've always been there for me. You've always encouraged me, complimented every drawing, every sketch, urged me to go to art college. You were there for me after Brendan. And you're here for me now. I'm embarrassed it's taken so long to appreciate that. You couldn't be more perfect.'

And then she smiles. 'Thank you.'

'No, Grace. Thank you.' She just needs a break. She's been under a lot of pressure, handling the boys by herself, Kevin working so hard. It'll get better. He'll miss her while she's away. He'll be more attentive when she gets back. More loving. It'll be fine.

~

Grace wants to clean up before facing everyone so she drops me at the villa and goes on to the apartment with Jason. I find the children indoors, playing an old board game of Toby's, Frustration. Rachel's sitting up on the back of the couch. Toby's draped across it. And Shane is surreptitiously picking his nose.

'Hi there,' I call.

They all look up. The boys say, 'Hi.' Shane asks where his mum is.

'Just gone up to the apartment to let Jase have his nap.' Rehearsed excuse, and partly true.

''K.'

'Would anyone like a drink?' I ask.

I've two takers – the boys. I quickly sort them out.

'Where's your dad?' I ask Toby when I hand him his blackcurrant juice.

'Outside.'

'Thanks.'

Greg's on the terrace. Just sitting. Not reading and sitting, or doing a crossword and sitting, not jotting down notes and sitting. Just sitting. He seems miles away.

'Hi!' I kiss his cheek.

'Oh, hi.' His smile is low voltage.

'You OK?' I ask.

'Mm-hmm.'

'I got you a tonic on the way back from the airport. Grace was saying you're feeling a bit drained.'

'I'd have come to collect you, but I just didn't have the energy.'

'Not to worry.' I pull up a chair beside him. 'Miss me?'

'Mm-hmm.'

'That much?' I joke.

When he smiles, it seems forced.

'How did you all get on?'

'Fine,' says the man who never uses one word if fifty will do.

'So, what did you get up to?'

He thinks for a moment, then abandons it. 'Not much.'

'Are you pissed off with me or something?'

He looks surprised. 'No.'

'Well, what's wrong? You're very quiet.'

He shakes his head. 'I'm fine.'

I try a few openers, including how the 'brainstorm' went. He barely blinks. The only time he shows any interest is when I tell him that Grace is unhappy with Kevin. He's sympathetic to the point of appearing personally sad about it. I take out the tonic and suggest two spoonfuls as a kick-start.

Later, when everyone's asleep, I slip into his bedroom. And bed. In all the weeks we've been together, this is the first time I've initiated sex. He does get into it, eventually, but his enthusiasm doesn't see him through. He can't maintain an erection. This has never happened before. I don't know what to say, or even if I should say anything. He doesn't want to talk about it, just turns from me, saying he's tired. I should have just accepted the fact that he was exhausted and left it at that. I wait until he's asleep to leave.

~

The children have not commented on the fact that I'm still staying at the villa, perhaps because they've become used to me being around – as long as I stay in the guest room. And perhaps they, too, are nervous that their dad might revert to old ways.

In any case, there's no room at the apartment for me now. Which is fine. The villa's a very different place – with air conditioning, without Hilary, and with Greg back to normal. The office has changed, too. Gone are the chaos and noise. I work alone in the mornings while Greg sleeps. Grace insists on minding the children, with Rachel a willing and able helper.

One morning, I'm busy working on the supermarket job, which, to my humiliation, I'm now doing in conjunction with Sebastian, when Greg appears. He's getting later and later. It's practically lunchtime. I smile hello and watch him settle at his computer. His edits are finished and he's attempting a new novel.

At first, I don't notice that he's having problems. It's the silence that draws my attention. There's none of the usual frantic keyboard tapping I associate with Greg. There's no sound at all. He's sitting, staring at the screen, fingers ready but not moving. I pretend not to notice and carry on with my work. But then he slams a fist on the desk.

'Just one clear thought, is that too much to ask?' He leaves before I can react.

After half an hour, I go looking for him. I find him lying on his bed, staring at the ceiling. I don't go in. Just close the door. He needs peace, a quiet place to think about Cooper and plots and pace and all those things writers have to get right. I wonder what it must be like to be expected to come up with something fresh and creative and not be able to. What am I talking about? I do know. I'm going through it. And I appreciate that you just have to keep pushing through to the other side. Then again, a design isn't a whole novel. Maybe that's what's stopping him, the magnitude of what's ahead. Knowing there's nothing I can do to help, I return to my own work.

Over the next few days, Greg spends less and less time in his office and more and more time lying down. When he's up, he mopes in a chair, doing nothing, nothing at all. Except smoke.

'Dad, are you coming for a swim?' Rachel tries.

He doesn't hear.

'Dad?'

'Hmm?'

'Are you coming for a swim?'

'No. No, thanks. You go ahead.'

'OK.' She walks off, looking back at him.

I sit beside him. 'You OK?'

'Yeah, fine.'

I know he's not. 'I'm sure all writers go through this. I wouldn't worry about it, Greg.'

'I haven't been a good father, have I?'

What? 'You're a great father.'

'I've neglected the kids. Neglected you.'

'Come on, Greg. Forget about that. You've been fine since we talked. Everything's OK now.'

'No.' The word seems to reverberate in the silence that follows, making me realise the truth. This is more than writer's block. This is more than Greg being run-down. I remember the websites on amphetamines and the list of symptoms caused by withdrawal. It's like a blow to the chest. All of this has been about drugs. Which means: one, he's stopped. And two, he lied.

'I think I'll lie down for a while,' he says.

I could do with one myself.

He heaves himself up from the chair as if it takes all the energy in the world. And as I watch him go, I tell myself: *It'll be OK. In a few days, it'll be OK.*

~

But it's not OK. In the days that follow, rather than improving, Greg stops communicating completely, not only with us, but with the world at large. Phone calls, post, emails are all ignored. It's the same with TV, radio, newspapers, even books. The only thing he embraces is drink. From mid-afternoon on, he's nursing something. If it's to lift his spirits, it doesn't work. And it sure doesn't do anything for mine.

Down, down, down everything goes – his head, shoulders, the edges of his mouth, his mood, even his voice. Every movement looks like it requires huge effort. Everything he does is in first gear.

He's still in bed, one afternoon, when his father-in-law rings. 'How is everything?' Ben asks me.

'Fine, Ben, thank you.'

'And the children?'

'Very well, thanks. Would you like to speak with them?'

'Yes, yes, in a moment. Could I have a quick word with Greg first, please?'

I'm not telling him he's in bed, not when he's so obviously called to check up on him. 'Just a moment and I'll find him.'

I go up to the room. It's dark, stifling, shutters and windows closed. Air conditioning off. He's lying on his side, a pillow over his head.

'Greg?'

He doesn't answer.

'Ben's on the phone.'

'Tell him to fuck off.'

I laugh, assuming he's joking, then turn on the air conditioning.

'Go away,' he says.

'I'm sorry?'

'Please. Leave me alone.'

'What is *wrong* with you?'

'I just need peace. Is that too much to ask?'

'OK, OK, I'll tell him you'll call back.' *Jesus.*

'And turn the air conditioning off. The noise drives me mad.'

Biting my tongue, I do as he asks, then head for the door.

'Lucy?'

'What?'

'Can you keep them a bit quieter?'

The children aren't making a sound. I say nothing, just go back to the phone. Ben's hung up. I find his number on Greg's mobile and call him back.

'Ben, I'm sorry for keeping you. I was working when you rang and hadn't realised Greg's actually taken the children to the beach. I'm sorry. I'll get him to call you when he comes in.'

'Is everything all right?'

'Everything's fine. I'll get Greg to call you.'

'All right,' he says, not sounding happy.

'Thanks for calling.'

~

When Greg does appear, an hour later, he doesn't look like a man who has spent the day in bed. He looks like he could do with one. I remind him of the phone call. This time, he rings Ben back. And I hope he's a bit more charming than he was with me.

At dinner, he won't eat. Instead, he drinks. Wine. Then whiskey.

Later, on the terrace, while he stares off into the distance or absently watches two geckos scale the wall of the villa in search of moths, I try to read. I go inside to get a drink. When I come back out, he's picked up the autobiography I was reading and is examining the cover. He opens it and runs his finger under the first line. He goes back over it. Can't seem to get beyond that. Over and over it he goes until he slams the book shut. I watch, in horror, as he flings it through the air. It lands in the pool with a splash.

'I was reading that!'

'*That?* The guy's a writer, you'd think he'd know what plain English is.'

'Maybe I'd have liked to have decided that for myself. For God's sake, Greg. You've just ruined my book.' I go get the net to fish it out of the pool.

His eyes register what he's done. 'Sorry. I didn't mean to destroy it. I just got so *frustrated*. I couldn't get beyond that first line. Here, let me do that.' He reaches for the net.

I give it to him and he goes to fish the book out of the pool.

'You might as well bin it,' I say, when he gets it.

'Sorry,' he says again.

'What's wrong with you, Greg? Why are you like this?'

He walks back to the table, reaching for the whiskey bottle.

'Drinking isn't going to help.'

'I'll drink if I bloody well want.'

'Right. Fine. You do that. Just don't expect me to hang around and watch. I'm going. I can't take this any more.'

'Where?' He sounds panicked. 'Where are you going?'

'I don't know . . .' Then, suddenly, I do. 'The apartment.'

'Don't.'

'I've had enough for one night. If you insist on being miserable, fine, be miserable, but don't take it out on me.' I leave, wondering how I ever thought that depression would be acceptable over a high.

23.

'You OK?' Grace asks when she opens the door.

I shake my head and the tears come.

'Greg?'

I nod. She puts an arm around me and walks me into the sitting room, where she sits me down on the couch.

'It's all gone wrong.' I cover my eyes with the heels of my hands. 'He's miserable. He's drinking. He snaps at me for the least little thing.'

'Shhh, it's OK,' she says, rubbing my back.

'He's so down. He has no energy, can't work, won't eat. He's grinding to a halt, Grace. I keep telling myself it's because he's come off drugs, but he's getting worse, not better.'

'Did he *tell you* he was on drugs?'

'No. But what else could it be? He has all the signs . . .'

'Have you ever seen any evidence of drugs?'

'No. But it has to be . . . He was talking gibberish. His writing was bizarre.'

'Can I ask you a question? When he was high, was he overspending, making any impulse buys?'

How could she possibly know? 'Why? It's not a medical complaint. Is it?'

She takes a breath. 'It can be. Sometimes.'

'Of what?'

'What kind of things did he buy?'

'A Porsche.'

She raises her eyebrows.

'A diamond earring – for himself.'

She nods.

'He dyed his hair white.'

I watch jigsaw pieces click together in her eyes. She scratches her hand, the way she always does when nervous. 'Lucy, there *is* one other thing that maybe we should consider . . .'

'What? What is it?'

'I've seen patients with symptoms similar to Greg's.'

'And?'

'Well, something I might have considered with them was bipolar disorder. Have you thought of that?'

My world stops. 'No. No way. He doesn't have a mental illness. He couldn't. Not Greg.'

She clears her throat. 'I'm not saying that's it. Only that it's a possibility.'

My mind is racing. 'Spike Milligan had it. I remember now. Oh, God. It never goes away. You have it for life, don't you? It's up and down and up and down. And you can get hallucinations. And . . . Oh my God . . .' I'm twisting my hair round and round until it's tight like a rope.

'Lucy. It can be treated – successfully – with medication. It's caused by a chemical imbalance in the brain and that imbalance can be adjusted with medication. And I'm not saying that he has it, only that it's one option. There are others . . .'

'But if he has it, if he is bipolar, why didn't he tell me?'

'He may not know. It can come on at any stage . . .'

'What if he *does* know? What if he's just not telling me?'

'No, Lucy. Think about it. If Greg had been diagnosed with bipolar disorder, Rob would have been alert to the symptoms.

Families have to be. If he'd noticed a change in Greg's behaviour, as he did at the barbecue, he'd have been very concerned, seen it as a warning of an approaching high. No. If Greg is bipolar, this is his first episode.'

'Oh, God.'

'Lucy, there are loads of other reasons Greg could be depressed – coming off speed, if he was on it, ME, glandular fever, brucellosis . . . Bipolar disorder is just one possibility. Greg does need to see a doctor, though, ideally back in Dublin. You should try to get him home. The sooner the better. I'll come back with you, speak to a friend of mine, Karl, a really great GP. He's so copped on. He'd be a friendly face who could give Greg a thorough general examination.'

One of the boys starts to cry. Sounds like Jason.

She rolls her eyes. 'Timed beautifully, as usual.' She sighs. 'Back in a minute.'

I watch her disappear down the hall and try not to envy her the normality of her life. Try not to envy her relationship, a relationship that may be under pressure, but at least is normal. Mental illness. This is the kind of thing that happens to other people, not me. I'm not strong enough for it. I don't want to be. I want to run. Far away. But it might not be mental illness. It could be brucellosis . . . Brucellosis; I thought cows got brucellosis. Or it could be ME. If it *is* bipolar disorder, then none of this is his fault. He hasn't lied. He can't help it. He can't control his moods and doesn't understand why. If that is what's happening, how can I walk out on him? I wouldn't expect him to do it to me.

~

The following day, Grace takes Rachel and Toby off so I can talk to Greg. Who is still in bed.

'Let's go out,' I suggest, hoping that we might be able to talk, away from the villa.

'I don't want to go out.' This is the man I couldn't keep in.

'Come on. Your edits are done. No more deadlines. Let's forget our responsibilities and just go to the beach like normal people.'

'What do you mean, "normal people"? Are you saying I'm not normal?'

'No. I just said we should go to the beach, not work so hard.'

'You said, "like normal people", implying I'm not.'

'That's not what I meant. I wasn't implying anything. We work too much and I just think we need a break.'

'There's nothing wrong with me.'

'I know. I know that. Of course there isn't. I just think that maybe you could have a shower, get dressed and we could go out, the two of us, get a bite to eat. We haven't been out in ages.'

'I don't want to.'

'It'd do you good.'

'I. Don't. Want. To. Go. Out.'

'OK, OK. Jesus.' I get up to go. No point talking to him when he's like this. 'It doesn't matter that *I* might like to go out, I suppose?' I grumble my way to silence.

'You don't love me,' he says.

That stops me. I turn.

'And I don't blame you. I've been a bastard.'

I come back to him, sit down. 'Greg, of course I love you.'

'I'm old, incompetent. I can't even get it up, for fuck's sake.'

What I say now seems very important. I take a deep breath. 'Greg. No man can be expected to perform a hundred per cent of the time.'

'Perform. That's it. I can't perform. On any front.'

I'm not letting the conversation down that route. 'I love you, Greg.' I lie down, facing him.

'You're lying.'

I sit up. 'I'm *not* lying. If I didn't love you, I wouldn't be here.'

'You're going.'

'I'm going to Dublin tomorrow, for the supermarket pitch, that's all. I'll be over and back in the same day. If I could get out of it, I would. But I can't. This is a big deal for Get Smart. I can't let Fint down. Grace will be here.'

'You're going to leave, like Catherine left . . .'

'Catherine *died*.'

'Because of me.'

'That's your father-in-law's logic. Not yours.'

'I made her pregnant.'

'Stop this.'

'I killed her.' He squeezes his eyes shut. I've never seen him cry.

'Greg, please. Don't do this. It wasn't your fault. You know it wasn't.'

'If I'd only kept my stupid dick to myself.'

'OK. That's enough. You're being ridiculous, and you know it. Let's go home. Let's just go back to Dublin.'

He's silent.

'You're depressed.' There, I've finally said it. It's an actual relief.

'I'm fine.'

'No, you're not fine. You're definitely not fine. I'm worried about you, Greg.'

'I'm not going anywhere.'

'You need to see a doctor.'

'What kind of doctor? A shrink, is that what you mean?'

'I don't *mean* anything. All I know is that you're depressed. And we need to do something about it. You need to see a doctor, someone who can just tell us what's wrong.'

'I can handle it.'

'Please, let's go home.'

'I *said* I can handle it.'

'Well, *I* can't. I'm about to crack up, here. We have to go home. We have to sort this out.'

He closes his eyes, blocking me out.

'Is it drugs? Were you taking drugs? Are you having withdrawal symptoms? Is that it?'

He looks at me slowly. 'Lucy, I have never in my life taken drugs.' His voice sounds tired – exhausted, but honest. And I believe him.

'Have you ever been depressed like this before?'

'When Catherine died . . .'

'No, I mean when there was no reason to be?'

He suddenly seems to realise where this is leading. 'I'm not depressed, I'm just exhausted. Burned out. I'll be fine. Just let me sleep.' He turns his back to me.

I leave the room, feeling like a failure.

When Grace arrives back with the children, she looks at me expectantly. I shake my head.

'I shouldn't go tomorrow,' I say in a low voice.

'You have to. I'll be here; don't worry. And, Lucy?'

'Yeah?'

'I didn't expect him to say yes immediately. It's not easy to admit you're in this kind of trouble.'

~

Colour is leaking into an indigo sky when the alarm goes off. Careful not to disturb anyone, I get ready, but can't pass Greg's room without checking on him. I know instinctively that he's awake.

'Are you OK?' I whisper.

No answer. He's breathing through his mouth, head turned into the pillow. Silently crying.

I sit on the bed beside him, take his hand in mine. 'I'll be back later. Grace'll be here.'

He nods.

'I love you, Greg. You know that, don't you?'

He turns to me. 'Why, Lucy? Please, tell me why.'

The need in this once confident voice almost breaks my heart. I think back to when we met. 'Greg, I was asleep until I met you. You made me see the world from a different place. You taught me so much – how to let go, take risks, have fun, laugh. You inspired me. Taught me passion. Love without fear.' I'm in tears now. I miss him so much.

'Do you know that I wake up, every morning, with such a sense of dread that I can't move, asking myself how I'm going to make it through another entire day . . . I don't know what's wrong with me, Lucy. I'm so lonely.'

'How can you be lonely?'

'I don't *know*.' He sounds totally exasperated with himself.

'You've Rachel and Toby and me. And we love you so much.'

He sighs the deepest, most hopeless sigh.

'I won't go,' I say, deciding.

'No, you have to.'

'No, I don't.'

'Lucy, go. Please, I want you to. I'll see a doctor while you're gone.'

'You will?'

'Yes.'

'Oh, Greg, that's great. It's the right thing. I know it is.' I hug him, believe him.

24.

Fint is wearing his favourite suit, his lucky tie. It's pre-pitch fever, a bug I normally catch. When we run through the presentation and I can't work up the necessary enthusiasm, Fint suggests that Sebastian presents the company blurb, while he pitches the proposal. Fine by me.

As soon as the potential client walks into our meeting room, I get a bad feeling. The MD hasn't bothered to turn up; it's just Frank Haddon, Marketing Director. And he's late. He doesn't apologise. His air is of practised disinterest – he has something we want and he knows it. Normally, this would stimulate me into action, motivating me to convince him he'd be mistaken to go with anyone else. Now, I'm just furious. His is the attitude of a man who has already decided, without even seeing our pitch, not to go with us. Oh, I know the type – insecure execs wanting to make the right decision, going for the safe option – the biggest, most expensive firm, the internationals. That way, if things don't work out, they have a fall-back for their bosses: 'I picked the market leaders.' So, why didn't Haddon just go with the big boys first instead of using up our man-hours? Because the smaller houses often have the best ideas, ideas that can be 'adapted'.

He has wasted our time. Not just the time we're spending looking at his ugly mug, or the time all three of us have put into preparation, but the time I could have spent with Greg, convincing him to come home. Well, I'm *sick* of being pushed around by people like him. Does he think he can just swan in here and treat us like this without any repercussions?

When Fint has finished his presentation and Haddon hasn't come up with a single question – interesting or otherwise – I ask, with an innocent smile, 'So, where's your managing director today?'

He looks surprised, marginally uncomfortable. 'Important meeting he couldn't get out of, I'm afraid. Sends his apologies.'

'Pity he didn't try to reschedule.'

'Didn't want to put you out, I expect.'

'Nice of him.' My tone is sarcastic.

'Quite.' He looks annoyed.

Fint is glaring at me.

I ignore him. 'So, how many other agencies are you seeing?'

He clears his throat. Smiles. 'Two or three.'

'And will you turn up late for them, too?'

'Excuse me?' He laughs.

'I was just wondering if you'll turn up half an hour late without an apology for them, too.'

'Well, I . . .' He looks at Fint and Sebastian, presumably to be bailed out.

'Thank you, Lucy,' says Fint, and looks at me as if to say, 'Shut the fuck up.'

I carry on. 'It's just that I wonder if you appreciate our time, Mr Haddon.'

He starts to shove his phone, car keys and the jotter and pen we supplied into his briefcase. He stands abruptly. 'Well, then, I won't keep you another moment. Thank you for your presentation.' He nods at Fint and an appalled Sebastian. He starts to leave, without a glance in my direction.

'Ah, I'll just show you out,' says Sebastian.

~

As soon as the door closes behind them, Fint rounds on me. 'What was *that* about?'

'I'm sorry, he just pissed me off. We've been here before, too many times. Snotty-nosed marketing hotshot with his yaw-yaw accent.'

'So, you decided to take him down a peg or two? That showed him, all right.'

'We weren't going to get the business, anyway.'

'Is that right?'

'That's right.'

'And how do you work that one out?'

'I knew the minute he walked in the door. Didn't you? Rude bastard. Didn't even apologise. And the attitude of him. Who did he think he was? These people think they can just waltz in here and steal our ideas. I really think we should stop getting involved in competitive pitches . . .'

'Do you know how much work Sebastian and I put into that pitch?'

'Do you know how much work *I* put into that pitch?'

'So, why did you just go and blow it? Did it make you feel better to watch him squirm? So what if he's a prick? So what if he's rude? A lot of our clients are, but they pay the wages. We're in no position to start getting fussy.'

'OK, I'm sorry . . . I'm just not in good form.'

'Well, don't take it out on the business, Lucy.'

I sigh. 'Sorry.'

'Fine for you. Jetting back off to the Riviera to your millionaire lifestyle. Some of us have to earn a crust.'

'That is so not fair.'

'You've lost your edge. You've lost your hunger. You used to be good, Lucy. Better than good. You used to be great. Where's it all gone?'

'Stuff you,' I say. And walk.

Flying down the stairs, feet pumping, I visualise that little pipsqueak sitting there so smugly, stealing our ideas, using us, and Fint fooling himself – he knew, deep down, that we hadn't a hope. Well, I'm glad we didn't get the business. Imagine working for that wanker.

But by the time I'm on the plane, fastening my seatbelt, ready for take-off, I'm seeing the situation from Fint's perspective. *What* was I doing? *What* was I hoping to achieve? Get Smart is not my business alone; I'm a partner. I should behave like one. If I want to go blowing contracts, then I should work for myself. If Fint had done that to me, I'd have killed him.

~

In the taxi on my way to the villa, the sun is sinking behind cypress trees, bathing everything in warm, glowing, optimistic light. If only I'd never left. I wouldn't have ruined everything, behaved like a lunatic.

It's nine when I finally push in the front door. All is quiet.

Grace comes to greet me. 'Hey! How did the meeting go?'

'Disaster.' I drop my briefcase to the ground. She opens her mouth to speak. 'Don't ask.'

In the kitchen, I pour myself a juice. 'Where is everyone?'

'Bed.'

'Already?'

'Rachel's reading in her room. Jason's asleep.'

'Where's Shane?'

'Having a sleepover in Toby's room.'

I smile, imagining them.

Grace's face is suddenly serious. 'Greg is really low. You have to get him home.'

'What did the doctor say?'

'What doctor?'

'He said he'd go to the doctor today.'

'He didn't budge out of bed all day. I brought him up lunch, but he didn't eat. He barely drank anything. All he did was smoke. I hid the whiskey.'

'Shit.'

'This is very serious.'

'I know. But what can I do? He won't listen to me. I can't force him.'

'You'll have to.'

'How?'

'Scare him. Bluff. Give him an ultimatum – either he goes home with you or you leave – for good.'

I look at her. 'What if he tells me to leave?'

'You have to get him home, Lucy. Concentrate on that, and you will.'

'He doesn't listen to me.'

'You have to make him. If he is bipolar, and I'm not saying he is, but *if* he is, his moods and feelings are out of control. It's up to you to get him home. Be brutal if you have to. But get him home. I'll come with you. I'll help you through.' She holds my hand. 'I promise.'

'But you have your own life, your own marriage . . .'

'I know. And I need to get home and try to sort that out. I can't do it from over here.'

'Oh, Grace, I'm glad.' I hug her. 'I knew you just needed a break from each other for a while, that's all.'

'Let's just get Greg home, OK?'

I nod. 'OK.'

~

There's never going to be a good time. So I pick what I hope is the least disastrous time. Late afternoon, next day. Greg's up. And hasn't started drinking – the whiskey's still hiding. Grace has taken the children to Aqua-Splash. Greg's sitting with his head leaning back over the top of one of the couches, eyes closed.

I sit beside him.

'What did the doctor say?'

He lifts his head like it's made of lead. 'What doctor?'

'The doctor you were supposed to see yesterday.'

'Oh,' he says quietly. 'I didn't go.'

'It's time to go home, Greg.'

'Not this again.' He pushes himself up from the chair and leaves the room.

I follow him, trying to keep calm.

He stands at the window of the office, arms folded, staring ahead. Blotting me out.

'Greg, this isn't going to get better by itself.'

He ignores me.

'It has to end. Now.'

'Really?'

'Yes. We're going home. And we're going to a doctor.'

'The last person who tried to bully me was fired.'

What's he talking about? He fired Hilary because she came on to him. But I'm not going to think about her now. I'm not going to get distracted. 'Here's the thing: If you don't come home to Dublin with me now, I'm leaving you. I'm going. I'm not staying to watch you ruin yourself. And I'm not letting you take me down with you.'

'All right. Go then.' He doesn't budge.

'Fine. I will.'

I turn and walk, thinking *Damn, damn, damn.* But I've gone this far. I have to keep going. He has to believe I mean it. Maybe I do. Maybe I *have* had enough. I pull my case out from under the bed, march to the wardrobe, snatch clothes from hangers. I throw them onto the bed and start to pack. How far will he let me take this? All the way? Just like that? Relationship over?

I sense him at the door. I don't look, afraid he'll see weakness in my eyes.

'Don't go,' he says, his voice gentle.

I look at him.

'I just have to control it. I can do it, Lucy. It's mind over matter.'

I put my not-so-red sandals into their canvas bag. 'I meant what I said, Greg.'

'Don't force me, Luce.'

I turn my back to him, and when I start to cry, it's because I know, all of a sudden, I'm going through with it, all the way. I turn slowly and meet his eyes.

'I'm going, Greg. I don't want to, but I am.'

I zip up my case then remember my toiletries. I go to the bathroom and start to fill my make-up bag. My hands are shaking, my legs weak. This is it. It's over. I reach into the bathroom cabinet. Toiletries begin to tumble out, landing in the sink and clattering onto the tiled floor. I drop to my knees to scoop them up. This is it, my lowest moment. I pull myself up using the side of the bath and see him, at the bathroom door, looking wretched.

'All right,' he says, letting his head fall forward as if conceding victory. 'I'll come home.'

I look at him, waiting for the catch.

'But I'm not making any promises about a doctor.'

'No, Greg. Not good enough. All or nothing.'

I walk past him, open the case and squash the make-up bag in. I zip it shut, lift it off the bed, pull up the handle and begin to wheel it behind me as I make for the door.

'All right. All right. I'll see someone, OK?'

'You mean like you promised to do when I was away?'

A wave of guilt crosses his face. 'I'll go. In Dublin. I promise.'

'You really promise?'

He crosses his heart like he did when we first met. And I want to cry.

'Thank you.'

25.

I move immediately to get us out of there, booking us all on the first available flight.

Greg tells Rachel and Toby we're going home.

'Already?' asks Rachel.

'Why?' asks Toby.

'I'm not feeling the best. The heat – it's making me tired.'

'Oh,' says Toby. 'So, if we go home will you be able to play with us, again?'

'Mm-hmm.'

'You won't stay in bed all day?'

'No.'

'Is it a deal?'

'Deal,' says Greg.

'Shake on it.'

He shakes.

Toby nods. 'OK, so, let's go.'

'What about the guys?' asks Rachel. 'Are they coming back to Dublin, too?'

'Yes.'

'Will we see them there?'

Greg looks at me.

'Sure,' I say.

Rachel takes Toby off to pack their things.

~

Rachel walks ahead of us at the airport, posture perfect, like a mini airhostess, pulling her case behind her. Her sense of purpose gives me hope. Whatever this is, we're sorting it out.

On the plane, Greg eases back his seat, closes his eyes and opts out. Toby, next to me, is busy with an activity book. Rachel's playing peek-a-boo with Shane, who's seated in the row in front with his mum and brother.

When we get to Dublin, Kevin is there to pick up his family. Shane runs to his dad and is scooped up. When Grace, carrying Jason, reaches Kevin, there's a tension between them I've never noticed before.

Grace turns to me and offers a smile of encouragement. 'I'll call you.'

'Thanks, Grace, for everything.'

As I watch them go through the sliding doors, I hope that they'll be all right.

The rest of us get a taxi, leaving the airport under a grey sky, everyone quiet.

When we get to the house in Dalkey, there's a crisis. Toby runs to Hilary's room, expecting her to be there. It's empty. She's taken her things. Of course she has. It makes total sense. Not to Toby.

'But where *is* she?'

It's Greg who should explain. But he's downstairs, slumped in a chair.

I squat down to him. 'Hilary's working somewhere else now, Toby.'

'But why?'

'Well, sometimes in life, a time comes for a change, for people to move on. But other people come instead, like Grace and the boys.'

'They're gone, too. Everyone goes.' The corners of his mouth turn down and his eyes fill.

'No. They're not gone. You can see them any time you like. They're kind of like your cousins, really,' I say, to cheer him up.

'Really?' he asks.

'No,' says Rachel. 'They're not our cousins. Because Lucy is not related to us.'

'Oh,' says a disappointed Toby.

'Well, Toby,' I say, trying to move on from my stupid mistake, 'your dad's not gone. Your dad's still here. He'll always be here.'

'Why did Hilary go?' he asks.

'Well, it was just time for a change . . .'

'Not true,' says Rachel. 'You asked Dad to fire Hilary, remember?'

'No, Rachel. I didn't . . .'

'Forget it,' she snaps. 'Come here, Tobes, I'll look after you. I'm not going anywhere.' She glares at me as if to say, 'But *you* will be.'

Grace has made an appointment for Greg with her GP friend, Karl Brennan, who has a special interest in psychiatry. Greg knows nothing of the special interest. And I hope he won't need it, that this will be something physical. All Greg cares about is discretion and getting it over with.

He wants to go alone. And I have to trust that he'll get there. He takes a taxi, lacking the energy or concentration to drive.

I can't stay still from the moment he leaves.

By the time he gets back, the place is spotless; the holiday clothes washed and in the process of being dried, cases put away. He walks past me, into the kitchen.

I follow. He's standing at the window, staring out.

I go to him. 'How did it go?'

'I thought he was supposed to be good,' he says, looking at me as if I've done something wrong. 'He hadn't a fucking clue.'

'What did he say?'

'He wanted me to see a shrink. A fucking shrink.'

Everything stops.

'Today. Would you believe that?'

I force the next question. 'Did he say what he thought it was?'

He doesn't answer. And, to be honest, I don't want him to.

We're stuck.

'Maybe he's making a mistake,' I say, hoping.

'Of course he is. Bloody quack. I thought Grace knew what she was doing. Why the fuck did she pick him?'

'Did he think you were depressed?'

He turns to me, his face bitter. 'Oh, no. Nothing that simple. He thinks I'm *manically* depressed. No, no, sorry. He thinks I'm *bipolar*, the politically correct tag. I mean, who're they trying to protect? Do they think that by changing the name it changes what it is? It's a joke.'

His anger makes everything clear. He does believe the GP. Otherwise he'd simply have dismissed him. He believes him, but he doesn't want to. And, my God, I don't blame him. I want to put my arms around him. I want to tell him that everything will be OK. But I'm paralysed. Will it? Bipolar disorder. It seems so huge, like a dark grey rug being thrown over us.

I have to assume he's going. It's my only hope of getting him there. 'What time is your appointment?'

He throws me a look that says, 'Are you mad?' 'I'm not going. Waste of time.'

'Greg, you have to go. You've got this far.'

'I said I'd go see a doctor and I have.'

'Yes, but you have to do what he recommends, or else it's like you haven't gone at all. I know it sounds like he's making a mistake. I'm sure he is. But go to the psychiatrist and get the all clear so we can get on with our lives. Please, Greg.'

'What if he's right, Lucy? Do you want that? Do you want me to be a maniac who gets depressed?'

'Greg, you either have this or you don't. And if you have, let's just deal with it, OK?'

'He thinks the psychiatrist will admit me.'

'To hospital?'

'St Martha's Hospital.' His head lowers. 'Psychiatric ward.'

This isn't happening.

'He wants me to bring my stuff with me in case I have to go in.'

'When's your appointment with the psychiatrist?'

'As soon as I'm ready. He's expecting me.'

I see now why denial is such a tempting option.

'What about the children?' I ask. What will he tell them? Who'll mind them? And how will they cope with yet another separation, this time from the most important person in their lives? I've just told Toby he'll always have his father.

'That's what I'm saying, Lucy. If I go in, I won't be coming home. Not for weeks.'

Weeks? I'm too shocked to speak. But I have to speak, to pretend I'm not shocked. '*Okaay* . . . We can manage that. Let's think. We'll have to get someone to mind the children, someone they know and trust, someone who's free . . . Rob. Of course! He's a teacher. He'll still be on summer holidays. We'll ask Rob.'

He looks hurt. 'Why not you?'

'Me?' I'd be useless. They're not my children. Rachel hates me. 'Greg, they need family.'

'You are family.'

'They don't see me that way.'

'Please, Lucy, look after Rachel and Toby for me and I'll go in.' His eyes are searching mine. He's waiting. If I say no, he won't go.

I close my eyes and find my head nodding, my voice agreeing, 'OK. I'll do it.' I try not to think about what will be involved.

'Thank you.' Such relief in those words.

We gaze out at the children, busy in the garden, Rachel trying to save the plants from drought, and Toby reaching under a shrub for something. We stand in silence for a long time, neither of us wanting to move forward.

'Do you want me to pack some things?' I ask, eventually.

'Hmm?'

'Will I pack for you?'

'Would you, Luce? I can't seem to get my head around what I need.'

'I'll make some tea, then throw a few things in a case, OK?' I try to sound casual, and not think about the fact that this will be the last tea we'll share for I don't know how long.

~

I bring a packed bag downstairs and start to look for the car keys.

'I'll go in on my own,' he says.

'Oh, Greg. Let me drive you.'

'No. I need to handle this myself. I'll get a taxi.'

The thought of him heading off alone kills me. But he has his pride.

'We'd better tell the children,' I say.

His eyes widen in panic.

'Just that you might be going into hospital. Not *why*.'

'You're right. Of course. I'm not thinking. But don't tell anyone about this, Lucy. Not one person, OK? If this gets out, I'm ruined.'

I nod, my heart breaking for him.

We call the children in. Toby comes running, shouting, 'D'you want to see my snail collection? It's brill. I've five of them. My favourite's the small one, but I like them all, really. D'you want to see, Dad?'

Greg looks at me, his face a question. How can I leave my boy?

We sit, the four of us, at the kitchen table. Rachel regards us carefully. Toby's oblivious, poking his box of snails under Greg's nose.

'Dad, can I've some lettuce for them? They ackshilly love lettuce.'

'Guys,' says Greg, 'I've something I want to tell you.'

Toby stops, looks up at his dad, big brown eyes wide. Rachel looks like she wants to run.

'I haven't been feeling the best.'

'I know,' says Toby. 'But you're home now. And it's freezing. Are you better yet?'

'No.'

'But you said . . .'

'Yes, I said that when we got home it wouldn't be hot and I'd be fine. But I was wrong. I'm not fine.'

'But we shook on it.'

'I was wrong. I'm sorry, pet. I'm still sick and I have to see a doctor.' He ruffles Toby's hair. 'I might have to go into hospital for a while.'

'No,' says his son. 'You can't. You have to stay here with us. You can't go away. I won't let you.'

'Come here, Tobes.'

Greg sits him up on his lap.

'You can't go, Dad. You just can't.' He clings to Greg, cheek against chest. Greg wraps him up in his arms.

'You want me to get better, don't you, Tobes?'

Toby doesn't answer.

'And you're a big man now, aren't you?'

Silence.

'What's wrong, Dad?' asks Rachel.

'I just haven't been feeling the best.'

Toby sits back from Greg. 'D'you have a pain in your tummy?'

Greg rubs Toby's cheek with the backs of his fingers. 'No, no. No pain.'

'Well, what is it, then?' asks Rachel. 'Not cancer?'

How does she know about cancer?

'No,' says Greg. 'Not cancer. It's just that I'm exhausted and I need to rest, that's all.'

'Go to bed,' says Toby.

'Stop, Toby,' orders Rachel. 'If Dad has to go to hospital, Dad has to go to hospital.'

Toby's little face crumples.

'Ah, don't cry, pet,' says Greg, hugging him. 'It'll be OK. I'll be back soon.'

'When?'

'In a few weeks.'

'A few *weeks*?' Toby and Rachel say together.

'Why weeks?' Rachel asks. 'Eva had her whole appendix out and she wasn't even in for one week. What is it, Dad? Is it really bad?'

His smile looks forced. 'I have to see this doctor, OK? And he'll decide if I have to go into hospital or not, and, if I do, how long I'll stay. Let me go see him and see what he says, OK? Let's just take this one step at a time.'

'So, you mightn't be going in?' Rachel confirms.

'I probably will, pet.'

'Who'll mind us?' she asks. 'Rob?'

'Lucy, of course. Rob will help out.'

Both heads swivel in my direction. Then Rachel shakes hers. 'No way.'

'Rachel,' says Greg.

'But I don't want her . . .'

'Look, I'm only going to say this once: I don't like being sick and, if I had my way, I'd be staying right here. But sometimes we have to do things we don't like to make things better for everyone. Lucy will have a lot on her plate, and the last thing she needs from you is trouble. Do you hear me?'

She lowers her eyes. 'Yes, Dad.'

'I want you both to help Lucy. OK? I want you to keep your rooms tidy, clean up after yourselves and help out. Is that clear?'

'Yes, Dad.'

'Now, give me a hug.'

And they do.

'I'll ring as soon as I know what's happening, OK?'

'OK,' we all say together.

~

The taxi pulls up outside. Looking like a man who's lost a battle, Greg gets in. I put his bag on the seat beside him. Even it looks sad. I don't want to fuss, so I just say, 'Talk later,' but then I can't let him go without kissing him and adding, 'Love you.'

He's looking straight ahead, as if finally accepting his fate. I close the door and stand back as the taxi pulls away. The sound of a lawnmower coming from a nearby garden seems at odds with what's happening. Nothing else should be normal. Not today.

'He didn't wave goodbye,' says Toby.

The taxi is at the top of the avenue. It indicates and turns right, taking with it the only thing I have in common with the children. For a moment, we just stand, not looking at each other. Flattened. Then Rachel lifts her brother, turns and walks towards the house.

I look back up the avenue. A young couple strolls by, bodies glued together, each with a hand slipped into the other's back pocket. They stop to kiss and gaze into each other's eyes. Wasn't that the plan? I look away and make for the house.

Rachel hasn't closed the door on me. It's a start.

26.

The children are off limits, hidden away in Rachel's room, a place that, when I first saw it earlier today, reminded me of what an enigma she is to me. I've never met a child so tough, yet her room looks like it belongs to a girl who dreams of turning frogs into princes. It's pale pink with a crystal blue chandelier and a muslin drape falling over brass bedknobs. Her colour-coordinated furniture is prettily ornate, as if taken from a doll's house and magnified.

I take a step towards the door then stop. What could I possibly say that would reassure them? With Toby, I mightn't have to say anything. I could just hold him. But with Rachel, I need a miracle. Wringing my hands, I walk away.

In my room, unable to sit still, I call Grace.

'I'm coming over,' she says.

'Grace, there's no need,' I say, conscious of her own problems.

'I think there is.'

'What about Shane and Jason?'

'I'll drop them at Mum and Dad's.'

'Don't tell them!'

'I'd never . . .'

'Don't even tell Kevin. He's terrified people will find out.' I hold my forehead.

'Don't worry, Lucy. I won't say a word to anyone.'

~

She arrives half an hour later. I'm at the front window, pacing like a sentry. I open the door before she gets to it. We hug. I burst into tears. Grace just holds me.

'I'm OK,' I say at last, pulling back.

'Where are the children?'

'Upstairs.'

'Where's the kitchen?'

I point down the hall.

'Right. Come on.'

She closes the door behind us.

We sit at the table.

'Will he be admitted?' I ask, willing her to say 'No,' 'Probably not,' 'Unlikely,' or any other version of negative.

'To be honest, Luce, while Karl has a lot of pull with the hospital, he wouldn't have got Greg seen today if it hadn't been urgent. And he wouldn't have asked him to pack unless he expected him to be going in.'

I close my eyes. 'That's it, then. It's definitely bipolar disorder.' I wait for her to say something. But she doesn't. I look at her. 'But why hospital, Grace? Can't they just, I don't know, give him some antidepressants or something and send him home?'

'He's very low, Luce.'

'We've all been low. Doesn't mean we have to be admitted to a psychiatric ward.'

'This isn't just feeling down. The chemical imbalance takes time to readjust. And they'll need to keep an eye on him while they do it.'

'But weeks, Grace. He said it would be for weeks.'

'Hospital's the best place for Greg, now.' She holds my hand. 'I know it's hard, but when you're as low as Greg is, ordinary life can seem too much to cope with. Hospital can provide a sanctuary. And, Lucy, he won't be in there for a solid block of weeks. As soon as he starts to improve, they'll begin sending him home for short periods to see how he gets on. Weekends at first, then maybe longer. The good thing is, they'll only discharge him when he's ready.'

'How'll I manage? I've the children and work and I'll have to find time to visit him . . .'

'I'm here. I'll help with Rachel and Toby, the house, whatever. You'll probably have to talk to Fint about work, though. There's no way you'll be able to go back full-time.'

'I know, but how'll I tell him? I'm already in his bad books.'

~

We're preparing dinner when the phone rings. I rush to it.

'Hello, is this Lucy Arigho?' A female voice.

'Yes?'

'This is Staff Nurse Betty O'Neill, from St Raphael's Ward at St Martha's Hospital.'

My heart skitters. 'Is Greg all right?'

'Yes, he's fine. Professor Power, one of our psychiatrists, has just admitted him. He's resting now. He asked me to call you to say he'll talk to you tomorrow.'

'Oh.'

'He's tired. It's been a long day. And, of course, a big shock.'

'I was going to come in and see him in a little while . . .' I look at Grace who has offered to stay with the children.

'Well, maybe not this evening. Better to let him settle in a bit.'

'He's all right, though? It's just I was expecting him to call.'

'Yes, I know. But Greg doesn't feel up to much at the moment.'

'I'll come in, first thing.'

'Actually, if you don't mind, we usually encourage visitors to wait till after five. That gives patients time to rest, attend group sessions, talk.'

'OK. Thanks for ringing,' I say, dropping the phone and bursting into tears.

Grace scoops me up in her arms. 'It's OK. This is the worst time, Lucy. It'll get better. I promise.'

'You said that already,' I wail.

When I look up, Rachel and Toby are standing in the doorway. I pull back from Grace, wipe my eyes and paste on a smile.

'Was that Dad?' Rachel asks.

'It was the hospital. They were just ringing to say he's fine.'

They speak together.

Toby: 'So, why are you crying?'

Rachel: 'He said *he'd* ring.'

I answer Rachel; it's easier. 'He's resting.'

'Can we go see him tomorrow?' asks Toby.

'Maybe not tomorrow, Toby. Let me just go in and see how he is . . .'

'Why do you get to go and not us?' Rachel demands.

'Can we ring him tomorrow?' asks Toby.

I don't need this. I seriously don't need this. But then I look at their little faces and see how distressing this is for them, their only security in life gone.

'We might just let your dad rest tomorrow,' I say. 'When I go in, I'll bring my phone. And, if it suits everyone in there, I'll call you so you can talk to your dad. I can't promise, though. Because I'm not sure yet, OK?'

'OK.'

'But I'll do my best.'

'Yeah, right,' says Rachel.

Grace looks at her. Then at me.

~

Grace leaves to collect the boys and bring them home. I serve up a dinner that no one eats. Rachel mothers Toby, putting him to bed and reading to him. By ten, I'm locking and bolting up the huge, unfamiliar house. Outside, it's twilight and the garden is full of shadows. I wrap my cardigan around myself and go to my room, hoping that things will seem more manageable in the morning. Two things keep me awake – fear of not being able to cope and guilt that I don't want to.

~

I wake early and get up. If I keep busy, I won't have to think. On the landing, Toby is at the airing cupboard, jumping up, trying to reach something. He's naked.

'Toby, are you OK?' I ask quietly, trying not to startle him.

He covers himself with his hands. 'I . . . I . . . was just getting some sheets.'

Ah, God. 'Here. Let me help.' I find what looks like Bart Simpson bed linen. 'These yours?'

He nods, holds his arms out for them. His skinny body is covered in goosebumps.

'It's OK,' I say. 'I'll carry them for you. They're heavy.'

In his room, the smell of urine lingers. He's tugged off three corners of his sheet. The fourth is held fast against the wall. His soggy pyjamas are in a heap on the floor.

'I'm sorry,' he says, head hanging.

'That's OK. It's just a little accident. Everybody has accidents.'

'Don't tell Rachel.'

'Cross my heart.' It's catching. 'I'll just go get you a towel.'

I return with a warm bath towel and wrap him up in it.

Eye to eye, I say, 'Everything'll be all right, Tobes.' I hold his chin between my finger and thumb and give it a little shake. 'I bet you're the kind of man who likes bubbles in his bath.'

He smiles.

He follows me into the bathroom, where I put down the toilet lid for him to sit on, while I fill the bath. Cold first, I remember from Grace's boys. As it fills, I nip back to his room to remove the evidence, in case Rachel stumbles on it. I open the windows and close the door.

Back in the bathroom, I can't find bubble bath. So I retrieve my Molton Brown shower gel. I test the water with my elbow the way you're supposed to with children, or is that babies? Toby is in charge of pouring the gel. He isn't stingy. Once, that might have bothered me. Once, I was a person who thought things like shower gel precious. Slow to leave him alone in the bath yet wanting him to have privacy, I busy myself tidying. Without directly looking, I notice that he's just sitting there, surrounded by bubbles.

'Do you want to mess around with this?'

I hand him the empty Molton Brown bottle.

'Yes, please!' He submerges it, filling it with bubbly water. He lifts it up and tips it over. He starts to hum.

'Can you wash yourself if I give you a cloth, or do you need a hand?'

'I can wash myself.'

'What about your hair?'

'I might need a little hand.'

'OK, bud.'

After the bath, I wrap him in a fresh bath towel and carry him to his room. We pretend he's a baby dinosaur that's just hatched. And suddenly I feel just as protective as a mummy dinosaur.

Later, as I'm giving him breakfast and he's chatting about snails, Rachel appears with her usual cloud. She ushers her runaway fledgling back under her wing. I wish she'd allow herself to be the child she is, rather than the adult she insists on being. I'd look after her, if only she'd let me.

~

In the afternoon, Grace arrives with the boys and I leave for the hospital. When I arrive, rather than ask where the psychiatric ward is, I try to remember the ward name the nurse mentioned on the phone. I check the list of wards displayed. St Raphael's sounds familiar. I follow the signs.

The doors to the ward are closed, I assume locked. I'm searching for a bell when someone simply walks through. I take a deep breath and follow. The mad bustle of the corridor outside dies. White walls are replaced by lavender. I wait for the impression of peace to be shattered by some patient going rogue.

I pass a television room to my left. Its occupants – a young, attractive man and a tiny, grey-haired woman – are dressed in outdoor clothes. They sit, five armchairs apart, ignoring each other, staring at the TV.

A woman's coming towards me, dressed in black – polo-neck top, trousers and flat shoes. She makes eye contact. I stop, hoping she can help.

'Hello. Excuse me. I was wondering where I might find a nurse.'

'You're talking to one,' she says. 'I'm Betty O'Neill. Can I help you?'

'Oh. Yes, Betty.' The relief! 'I think we spoke yesterday? I'm Lucy Arigho. You rang me about Greg Millar?'

'Yes, of course.' She smiles. 'I'll take you to him.'

We walk, side by side, in silence. Finally, she stops at a two-bed ward and gestures to the bed nearer the door, which has its curtain pulled around it.

'Is it OK to go in?' I ask.

She nods. 'He just wants privacy. Go on in.'

~

Greg's lying with his back to the door, still in the clothes he was wearing when he came in. If he hears me, he doesn't react.

'Greg?' I whisper, in case he's asleep.

He turns.

I smile. 'Hi.'

He drags himself into a sitting position, his clothes crumpled, his pillow flattened behind him. 'Where are the kids?'

'At home. With Grace.'

He sits forward, suddenly. 'Jesus! You didn't tell her, did you?'

I look at him in all his pain and wonder if I should lie. But what'll we be left with if we can't hold on to honesty?

'I didn't have to tell her, Greg. She's a doctor. She worked it out for herself. And don't worry, she won't say a word to anyone.'

'Not even Kevin?'

'Not even Kevin. Can I sit down?'

He nods, and I perch on the edge of the bed, facing him.

'You didn't tell anyone else?'

'No.'

'Well, don't. OK?'

'What about your family?'

'No.'

'What if they're looking for you?'

'Make up an excuse. Lie if you have to. Just don't tell them. Especially not my mother. Do you understand, Lucy?'

'Yes, yes, of course I understand.' *I'm not stupid.* 'But I really think you should tell Rob.'

'No.'

'Greg, you'll be in here for weeks. Won't you?' I hold my breath, make a wish.

'Looks like it.'

'Well, what if Rob calls over and the children tell him you're in hospital? What'll he think? And don't tell me to keep him away. Rachel and Toby need all the familiar faces they can get just now. You're suddenly gone. Hilary's gone. And they're left with me. It's not like I'm their favourite person in the world.'

He drums his fingers on the bed for what seems like ages. 'OK. Just Rob . . . But *I'll* tell him.'

'Fine . . . What'll I tell your mother if she calls?'

'Let me think about it, OK? Let me think. You can't tell her . . . Promise me you won't.'

'I promise.' I sigh deeply. He's not exactly making this easy. 'Rachel and Toby made these for you,' I say, opening my bag and pulling out two cards.

Rachel's has a smiley, happy sun. Toby's has a rocket.

They have the opposite effect to what was intended. Greg puts them down as though they weigh a ton. His once blue, now pewter eyes well up. It kills me to see him like this. I pick up the cards and stand them on the locker. I reach for his hand. He pulls it away.

'We've done the right thing, Greg. I know we have. This is the first step to your recovery. Things will get better from here.'

He gives me a cynical look.

'What was Professor Power like?'

'Does it really matter?'

'Did he start you on medication?'

Another deep, deep sigh. 'For what it's worth.'

I look at his dinner tray, lying untouched. 'Will we ring the kids now?'

He closes his eyes. Then takes a deep breath. Finally, he nods.

I dial the number, expecting Grace.

Rachel must have beaten her to it. 'Hello?' she says, so hopefully.

'Rachel, it's Lucy. Your dad wants a word.'

'OK.'

As I pass the phone to Greg, I hear her calling Toby.

'Hello, pet,' says Greg. 'I'm fine. How're you?' He pauses to listen. 'It's fine . . . Soon . . . I'm not sure . . . She's doing her best, Rachel . . . I'll call you tomorrow, OK? . . . Love you, too.' Another pause, then, 'How's my man? . . . I miss you, too, Tobes . . .' His voice is rising. 'I know . . . Very soon . . . I'll talk to the doctor, OK . . . And I'll ring tomorrow . . . Are you minding your sister?' A pause. 'Good boy, good man.'

I know he's not up to me staying, and, clearly, he doesn't want to be touched. So I say goodbye, tapping the bed with my hand.

On the way out, I see Betty O'Neill ahead of me. I hurry to catch up.

'Betty? Hi. Excuse me. Would you have a moment?'

'Yes, of course. Why don't you come in here?'

I follow her into some kind of office.

'How is he?' I ask.

She folds her arms, smiles in an apologetic way. 'I'm sorry, Lucy, but Greg has asked us not to talk to you about his condition.'

'Excuse me?'

'Greg has asked us to respect his confidentiality. He doesn't want us to talk to anybody about his condition.'

'Not me, though, surely.' *He loves me. He trusts me.* 'I've been living with him through this. I'm his fiancée.'

Her voice softens. 'I understand that. But I'm afraid he was very clear. And we have to respect our patients' wishes. I'm sorry. If Greg doesn't wish us to talk to you, we have to respect that.'

'I don't understand.'

'This isn't unusual. Greg's very down at the moment, but, as his condition improves, I'm sure he'll open up. For now, though, we have to respect his wishes.'

I can't believe he's excluding me.

'I can't talk to you about Greg specifically,' she continues. 'But I can give you these.' She holds out a bundle of leaflets and booklets. 'You might find them helpful.'

I have to stop myself telling her where to shove them.

27.

Evening. In a house that is not my own, with none of my things around me. Where there are too many rooms, all of them huge. Where the shadows and creaks are unfamiliar. Where my bedroom is the only place I can relax. I take out one of my step-parenting books. It's my second time reading it. It's either that or the leaflets.

My mobile rings.

'So you're home,' Dad says, accusingly.

'Yes.'

'When were you going to tell us?'

'I was just about to call you.' Slight exaggeration.

'We wouldn't even have known if Grace hadn't let it slip. It is nice, *occasionally*, to know what country your daughters are in. Your mother's upset, Lucy. You're home days and you never called.'

'Three, Dad.'

'She may not be your favourite person in the world, but she *is* your mother. She does love you. She does get hurt.'

'I know. I'm sorry. I'll call round. OK?'

'When?'

'I don't know. Soon.'

'Hang on a minute, your mother's saying something . . . Why don't you all come over tomorrow for dinner?'

'It might be difficult. Greg's very busy at the moment.'

'Surely, he has to stop to eat?'

'Well, it's just that he has this deadline and he's way behind. He's working flat out.' I hate lying, but am surprised at how easy it is.

~

Speaking of work, I have to face Fint. How can I tell him I'm home but not office-bound without admitting the truth? Does Greg realise the extent of what he's asked me to do? Fint's my best friend. We've always shared our problems. Outside of that, as my partner, he deserves an honest explanation as to why I can't go in and why I behaved so appallingly at the pitch. But I promised Greg. And if a nurse at the hospital can respect his privacy, surely I can.

It's noon the following day before I finally work up the courage to ring Fint.

'Ooooh, it's the globetrotter gracing us with a call.'

I force a laugh. *He's joking, right?*

'Let me guess, you're ringing from Monte Carlo, where you're visiting dignitaries.'

'I'm home.'

'Oh. Great. So, what's keeping you?'

'I can't come in, Fint. I need to continue working out of the office for August. I hope that's OK.'

'No, actually, Lucy, it's not. I need you in here. We might be able to win the odd pitch if we could actually put our heads together on something.'

'Fintan, I'm sorry about the pitch. I was out of line.'

'You sabotaged the whole thing.'

'I know. I'm sorry.'

'I've been patient, Lucy, but this is a business. It requires effort. New accounts don't just sail in without a bit of blood, sweat and tears . . .'

Speaking of tears . . . 'You have no idea how much effort I've been putting in. You've no clue what's going on in my life, how this is the last thing I need right now. Oh, forget it.' I hang up.

It rings.

'I'm sorry,' says my business partner.

I say nothing.

'Are you OK?'

'No.'

'What is it?'

'Nothing.' I stifle a sob. 'I just need to be around here for a while.'

'OK. Fine. Just tell me why.'

'Things are tricky right now. I'm minding Greg's children.'

'Why? Where is he?'

'I can't say.'

'What do you mean you can't say? This is me, Fint.'

'It's awkward.'

'Is he all right? Are you all right?'

'I'm OK, but I'm not "swanning around" and I'm not having a good time; I'm trying to cope. And because Greg's children are my responsibility now, I have to work from home. Or quit.'

'Well, that's not an option.'

Even the thought of working seems too much.

'I wish you'd confide in me. I might be able to help.'

'Believe me, you wouldn't.'

'Is he ill?'

He deserves to know that much. 'Yes. But don't ask me any more. Please. I promised him I wouldn't talk about it.'

He's silent for a moment. 'Can I do anything?'

'Just hold the fort for a little while longer. I'll be back in a few weeks. And I'll make up for it. You can take months off. A year. I don't care.'

'That's the only way I can help – work?'

'Yes.'

'OK.' His voice is tight, hurt.

'I'm sorry, but I promised Greg.'

'No, I'm sorry. I've been . . . a bit uptight. I shouldn't have snapped.'

'You had every right to. I haven't exactly made life easy for you, lately.'

'Forget about it. Do what you can, OK?'

'I could make client meetings . . .'

'Let's just see how it goes.'

'Fint, there *is* another option.'

'What?'

'Buy me out of the business.'

'Forget it, honey. We're stuck with each other. Wouldn't trust anyone else.'

~

Later, I'm mopping the kitchen floor, trying not to think, when the doorbell rings.

It's Rob. 'Are you OK?' he asks, his voice filled with concern.

'So, he's told you.' It's such a relief.

'Yeah, though I'm not to tell anyone else.'

I half smile.

The children come bounding down the stairs.

'Rob, Rob,' Toby shouts, hurling himself at him and clinging to his leg like a lonely koala.

'Hey, bud,' says Rob, rubbing the top of his head with his knuckles. 'How's the champ?'

'Fine. Dad's in hospital,' Toby announces.

I look despairingly at Rob. *How am I meant to keep this a secret?*

'He's exhausted,' Toby continues.

'I know,' Rob says, nodding slowly, probably trying to gauge how much they know. 'Lucy, I was thinking of taking the guys out for the day, if that's all right with you? Might give you a bit of time to catch up on things and maybe see Greg later if you like.'

'Are you sure?'

'Absolutely.'

'Aw, that would be great, Rob, thanks. I'm sure they'd love a break from me,' I joke.

'Ye-ah,' says Rachel.

Rob throws her a surprised look.

'Where're we going?' asks Toby.

'Up to you. We can decide in the car.'

Rob's so at ease with them, it makes me realise how tense I am in comparison, holding myself as though expecting a blow to the back of the head.

He winks. 'See you later.'

'Ah, Rob? What time will you be back? Just so I can make sure to be here.'

'Eight OK? Would that give you enough time?'

'Yeah, that'd be great. Thanks a mill. Really appreciate it.'

'No probs. See you later.'

~

I call my parents to keep them at bay. After an exhausting performance of 'All's well', I visit Greg, only to discover that the man I've promised to spend the rest of my life with won't talk to me. He won't even look at me, making me feel that it might be easier for him if I wasn't here. My attempts at optimism sound trite, even to me.

I get back to an empty house feeling drained. And cold. I climb the stairs and crawl under the duvet fully clothed. If only I could get warm.

I wake. It's dark. The house is quiet. I check my watch. It's nine. I jump from the bed and hurry downstairs. I'd have woken if they'd knocked, wouldn't I?

I bump into Rob in the hall.

'Jesus,' I say, my hand going to my chest.

'Sorry. I thought you were still out.'

'No. I just lay down for a second. Didn't plan to sleep. Where are Rachel and Toby?'

'In bed.'

'I'm *so* sorry, I didn't mean to nod off.'

'You must've been tired.'

'Cold. I was freezing. Anyway, sorry. Thanks so much for looking after them today. It was such a great help.' I'm walking him to the front door.

'Don't I get a cup of tea?'

'Yes, of course. Sorry.' I touch my forehead. What's wrong with me?

In the kitchen, he pulls out a chair. I put on the kettle.

'How was he?' he asks.

I sigh and join him at the table. 'To be honest, Rob, I don't know. He won't talk to me. He says he wants to handle it.'

'Now, why doesn't that surprise me?' he asks, surprising me.

'What do you mean?'

'It's just the way he is. He doesn't rely on anyone, especially family. When Catherine died, I got the same – "I can handle it." The only person he allowed to help was Hilary, and that was only because it was her job. I bet he opens up to the nurses and doctors in there.'

'I don't know. He won't let them talk to me.' I sigh. 'Why is he blocking me out? All I want to do is help. We're engaged, for God's sake.'

He shrugs. 'Survival instinct, or some shit. Ever since our father died, he's always been the responsible one. It's like his role, or something.'

'But he should trust us.'

'He thinks he's protecting us.'

'But it means we can't help.'

'You *are* helping, Lucy, by being here, by looking after the children. When Catherine died, that's how I did my bit – with Rachel. I'd take her off, distract her, giving him time for himself. It did help. I know it did. Of course, I couldn't let on I was deliberately helping.'

'Is that what you were doing today?'

He shrugs. 'Helping you is helping him. Speaking of which, I'd like to take Rachel and Toby for a few hours every evening. You could go see Greg.'

'That's too much, Rob. I'm sure Grace will do some nights. You have a life.'

'I want to do it. It's always been one-way with Greg and me. In fact, I don't just want to help; I need to.'

'And I get that, but you'll want to see him yourself . . .'

'I'm off for another few weeks. And when school starts again, I'll work something out.'

'Well, then, have dinner with us when you come to collect Rachel and Toby.'

He smiles. 'That'd be nice.'

I wake three times during the night from the same nightmare. I leave the children to sleep on the street, overnight, while I check into an upmarket hotel. I go back out to the street, tuck them up in sleeping bags and leave them again, hoping they won't wander off or be attacked. It never once occurs to me to bring them into the hotel.

28.

In the morning, on my way downstairs, I notice Rachel's bedroom door open, a rare occurrence that allows a glimpse of the bomb-site within. Her pretty room is overflowing with clothes, glasses, cups, books and dirty plates, scattered in random heaps. It's partly my fault. I should be able to say no when she heads upstairs with her self-made dinners, lunches and breakfasts. I should be able to say no to a lot of things. But I've a problem getting the word out with Rachel. Her dad's in hospital. I'm not her mum. She's a land-mine and I am a foot. But there's no sign of her now so I pop in to rescue uneaten food at the pre-fungal stage.

From across the corridor, I hear the toilet flush and the door open. A heap of clothes under one arm, a stack of plates in one hand and four glasses in the other, I turn. She's standing at the door looking like she's ready to blow.

'Get out of my room.'

'Sorry?'

'Are you deaf? I said, get out.'

'Don't talk to me like that, Rachel.'

'Then don't go into my room. It's my room. You can't just go in whenever you want.'

'I was just bringing down your dirty plates and the clothes that needed washing.'

'Did I ask you to?'

'No. But if you don't want me to come into your room, then please keep it tidy so I don't have to.'

'I'll do what I like in my own room. It's my room.' The tilt of her head and hips say more than the words.

'Rachel, honestly,' I say, in what I hope is a reasonable tone. 'How do you expect your clothes to get clean lying here on the floor?'

'I'll clean them. At least I *can*, without ruining everything.'

'Fine, Rachel. Clean your own clothes. And leave your room whatever way you want. Just keep the door closed so I don't have to look at it.'

'Don't tell me what to do,' she shouts. 'You're not my mother. You can't make me do anything.'

'I wish you could hear yourself, Rachel.'

'I can. You're the one who's deaf.'

Now I know why Hansel and Gretel's stepmother left them in the forest. I count to ten. In French.

'Why won't you just go away?' she says, when I get to six.

'And why won't you be fair?' My arms and fingers are aching. If I don't put something down, it'll all slip from my grip. I rest the glasses on my forearm. 'All I was trying to do was help. All I've ever tried to do is help. And you've been nothing but ungrateful. You won't eat my food. You insult my clothes. You complain about the mess the house is in, but never lift a finger to help.'

'Look, nobody asked you to do anything.'

'That's where you're wrong. Your father asked me to look after you while he's in hospital. If I had a choice, by God, I wouldn't. Once upon a time, Rachel, I had a life. I don't need this from you, day in, day out . . .'

'So go.'

As soon as we arrive at this point, I realise it was her intended destination all along. I've just given her what she wanted, an admission that I don't want to be here. Despite knowing that it's too late, I try again. 'Why can't we be friends? Why can't we get on? I only want what's best for you and Toby.'

'You just said you didn't want us.' She looks triumphant.

'Rachel, what I meant to say was that it's hard to enjoy looking after you when you're being deliberately difficult. That's all I meant to say. Actually, I didn't even mean to say that.'

She doesn't budge, standing there, arms firmly folded.

'OK, you win,' I exhale. 'I'm going.'

I struggle down the stairs, my mind racing. How could I have said that? Why couldn't I have kept my mouth shut? She's a child. Remember that, Lucy. A child. Remind yourself every time she scowls at you, every time she pushes your buttons. Or just face facts: you're not cut out to be a parent – of any kind.

In the hall, Toby has the phone in his hand and is pressing the buttons. It melts my heart. I go to him, put down the glasses and plates, and let the clothes fall to the floor.

'You all right, Tobes?'

He's been chewing his sleeves. The cuffs are wet. Little holes have started to form, as if a family of moths has been on a picnic.

'What's Dad's number?'

'It's a little early to ring the hospital, pet.' And Greg's worst time of day. 'I'll tell you what, why don't you come into the kitchen with me and help me make . . . a Slush Puppie.' He loves Slush Puppies.

'Can you *make* Slush Puppies?'

'We can *try*.'

~

When Grace learned that no one at the hospital would tell me what was going on, she asked Karl to call and check on the patient's progress.

'It mightn't be the most ethical route in the world,' she said. 'But fuck that.'

Now she arrives with news, the boys and lunch. Shane runs uninhibited into the house. Jason, on hands and knees, isn't far behind. I catch Rachel looking down from the landing. Toby comes out from the kitchen.

'Hi, guys!'

'Hi, Toby,' everyone replies, in various stages of language development.

'Hey, Rachel, you coming down?' calls Grace.

'Yep,' she says, all smiles.

'Do you want to take Jase and Shane out the back to the swings?' Grace asks her.

'Sure.' She picks up the baby. He looks at her, grins, then yanks her hair. She laughs. 'OK, everyone, follow me.'

Grace and I watch them from the kitchen.

'Remind me to ask you over more often,' I say.

'I invited myself, remember?'

'Well, do it more often, then.'

We smile.

'So,' she says, all business suddenly. 'As I expected, they've started him on lithium and an antidepressant.'

'Oh, God. Hang on. Let me sit down for this.'

'Sorry. Will I make tea?'

'No, no. I'm fine now. Sorry.'

'Right, well, you know that lithium stabilises mood?'

'You told me.'

'And it's the standard treatment for bipolar disorder?'

I nod.

'Right, OK. Well, they've also started him on an antidepressant, for the moment.'

'How soon will it start working?'

'It'll take a week or two to build up in his system. They're also going to try and involve him in group therapy. So far, they haven't had much luck there.'

'I'm not surprised. He won't even talk to me.'

'These would be general conversations, you know, like what's in the newspapers.'

'What good would that do?'

'Get him out of his own head. But never mind that. They seem to be having some success on a one-to-one level. He's been allocated one nurse as a main point of contact. Someone called Betty. He seems to be opening up to her. Hopefully, in time, she'll be able to convince him to go along to psychotherapy – you know, group therapy, art therapy . . .'

'Art therapy?'

'Expressing yourself through art.'

'Sounds good.'

'At this stage, Lucy, Greg probably couldn't care less. Hopefully, once the drugs kick in, and once he begins to trust Betty, he'll get more involved.'

At that, the children burst into the kitchen looking for juice. Grace gets lidded beakers for her boys. Rachel takes over from there. We wait till they've gone. It takes a while; Rachel's making a picnic.

'When can he come off the drugs?' I ask, when the door closes behind them.

'Once he's out of the depression, they'll probably try weaning him off the antidepressant. The lithium is for life, Lucy.'

'Life.' Like a prison sentence.

'For most people, yes.'

'What's most?'

'Fifty to seventy per cent.'

'What about the others?'

'The lucky few who don't relapse? They might try weaning them off after, say, five years. But I don't want you to get your hopes up. For your own sake, you need to assume that Greg will be on it for life. But let's not think about that now. At the moment, he's in a very, very dark place. If he says anything hurtful, tell yourself that it's the illness talking. Try not to take it personally.'

'Easy to say.'

'All the more reason for you to have your own life outside this. Your job. Your interests.'

'Interests!' I laugh.

'I'm here, Lucy. You know that.' She takes both my hands in hers. 'You'll get through this.'

I said something similar to Greg. Did he feel as hopeless, hearing it?

'This doesn't have to spell disaster. Lots of people lead fulfilled and happy lives with bipolar disorder.'

Happy and fulfilled. Not normal, though. Not normal.

~

Art therapy is my chance to get involved. Or so I think. When I suggest it to Betty, she has a different view.

'Lucy, with all due respect, while Greg needs your support, he doesn't need your involvement in his care. You're not a therapist.'

'I need to help.'

'I understand that. But Greg has to be allowed to regain his strength at his own pace. If he had a broken leg, you wouldn't rush him to hop out of bed and run around. Think of this in the same way. Greg's in competent hands. You should be concentrating on your own health now. You need to keep your strength up – get plenty of sleep, fresh air and good food. Have you thought of joining a support group?'

'So, there's nothing I can actually do?'

'Have you read those leaflets I gave you?'

'Well, ah . . . Not yet.'

'It would help you understand some of what Greg's going through and why this takes time.'

And so it seems that everyone's telling me the same thing – I have to let Greg fight his fight alone until he's ready for me to join him. I'll do it, then. But it doesn't feel right.

~

On my way back from the hospital, I call in to see my parents.

Dad's in the front garden.

'Hi, Dad, is Mum in?' I ask, walking past him.

He looks surprised. 'Everything OK?'

'Yeah, yeah, fine. Is she inside?'

'Kitchen,' he says, trowel suspended mid-air.

In I go, a woman on a mission.

She's at the sink, her back to me.

I lean against the worktop. 'Mum?'

She turns, her rubber-gloved hands lifting out of the water. 'Lucy! Is everything all right?'

Is it so weird I want to talk to my mother? 'Everything's fine, Mum . . . Can we sit down?'

Looking concerned, she starts to peel off the gloves. She sits at the table, looking at me with such an intense look of expectation, I have to smile.

'I just wanted to say thanks for everything.'

She looks confused.

'Everything you've ever done for me, every meal you've ever cooked, every pair of jeans you've ever washed. I mean it, thank you, Mum.'

Her face relaxes into a smile. 'What's brought this on? Did you have a bad day with the kids?'

I think of Rachel. 'Was I *very* difficult?'

'No, Lucy.'

'I was, though, wasn't I?' I remember years of arguments.

'No more than any other teenager, myself included.' She smiles.

I can't imagine her as a teenager. 'I'm sorry, Mum.'

'There's nothing to be sorry for.'

'How did you do it?'

'Not perfectly, that's for certain. I've made my mistakes, Lucy. I pushed you too hard. So hard, I pushed you away.'

I squint at her. She *noticed*?

'Your father and I had a long chat when you were in France. I know you don't come to see us much at the best of times, but when you were away and didn't call, I got a bit down. It made me face up to the way things are between us. I talked to Dad about it.'

Wow.

'I'm one of life's worriers, Lucy. When it comes to my children, especially. The minute you tell me something, I'm worrying about the implications. And, instead of keeping all those useless fears to myself, I blurt them out. I'm trying to be helpful. But all I'm doing is interfering. In trying to protect you, I'm telling you how to live your life. And I'm sorry. I *have* been "working on it", as he'd say himself. I don't know if you've noticed?' She looks hopeful.

I don't tell her that I've noticed little outside of Greg and the children, lately. What I do say is, 'All I could ever see was what you were doing wrong. Never what you were doing right. And never the effort you put in – or the worry. I guess I just wanted to say I appreciate it now, if that's any comfort.'

'It is, Lucy. It is.'

We're holding hands across the table when Dad peeps into the kitchen. 'Crisis over?'

'No crisis,' says Mum, smiling at me.

There is affection in her eyes. Maybe it was there all along and I was too stubborn to notice.

'Good,' says Dad. 'Any more of that rhubarb tart left?'

~

'Something arrived for you,' says Rob as soon as I get back.

Submerged in water, in the kitchen sink, is an enormous bouquet of sunflowers. I look at him.

'There's a card with them.' I can tell he's curious.

I open it. And smile. Fint, offering his services in whatever way he can.

'Secret admirer?'

'No. Just a very good friend.'

29.

Rachel won't do anything for me. Neither will she go anywhere. Until I suggest visiting Jason and Shane. *That* she'll do. And so, we go.

'Hi, guys,' says Grace. 'What a lovely surprise!' And as Rachel and Toby troop in, she warns me, 'Dad's here.'

'What? His car isn't outside!'

'Mum went shopping in it.'

'Rachel! Toby!' I call, but they've already disappeared.

Grace grimaces. 'It *should* be OK. Dad's busy fixing the Hoover.'

'We won't stay long.'

We find Dad kneeling on the floor in the dining room, surrounded by bits of Grace's Hoover, a strip of black grease running down his nose. And Rachel standing over him.

'Hi, Dad!' I say brightly. 'We won't disturb you.' I widen my eyes at Rachel to get her to come.

She looks back defiantly, then turns to Dad. 'Would you like a hand?'

Crap.

'You know, that'd be great. I love a bit of company when I'm working. Lucy used to be my helper when she was little.'

She ignores that.

'Right, then. Hand me that screwdriver over there. The one with the red handle.'

Like a shot, she obliges.

Toby starts to look interested, so I offer him a drink.

I close the dining room door behind us, thinking *Holy Mother of God.*

In the kitchen, Jason's busy gnawing on building blocks. Toby finds a truck and begins to race Shane, who has a Ferrari. It's good to see him just play, with no one to smother him. Grace makes coffee and the two of us sit at the table, keeping an eye on the boys. I ask her what she and Kevin are doing to the kitchen cupboards. Work seems to be in progress.

She lowers her voice. 'Don't talk to me about those bloody cupboards. If I hear the words "Preparation is nine-tenths of the law" one more time, I'll scream.'

'Isn't it "*Possession* is nine-tenths of the law"?'

'Is it?' She bursts out laughing. 'That's the best news I've had all day.'

I smile. 'What are you doing, painting over them?'

'Oooh no, not just painting. That would be sloppy. First, we're sanding them down, then we're going to paint them. Sorry, *I'm* going to paint them. Kevin will project manage the job, supervise the entire operation. Give me practical little tips. Honest to God, there are times when I could throttle him. D'you know what I spent the morning doing? In between feeding and changing children, that is?'

'No.'

'Filling in holes and irregularities in the woodwork. I told him that it's wood, it's supposed to have irregularities, and d'you know what he said? There's other people's wood and there's our wood.'

I smile. To me, that sounds like such a simple, straightforward argument. No one being accused of not loving, not caring, deserting.

'If I suddenly jump up and start filling in the children's chicken pox marks with stopping, you'll know I've finally flipped.'

'What's stopping?'

'You don't know what stopping is?' she says in mock horror. 'Lucy, you haven't *lived*. You use it on wood instead of Polyfilla. It's *fantastic*. I'll have to get you some.'

I smile. 'Apart from the cupboards, though, how's it going?'

She sighs. 'I don't know. I'm trying, Lucy. Really I am.'

'Maybe it mightn't be the best time for DIY. Maybe you should just get out of the house, have fun together.'

'Kevin? *Fun?*' She sighs. 'Anyway, forget the perfectionist, how are you?'

'Freezing.' I run my hands up and down my arms. 'You don't have a jumper I could borrow, do you?'

Grace disappears and returns with a hoodie and socks. I'm especially thrilled with the socks. They're so snug and homely. I start to get teary. I know she's going to talk about it, so I stop her before she does.

After coffee, she shoos me away.

'Go on. Show your face at the office. They'll be fine here.'

'They'll be happier here. But what about you?'

'Lucy, you're doing me a favour. Shane and Jason are occupied. And when Rachel's finished in there, she'll take over. Honestly, go. It's easier for me with them here.'

I hope that Dad will work in his usual way – in silence – and that my mother will be back shortly to collect him.

~

Fint and I hug, everything forgotten without a word. He cancels his afternoon and takes me through all that's been happening – staff issues, proposals they've been putting together, current clients. We troubleshoot, brainstorm. Work. It feels good to be listened to, my opinion counting for something, to feel the adrenalin of an office environment, to be reminded that I have a brain. I leave with two not so major jobs to get working on. Grace was right, I needed another focus.

~

I collect the children and bring them home. They watch a video while I tackle the mess. I'm collecting a pile of laundry when I feel someone behind me.

It's Rachel.

I brace myself for a complaint, an unreasonable request – a problem, basically.

'You've a nice dad,' she says, almost shyly.

I remain cautious. 'Did you have a good time?'

She nods. 'I like helping out.'

'Good.'

'I used to help my dad all the time . . . Before.'

I straighten up, surprised that we're still having – I'm still not sure – our first proper conversation?

'Do you think your dad would ever need a hand with anything else?'

I hide my surprise. 'I'm sure he would, Rachel.'

'Can you ask him?'

'Yes, of course.'

'Thanks.' And then she's gone.

~

Later, when they're asleep, I call Dad. 'You were a big hit, today.'

'Ah, she's a little dote.'

Strange. Though she's a child, I've never seen Rachel as little. And *never* 'a dote'.

'She reminds me of you.'

'She's not a bit like me.'

'No?'

'No.'

'She's very quiet,' he says.

I say nothing, which I realise, too late, probably proves his point.

'Angry,' he says.

'You can say that again.'

'I used to know a little girl like that.'

Listen to the psychologist. 'If you're talking about me, you're wrong.'

'Your mother didn't make you angry?'

I'm not going to admit to anything.

'And your sister?'

'Wrong. I was never angry with Grace.' *I might have been jealous . . .*

'What did you call her, again? Little Miss Perfect? Don't tell me you weren't the teensiest bit angry?'

'Guess who's making me angry now? Anyway, I just called to say thanks. You seemed to cheer her up.'

'That's all right, love. I enjoyed her company. As I always did yours . . . My little helper.' Why does that make me feel weepy? 'You know, maybe you should think about letting her help around the house.'

'She'd never do anything for me.'

'Let her think it's her idea.'

'I don't know.'

'Well, why don't you let her come over here some afternoon? I'll think of something she can help me out with. And you could probably do with a break from each other.'

'Probably.'

'That settles it, then. And sure, bring the little fellow as well. Toby. Your mother took a big shine to him.'

Can I risk it? Maybe I've no choice. This is something Rachel very clearly needs.

~

The following morning, my phone rings.

'Is that Lucy?'

'Ben.' I close my eyes; I forgot to tell them we were home.

'I got your number from Hilary. I've been ringing the villa for days. I've been trying Greg's number . . .'

'Oh, I'm sorry, Ben, I think it needs recharging.'

'Why haven't you been contactable? We've been so worried. We were going to fly over when Hilary gave us your number.'

Hearing Hilary's name has the same effect as always. It's like receiving bad news. 'Ben. We're home.'

'You're home? In Ireland?'

'Yes. I'm sorry we haven't got around to calling you. Things have been a bit hectic.'

'How long have you been back?'

'A few days.' Over a week.

'And you didn't think to let us know our grandchildren were in the country? We do have a right to know where they are, Lucy.'

'I realise that,' I say, struggling to remain calm. Why is he talking about rights?

'What are you doing back? Was there a problem?'

'Yes.' I've worked it out. 'The heat. It was too hot for the children.'

'Ah, yes. As a matter of fact, I'm surprised you didn't come home sooner.'

'Well, we're back now.'

'Is Greg there?'

'Not at the moment.'

'Why is he never available when I call? Is something going on, something I should know about?'

'Ben, nothing is, as you put it, going on. You can see your grandchildren any time. I'm sorry you had a problem getting through, but everything's fine. We're just settling back in.'

'We'd like to see the children.'

'Of course.' *Shit.*

'Maybe you could drop them to us?'

What am I, his personal slave? 'When would suit?'

'Next Saturday?'

God. 'What time?'

'Three?'

'Fine. Rachel will be able to show me where you live, I'm sure.'

He gives me the address anyway. Just in case.

I have five days to figure out what to do.

I've no sooner hung up when Greg calls. He gets straight to the point.

'Professor Power wants me to explain to Rachel and Toby why I'm in hospital.'

I don't know what to say. 'Oh,' I manage finally.

'He thinks that the truth is preferable to imaginary fears.'

But it's a pretty heavy truth. 'Are they old enough, Greg?'

'He thinks so – as long as I keep it simple.'

'When does he want you to do this?' It had better be after Saturday. I'm not sure Ben and Ruth are ready to hear – from the mouths of babes – that Greg's in hospital suffering from a psychiatric illness.

'He thought maybe you could bring them in this afternoon and we could all go for a walk together and I could tell them then.'

I remind myself to breathe, tell myself it'll be OK. I'll postpone Ben and Ruth – indefinitely.

'OK', I say finally, on the basis that the doctor knows what he's doing.

When I hang up, I tell the children that they're going to see their dad.

There follows a frenzy of activity. We buy a hanging fern and a little red watering can – Rachel thinks Greg should have something to look after. Toby remembers wine gums. We make posters for the ward. Toby hums while he works. Rachel forgets to snap at me. Art therapy has a convert.

I've arranged to pick Greg up from the hospital entrance. As we approach, I'm hoping he'll be there, that he'll have remembered to shave and that the kids won't notice how pale and gaunt he's become. All three of us peer out for the first sight of him.

'There he is!' Toby shouts, pointing to a lone, thin figure.

And when Greg smiles, I see the effort he's making.

I pull up in the Set Down area. The children jump out and run to him. I'm about to go help him to the car then remember he's not an invalid. Behind me, a car honks. Rachel turns and gives the driver the finger. I'm shocked, but strangely proud.

Driving away with everyone aboard, I'm gripped by a *Thelma and Louise* urge to keep going, never return to the hospital.

It's a short trip to Sandymount Strand. The children bombard their father with questions all the way. And as he struggles to keep up, I worry that he's not ready for this.

We make it to the strand and walk, together, down onto the beach. The tide is so far out, the balance of sand to sea seems wrong, as if the moon has pulled too hard, leaving a margin of blue at the edge of a golden page. The sky seems to stretch forever in all directions. The sand, at first, is dry and loose, then damp and corrugated. Little saltwater streams and pools, left by the outgoing tide, glisten in the sun, reminding me of milk on a surface of porridge.

We take off our shoes, roll up our trousers and walk. Huge brown jellyfish lie stranded, like alien spacecraft that have landed for a convention. A giant seagull struts by as though he owns the beach. As we get closer to the sea, the line of white dots at the water's edge becomes a flock of seagulls. A dog runs among them, causing them to lift and fall like a Mexican wave.

But, no matter what the beach has to offer in terms of fun, adventure or excitement, the children never leave their father's side. Toby slips a hand into Greg's and starts to skip, his skinny body light and carefree. It's so good to have Greg back with us again, breathing the salty air, experiencing the breeze on his face. We spend at least an hour on that beach.

Almost back at the car, Greg stops at a wooden bench that looks out onto the strand.

'Let's sit for a while.'

My stomach tightens.

Greg settles at one end of the bench, Toby on his lap, Rachel next to them. I'm at the other.

Bookends.

'Guys,' Greg says, 'I want to explain why I'm in hospital.'

'It's OK, Dad. We know,' says Toby. 'You're exhausted.'

'Well, it's a little more than that.' He takes a breath. 'I have a sickness that makes me sad sometimes. Other times it makes me very excited.'

They take time to digest that.

Toby is first to speak. 'But it's OK to be sad, Dad. You said.' He looks at Greg for confirmation.

'I did. And it's OK to cry when something happens to make you sad.'

'Yeah, you're always telling us that.'

'It's just that if there's no reason to be sad and you're sad anyway – all the time – well, that's not good, is it?'

Toby shakes his head wildly. 'No, that'd be . . . sad.'

'And not good,' says Greg.

'No,' agrees Toby.

Rachel's quiet. Taking it all in.

'And it's OK to get excited, too,' continues Greg. 'Lots of things are exciting . . .'

'Like Christmas and birthdays and fireworks and when you get onto the next level in a game.'

'Exactly.' Greg smiles. 'But being hyper isn't good.'

'No.' Toby shakes his head again. 'When you have Coke or Skittles or something, you get hyper. And that's not good 'cause you go bananas. Isn't that right, Dad?'

'Yes, son.' Greg kisses the top of his head. 'But you eventually go back to normal, don't you?'

'Yeah.'

Rachel, eyes fixed on her father, is oblivious to the breeze whipping her hair across her face.

'Well,' says Greg, 'I've a sickness that makes me hyper for weeks. And that's not good.'

'No.' Toby squints. 'Why not, again?'

'Well, it can make me do silly things, and can make me hurt people.' He looks at me.

'Did you hurt someone?' asks Toby.

'I think so,' Greg says, his eyes finding mine.

My throat burns. Tears well. I smile.

'Who did you hurt?' asks Toby.

'Well, in France, I think I hurt you all.'

'No, you didn't,' rushes Toby. 'You never slap us.'

'I wasn't very nice to you, though, was I? Remember? I was hyper and I forgot about you, the people I love. And that wasn't right, was it?'

'Is that hurting?'

'Yes, Toby.'

'Is that because you were sick, Dad?' asks Rachel. 'I thought you were just cross with us.'

He puts his arm around her. 'No, Rache, I wasn't cross with you. You didn't do anything wrong. If I snapped at you, it was my fault, not yours. I wasn't well. I had – still have – this sickness. This sickness called bipolar disorder.'

'Dad?'

'Yes, Tobes?'

'Was it the sickness that made you talk funny?'

Greg nods. 'Anything I did in France that I don't normally do was because of the sickness. And I'm sorry. So sorry. I didn't mean to frighten you or upset you . . .' His voice falters. I'm afraid his tears will upset them. But that only shows how little I know about children.

They put their arms around him. 'It's OK, Dad. It's OK.'

And so, four people sit on a bench. Two in tears – the adults. And two comforting one of the adults and, thankfully, not noticing the other. Greg pulls a handkerchief from his trouser pocket and runs it over his face. He sighs.

'You're such good kids. I'm glad we had this chat. I wanted to explain, in case you were worried about what happened in France. Were you?' He looks from one to the other.

'Kinda,' says Toby.

'Yes.' Rachel.

'Well, everything's going to be OK. I'm taking medicine. And I'm not so sad now . . .'

'And you're not hyper,' reassures Toby.

'No.'

'Poor Dad,' says Toby, snuggling into him.

'Hey, guess what? The doctor said you can come and see me every day, if you like.'

'Yaay!' they say together.

'And soon I'll be coming home for a weekend.'

'When?' asks Rachel.

'Well, maybe not this weekend. But next weekend. Maybe. How's that?'

'Great,' she says.

'Good,' says Toby. 'Can we go and get your presents now? They're in the boot. They're really good.'

'Let's do that.'

The children hop up. Greg reaches out and takes my hand, the first time in weeks that he's voluntarily touched me. As we return to the car, I marvel at how straightforward bipolar disorder can be when explained a certain way – a sickness that makes you sad and excited. Not something to be ashamed of. Just something that happens. Of course, that's when you're talking to children. With adults it's different. With adults it's more complicated. And with Ben and Ruth, I guess, it will be impossible. They'll never understand.

At the hospital entrance, I'm about to start the goodbyes when Greg asks the children if they'd like to see where he sleeps. Another surprise. Another step forward.

~

That night, as darkness falls, I have a visitor. I'm surprised to see Hilary, but more surprised at how she looks, almost unrecognisable because of the amount of weight she's gained. Her face has changed shape, the lower half dominating, her features losing prominence. It doesn't help that her hair is greasy and scraped back.

'I need to talk to Greg.'

I notice a stain on the front of her sweatshirt. 'Sorry, he's not here.'

'Yes, he is. I know he is. He just doesn't want to talk to me.' She steps closer.

I hold the door and am firm when I repeat, 'Greg. Isn't. Here.'

'Well, where is he, at this time of night?' she asks, as if trying to catch me out.

'Hilary, I don't think that's any of your business, and, frankly, you've a nerve showing up here after what you did.'

'What, exactly, am I supposed to have done?'

I realise my mistake – the last thing I should be doing is engaging in conversation with her.

'Nothing. Forget it. I'll tell Greg you called.'

'If you're talking about Ben and Ruth, I just told them the truth.'

'What do you want, Hilary?' I make my voice sound tired.

'To talk to Greg.'

'Fine. I'll tell him you called. He has your number.' I go to close the door.

She takes a step forward. 'Why isn't he answering his phone?'

I slip my foot against the door. 'I don't know. I'll get him to call you, OK? Goodnight.' I close the door. Lean against it. Don't move. Listen. Hoping she'll go. I hear nothing. After what seems like an age, I hear footsteps walk away. I breathe a sigh of relief. *It's just Hilary. What can she do?* But there's something invasive about her coming to the house. It reminds me that she could do so at any time. During the day when the children are around. Any time. It would be so easy to make a scene.

30.

Dad needs a hand to re-grout the bathroom, as well as fix a doorbell and a leaking tap. Mum requires assistance in the kitchen. Rachel is called in on maintenance duty. Toby's culinary expertise may stem the domestic crisis.

I make a much needed appearance at the office, where I complete one of the jobs I've been working on and make good progress on the other.

When I get back to collect the children, they nag me to stay for dinner. After all, Toby's cooked it single-handedly, with just a little guidance.

'I'd love to stay, but we're having Rob for dinner.'

'Why don't you just ring him and invite him here?' Mum says. 'And Greg, of course. We've made plenty. Or should I say, Toby's made plenty.' She puts a hand on his shoulder.

He looks so proud.

'Greg can't make it, Mum. He's up to his tonsils.'

'Yeah, he's in hospital,' explains Toby, helpfully.

Both parents look at me, then at each other.

'In hospital?' My mother looks at me.

But Toby's already answering. 'Yeah. He's sad, but not hyper, and he'll be able to come home – not this weekend, but next weekend.'

'It's bipolar disorder,' confirms Rachel.

'Yeah. He has to take medicine,' says Toby as my parents stare at me. 'I saw his bed. It's boring. But we brought in lots of stuff, so it's much nicer now.'

In fairness to Mum and Dad, they say no more. Mum opens her mouth, but shuts it again.

'Come on,' I say to the kids. 'Let's go. Thanks, Mum and Dad.' On the surface, I look calm. Inside, I'm freaking. What will I tell Greg? And how can I bring the kids to Ben and Ruth's now?

'Wait a minute,' Mum says, disappearing into the kitchen. Toby follows.

Then they're back with a big Tupperware container filled with dinner.

'You have to try this,' Mum says. 'It's delicious. You carry it, Toby, seeing as you're the chef.'

He smiles proudly and puts out his hands.

'Bye, my darlings,' she says, kissing them both on the top of the head.

Dad does the same.

'Can we come again?' asks Rachel.

Everyone looks at me.

'Of course. If it's OK with you,' I say to my parents.

'We'd love to have Rachel and Toby, any time.' I almost hear them thinking, *Especially now.*

~

When we're in the car and driving off, Rachel says, 'Is it a secret that Dad's in hospital?'

'Well. It's not a secret . . . as such. It's just that your dad, well . . . He isn't ready to tell everyone yet.'

'Why not?'

'He just wants peace and quiet . . . for the moment. And . . . if everyone knows he's in hospital, they'll all come and visit, and he's not ready for that yet.'

'But he's sad,' says Toby. 'Visitors will cheer him up. They can bring presents like we did.'

'I know. It's just that, well, your dad doesn't have the energy for any visitors other than us and Rob, at the moment.'

And though it's the truth, it's not the whole truth, and I know for a fact that Rachel cops that.

As soon as the children are in bed, I phone Ben to postpone. He's not pleased. He wonders if he should worry. I feel like telling him to go right ahead, he seems to enjoy it. Instead, I arrange their visit for the following Saturday and try to put worrying on hold.

Since Greg's chat with the children, our routine has changed. Rob comes with us to the hospital, we collect Greg and go for a walk or a coffee, then, when it's almost time to head back, Rob takes the kids off for ten or fifteen minutes while Greg and I have time together. Having everyone there makes things easier for me as Greg makes more of an effort. I worry, though, that it tires him.

We're feeding ducks in Herbert Park when I tell him about my parents knowing.

'I'm sorry, but the only way to keep this a secret is to lock up the children.'

He's quiet for a moment. Then he looks at me sideways. 'Where'll we lock them?'

One small joke, but it seems monumental to me. I smile when really I want to throw my arms around him.

He shrugs. 'Forget about it. Nothing you could have done.'

'No.'

We circle the pond.

'Rob says you're doing too much,' he says.

For him to think like that, outside his own head, is major progress. 'Greg, I'm fine. I'm great. I don't know why he said that.'

'I asked him.'

'Well, he's wrong. Really.'

'Is he, though? Your job, the kids, the house, me. You can't do it all.'

'I can. Honestly. It's not a problem.'

'Cut back on something. Maybe you don't need to see me so often?'

'Are you kidding? *You're* my priority in all of this.' That, I realise, gets forgotten in the day-to-day hassle of survival. 'I love you, Greg. I want to be with you.'

'What about work? You don't need to, you know. I can support you, Luce.'

'I like my job. I need to work.'

He scratches his head. 'Thought you might say that.'

I watch our feet as we walk in silence.

'How're you paying for things?' he asks.

'Greg, please, don't worry about money, everything's fine.'

'Let me give you my bank card and PIN.' He stops, begins to tap his pockets.

I did resent paying what seems a huge amount to run a house and look after two children, but now that he's offered, I don't want his money. We're supposed to be a team.

'Greg, please.'

He finds his wallet, pulls out his card. 'Here, take it. The number is . . . Hang on. What's the number? Jesus.' He hits his forehead with the heel of his hand. 'OK. Don't worry. I'll sort something out with Rob . . . And I want you to get a cleaner. Rob will organise it, don't worry.'

Maybe it would be good.

'What about a part-time childminder?'

'No, Greg. Let's not land someone new on Rachel and Toby. Let's see how we cope, alone. In a weird way, it's an opportunity for us to crack this – it's them and me. Sink or swim.'

~

The inevitable phone call comes at nine. Dad. Timing it beautifully. I can picture him working it out: 'What time d'you think she'll be back from the hospital?'

'Hi, Dad,' I say, tired.

'Hello, love.'

I wait.

He waits. Then, 'Why didn't you tell us?'

'Greg doesn't want anyone to know.'

A second's silence. 'Understandable.' A pause. 'How's he doing?'

'He seemed better today.'

'Will I come over?'

'I'm a bit tired, Dad.'

'All right, love. I just wanted to say that your mother and I want to help. Are you getting any time on your own?'

'I'm grand, thanks. Grace takes the children if I have to go into the office.'

'Grace *knows*?'

'Yes, Dad, Grace knows. I asked her advice before I knew what was wrong. Then I had to ask her not to tell. Sorry.'

'Lucy, there's nothing to be sorry for. I'm glad you've had Grace. We want to help, too. We'd like to take the children for a few hours, every day. We'd love to have them. We've been feeling a bit lonely lately and they're little dotes.'

'And that's the only reason?'

'Well, you could do with a bit of time on your own, even just to spend it at the office. At least you'd be getting away from things for a while. You're still a young woman.'

Sadly, I needed the reminder. 'I suppose I could do with showing my face in there a bit more often. Actually, Dad, that would be great – if you don't mind.'

'We wouldn't have offered . . .'

'Yes, you would.'

'Put it to the children. See what they think. If they're all right with it, that's what we'll do.'

'Thanks, Dad.'

'Thank your mother. It was her idea.'

~

Rob hires a cleaner through a local agency to do three hours, twice a week. Tracy arrives like a fairy godmother. All she's missing is the gold dust. The laundry basket stops overflowing. The Mount Everest of ironing vanishes. It's possible to see whole pieces of furniture again and rooms as they're supposed to look. Hearing the Hoover is a relief.

Next time, she says she'll do the brass on the front door. *There's brass on the front door?* I've been struggling, on an endless production line of cleaning, ironing, cooking, Internet shopping, so tired that my head has become hard to hold up. The number of times I've caught myself leaning my forehead against cupboards, tables, the steering wheel, the wooden slats in the airing cupboard, so hard to lift back up, so much energy required. Even listening takes such concentration. And now here's Tracy. Like the sun coming out.

~

Over a two-week period, I've fielded four calls from Phyllis, Greg's mother. Rob made the mistake of telling her we were back. He knew not to mention where Greg was; something, at least. When she calls, I tell her Greg's out. Then I ring the hospital. Greg waits a while, then calls her back. It's been working, except for one thing: Why, she wants to know, hasn't he invited her round for Sunday lunch?

So, instead of Greg using his first day at home to relax and try to settle back into normality, he decides to put on a performance. Without consulting me, he invites her to lunch. When I hear that, I nearly explode. He doesn't need that pressure. *I* don't need that pressure. What if the children mention the hospital? What if she sees for herself that he's a changed man? He *is* her son.

When we collect Greg, he's looking better, his blue shirt picking up the colour of his eyes, making him look less pale. He's had a haircut and is cleanly shaven. All round, a big improvement. But enough to fool his mother?

We get to the house in plenty of time and wander down to the sea, something Greg misses. Toby and Greg roll up their trousers and paddle on the steps. Rachel collects stones for skimming. I perch on a rocky outcrop, staring off out towards Bray Head and the Sugarloaf Mountain. But when Greg starts to explain to the children why they 'shouldn't upset Gran' by mentioning that he hasn't been well, I slip away to the kitchen.

Apparently, she likes pork steak, cut into slivers, covered in flour, then fried. I take the meat from the fridge, cut open the plastic wrapping and watch watery blood ooze out. No matter how many times I've cooked it for the children, I still haven't got used to raw meat. There's no getting away from the fact that it was once a living creature.

It smells, but as I've never experienced the pleasure of raw pork steak before, I can't tell whether it's a normal or an abnormal smell. I check my watch. Too late to make it to the supermarket and back.

I ring Grace.

'What does raw pork steak smell like?'

'Seriously, Lucy, how can I describe the smell of raw pork steak? It smells like raw meat, what can I say?'

'I know, but how do I know if it's gone off?'

'It smells gone off.'

No help. 'What else?'

'Does it look sort of greeny-grey?'

I lift it with a piece of kitchen paper and slowly twirl it around. 'It *looks* OK.'

'Then it probably is, Luce.'

'I don't want to poison her.'

'You sure?' She laughs. 'Listen, I've got to go, they're killing each other here. Cook it, Lucy. It'll be fine. Got to go.'

~

Phyllis, as is her custom, arrives by taxi. I stay at the door while Greg and the children go to greet her. Greg helps her from the car. She has gifts and hugs for Rachel and Toby.

'Come meet Lucy, Ma,' says Greg, his arm around her.

She looks at me as if remembering, with grave disappointment, that I exist. Then she starts towards the house. She's about ten years older than my mum, but looks more – thin, short and slightly stooped, her face a road map of lines, her silver hair yellowing at the front. She's wirier than I expected, though, and when she speaks, her voice is deep and hoarse.

'Lucy,' she says, like it's a statement of my existence rather than a greeting. She doesn't smile.

'Nice to meet you,' I lie – for Greg. I extend a hand.

She shakes it, loosely at first as if testing my grip, then tightening into a squeeze, before letting go. I catch her looking at my toe ring.

In the sitting room, Greg pours drinks.

'Aren't you having one yourself, Greg?' she asks.

'Not today,' he says. 'Rough night.'

She starts rooting in her bag. 'I know it's a mortal sin to smoke indoors, but mind if I have a quick one?'

'Go ahead,' he says.

I take myself off to the kitchen where I make a semi-success of lunch. Rachel, under her father's instruction, helps me serve.

We sit down to eat.

While Phyllis asks the children if they're looking forward to going back to school, I check faces as they bite into their pork.

She turns to me. 'And what do *you* do, Lucy?'

'I'm a graphic designer.'

The children eye me with interest.

'And what's that when it's at home?' Her laugh is husky.

'We design packaging, logos, book covers, pretty much anything really. We . . .' She has stopped looking at me. Has she stopped listening? Am I boring her? I let my voice trail off. If she wants to know more, she'll ask.

'Don't stop now, this is fascinating,' she says in a bored tone.

I look at Greg, bemused.

'Lucy's an artist,' he says, smiling at me.

'I *knew* you were good at drawing,' says Toby.

'I'm learning how to sew, Gran,' says Rachel. 'Lucy's mum is teaching me. She's really good.'

'You see Lucy's parents?'

'Yeah, we go all the time, when Lucy's at work,' says Toby cheerfully.

She turns to Greg. 'Is Lucy *living* here? Where's *Hilary*?'

There's an awkward silence.

'Yes, Lucy is living here,' says Greg.

'Just until Dad gets out of—' Rachel stops.

'We let Hilary go,' Greg says.

Phyllis's eyes widen. 'You fired her? Why?'

'It wasn't working out,' he says.

'But she was so good with the children.'

'I know,' says Rachel, narrowing her eyes at me.

'I'm shocked,' Phyllis whispers.

No one speaks.

She lifts a piece of pork with her fork, examines it and shakes her head sadly. 'They make such good meals at the home.'

Greg looks at me as if to say 'Don't mind her.' But he doesn't say anything.

'Catherine was a great cook,' she says, staring off into space as if dreaming of wonderful times gone by. 'Speaking of food,' she says, turning to her son, 'are you eating properly? You've lost weight. You don't look well.'

He pretends he hasn't heard, cutting into a piece of meat.

'You work too hard, Greg. Always have. You should let Lucy take care of you. Ah, but Lucy has her own priorities.'

What have I *done* to the woman?

'It's Catherine's anniversary next week,' she continues. 'I think we should do something.'

'We'll talk about that another time,' Greg says.

'We should put an announcement in the paper.'

'We'll discuss it later.'

The children's knives and forks are suspended as though they, too, are listening.

'Such a great loss, she is. Such a good wife. And mother.'

'*Fine*, Ma.'

'She could handle anything, could Catherine. Then again, she *was* older.'

I excuse myself.

Greg follows me into the kitchen. 'Don't mind her.'

I turn to him. 'How can you let her go on like that? Catherine this, Catherine that. As if I'm chopped liver.'

'She doesn't mean anything by it.'

I stare at him. 'I'm not going back in there. I'm going for a walk.'

'OK, fine. Run away.'

'Don't think I'm not tempted, Greg Millar, a million times a day.'

He looks shocked, wounded.

'I'm sorry. I didn't mean that.' But, in a way, I did. And he knows it. Looking like I've speared him in the heart, he turns and goes back to his mother.

31.

I stand at the sink, looking into dirty pots, reminders of the effort I made: the remains of potato I carefully mashed, pork steak I fussed over, broccoli I didn't overcook, carrots sliced longways, the way she likes them. The old bat. She's probably in there planning another offensive. I'd been doing so well with Greg, fighting all urges to admit how hard I'm finding everything. And now I've gone and sabotaged that with one thoughtless remark.

I go back in and sit at the table. I make eye contact with him and mouth one word. 'Sorry.'

'Oh, Lucy, you're back,' she says.

Round Two.

'I was just telling Rachel about the time her mother discovered she was pregnant with her. She was so happy . . .'

What about Toby? How can she even bring up the pregnancy?

'Toby, are you finished?' I ask.

He nods.

'Come on, I want to show you something in the kitchen.'

'OK.'

'We'll see you later,' I say into the general air.

'What d'you want to show me?' he asks when we get to the kitchen.

I think fast. 'Bubbles.'

'Bubbles?'

'Yeah, let's make some. Let's make a load. Let's fill the kitchen with bubbles.'

'OK,' he perks up.

I sit him up beside the sink, put in the plug, hand him the washing up liquid and blast on the water.

'OK, squirt it in. Go mad.'

Bubbles multiply like happily dividing rainbow cells. She doesn't matter. Only Greg does. And I've hurt him. When it's the last thing he needs.

~

And so, when she's leaving, I bring Toby out to say goodbye.

As the back of her tiny head disappears up the driveway, the children go inside.

'I'll get a taxi,' Greg says.

'Greg, I'm sorry. I didn't mean that. I was upset.'

'I wouldn't blame you if you did.'

'I didn't, though. Honestly. Why don't you come in and I'll make a cup of tea.'

'I need to go back, Lucy. This was a mistake.'

~

We stand at the door, watching him go. Toby waves.

Back inside, the kids turn on the TV. I'm stacking the dishwasher when I hear someone's runners squeak on the floor behind me. I wipe away my tears and turn. It's Rachel, carrying a heap of plates in from the dining room. The gesture seems enormous.

'Thank you,' I say.

She half smiles and goes back out. When she brings in her grandmother's plate, she heads straight for the bin with it, as if trying to hide the fact that it's hardly been touched.

We work together in silence.

Eventually, she speaks. 'She was kind of mean to you, wasn't she?'

I shake my head. 'It doesn't matter.'

'Especially when you made her favourite dinner.'

I smile.

She tucks back the hair she normally hides behind, then fiddles with the coloured charity bands on her wrist, before looking up at me with those dark eyes of hers.

'It's not just you, you know. She's like that with Rob's girlfriends, too.'

'She is?'

She nods. 'She made one cry.'

'Well, that makes me feel a whole lot better. Thank you.'

'It's OK.' She looks out of the window.

Suddenly, I feel for her. 'Things will get better, Rachel.'

She looks at me with such hope.

'You're a good kid.'

She gives me a 'You can't be serious' look, then heads for the door.

~

That evening, around ten, the doorbell rings. I think of Hilary and peer through the peephole. When I see that it's Rob, I open up.

'Hey,' he says. 'Kids in bed?'

'Rob, if they're not at the door two seconds after you arrive, *assume* they're in bed.'

He smiles and heads for the kitchen.

'So, how did it go?' he asks, tipping back onto two legs of a chair.

Realisation dawns. 'That's why you're here, isn't it? You knew it would be a disaster.'

'Let's just say, I know my mother.'

I pull a Heineken from the fridge. 'Want one?'

'Only if you're having one.'

'Try and stop me.' I crack open two cans. 'Let's go inside.' I need to get out of that kitchen.

'So, how awful was she, on a scale of one to ten?'

'Five hundred – and three.'

'Ouch.'

I give him an outline.

'If I *ever* get married, remind me to live abroad,' he says.

'I don't know. You might be OK. She liked Catherine.'

He throws his head back and laughs. 'Are you serious? Catherine and my mother? They hated each other. Catherine refused to be in the same room as her.'

'But she said . . .'

'Lucy, if my mother was talking Catherine up, it was to bring you down.'

'It did feel like that.'

'Don't take it personally. Nobody's good enough for her boys, especially her eldest.'

So, Rachel was right.

'Take a leaf from Catherine's book. Don't put up with any crap. When the Old Dear was visiting, Catherine would always arrange to be somewhere else.'

'And Greg was OK with that?'

He shrugs. 'I doubt he had a choice. Catherine did her own thing. In fairness, I think she was right. She was straight. No bull. But no saint. Well, not till she died. Then my mother canonised her.'

'Well, I'm not about to keel over to keep Phyllis happy.'

'Take my advice and stay out of her way. She's happiest when she can have her sons, especially her elder, all to herself.'

'But why didn't Greg tell me that?'

'You have to understand something: Greg has always been protective of her – ever since our father died. He lets her away with anything, won't have a bad word said against her. I don't see that changing. Learn from Catherine. Love him, but don't take any crap from his mother.'

I stare into my beer. 'I should be more like her, shouldn't I, Catherine?'

'Just in *that* sense.'

'Sometimes I think Greg was looking for another Catherine when he met me.'

'What makes you say that?'

'Don't you think we look alike?'

He squints at me. 'OK, you're dark like she was, but that's it. Your face is softer.'

And then I'm sharing it, the worry that has started to grow in my mind. 'Maybe Greg didn't fall for me at all.'

'What are you talking about? He's mad about you.'

'Greg was probably hypomanic when we met.'

'Come again?'

'Hypomanic: the earliest stage of mania. Remember the barbecue? Remember how you thought that he was acting out of character? Well, maybe he was. Maybe he was at the beginning of his first high. Maybe he didn't fall for me at all, but an idea of what I was.'

'I don't believe that for a second.'

I lean forward. 'I've been reading all this stuff the hospital gave me and visiting website after website. Things keep hitting me. Like the fact that rejection triggers depression. Rob, after Greg's high,

I told him I was leaving, that I couldn't take any more. What if I caused his depression?'

'Or *what* if it was the disease just running its course? Lows follow highs. Or maybe something else triggered it, a stressful event. You don't know it was you.'

But I'm not listening. 'And then today I sent him tearing back to the hospital. Do you know what I told him? I told him I thought of running away, a million times a day. I'm afraid of what I might have done to him.'

'Look, Lucy, I'm no expert. But I know one thing: Greg loves you. Even when he's down, he's thinking about you. He's always asking after you. "Is she doing OK? Is she doing too much?" He's never asked for my help before. All of a sudden, he's asking me to organise money for you, a cleaner . . . I mean, no offence, I'm delighted to do it. You know that. I'm just making a point. He rang me, about an hour ago, and asked me to call over to make sure you were OK. He's about as low as a guy can get and he's still thinking about you. In my book, that says something. I know my brother. He loves you. Maybe you should stop reading all that stuff. Just go see him. Steer clear of my mother. And hang out with wonderful people like me.' He grins.

I smile.

'You'll get through this. I know you will. Trust me, I'm a teacher. We know everything.'

Funny how, of all people, it's Greg's happy-go-lucky brother who is holding our relationship together.

~

Next day, walking into the hospital with Rob and the children, I've no idea what to expect. I'm terrified that he'll have regressed. I'm even more terrified when we get to the ward and he's not there. His roommate directs us to an exercise room I never knew existed.

We find it. And Greg. Pummelling a punchbag. I don't know whether it's all that action or the fact that punchbags automatically make the puncher look more masculine, but he looks great, moving with determination and force.

'Dad,' says Toby. 'Can I've a go?'

He turns. Smiles. 'Hey,' he says, very Rocky. 'OK. Come on, a quick one.'

Greg stands behind his son as he throws a few wobbly punches.

'Cool,' says Toby.

'Right. Let's go,' says Greg, grabbing a towel, running it over his face and throwing it across his shoulders. Rob and I exchange a surprised glance as we follow him from the room. We drive to Greg's favourite destination, Sandymount Strand. Rob takes the children off for ice cream while Greg and I sit together on the same bench where he told Rachel and Toby about his bipolar disorder.

'I started group therapy today.'

'Oh, Greg, that's great.' But I don't understand; I rejected him *again*. The opposite should be happening.

'I made a decision. I'm going to get out of this. I'm going to do the art therapy, the group therapy, the psychotherapy, every bloody therapy they have.' There's colour in his cheeks, determination in his eyes.

'That's so great.'

'I'm sorry, Lucy. I've been an idiot. I should have involved you. I was trying to protect you, but all I did was push you away. No wonder you wanted to leave. I don't ever want you to feel like that again.' He takes my hands in his. 'I'm sorry about my mother. I should never have invited her. I should have known she'd be difficult.'

'Don't worry about it.'

'In future, I'll take her out to lunch with the children, and maybe Rob – if that's OK with you.'

'That's a better idea.'

'It was Betty's.'

'Clever woman.'

'She said something else.'

'What?'

'Most first trips home end in disaster.' He bumps me with his shoulder.

~

Hilary keeps phoning the house in search of Greg, then hanging up when I tell her he's not here. I'm not surprised when she turns up at the front door, late one evening, but I'm determined to end this.

'Greg's not here,' I say, beating her to it.

'I don't want to talk to Greg. I want to talk to you.'

I fold my arms. 'I can't help you, Hilary.'

'I don't want your help. I want to tell you something. About your precious boyfriend.'

I don't want to hear this. But I do.

She tries to come in.

I block her. 'Whatever it is, you can tell me here.'

'Suit yourself,' she says with a tilt of her head. 'He hasn't exactly been faithful to you, you know.'

No matter how untrustworthy the messenger, it's never something you want to hear.

I work hard at sounding bored when I say, 'Hilary, your lies are getting predictable. Don't you think Greg and I talk? Don't you think I *know* there were no other women, no private jokes at my expense?'

'OK. Maybe not women, but there was *a* woman.'

'Sure.'

'Oh, I'm sure all right. Because it was me. Why d'you think he sacked me?'

'He told me why. You came on to him.'

She laughs. 'Actually, he came on to me. Not that it matters. The end result was the same. He fucked the hired help, and didn't feel too good about it. Why d'you think I've been ringing him? Because he can't get off that lightly. You think you're so goddamn wonderful. Well, you're not . . .'

'OK. You've had your say.' I close the solid walnut door and slide down it. I wrap my arms around my legs and place my chin in the safe place between my knees. *He didn't do it*, I tell myself. *He wouldn't.* But I remember back. He was out of control, fired up, over-sexed. And it wouldn't have been his first time with Hilary.

~

Fingers fumbling, I call Grace.

'I have to ask him, straight out.'

'No. You can't confront him now. You have to wait until he's up to it. Then you can talk. For now, you have to believe that whatever he did when he was high doesn't count. Off limits.'

'I can't. If he and Hilary . . .'

'Stop, Lucy. What's important is how Greg is normally. That's all.'

'So I should let him off? He can do anything he likes when he's high and I can't say a thing?'

'You're actually accusing him of something he probably didn't do.'

'You don't know that.'

'Lucy. Stop. You said yourself, you can't believe anything she says.'

'This time I do.'

'Talk to Rob.'

'Why? He wasn't there.'

'No. But he knows what Greg's normally like . . .'

My God; I *don't.* The words come slowly: 'I don't know what Greg's normally like.'

'That's not what I said.'

But it's true. If he was hypomanic when we met, then I don't know what he's like when he's not. The very things I fell for in Greg are also symptoms of hypomania: enthusiasm, optimism, impetuousness, wit, energy, adventurousness, a busy mind. What if I didn't fall for Greg at all, just a bunch of symptoms? What if I love an illness, not a man? Do I even *know* him?

'Lucy? Are you there?'

I can't speak.

'You have to give him the benefit of the doubt. Be fair.'

'I'm sick of being fair.'

'Talk to Rob.'

'No. This is too big for me. I don't want it. It's not worth it.'

'Talk to Rob.'

'No, Grace. I've had it. I want out.'

'Listen to me. If anyone should leave their relationship, it's me. I don't have what you have. I never did. You're mad about each other. The way you look at one another, the way you touch. The first time I saw you together I knew what was missing between Kevin and me. Passion, love . . .'

'But—'

'You've been through so much and you're still together. Don't give up now when things are about to get better just because that manipulative bitch shows up on your doorstep. Wait till he's ready, then hear his side. Don't give up on what you have, Lucy. Not everyone has what you have.'

'But *do* I have it?'

'Trust me. You do.'

'How does this always happen? How do I consistently end up in a mess?'

'At least you didn't create it. I've no excuse. I walked into this marriage, trying to do the right thing for the wrong person. It's not going to get any better for me. Kevin will always be Kevin. He'll still be checking my legs for cellulite when I'm ninety. He'll still be expecting perfection – from me, from the boys. Greg will get better, Luce. And you can try again. Give yourselves that chance.'

'But what if it doesn't work out?'

'Then it doesn't work out. But you'll never be able to blame yourself for not trying. Not all relationships can withstand the pressure of bipolar disorder. There's no shame in it not working out. I just think you should at least see how things go when Greg has stabilised. I think you should give your relationship that chance.'

32.

Three weeks since Greg was hospitalised and he's due home for a full weekend. Considering the last visit and what's going on in my mind, I'm dreading it.

The children and I spend the afternoon making a vegetable curry. At five, we collect Greg. Toby talks, without pause, all the way home.

We eat together. Then Greg spends time with the children, curled up on the couch, watching a movie.

'I can't get over Rachel,' he says after they've gone to bed. 'She's making such an effort.'

'Huge. Tidying her room, helping around the house . . .'

'You seem to be getting on better?'

'Ever since your mum's visit.'

'Don't mention the war.'

He can still make me smile. 'Rachel was so sweet to me after you left that day.'

'Sorry I wasn't up to staying.'

I remember what Grace said about hospital being a sanctuary. 'I'm sorry too – for what I said.'

'No. I'm glad you said it. It woke me up. Lucy, I want to thank you. For everything. For sticking by me, for taking such good care of the kids. I knew you would. At times, I may not sound like I appreciate you, but I do. So much.' He closes his eyes.

'I know.'

'I'm sorry for anything I've ever said or done to upset you . . .'

I think of Hilary. 'It's OK. Forget it.' Can I, though?

'When I think of what I've put you through, I just can't . . .' His voice is crumbling.

'Greg, I understand. Honestly.'

'I love you.'

'I know. I know you do.'

'And I know you love me,' he says.

God.

'You wouldn't still be here if you didn't. You wouldn't be minding the children, coming to see me every day . . . I've been trying, Lucy.'

'I know. I know you have.'

'Attending every therapy, talking myself stupid. Forcing myself to get up, shave, get dressed, make an effort, eat . . . OK, I still can't sleep, but it's a matter of time. It's just a matter of time.'

'You're doing great.'

'I have to fight this, keep fighting it. I'll get out of it. I know I will.'

'You've already started.'

He smiles crookedly. 'Never thought *I'd* be the one they'd be telling, "Keep taking the tablets."'

~

We head up to bed early. Outside my room, he stoops to kiss me goodnight. It's our first kiss in weeks, a simple peck. I force a smile, but break down as soon as the door is closed behind me.

Somewhere in the house, the phone rings – and is answered. I freeze, hoping it's not Hilary. I pray that she's not hounding him, right now. I haven't told him about her calls, to protect him from that stress. But if it *is* Hilary, I've wasted my time.

To distract myself, I dress for bed and wash my face and teeth. I root in the drawer for one of my dog-eared books on step-parenting and climb into bed.

There's a gentle knock on my door. Greg pops his head in. 'Sorry for disturbing you, Lucy.'

I hold my breath.

He comes in. Closes the door. 'That was Ben.'

'Ben? What did he want at this time?'

'To know if it would be OK for Hilary to be there tomorrow when we take the kids over for their visit. He read somewhere that cutting off contact abruptly with childminders can be traumatic for children. He thought it would be good for them to see her.'

'And he didn't mention, *at all*, did he, what *Hilary* might like?'

He smiles. 'I've always loved you when you're angry.'

'I hope you said no.'

'Of course I said no. I haven't completely lost my marbles.'

I smile at that. 'What excuse did you give?'

'I just told him you don't like Hilary.'

'You did *not*.'

'No, I did not.' He smirks.

I fire a pillow at him.

He puts his hands up. 'Careful. Delicate man, here.'

And I'm smiling again. 'So, what *did* you tell him?'

'Just that I'd prefer if she wasn't there. And, in his usual, reserved way, he didn't ask why.'

'So, that's that, then.'

'That's that.' His gaze lingers. 'You look nice.'

No make-up, grey T-shirt over pyjama bottoms, I don't think so.

He comes over, stoops and kisses me slowly on the cheek. 'Goodnight.'

''Night,' I say hoarsely.

And when he closes the door, it hits me with force – I need to talk to Rob.

~

The day I've been dreading arrives. Though Greg has asked the children not to worry Ben, I'm terrified that something will slip out during the interrogation that their grandfather will, no doubt, subject them to.

Their Glenageary home, a two-storey-over-basement red-brick, is on one of Dublin's most prestigious roads. It is in mint condition, with a glossy black door and gleaming brasswork. Rich, heavy drapes are visible through the windows. Perfectly maintained box plants fill the matching metal window boxes that adorn each sill.

We climb the dust-free, granite steps.

Both grandparents appear at the door almost immediately after we knock.

'Children, Lucy, Greg,' exclaims Ben. 'Good to see you.'

'Hi, Granddad, hi, Gran,' say Rachel and Toby together, walking past them into a tiled hall.

Ruth follows, chatting to them, quietly stroking Toby's hair. It's clear she loves them.

'Bye, guys,' Greg calls.

They turn. 'Bye, Dad.'

'Would you like to come in?' Ben asks, his voice empty of welcome.

'No, thanks, we're off to the movies,' says Greg, almost inviting ridicule.

'Good, well, I'd better go in. We'll see you later, then? What time will you be here to collect them?'

'When the movie's over. Six-ish?'

I feel that Ben would like the time pinned down, which is probably why Greg is keeping it open.

'Good, good. See you then, then.' He closes the door firmly.

'I wish we didn't have to leave them there,' I say as we get into the car.

'Don't worry. They won't say anything.'

Much to my relief, Greg proves to be right. When we collect the children, Rachel boasts of how she stopped Toby from spilling the beans. Toby denies this and a fight breaks out, each claiming to be best at keeping secrets. I worry about how much we're asking of them.

On Sunday, Greg takes his mother out to lunch with Rob and the children. I make a long-overdue visit to my neglected apartment. So glad to be home, I kick off my shoes, throw my keys on the counter, open all the windows, check what's in the DVD player: Barbara Streisand and the Bee Gees. That'll do.

I take a Coke from the fridge and lounge across the couch. My eyes take a slow trip around the familiar, alighting on the paintings I've collected over the years, ever since my first pay cheque – the sparseness and simplicity of Robert Ryan, the richness of Stephen Cullen and the special attachment I feel to works done by friends.

I gaze at the Shona sculpture Brendan bought me in Sonoma Valley on that magical Californian holiday when he proposed. 'The Lovers' is carved from soapstone and features a man with hair like ropes, his arms wrapped protectively around his woman. I love it. Always have. I close my eyes and try to visualise Brendan's face, his smile. In the end, I have to find a photo. I run my finger over his tanned, vibrant face, then close my eyes. *Help me, Brendan. Please. Tell me what to do. Keep going? Or come home?*

I close my eyes and pray for a sign to take the decision from me. I've done this before – and nothing. But I open my eyes, anyway. Again, nothing. At first. Then in through the window flutters a tiny butterfly in chaotic, bouncy flight. It is such an unusual colour. Iridescent blue. I don't remember ever seeing one like it. It has no goal, no sense of direction; its flight light, optimistic, happy. And suddenly I know what to do – give Greg and our chaotic relationship a chance, talk to Rob, and try harder to understand. I stay watching that butterfly until it flies free, then it's time to go.

I begin to lock up. On my way out, I stop at the Shona sculpture, run my hand over its cool, smooth surface, and lean to kiss it.

'Thank you,' I say to the man who was my life.

~

Mid-afternoon, Rob returns to the house with the children, having dropped his mother to her home and Greg to the hospital.

'He's great, isn't he?' he says enthusiastically.

'Much better,' I agree.

'So much fitter, brighter. I know a lot of that's pure effort and he probably collapsed as soon as he got back to the ward, but, still, he's trying.'

'True. Rob?'

'Yeah?'

'Have you any plans for the rest of the day?'

He looks at me, knowing something's up. 'Nope.'

'Will you stay for a while?'

'Sure.'

I try not to think about what I have to ask him, and simply enjoy the entertainment the children are providing. Rachel's acting as seamstress. With needles, thread and felt that Mum gave her, she's for some reason making a pair of white felt underpants for Toby, opting for a simple design – two pieces of (stiff) cloth, cut into the shape of a T. Without realising it, she's making her brother a thong. She holds it up against his skinny little body and nods in silent satisfaction. Her stitches are big and blue.

She has to bribe him with sweets to model it. When he tries it on over his trousers, the seams burst. But he's done the job and wants the sweets. No sweets, Rachel insists, until she fixes the problem and he tries it on again. Toby's having none of it.

I broker a deal – one sweet now, and the rest after the next *and final* fitting session.

Peace reigns in time for dinner. Then, I free the thonged superhero from the sewing enthusiast and give him a quick bath before bed.

Wrapped in a towel, with another draped over his head, he looks like a nun. A cute nun.

'Who are you, again, Sister Alfonsis Xavier? Or Sister Glorious Halleluiah? I can never tell you apart.'

He produces that adorable smile of his. 'Fonsis Zavier.'

'You're a sweetie. You know that?'

'Yup.'

I smile, kiss the top of his head, read *Captain Underpants*, hug him goodnight. It's great; we've moved on to hugging.

''Night, bub,' he says.

''Night, Captain Underpants.'

I'm alone with Rob. It's what I've been waiting for and simultaneously dreading all afternoon. Sitting on the couch, he looks so trusting, so bloody balanced, I know I can tell him.

'Rob, I need your help.'

'Sure. What's up?'

I try to organise my thoughts. 'Remember the other day, when I said I thought Greg may have been hypomanic when we met?' He opens his mouth to speak, but I have to keep going.

'It's just that if he *was*, then I've never known him otherwise – except depressed. I've never known him just as he is. And I need to. I need to know what was a symptom and what was really Greg. *You* know him, Rob. He's your brother.' He sits up. 'There's something else, and I can't get it out of my head. Hilary told me something happened between her and Greg on the night he fired her.'

'No way.'

'I keep telling myself that whatever he did when he was high doesn't count, that it's what he's *normally* like that's important. But I don't *know* what he's normally like with women. I don't know what he's normally like, full stop. I need to.'

'OK, firstly—'

'Rob, please tell me you won't go back to Greg with this.'

'Come on, Lucy. Give me some credit. This is the last thing he needs to hear.'

'I'm sorry. I want to trust my love for him – so badly – but I need to get to know him all over again, learn what's real, solid, what I can believe in.'

'I don't know where to start.'

'What's he normally like with women?' Trust is the biggest issue, I realise. Without it, there can be no relationship. 'Please don't keep anything from me. I need to know.'

'There's nothing to keep. After Catherine, there was no one. I tried to set him up a few times; he told me where to go. How did he put it? He had a wife to remember, children to raise and a book to write. If someone flirted with him, he skedaddled. He was a one-woman man. Until you.'

'Do you think he and Hilary ever . . . ?'

'No! Their relationship revolved around the children. I'm stunned by what you've said.'

Maybe Rob's not the best person to ask about women. 'Tell me about Greg before I knew him, before all this.'

'What do you want to know?'

I remember what attracted me to him. 'Was he always an optimist?'

'An optimist?' He makes a face. 'I wouldn't say an *optimist* . . . More a realist. He's always looked to a better future, but worked hard for it, you know?'

Immediately, I rationalise. To be optimistic would have been naïve; blindly believing that good will happen negates the need to work for it. It strikes me: not only do I have to uncover the real Greg, but I have to re-evaluate the qualities I once thought important. Can I do that with everything?

'But he was always sharp, right?'

'Sharpest tool in the shed. Always.'

'He took life pretty seriously, though, didn't he?' I don't want a yes here.

'Yeah, but he could be fun. He's always had a sense of humour. When we were kids, if I'd had a really bad day at school, to cheer me up, he could be so fucking funny. He'd mimic one of the teachers – any of them – he had them all down to a T. He'd have me cracking up.'

I smile, remembering how he used to do that with Matt. How simple and uncomplicated everything was then, when he was just this great, fun guy who embraced life and me. I miss him so much.

'Lucy, I could talk and talk about Greg. But you'll see for yourself if you just wait. He's a great guy – a special guy, actually. I've seen him through the best and worst times, and, to be honest, I wish I were more like him. That's all I can say. You just have to hang on – like he has to. Just hang tight till he gets through this. The good times will come again.'

I nod. I might not be able to trust the times we've had, but if I hold on until Greg has stabilised, then I can judge. Like Grace said, if Greg comes out of this and it's not working, then we can end it, knowing we gave it our best shot. So I'll wait for the boy who brought up his kid brother. I'll wait for the man who survived the loss of his wife and raised his children alone. I'll wait for Greg to fight his biggest fight, this unfathomable illness that has taken his mind hostage. If anyone can get through it, he can. And yet, the insecurity of not knowing who will emerge at the other end remains. Maybe Greg Millar doesn't need to be impulsive, fun, impetuous and gregarious for me to love him. But those are the things I fell for. If they're gone, what will be left behind?

33.

A few days before the children return to school for the autumn term is too late to get organised, I discover – the hard way. I have to queue with them for books, uniforms, shoes and haircuts. First day back, we're twenty minutes late, teaching me the valuable lesson of how long it takes to get two children ready to a deadline.

School has its tests, too. When collecting Toby, first day, I stand alone, watching mothers (who all seem to know each other) stoop to kiss and hug their children. I wait, feeling inadequate, insecure. Toby appears, his eyes searching the mums. When he sees me, he smiles and starts to run. My heart soars. I squat. He nearly knocks me over. Can what I'm feeling really be love?

When Rachel comes out, half an hour later, it's a different scene. The older children talk together in small groups until they see their parents, then just walk to them. No big deal. No hugs. The relief I feel reminds me that, while Rachel and I may be getting on well, our relationship does not extend to physical contact.

Now that the children are back at school, my parents mind them in the afternoons, allowing me to return to a full day at work. I take a late lunch and nip to the school to taxi the kids to my parents'. Dad would willingly do this, but I want to be there for them when they come out. I also want, I discover, the same things for

Rachel and Toby that a real parent might – to like their new teachers, find work easy, be happy, fit in.

One day, I overhear a woman invite her daughter's friend over for the afternoon. I ask Rachel if she'd like to do the same. She would. And does. I take a half-day and a girl called Keelin comes to visit. To distract Toby from following the two of them around, I decide to take the stabilisers off his bike and teach him to cycle. I hold the saddle, instructing him to keep his weight in the centre and look where he's going rather than at the pedals. The girls potter around. I so like this, I so don't like that. It reminds me of how young Rachel is, but how old she wants to be.

~

It never occurs to me that Greg might have liked to be the one to teach his son to cycle, until I see his face when I tell him I have. It's then I appreciate that, in trying to do my best, I've started doing too much. Roles are blurring. I have to step back.

When Toby decides to take up hurling, I see my chance. Maybe Greg would like to be there for his first lesson?

He would.

It's a Friday. I collect Greg. Together, we pick the children up from school. We drop Rachel off at hockey then drive to the Gaelic sports grounds with Toby. He jumps out and runs to catch up with friends from his class. He's given a bright blue helmet and a hurley stick. So cute – the helmet's almost bigger than him.

Before long, there's a hall full of what look like mini aliens racing around in circles. They have no fear, tearing after the ball, sticks swinging wildly and the sound of clashing wood echoing. Toby's a little flier. And a great man for stopping the ball. He isn't like I used to be at sport – an eye-closer. I'm so proud of him.

'Come on, Toby, whack it.' *Was that me?*

Greg looks at me and laughs. Actually laughs.

In the car on the way back, Toby is animated. 'That was the best day of my life. I was Man of the Match, Dad. Did you see that?'

Greg turns around to him. 'You were great, Tobes.'

'Was I?'

'Exceptional.'

'Was I better than exceptional?'

'You were spectacular.'

'Was I better than spectacular?'

'You were splendiferous.'

'That good?'

'That good.'

I look in the rear-view mirror at a flushed and beaming child. And I have a flavour of what it must feel like to be a real mum.

That evening, while two exhausted children watch *Finding Nemo*, Greg decides to go for a swim. I throw on a hoodie and we make our way to the end of the garden. The breeze carries a September chill, and already the light is beginning to fade. The water is grey and choppy. The surface is thick with bladderwrack.

Greg wades, knee-deep, preparing to dive off.

'You're mad,' I call, then realise what I've said.

'You're only realising that now?' He smiles, then dives in and swims out with a strong overarm. 'Come on in,' he calls. 'It's . . . freezing.'

'Tempting. But I think I'll pass.'

He swims for a good five minutes, then back in, runs up the steps and shakes himself on me. I scream, jump out of the way and throw him his towel. He snatches it mid-air and begins to dry himself. I'm surprised by the shape he's in. He's heading for a six-pack. I feel something I haven't felt in weeks. It catches me by surprise as it did that first time, in a snug on the outskirts of Dublin.

'That'd cure any man's depression,' he says, dragging on his denims. I hand him his shirt. He takes it from me and kisses me quickly. His lips are cold and salty. Alive. I look into his eyes and return the kiss. Properly. He pulls back, his eyes searching mine as if to say, 'Do you really want this?'

'Don't stop,' I breathe.

Then his mouth is on mine, icy fingers cupping my face. Oh, God. I've missed this. Freezing hands slip up under my T-shirt. He groans when he reaches my breasts. Our hips press together, our kisses urgent now. He lifts my hoodie and T-shirt up over my head. Our mouths meet again. He lifts me up. I wrap my legs around him, my nipples brushing against his chest. He carries me to the changing area, where, in the company of the swirling September breeze, he lies his damp towel down, and we at last let go of our worries, fears and thoughts of tomorrow.

~

Saturday. The children visit Ben and Ruth. There's a keeping-secrets competitiveness between them now that worries me; they shouldn't have to hide things from their family.

When we collect them, we have lunch together, then Greg spends time with them, while I go shopping.

Later, Rob babysits, while Greg and I go out for a meal. It's such a treat to have a normal conversation about nothing in particular. Like old times. Which are still relatively young times.

Sunday, we get up late and take it easy. Then Greg, Rob and the children go out for lunch with Phyllis. This time, Greg returns to the house. Only at the very last minute does he prepare to head back to the hospital. I feel like a school-hating child on a Sunday night, longing for just one more day. That changes when Greg says, 'I'm ready to come home.'

I stop folding the hoodie I've been packing.

'I'll tell Betty when I get in,' he says with a certainty I don't share.

We've discussed the logistics of his coming home. I'm supposed to stay living in the house until he's feeling better. I'm to monitor his moods and call the hospital if I feel he's becoming too animated or too down. I was fine with that – happy, even, to be finally included in his care. But his sudden announcement changes that. Am I really the right person to do this? Wouldn't Rob be better? He's known Greg his entire life. How can I tell the difference between a normal mood swing and an abnormal one? I don't want to ring the hospital, worried, only to discover he's just fed up about something anyone would be.

'OK,' I say with a brightness I don't feel. Now that he's finally making progress, I'm not going to be the one to stop it.

Two days later, Greg comes home for a trial period of a week. As advised, we try to settle into a routine. With Fint's agreement, I go back to working from home. I think it best that the children continue to go to my parents' in the afternoon, although for shorter visits. I don't want to land too much on Greg, and, although I don't say it, I feel it wise to stick to the routine, in case things don't work out.

After three days, I ring Betty, worried about his progress.

She establishes that he's getting up in the morning, eating and sleeping at night, then hints that the problem might be mine. She talks of letting him take his first steps himself, encouraging him and appreciating that even the smallest steps will be monumental to him. She suggests I get out of the house for a few hours in the morning. And so, it's back to half-days at the office.

When Greg is officially discharged a week later, he does everything by the book. He takes his little white tablet every night and the coloured ones during the day. He attends every appointment: Prof Power fortnightly, anxiety management once a week, outpatients every two weeks to have his lithium levels checked. Getting better is a full-time job. I do my bit, keeping a nervous eye out for mood swings.

Betty's right. The small steps, when made, do seem monumental, even to me. An offer to help with homework. A dinner prepared. Another quiet, but firm refusal to drink. The very first time Greg gets up before eleven – especially that.

'Thank you, Dad, for the lovely dinner,' says Rachel.

'Thank you, Dad, for the story,' says Toby.

They notice every little thing he does for them. And he notices them noticing. It makes him try harder. He starts to swim, every morning. It gets him out of bed, kick-starts his day. We buy a punchbag and install it on the landing, so we can all have a swing at it whenever the mood grabs us. Toby takes a particular shine to it, contributing as it does to his ambitious muscle development programme.

As the weeks pass, Greg begins to collect the children from school. Twice a week, they go to my parents'; otherwise, Greg brings them to whatever activity they have on, or else home. That the children are increasingly happy is evident from random snatches of conversation.

'What's Mr Incredible called again?' Toby asks Rachel.

'Bob.'

'Oh, yeah.'

Not so long ago, Mr Incredible wouldn't have mattered.

With every new responsibility he takes on, Greg moves towards recovery, regaining his pride, his life. Not yet ready to resume writing, he finds an outlet for his creativity in the garden, a place that's tolerant and forgiving of his lack of concentration and slowed mental agility. He and the children begin to plan a vegetable patch. They look up books, consult the local garden centre and map out the garden. Then they get going. To look out and see three backs hunched over together, busy planting, is to imagine a brighter future.

~

When Greg finally feels up to greeting the outside world, he recharges his iPhone and switches it on. It's a big step. Which is ruined by Hilary. Within hours, she calls. The first I learn of it is when Greg comes to my bedroom, all colour gone from his face.

'Did Hilary call here?'

I put down the book I've been reading, knowing instinctively that this is it. The Hilary showdown has arrived, I fear, before he's ready. 'Yes.'

'What did she say?'

One thing I've learned is that when you're dealing with Hilary, it's wise to be straight. 'That you sacked her because you and she . . .' I finish the sentence with my eyes.

'Shit. Why didn't you say anything?'

'I was waiting till you were ready, Greg.'

'Jesus.' He runs his hand over his mouth. 'What, exactly, did she say?'

'That you came on to *her*, not the other way round.'

'Not true.'

'She said that it didn't matter, either way, because the end result was the same – you fucked her, then fired her because you couldn't admit to what you'd done.'

'Christ,' he whispers.

'What happened that night, Greg? I need to know.'

He nods. 'When you left the villa, Hilary came downstairs. She started the same thing about me needing to see a doctor. I didn't want to hear it, not twice in one night, not when I knew there was something in it. But she kept going. Then she started on about you not understanding me like she did, not seeing that anything was wrong. She said I was making a mistake with you. And then, well, basically, she . . . started to get physical. I'm going to be honest with you, Lucy. I was tempted – not because it was Hilary, but because I was high as a kite. I'd have jumped on a goat. But I didn't. I swear. I left. Drove. Tried to sort my disorganised, wired-to-the-moon mind into logical thought. I decided she had to go. It was the only way. To keep her on, knowing how she felt, would have been dishonest. To everyone.'

'Why didn't you tell me the next day when I asked what happened?'

'You know the way I was. Everything was spinning out of control. I couldn't organise my thoughts. I couldn't trust myself to tell you and not botch it. Lucy, I love you. I'd never consciously do anything to hurt you.' His eyes are so sad when he says, 'But, somehow, I always seem to manage it.'

'But why does she keep ringing?'

He sighs. 'I was hoping to protect you from this.'

I give him a look that says, 'Enough protecting.'

'OK. When the calls started, she was looking for her job back, saying she'd made a mistake. I felt a bit sorry for her, then. I didn't know how she'd been with you. I knew she missed the kids. But I couldn't risk her coming back. I tried to explain that she needed a life apart from us. She wouldn't listen. Then she changed her attitude completely. Started to threaten me. She said if I didn't take her back, she'd sue me for sexual harassment.'

'What? Oh my God!'

'I hoped she was bluffing. Waited for the solicitor's letter, but none ever came. Then one day she rang to ask if I'd enjoyed the visit from Ben and Ruth. I felt the pressure building. I was dealing with a loose cannon. She seemed intent on causing trouble. I sometimes wonder if the pressure of all that sent me into the depression.'

'I can't *believe* the sexual harassment thing.'

'It would've ruined everything – our relationship, my reputation, career. God knows how I'd have kept it from Rachel.'

'Why d'you think she didn't go through with it?'

'I don't know. Maybe she got legal advice. Maybe it would have cost too much. Or maybe it was just a threat she never intended to carry out. I don't know.'

'What did she say, just now?'

'That she hoped you'd got over the news OK.'

I shake my head. 'I can't understand how she thinks that this kind of behaviour will get her job back.'

'It's gone beyond that, Lucy. She knows there's no hope of that now. It's gone to another level. She wants to cause as much damage as she can.' He sits on the bed and reaches for my hand. 'Thank God, you didn't believe her. Thank God, you had faith in us.'

I can't look at him.

'Lucy?'

I meet his eyes.

'You do still love me?'

I nod.

'If you've changed your mind, I'll understand. I've put you through so much. And who knows what's ahead? If you want to leave, then maybe now would be a good time.' He's looking at me as if he knows everything that has been going on in my mind.

'I'm not leaving.'

'Think about it. Your life would be easier, freer, less complicated. You could start again with someone else – someone who doesn't have . . . this.'

'I don't want anyone else.'

'We're not married; we're not tied to each other. Don't feel guilty if you want to go. Just do it. Please. I don't want to live with a martyr.'

I leave my spot on the bed, crawl to where he's sitting and put my arms around him. 'I love you, Greg. I'm going nowhere.'

We hold each other for a long time until one thing leads, happily, to another.

I fall asleep with his arm around me.

In the morning, when Greg is returning to his room before the children wake, he speaks decisively.

'It's time to put a stop to Hilary. We need to talk to her as a couple – present a united front. The reason she's got away with this for so long is that we haven't been united. We are now. And we need to tell her nothing she does will break us. She'll give up; she'll have to.'

I look doubtful.

'We have to end this, Lucy. Once and for all.'

~

Hilary calls at the house the following morning. She's made an effort with her clothes, wearing a clean, white shirt and a long, navy skirt. She has also washed her hair.

'You never said *she'd* be here,' she says as Greg shows her into the sitting room.

'Hilary, why don't you sit down?' says Greg, taking control.

She does.

We all do.

'Hilary,' he says. 'The reason we're both here is to show you that we're still very much a couple. Whatever you do to try to spoil that only brings us closer. I'm sorry if you ever got the impression that your job was more than a job. That was partly my fault. I made a mistake a long time ago, and I'm very sorry about that. You were a great nanny. The best. But you stepped over the line. I love Lucy. And that's that. It's time you moved on now, built your own life, around yourself.'

'End of lecture?'

Greg raises an eyebrow.

'I've invested years of my life in this family,' she says. 'I won't be discarded like a used cloth. I love Rachel and Toby. You can't keep me from them. And, let's not forget, you were the one who stepped over the line back then, not me.'

'Hilary. You've done nothing but lie. You tried to turn Lucy against me, the children against Lucy, Ben and Ruth against us. We can't trust you.'

'You can, you can. I'm sorry about that. It was a mistake. I was afraid.' She's leaning forward, clutching her mini rucksack. Her fingernails have been bitten so low, the fleshy parts of her fingers are peeping over the top.

'Hilary,' says Greg, 'it's time to move on, start your own life, separate from us.'

'Don't sit there so smugly and tell me what I need. How do *you* know what I need? Who are you to decide? Who are you to take the children from me? You can't just dismiss me with the snap of your fingers after all I've done for you. I'm a person. I have feelings. You can't treat me like this.' She breaks down.

I remind myself of what she's done, how she's created this situation for herself.

She wipes her tears impatiently, stands suddenly. 'This isn't over. I'll find a way. I won't give up. I'll bide my time. Do it right. You'll see.' She storms from the house.

My heart's hammering. 'Oh, Greg! This was a mistake. It was like two against one. Maybe you should have met her alone.'

'No. She had to see that we're a couple. She had to see that we won't be bullied.'

'But we've only made her madder than ever. She wants revenge. I feel she's going to do something, I really do.'

'Don't worry.' He puts an arm round me. 'It'll be fine.'

I wish I could believe him.

34.

Weeks pass with no word from Hilary. We begin to breathe again. Maybe Greg was right. All she needed was to see that we're together, properly together. As Christmas approaches, she starts to fade from my mind. Toby's questions begin as soon as the decorations make their first shimmer in the shops. Are Santa's elves slaves? Is he *covered* in soot when he gets back to the North Pole? Has he only one suit?

As soon as Toby sees cars going by with trees strapped to their roofs, the requests begin for ours. Before long, we are inhaling pine, listening to Frank Sinatra and imagining chestnuts roasting on open fires. I still prefer 'The little Lord Jesus lay down his sweet head . . . The little Lord Jesus asleep on the hay,' which is being sung over and over by Toby as rehearsals continue for the school play.

Rachel makes a crib out of three black cardboard sheets stuck together into a triangle, the Get Smart logo turned in. You can tell, by the care she takes, that this isn't just a crib, but a home for Mary and Jesus. It's their first year without Joseph, who met an untimely death last Christmas when he fell and his head rolled under the fridge. Mary stands guard behind Jesus. The Three Wise Men and shepherds line up on the right-hand side of the crib, the animals on the left. Nice, orderly crib. And still I wait for her to turn to me and ask where I'll be spending Christmas. Greg seems to assume that we'll be together. But it's such a traditional time and I don't want to upset anyone. And so, one night, I ask him.

'Here,' he says. 'Of course.'

'But Rachel . . . ?'

'Has already asked if you can spend Christmas with us.'

'Really?' I touch my heart. My eyes fill. It is the best gift I could get.

Greg and I shop together when the children are at school. That they both want surprises forces me to really think about their personalities. Walking around the shops, I realise that I have started to know them. It no longer seems impossible that one day we might become a family.

The Christmas plays signal the final run-in. Toby's is first. He is Rudolph. The spotlight is on his nose when he picks it, demonstrating that even legends can have bad habits. To prove the point, he removes his cardboard antlers and begins to chew them. When we go up to the stage to collect him, we overhear him say to another reindeer, probably Donner or Blitzen, 'I'm so proud of myself. Are *you* proud of *yourself*?' One thing's for sure. I'm proud of him.

Rachel, for her performance, swaps with someone, to become one of the Three Wise Kings. Angels are so boring. She makes a very beautiful, very wise king. My claps might be loudest.

It's customary, on Christmas Eve, for Ben and Ruth to break with tradition and come to the house with their gifts. It's a simple enough evening. Their focus is on the children. They sit, a little less straight-backed than usual, sipping politely on sherry, commenting on the decorations and weather. They leave before nine.

On Christmas morning, Greg slides an arm around me as we watch the children rip open their surprises. And while they're busy with their newly discovered treasures, we slip into the kitchen to exchange gifts. I found it hard to choose for him – everything has been so delicate between us – but, in the end, I settled for a giant telescope so he could look to the stars.

'Excellent. I've always wanted to spy on the neighbours.'

The oil painting he gives me means so much. Not just because it is beautiful and by one of my favourite artists, but because, for the first time, I have an excuse to hang something of my own here. I have my own little space.

Turkey in the oven, we go to Christmas Mass, then on to my parents'. As requested, the children have made, rather than bought, their gifts: Toby, an apple tart for my dad and shortbread biscuits in the shape of angels for Mum. Rachel has sewn a pink gingham apron for Mum. For Dad, she has fashioned a kind of holder for his tools. Made from heavy fabric, it ties around his waist so that, when he's working, everything is at hand. My parents are thrilled. Grace and Kevin arrive with the boys, and the tempo rises. I notice the lack of eye contact between my sister and her husband; independently, they focus on the children. Neither smiles at the other as if to say, 'Aw, look at that.' There isn't one look, one word between them to reassure me. I want to wave a magic wand and make it right. More than anyone, Grace deserves happiness.

We arrive back to the smell of turkey, which has been roasting away all by itself. Within the hour, Rob and his mother arrive for Christmas dinner. I've had a few glasses of wine, which softens the edge of Phyllis. I ignore her comments, concentrating instead on how far we've all come in the last few months.

On St Stephen's Day, I go horse racing at Leopardstown with Fint, a sacred tradition that can't be broken. We put our money down, lose it all, eat steak sandwiches and warm our insides with port. I make an early New Year's Resolution to spend more time with friends.

New Year's Eve sees Greg and me return to the restaurant of our first date. I look across at him, as handsome as ever, but with eyes that seem more knowing and humble. So much has happened between us in so little time. There's a temptation to say, 'Let's forget it all and start over.' Neither of us does. We've seen each other raw, laid bare, and, hard though that's been, to lose it would be a mistake. It's part of who we are now.

Still, at midnight, we toast to a year that will be nothing like the last.

~

January sees Greg sitting down to write again. It's like going back in time. He stares at the screen, stuck.

'I can't do this,' he says, eventually. 'It's cotton wool in here,' he adds, tapping his head. He looks at me. 'How can I be creative with my thoughts reined in by lithium?'

I don't have an answer. But I try. 'Maybe if you just write something to get started. Anything. And just keep going till you reach the end, *then* worry about what you've written. Isn't that what Stephen King says?'

'Stephen King. The fucking expert. Bet *he's* not on lithium.'

'Well, coming off it isn't an option, Greg.'

He pushes back his chair. 'Why not? I'm fine. If I stop and get a bit high or low, I'll just take it again.' He's looking at me as if it's a great idea.

'If it was that easy, they wouldn't spend so much time warning you against it.'

'They just say that to be on the safe side. I bet some people can control it, once it's been tamed. I bet I can. I know I can.'

'Greg, don't risk it. Everything's coming together for us now, finally. The only problem is the writing and . . .'

'Writing's my life. If I can't write, I *will* get depressed.'

A point.

'Have you any idea what it's like to have to take pills every single day for the rest of your life?'

Another point.

'Every time I reach for one, it reminds me that I've a mental illness.'

Make that three.

'Lucy, if I come off, you can keep an eye on me, tell me if I'm heading up or down. I'll go straight back on them, I promise.'

I've made another New Year's Resolution: to move back to my apartment and return to work full-time. That won't happen if Greg stops his lithium. I'll have to hang around the house watching his every move. And so, because my motivations aren't entirely pure, I feel guilty. Which weakens my resolve. Especially as he keeps on about it over the next few days.

But then I speak to Grace.

'Lucy, this happens all the time. As soon as people feel well again, they think it's OK to stop. It isn't.' She's unpacking Shane's lunch box.

'But the lithium is making his head muzzy.'

She turns to me, Tupperware in one hand, bread crusts in the other. 'No, it's not. It might be slowing things down a bit, but it doesn't cause muzziness. It's probably the antidepressant.' She throws the crusts in the bin, the Tupperware in the dishwasher, rubs her hands together and joins me at the table.

'He's convinced it's the lithium,' I say.

'Well, unconvince him. You have to make him stay on it. It's that simple.' She sips the coffee I've made her.

'He thinks he's different from everyone else. He thinks he can control it, that he can take the lithium again if his moods start to change.'

'And that's exactly what has sunk so many people. The next "up" could be way up, the next "down", further down – and harder to get out of. Greg needs to keep taking the lithium. And it's up to you to convince him to.'

'How, though?'

'Remind him what he was like. Warn him you won't go through it again. Tell him you'll leave.'

'Do I have to spend my entire life bullying him?'

'If it means he'll continue to take his lithium, yes. Look, no matter how sensible or rational or frustrated he gets, you can't let him stop. Go see Professor Power. He'll know a way around this. Maybe he'll cut down the dose of the antidepressant.'

'Hmm.'

'Lucy, don't make the mistake of forgetting how bad it got. Don't forget what it was like coming down that mountain.'

I let out a long breath. 'OK. I'll try to get him to see Professor Power.'

'Well, do. Otherwise he might just stop and not tell you.'

That convinces me. Now all I have to do is convince Greg. And I do. I take him back, make him relive his high from our point of view. Remembering it all, I get upset, distressed. When I say I can't go through it again, I mean it.

We go to see Professor Power together, who reduces the dose of the antidepressant and explains that this is the beginning of weaning Greg off. He suggests waiting a week or two before trying to write again.

~

'Why did you stay with me?' Greg asks that evening, staring into the fire.

I sit on the arm of his chair. 'Because I love you.'

'But I treated you so badly.'

'*You* didn't. The illness did. I only told you how bad it got so you'd stay on the lithium. It's over now. I just want it to stay that way.'

'I knew it was bad. I knew I hurt you. But . . .'

'It wasn't you.'

'You didn't know that.'

'I loved you.' It's the truth. And I love him now. Does it matter that I had moments of doubt? It may be a different kind of love from the one we started out with, but it's stronger. I feel it.

35.

After two weeks, Greg tries writing again, this time in longhand. One evening, I'm glancing across at him. Spiral notebook on his lap, he's spending more time sucking his pen than using it.

'Why don't you forget Cooper? Write something else.'

He takes the pen from his mouth, looks over. 'Like what?' The question lacks optimism.

'I don't know. Something completely different. Something from the heart.' I think for a second, then shrug. 'What it's like to have depression?'

He groans.

'Why not?'

'Too depressing.'

I smile and rethink. 'How about just documenting what you've been through.'

'I couldn't put that in a book.'

'You wouldn't have to. Do it for yourself.'

'Why?'

'Just to get you writing again.'

He seems to consider it.

'You could give it a simple structure. Something short, like a letter . . .'

He's listening.

'You could write it to me. To help me understand what it was like for you.'

He looks hesitant. 'I don't think so.'

'You've always said you find writing easier than talking.'

'I don't know, Lucy. Let me think about it, OK?'

'OK.'

Two days later, he begins to write. I don't ask what. He's off, though. That's the main thing. He writes longhand at first, then transfers back to the computer. Soon, he's flying.

We settle into a new routine. Greg drops the children off at school and writes in the morning while I head to work. On the two afternoons the children are with my parents, he also writes. Otherwise, he's there for them. Sometimes, after dinner, he disappears to his office for another hour or so.

Two months after the coming-off-lithium scare, he has forgotten all about it. He is engrossed in his writing and his life. I feel it's time for him to become fully independent. We agree that I should move back to the apartment.

It seems very quiet there.

~

For months, Greg writes. In April, he gets a call from his editor wanting to know how he's getting along with the next Cooper book. That focuses his mind.

'What'll I tell her?' he asks me.

'You're working on another project?'

'That would make me in breach of contract.'

'Oh.'

'And, anyway, what I'm writing is not for publication.'

I look at him.

His expression softens. 'It's for you. My trip through psychosis.' He smiles awkwardly. 'I'm bringing you with me. If you still want to come.'

I sit on his lap and snuggle into him. 'I do.'

'There won't be a Cooper book this year, at the rate I'm going.'

'I suppose you'd better tell them.'

He does. They're not impressed. They've promised the book trade another one. What will they give them instead?

I remember a book cover I did for a collection of articles and essays by another well-known novelist. I thought it a bit of a cop-out at the time. Now I see it as a way out. I suggest to Greg that he publish a collection of short works he's already written. He takes the idea to his agent, who passes it on to Copperplate like a relay baton – embellishing it before handover. Copperplate buys it. It means nothing to them that little effort will be required from Greg. All that matters is that the book will sell. International publishers share Copperplate's enthusiasm. Greg has time to breathe.

~

We spend summer in Dublin, Greg writing, me working and the children attending summer camps with their friends, something they've always missed out on by going to France.

By mid-August, Greg's finished. He holds what has become an entire manuscript in his hands.

'Are you sure you want to read this?' he asks.

'Try and stop me.'

He hesitates. 'There are things in here I haven't told you. Couldn't.'

'That's OK,' I say, but I've started to worry.

'I love you, Luce. I want you to know that before you read it. I've always loved you, however low I got. I want you to understand that.'

Oh, God. What's in it? 'I do, Greg. I do.'

He hands over the wad of A4 pages. I smile to hide my fear. Will I be able to hide my reaction to what he's written, though? 'I need to read this on my own, Greg. Is that OK?'

He nods. 'Better, actually.' He smiles then, and I know I'm not alone in my fear.

Suddenly, I want to throw it away. Not know. Things have been so good between us.

He takes me in his arms and holds me tight. He kisses me, then lets me go. And when he looks into my eyes, it's as if he's hoping it won't be for the last time. I want to thrust it back into his hands, tell him we're fine now, we don't need it. But he has taken this step, this hugely courageous step for me, for us. And I can't stand back from it now. It's what I've always wanted, to share his journey. I just have to find the courage. From somewhere.

~

In the apartment, though it's half eleven on a Saturday morning, I climb into bed with the truth. I take a deep breath and turn the cover page.

He starts by taking me back to when we first met, explaining that, driving to the meeting, he was feeling the best he'd felt in his life, the most energetic, powerful, alive. Why? Because he was hypomanic.

I bite the back of my hand. *So, he didn't love me.* But then I remember his face when he handed the manuscript to me, and his declaration of love, as if he knew I'd need to hear it. He wanted me to keep going. I close my eyes, take a moment. And pick it up again.

Greg explains that, if he hadn't been hypomanic, he'd never have had the confidence to pursue me; he'd have taken my refusal at face value. His optimism stills me. Rather than doubting his love because of hypomania, as I have done, he *appreciates* it for getting us together.

Reading on, I come to understand Greg's high from his point of view: how he wanted everything to happen immediately, including marriage; how he believed that he was indestructible. He could outsmart, outwrite, outdrive anyone. He truly believed he could do anything. Bring on the adventure. Bring on the challenge. Nothing couldn't be conquered. The world needed to witness his genius, his way with words, his great sexual feats. I remember that time in the restaurant. If I could have looked inside his mind back then, it would have explained so much.

I have to keep readjusting my perception of the past. Intense experiences we shared, I'm reliving from Greg's point of view. The time I confronted him about drugs: he wished he had been on something because he'd have had some explanation for his behaviour. When he accused me of having problems, he wasn't just trying to deflect attention away from himself, he really did think there was something wrong with me – I was doing everything so slowly. And I never knew, never imagined, that one of the reasons Greg avoided us during that time was because he couldn't take the fear he saw in our eyes.

After the thunderstorm, when I told him I couldn't go on, and he began to behave reasonably again, he wasn't responsible for that. He had started to come down from his high naturally. It had nothing to do with our conversation. It was the result of brain chemicals.

The struggle to keep going, to keep doing those simple things that had once been automatic, was enormous. Everything that had given him joy became impossible – writing, reading, communicating, living. The man whose life had been books could no longer read to the end of a sentence let alone steer his thoughts into writing one. And the reaction of the people he loved only served as a reminder that something was desperately wrong.

I learn the enormity of what I was asking Greg to do in seeing a doctor. I was urging him to admit failure, to relinquish his role as hero to his children. How could he be their hero and have a mental illness? And how could he even look after them, if he couldn't look after himself? Despite all that, he went to the doctor because he loved me and didn't want to lose me.

And I doubted his love.

All day, I read, unable to stop, to detach, to move from the bed.

When Greg told me he was trying to protect me by isolating me, I never imagined the extent of what he was trying to protect me from. When he was admitted to hospital so quickly and for so long, I never dreamed it could have been because he was suicidal. He thought of ending his life, constantly. He even planned it. Genuinely planned to take his life, to leave us. I feel my heart break, actually tear open, rip apart. The tears I'm crying must be made of blood. Because ordinary tears just aren't enough. Pages fall, scatter. I want to shake him and scream, 'Why?' But the answer is lying, silent, on the bed. Waiting.

He felt so far away. He wasn't just down; he was underground, in the dark, cold earth, already in the grave, but living. There was no escape in sleep, because he could not sleep. He'd lie awake watching the sunrise, wondering, as he'd once said to me, how he'd get through another entire day. Greg was in a tunnel with no light at the end. Then suicide became the light. It made absolute sense. What was the point in living when he already felt dead? Better to end it and save everyone the pain of living with him.

That I was so concerned with my own survival at that time, with no clear understanding of what *he* was going through, makes me feel insensitive, clumsy, stupid and, of course, guilty.

Greg took his medication with absolutely no hope that anything would improve. But slowly, very slowly, the opaque screen that had been shielding us from him began to fade and he remembered why he loved us. He realised that he needed to fight for us. There were things that helped: certain things I inadvertently said; being able to explain his condition to the children and their acceptance of him; being able to talk to Betty, then me; exercise; the hospital chaplain; getting home; and yes, even group therapy.

He has changed, he writes: quicker now to give people the benefit of the doubt, more appreciative of his family and the people who stuck by him, and more than willing to take one day at a time.

I put the last page down. Outside it's dark. And quiet. One question rings in my mind. How could I ever have considered leaving this person? I check my watch. Eleven. I grab my car keys and run.

I let myself in and find him in the sitting room, reading by a blazing fire.

'Hey,' I say.

He looks up, his eyes searching mine.

I go to him, take the book from his hand and place it upside down on the table. I ease myself onto his lap and snuggle up to him. 'You're wonderful.'

'So, you're not leaving me?' He smiles.

'Not for the moment.' I stretch up to kiss his cheek, then rest back against his chest. 'I can't believe what you've been through.' My voice starts to crack.

He puts his arms around me, kisses the top of my head.

'Thank you for writing this, for letting me in.'

He rests his cheek against my hair.

'I love you so much,' I say into his chest.

For a long time, we're quiet. I'm so grateful to be here with him, to have a second chance. To *understand*. I sit up suddenly. 'You have to publish it.'

He smiles as if humouring me.

'It's brave, honest, from the heart . . . and it would help so many people.'

'It's private, Lucy. I wrote it for you.'

'I know, but think of the people out there who're going through what you've been through, not knowing what's going on, their families totally at sea. If someone as high-profile as you stood up and said, "I have bipolar disorder and it's not the end of the world," think of what it would do.'

'Yeah, end *my* world. People would run a mile. From me. From my books. Bye-bye, income. Bye-bye, security.'

'I don't think they would. OK, they might buy the book out of curiosity, but once they read it, they'd see the reality – you're the same person, only stronger because of what you've been through. Imagine what that would do to the stigma of mental illness.'

He looks dubious.

'Look at the alternative. Spending our lives hiding, covering it up, pretending, hoping the children won't say anything . . . Greg, publishing this would help us, too.'

'You're overestimating it.'

'Don't you want to help people?'

'I don't want the world knowing my business.'

'Even if that helps people out there on the verge of suicide?'

'Lucy, I can't tell my mother I'm bipolar. So that's the end of it.'

'Why not? Better to hear it from you than the children. At least if you tell her, you control the way she hears it. And, anyway, it's not good for Rachel and Toby to be keeping secrets. There's pressure in that, you know?'

'Lucy, I need to get up.'

I get up, so he can.

He paces in front of the fire. Eventually, he stops and looks at me. 'There's something I haven't told you. Something that happened when I was a child.'

I look at him.

'My father had depression. He took his own life. If my mother hears I have depression, it would kill her.'

'I'm so sorry.'

'Never mention this to Rob, OK? He doesn't know. No one does except my mother, the GP and me.'

'But how do *you* know?'

Pain passes over his face.

'Oh God. You found him, didn't you?'

His sigh is filled with sorrow. 'Hanging from his dressing gown belt. My mother sent me to call him for breakfast; he never could get up in the morning.'

'Oh, Greg.' I go to him and sweep him up in my arms as if he's still that ten-year-old boy.

'That's what he left me, Lucy – that memory. I can't think of him without thinking of that. So I don't think of him. Don't talk about him.'

This is why Rob could talk endlessly about his childhood, while Greg has always refused to. It's not the same childhood. Rob has a cloud-free version while thunderstorms rumble above Greg's. There's something else . . .

'When you started feeling depressed, didn't you worry that you had what your dad had?'

'It crossed my mind,' he says bitterly.

'But I don't understand. How could you have even *considered* suicide, when you know what it does to the people left behind?'

'My logic was very different. I thought: *Better to get the inevitable over quickly. Save all that pain.*'

36.

Rob calls Greg. To apologise. Phyllis knows that Greg is bipolar. She and Rob were trying to work out when exactly her nursing home had increased its fees. Rob remembered that it was around the time Greg was in hospital. She pounced, saying that she *knew* something was up. She wormed the truth out of him. In fairness to Rob, he didn't know the full significance of keeping the news from her. And he *has* told Greg straight away. I'm not sure that Greg appreciates either of those points, though, as he hammers the punchbag, something he hasn't done in months.

'I can't believe it. I can't fucking believe it.' Wham!

'You'd better get over to her,' I suggest.

The bag rebounds as another punch lands. 'I knew we shouldn't have told Rob.'

'I couldn't have coped without him. And you can't hide everything. This just proves it.'

'Fuck!'

'It might not be the end of the world. At least you can be honest with her now. I mean, that's good, isn't it? All those secrets, Greg. No wonder you got sick.'

He swivels around. 'Bipolar disorder is biological; it has nothing to do with secrets.'

'Your mother's a coper. Look at what she's lived through.'

'I'm responsible for her.'

'You can't protect her from everything. You can't protect her from life. You're human. You can't manage the world.'

'That's for sure,' he says in a defeated voice. He pats his trouser pocket for his car keys. 'I'd better go.'

I kiss him. 'Good luck.'

~

'Will you braid my hair, Lucy?' Rachel asks, from her bedroom.

'Sure.' I go in, remembering a time I was barred, a time when she'd have died before asking me to do anything for her. She has grown up so much, become so confident, and calm. Clothes are a big thing now. She has developed her own style that ignores trends. She has let her fringe grow out, taking her face from the shade. She is a beautiful girl.

She sits on her bed and I kneel behind her, holding brightly coloured braiding in my mouth.

'Remember when you were five and you climbed out of your bedroom window and sat on the ledge?' she asks.

'Who told you that?' I laugh. It can only have been Dad. Ever since the kids first started visiting my parents, he has taken it upon himself to tell them stories about when I was a child. Not all of them cute. His rationale, I discovered when I confronted him, has been to present me as a real person as opposed to the stranger who landed into their lives without their say. The whole thing has mushroomed.

'Did that really happen?'

'Mm-hmm.'

'Was it because you were looking for attention?'

'No! I was just getting fresh air.'

'But Joe said you were looking for attention. He said you were jealous of Grace.'

'Well, he's wrong. I sat out on the window ledge because it was peaceful and quiet and away from everything.' I've made it sound too tempting. 'But, of course, it was very dangerous.'

'*Were* you jealous of Grace?'

'I don't know. Maybe. Sometimes.'

'Are you still?'

'No. I appreciate Grace now.'

'And were you really engaged before?'

'Yup.'

'And did he really die?'

'Mm-hmm.'

'Were you sad?'

'Very.'

She is quiet for a moment. Then she turns her head and I have to move my hands to avoid pulling her hair. 'If he hadn't died, you wouldn't be here now, on my bed, would you?'

'No.' I smile so she doesn't think I regret it.

'So, sometimes, good things can happen, can't they, because of bad things?'

'How wise you are.' I think about Greg's illness. Would I have ever become so close to him or the children without it?

Toby bursts in, looking like a skater boy.

'You're supposed to knock, Toby,' says his sister.

'I've got onto the Genie level,' he shouts then sees me doing Rachel's hair.

'Will you spike mine? I'll get the gel.' And off he runs.

~

When Greg hasn't returned, I take Rachel and Toby to a movie. I leave a note and take my mobile. Even so, we get back before him.

When he finally returns, the children are in bed. I put down the novel I was trying to distract myself with.

'D'you want a cup of tea?' he asks.

'Please,' I say, trying to read his face. I follow him into the kitchen.

He puts on the kettle, leans against the counter and reaches for a schoolbook. He flicks through it. 'God, I was crap at Irish.'

'Greg, I'm dying here. What happened?'

He looks up. Smiles. 'Poor Rob. He didn't stand a chance. She dragged it out of him.'

'So, she was OK about it?' I gather from his face.

'She was upset that I hadn't told her and demanded to know everything. She had so many questions about depression. She really wanted to understand it – not just for me, but for herself. All our lives, we've avoided the truth; it was a heart attack, plain and simple. I've always tried to protect her and Rob from it. From everything, really. I'd failed my dad; I wasn't going to fail them, too.'

'You didn't fail him.'

'I didn't get to him on time.'

'Greg.'

'I know. I know. But that has always been my thinking. Anyway, she doesn't want my protection, she told me. That's why she moved into a home rather than here. She needs her independence. She can look after herself. She wants to.'

'You look relieved.'

'You have no idea how relieved – to finally admit the truth and be able to talk about it. I told her about what I've written. She wants to read it.'

'Does she know that you planned suicide?' I ask, warily.

He nods. 'We talked about it. I told her about lithium. And how you keep an eye out for mood swings and how supportive you are of me.'

I smile, knowing that she won't hate me any less.

'So, yeah, I think I'll let her read it. It's weird. I thought her finding out would be the worst thing in the world. It might just be the best.'

I think about that. 'Maybe it's time to tell Rob how your father died.'

His voice changes. 'That's different, Lucy. I've kept it from him for so long. All these years.'

'You've spent your life protecting him. And I understand why. But there's a downside. When you're in trouble, you don't let him in. He's wanted to help so many times, to pay you back for all you've done for him. But you turn him away. It happened when Catherine died. At least this time, you asked him to look out for us. He really appreciated that.'

'He told you this?'

'He's such an open guy. He's been so good to me, Greg, so good to the children. And so loyal to you. You said your mother is a grown woman. Well, Rob's a grown man. He can handle this. Tell him. It would explain a lot to him. I honestly think he needs it, deserves it. I think you do, too. You all do, as a family.'

For the first time, he isn't dismissive.

37.

Greg gives Phyllis the manuscript. For days, we hear nothing.

Then she rings. She wants him to come over.

After thirty years of trying to forget, to pretend it never happened, Phyllis has gained an insight into her husband's depression and suicide. The manuscript has brought her a kind of peace. It wasn't her fault, after all. If they'd argued less, it wouldn't have made a difference. If she'd been a better wife, it wouldn't have stopped him. It has to be published, she insists, for people like her who have had their lives ruined by an illness they underestimated. She is adamant. And calls him every day. Until, after two weeks, he relents.

He sends it to his agent, who reads it overnight and sells it, next day, to Copperplate Press and Greg's international publishers. From being a contract-breaker, Greg has become Mr Popularity. Publication will be rushed to have the book out in early January.

Greg did not include anything about his father in the book. That is his story, nobody else's. He does finally tell Rob, though, who reacts with fury at Greg having felt he wasn't up to the truth, at there having been a secret of such enormity between them for all these years, and at the only other members of their little family having conspired to keep him living a lie.

I call to see Rob. To explain that, at first, his brother and mother had just been trying to protect a little boy from something that had traumatised them so much; and, after that, they had tucked the past away, even from themselves. Ultimately, Rob sees the positives, as only he can. He has an explanation for all those times Greg pushed him away. Most importantly, there's no longer a need for Greg to do so.

~

The final manuscript is delivered to the publishers soon afterwards.

That evening, we're celebrating with hot chocolate and a blazing fire. On the couch, I snuggle into Greg.

'Can I have my ring back?' he asks.

I laugh. 'Feck off.'

'I'm serious,' he says gravely.

I sit up and look at him. He *is* serious. I don't understand. I thought we were OK. Better than OK. Heart pounding, I start to wriggle the ring – so precious to me now – off my finger. I hand it to him.

'Thanks,' he says, taking it.

'What is it?' I whisper.

He gets up from the couch. 'It's good we never got married.'

'What?' I whisper, tears threatening.

'You didn't know what you were taking on, Lucy.' He gets up from the couch.

'I know *now*.'

'You do.' He gets down on one knee and holds out the ring so reverently. 'Lucy Arigho, more than anything in the world, I'd love for you to be my wife. But I'm a different man and I'll totally understand if—'

'Shut up! Shut up! Jesus. Of course I'll be your wife! My God, Greg! You frightened the shit out of me.' I slip the ring back into position and feel right again.

'Sorry. That wasn't the plan. I just wanted to give you a chance to, you know, reconsider in light of . . .'

I get up, take his hand and pull him up. 'I love you, Greg. Now more than ever. And it *is* good that we didn't get married – because you'll always know that I stayed with you because I wanted to.'

He hugs me ferociously. And with my ear pressed against his chest, he asks, 'How does October sound?'

I smile. 'October sounds perfect.' But then I pull back. 'Do you think the kids will be OK with that?'

He raises an eyebrow as he looks down at me. 'Oh, I think so. Given that Rachel keeps asking me when I'm going to "get my act together".'

I laugh, so suddenly happy. I never thought this day would come.

~

Once, I dreamed of a wedding gown, of tuxes with white rosebuds, official photographs and a string quartet. That dream involved another man. With Greg – and Rachel and Toby – that kind of wedding would feel wrong. We opt for low-key, casual, cosy. Friends and family only. Thirty, max.

This brings its own problems.

I spend days looking at dresses. In desperation, I recruit my sister.

'What can a bride wear that's casual, but *appropriate*?' I demand. 'Tell me because I'd *love* to know.'

She smiles calmly. 'I'd go for a simple wedding gown, if I were you. At least we'd know where to *start*.'

I think about that. Rachel wants a proper flower girl dress anyway. And if *she* has one, then Grace, as bridesmaid, probably should, too. My sister is going to upstage me whatever I wear (it's her job), so I should probably glam up *a bit*. And why the hell am I worrying? This is supposed to be laid-back.

~

Somehow, on the day, I look out of the bedroom window and the marquee is standing where it should be, overlooking the sea. The catering company is setting up. The band is on its way. And I know (because I've asked him) that Greg remembered to buy the disposable cameras Toby will hand out to the guests instead of us having a formal photographer.

Rachel, Grace and I help each other get ready.

Rachel is stunning in purple.

And Grace? A vision.

I slip into a sheath of cold, cream silk.

Grace zips me up, then bursts into tears. 'You're beautiful!'

'I need a drink.' My knees are shaking. And my stomach is doing flips. I don't know why, because I want to do this more than anything.

Grace produces a bottle of champagne from her changing bag and two flutes.

'You girl scout,' I say.

'Hey, I've only ever been asked to be bridesmaid once. I'm going to do this right.'

The champagne makes me giddy. I wander over to the window. Down below, Greg and Toby are taking a manly stroll, in matching navy shirts and chinos. My heart swells with love. Like magic, I stop shaking. We have almost made it. We are almost, almost a family.

At last, it is time. Music starts up downstairs. The shakes are back.

I'm convinced I'm going to fall on the stairs. But I don't. I look up and Dad is waiting at the bottom with his arm crooked for mine.

In jeans and white shirt, he looks very Paul Newman. I ignore his arm and hug him.

'My little girl,' he says hoarsely.

Arm in arm, we walk outside. Entering the marquee, I see so much at once. Mum, Fint and Sebastian have broken the dress code and glammed up in dazzling and flamboyant silks. The fashion conspiracy makes me smile and I love each of them just a little bit more. At the top of the aisle, the best man is waiting in a white T-shirt and faded denim. Rob looks so good it's almost sacrilegious. But it's the groom who takes my breath away, my man, facing me now, eyes bluer than blue, teeth whiter than white. Or is that just me? I can't stop smiling.

And then we are walking. And the snappy dressers – all three – burst into tears.

'God, I love that woman,' Dad whispers.

I decide, right at that moment, that this is the happiest day of my life.

Greg and I lock eyes and everything else fades. The pull to him is magnetic.

Together at last, we hold hands.

And then the priest does his thing. We stand. We sit. We stand. And sometimes we stand instead of sitting and try not to laugh.

Then comes the moment. The 'for better or for worse' moment. After 'worse,' Greg pauses. He looks into my eyes as if to say, 'You can still change your mind.' I shake my head, tears not far off. And there must be something funny about the way I say 'I do', because a titter of laughter runs through the congregation. Maybe it was too loud, too definite?

Rob passes Greg the platinum band. Greg looks deep into my eyes before slipping it onto my finger, taking me in his arms and kissing me.

And then it's over. We've done it. Everyone's clapping and hugging us. Taking photos. Throwing confetti.

The speeches were meant to be short. But Dad gets all philosophical. Greg's speech – so appreciative, so honest, so loving – makes me cry. Rob's is outrageous – despite the presence of Phyllis. She and I avoid each other, even today. I guess that's how it will always be. But I'm used to the idea now: just because we both love the same man doesn't mean we have to love each other.

Rachel and Toby stay with my parents while we honeymoon in Sicily. It's our first time holidaying on our own together. I feel like a new bride should – in love and in lust. Hand in hand, we stroll along narrow, cobbled streets, wandering in and out of tiny shops, buying each other gifts that involve thought, not extravagance. We visit small harbours, Greek temples and a tiny mountain-top village with views of Mount Etna. It is like a sunny spell at the end of a grey summer.

When we get home, and I am so, genuinely, happy to see and hug Rachel and Toby, I know that it has happened. We have become a family. We are a unit. The world has become an optimistic, friendly place.

38.

In March, I'm sitting in the production studio of a national radio station, looking at Greg through a window. Headphones on, he's being interviewed about his new book, *At Least I Don't Snore*, chronicling his experience of bipolar disorder. He spent last night awake, convinced that he was on the verge of ruining his career – and life. Half an hour ago, waiting to go on, he was about to back out. The presenter, Gerry Glennon, came out to him. They sat and chatted about the type of questions Gerry would be asking. I could see Greg relax. Then it was time.

Now, it's as if they're having a quiet conversation between themselves, not broadcasting to a nation. And yet, Greg considers each question carefully as if searching for the most accurate answer. He's not trying to entertain, impress or be funny. Just to be understood. He speaks about his high, his low, and his decision to end his life. To emphasise the importance of staying on lithium, he relates the story of our mountainside descent, admitting to having put his family in danger. The producer begins to reorganise the programme, cancelling other guests and letting the interview run. Texts and emails flood in. The studio phones are hopping. People all over the country are wishing Greg well – fans, sufferers, doctors – and people with no connection who simply want to show support. The producer puts calls through to the studio. Greg handles each one with the same concentration that has characterised the interview.

When he finally emerges, the production team thank and congratulate him. Calls are still coming in.

Outside, I hug him. He's just glad it's over, and hopes it helped.

In fact, it's just the beginning. As soon as Greg turns on his phone, it starts to ring. He takes back-to-back calls all morning. Until, finally, he turns it off.

Over the next few days, Copperplate's publicist is on to him constantly. Newspapers want interviews; a late-night talk show wants him on. He has become a commodity. Which makes him nervous.

Public reaction is such that, within days of publication, a second, much larger print-run is ordered. By the time it arrives at the wholesalers, original stocks have almost been depleted. Matt takes his staff off current assignments to handle the flurry. He even personally delivers copies to the shops. Hundreds of fans turn up to Greg's book signing. Reviews are rave. Greg's reaction is one of relief.

~

Back at work, Fint sticks his head around my door.

'Come *in*.' He usually doesn't need to be asked.

He closes the door behind him, then sits on the corner of my desk. 'I wish you'd told me.'

'I'm sorry. I wanted to. Greg asked me not to say anything – to anyone.'

'I never imagined . . .' He pushes his glasses up his nose. 'It must have been a nightmare.'

'Hell, really. But it's a year and a half ago now. And he hasn't had another episode.'

He picks up my stapler and begins to fiddle with it. 'If I'd known, I'd have been more patient.'

'You were amazing, once you knew I was in trouble.'

'I listened to him, live. He had me crying, the bastard!'

I smile.

'Suicide.' He puts the stapler down. Then he looks at me. 'You'd be surprised how many people think of it, at one time or another.'

'*You?*'

He raises his eyebrows and nods. 'A long time ago. When I was at school.'

'*Why?*'

He shrugs. 'It was your typical all-boys' school. If you weren't into rugby, you weren't one of the lads. And if you weren't one of the lads, you were pretty much crucified. So, you'd pretend to be like them. But you weren't like them. You knew that. They knew that. You hated yourself. And so did they. They called you girls' names. Tripped you up. Let air from your tyres. Laughed in your face. For years. You couldn't see a way out. You couldn't tell anyone, especially not your parents; they had their expectations, and homosexuality wasn't one of them. Sure, it was against the law in Ireland.'

I shake my head in disbelief. Poor Fint.

'There was only one solution – or so I thought. Dad was in the army. He'd guns locked away at home. I knew where he hid the key. We all did. I got a gun, went to my room, loaded it as he'd taught me, put it to my head. But I couldn't do it. I left it on the bed and ran. For miles. I wasn't going back. But I did go back – at some point. When I got to my room, the gun was still there on the bed. No one had found it. I put it back, locked the cabinet, and returned the key to its hiding place. No one ever knew. I never tried again. I stuck it out at school, went to art college, and realised there were lots of people like me, and they were normal. It was OK to like beautiful things. It was OK to be myself.'

'What age were you?'

'Fourteen.'

'I'd never have met you.' The shock of that. 'I'd never have known you, Fint. We'd never have had all those laughs, set up our business, created all those designs.'

'And I'd never have fallen in love, tasted champagne, seen Paris.'

I think of his mum and dad, who are crazy about him. 'Your parents would have been devastated,' I whisper.

'I didn't see that, then. All I saw was this big secret between us. I thought they'd hate me if they ever found out.'

'But they're *fine* with it.'

'Now, they are. It took a while for my mother to come around.' He smiles. 'Funny, I always thought that it would be Dad who'd have the biggest problem with it.'

'You don't regret telling them?'

'Are you kidding? The relief of just being able to go home and be myself. No more secrets. The freedom of that.'

39.

A month after the publication of *At Least I Don't Snore*, Greg and I are having coffee in the kitchen. He's just back from a book tour of the US, and I've taken a few days off to be with him.

The doorbell rings.

Jet-lag-free, I go.

Standing outside is a small, thin woman in a grey business suit that has seen better days.

'Can I help you?'

'I'd like to speak to Greg Millar, please.' She has a package in her hand.

'Do you want me to just give him that?' I ask to save him getting up.

'No. I have to give it to him in person.' There is something about the way she says it.

'Just a second, then.' I go to get him, leaving the door open.

I return with Greg.

'Greg Millar?' she asks.

'Yes?'

She holds out a large, yellow, padded envelope. Greg is about to take it from her when she taps him with it, saying, 'You are served.'

'Sorry?' Greg asks, looking at the envelope that has been thrust into his hand.

But she has already turned and is hurrying away to a dusty Nissan Micra. She starts the engine after two attempts, and drives off.

Greg looks at me. 'Probably some chancer trying to get money out of my publisher or something. Wouldn't worry.'

In the kitchen, he examines the envelope. Turning it over, he starts to remove the clips securing it. He takes out legal documents. Eyes scanning them, his face changes.

'Shit.'

'What?'

'Fucking hell.'

'What?'

'They want the children.'

'Who? Who wants the children?'

'Ben and Ruth. They want custody of Rachel and Toby.' He looks up, wounded. 'They think I'm an unfit parent. They heard me on the radio. They read the book. They think I'm a danger to their grandchildren.'

My hands go, automatically, to my face.

'They think I'm going to top myself in front of the children, or drive off a mountain with them in the car.' He throws the papers onto the table, and runs his fingers through his hair. 'Fuck.'

I pick up the papers as if they might spontaneously combust. The first page is a solicitor's letter explaining that this is 'a court order, made ex parte, granting interim custody to the applicants, with a motion for a court hearing, grounded on an affidavit'. Whatever that means. It's like a foreign language. Which makes it even scarier.

'Are you sure that's what it means?'

'Read it. If we don't hand Rachel and Toby over to them within twenty-four hours, we'll be in contempt of court. They can get a bench warrant for my arrest for failing to comply with the terms of the court order.'

'But they can't do that! They can't just take the children.'

'Here, give me the letter.'

I hand it to him.

He underlines a sentence with his finger. 'It says here that, according to the Guardianship of Infants Act, they can. They think I'm mad. They think their grandchildren are in danger.' He looks at me. 'I shouldn't have written that bloody book. I should have kept my mouth shut. This is what I get for messing with stigmas.'

'No. It's an important book. It had to be written. But we should have talked to them before it came out. We should have explained.'

'Why the fuck didn't we think of Ben?'

I think back. 'Phyllis was our concern, remember? And then everything happened so quickly with the book. Then the wedding. Everything was going so well with Ben and Ruth at that stage, the children visiting them every week, we forgot what they'd been like when they thought there was a problem.'

He's pacing the kitchen. 'I'm calling our solicitor.'

After a brief conversation, Greg hangs up. He looks at me. 'We need a family law solicitor. Harry knows someone. He's calling her now and will get straight back to us.' He goes to the drinks cabinet and opens it, but, to my relief, slams it shut again, hands empty.

The phone rings.

Greg has a longer conversation with Harry.

'What did he say?' I ask as soon as it ends.

'They've gone to the High Court and convinced a judge that I'm a danger to the children. Without us even being *consulted*, she granted them temporary custody until a court hearing decides who they should stay with for good.' His voice falters.

'OK. We'll just tell the court the truth. You're not a danger. And that's that. When is the family law solicitor coming?'

'She's in court all day, and normally wouldn't be available after that, but, apparently, she owes Harry one. She'll be here as soon as she's free. In the meantime, she's sending a courier to collect the legal documents. She'll try to look at them in between cases and on her way out here.'

'Why are they doing this?'

'We lied to them, Lucy. We told them everything was OK. And they believed us. Now they know the truth. Hilary wasn't exaggerating. They think I'm a danger. And I don't blame them.' He sounds gutted. He finally sits, cradling his head in his hands.

'You'd never do anything to harm Rachel or Toby. This is ridiculous.'

'I've a mental illness. They heard me loud and clear on the radio saying how I put you all in danger. They heard me say I was suicidal. As far as they're concerned, it could happen again. And they're right. It could.'

'But you haven't had an episode in almost two years.'

'I could have one tomorrow.'

I start leafing through the stack of legal documents as though I can somehow single-handedly solve a problem I don't even understand. I look up. 'I don't believe it! There's something here from Hilary!'

'Hilary?'

I hand him a document.

His eyes scan quickly. 'Great! Just what we need! A sworn statement from the trusted, reliable nanny, going into vivid detail about how terrified she and Rachel were in the car in France, how out of control I was, and how I wouldn't listen to reason. It's all here. Black and white.' He slaps it with the back of his hand.

I feel sick. She has finally found a way. 'Sexual harassment seems minor by comparison.'

We look at each other.

'I think you should ring Ben,' I say. 'Try to explain, tell him we didn't want to worry them.'

'Why should he believe me now?'

'You could bring a letter from Professor Power saying that everything is under control, that you haven't had a relapse in almost two years.'

He looks doubtful.

'It's worth a try, Greg. Anything is.'

'Maybe I should check with Harry first.'

'OK. Yeah. Maybe.' I haven't a clue. I'm so out of my depth, I'm drowning.

~

According to Harry, it should be OK to call as long as we don't make any threats or say anything that could be used against us. This we interpret as 'Be nice'.

I hold my breath as Greg dials. Then watch as he drops the handset. He looks at me. 'It was Hilary. What's she doing over there?'

'We need that solicitor.'

But we have all day to wait.

Unable to stay still, we have to get out of the house. We find ourselves pacing Dun Laoghaire Pier, oblivious to the wind that has others stooped, heads down, hands in pockets. We're silent, each of us trying to work out a solution. Every so often, one of us stumbles on an idea. But we have no clue if any of them are relevant. Law is something you either know, or you don't. We don't.

~

It's time to collect the children from school. We go together. We do our best to act normally. But it's hard not to cling to them. We notice everything they do, every word they say. I cook their favourite – tuna pasta. It reminds me of that first day in France when Rachel said she hated me. It seems so far away. And preferable to this.

We let them watch TV and wonder how important homework really is in the scheme of things. I try not to think that they could be gone in under twenty-four hours.

~

Freda Patterson has a strong handshake. She delivers a brusque apology for being so late – apparently, there was a crisis at home. Her crisis means that Rachel and Toby are in bed when she arrives, which is something. It also means that, presumably, she has a family – so, hopefully, also empathy.

We show her in.

She slips out of her coat, but when I go to take it from her, she tells me, 'It's fine.' She folds it over the side of the armchair. In her business suit, she looks efficient.

'I'm sorry, I never offered you tea or coffee,' I say, getting to my feet.

'I'm fine. Thank you.'

I sit back down.

She pulls the documents from her case. 'Now . . .'

'Can they do this?' I ask.

She looks up, seems to consider me for a second. 'Yes. I'm afraid they can.'

'How?'

'Well,' she says, putting her briefcase back on the floor. 'They've based their claims on a published book, a broadcast radio interview and a sworn affidavit from what looks like a reliable childminder, given that she worked for you for five years.'

Even to me, it doesn't sound good.

'By granting this injunction, the judge has indicated that she considers the children's father a danger. And, in family law, the welfare of the children is the primary concern.'

What does she mean, "the children's father"? He's sitting opposite her. He has a name. 'Greg,' I say. 'The children's father's name is Greg.'

'Yes, of course. Greg. I'm sorry.'

'Is there anything we can do to stop them being taken tomorrow?' Greg asks.

'I'm afraid not. No.'

'There has to be *something*,' I say. 'You can't just go to court and swear that someone is a bad parent and have their children taken away. There has to be some safety net against that happening.'

'In this case, Greg has publicly admitted to endangering the children's lives by driving dangerously with them in the car. The fact that he still has the condition that caused him to do so means that, technically, there is a risk that it could happen again. In situations like this, where a serious yellow flag has been raised in terms of the welfare of a child, and where a relative or health board mounts a legal challenge, the courts will look at it. And they will consider the welfare of the child a priority.'

I am sick. *Sick.*

'What about Lucy?' Greg asks. 'Lucy's my wife and the children's stepmother. Doesn't her being here count for anything?'

Freda doesn't look optimistic. 'Lucy was in the car during the dangerous driving incident and allegedly unable to influence your behaviour. Her role in protecting the children could be legally challenged. Aside from that, step-parents are not considered, in law, to be as significant as flesh and blood. Legally, the children's grandparents have a stronger claim on them because there is a blood link.'

'But that's ridiculous!' Greg interrupts. 'Doesn't it matter, *at all*, who the children are closer to, who would do a better job of parenting them, who the children would prefer to be with?'

'Greg, if you were to die in the morning, Rachel and Toby would be removed from Lucy's care, immediately.'

We look at each other, eyes wide.

Then Freda adds, 'Unless, of course, you have adopted the children?'

'Adopted? Why would I need to adopt if I'm already a stepmo—'

Greg interrupts. 'Would it make a difference?'

'It would have, yes,' she says, speaking in the past tense. 'It would have created a direct link between Lucy and the children.'

'Why don't people tell you that?' I ask. 'How are you supposed to know?'

'Lucy could adopt them now,' Greg suggests.

'There would never be enough time. It is a long and arduous process.' Seeing our distress, her face softens. 'Having said all that, in this case, one thing has gone in your favour. Their solicitor has made, in my view, a slight cock-up. He has included Lucy's name on the order. That increases your relevance to the case,' she says, looking at me, 'and puts you both in a stronger position because they are effectively acknowledging your status as that of a parent. A parent who does not have bipolar disorder.'

'But, then . . .' starts Greg.

'Legally, it could still be undermined because the blood link is stronger. But it's something.'

I look at my husband, guilty that I never offered to adopt his children, and even guiltier that I am considered a better parent simply because I don't have bipolar disorder.

But Greg hasn't given up yet. 'Can't we argue that taking the children from their home would be extremely traumatic? They've already had to suffer separation when I was in hospital. Surely, a court should recognise this? And, surely, Ben and Ruth must come across in a bad light for not caring about that?'

'You can argue it, but not until the hearing. Temporary custody has been granted. A decision has already been taken, in court, that indicates that the judge is concerned about the children's welfare.'

Jesus.

'Couldn't we appeal?' Greg asks.

'Yes. You could. But it wouldn't be in your interest. An appeal would be based on a short affidavit only – not enough, in my opinion, to convince a judge. A full hearing is what you need, and that is already planned for three weeks' time. What we need to concentrate on now is being as prepared as we can for that hearing. We need to get a report from your psychiatrist . . .'

But Greg has stopped listening. 'Are you saying that the children have to stay with Ben and Ruth for three weeks? That's a ridiculous amount of time to separate children from their parents. It's unjust.'

'That's why I will begin negotiations tomorrow, for access,' says Freda in an assured tone. 'We should get daily access. It may have to be supervised. Indeed, we should request supervised access. It would increase our chances of getting it. I will argue for supervision to be carried out by a relative.' She makes a note of that.

'So, to be clear . . .' I say. 'We can't get the children back before three weeks, and there's a chance we may not even see them in that time, and then a court hearing will decide who they stay with permanently?'

'That would be a pretty accurate summation.'

I shake my head at the injustice of it.

'Who will you negotiate with for access?' asks Greg, who has started to take notes himself.

'The applicants, through their solicitor.'

'Who are the applicants?' I ask.

'The children's grandparents. They are the applicants. You are the respondents.'

'What if they don't agree to access?' Greg continues.

'Unlikely. Their solicitor will advise them to agree. Judges don't look favourably on denial of access. Even in child abuse cases, access is granted. Supervised access. But as there have been cases where applicants have not agreed to access, I will prepare a replying affidavit to bring a motion, returnable on the date of the court case, seeking interim access that day.' She makes a note of that.

'Sorry, what?'

'If they don't agree, the question of access will be before the courts in three weeks.'

'That's all we can do?' asks Greg.

'For the moment. Yes.'

'What about speeding up the hearing?' Greg, again, is asking all the right questions.

'I must warn you,' she says, 'the case may, in actual fact, be postponed.'

'What? Why?' I demand in disbelief.

'Their side is likely to apply for a Section 47 Report as soon as the hearing opens. If that happens, and don't be surprised if it does, then nothing can be decided upon until the report has been prepared. It may take weeks.'

'I'm sorry, you've lost me,' I say. 'What's a Section 47 Report?'

'It's a report carried out, for the benefit of the court, by an independent expert – a child psychiatrist or psychologist, usually – recommending which party custody should go to. The – probably psychiatrist, in this case, will be professionally trained to interview the applicants and respondents. He will also want to see how the children interact with both. He will, almost certainly, look for access to your medical records, Greg. These can, I'm afraid, be used as evidence against you.'

'If they're going to apply for a Section 47 Report anyway,' says Greg, 'would there be any advantage in us being the ones to request it, you know, to show we've nothing to fear?'

'No, the courts will make their decision based on the welfare of the children, only. And no, I wouldn't request one. Once evidence goes in, that's it, you can't take it back,' she says, leaving us in no doubt that a Section 47 Report would not be good news.

'Is there anything we can do to influence the report?' Greg asks.

I think it a wasted question.

'Two things,' she says. 'Firstly, it is well-known that some psychiatrists are more pro-men than others.'

'Really?' I can't help asking.

She nods. 'I'll go through the list of psychiatrists who do these reports and contact one I feel would be appropriate and see if he could start work as soon as possible. If the applicants request a Section 47 Report, they'll suggest a psychiatrist. If we don't agree with their selection, we can put forward the name of our man on the basis that he'd be ready to start immediately. Saving time would be seen as hugely advantageous to the court.'

'You said that there were two things we could do?' Greg asks, pen poised.

'Yes, we will also ask the psychiatrist you attend to prepare a report on your condition, treatment and prognosis. You're his patient. He's likely to give you a favourable report. However, I should warn you that a Section 47 Report, should it be requested, will override all others.'

'Is there anything, at all, in our favour?' I ask.

'Well, there's Greg's history as a good father.' She turns to Greg. 'You've been a parent for twelve years and – apart from that driving incident in France – nothing untoward has happened to the children while in your care. There is the fact that your condition is well-controlled . . . I assume it is?'

Empathy of a stone.

'I haven't had a relapse in almost two years,' Greg says, flushing under her scrutiny. I hate Ben, Ruth and Hilary for putting him through this.

'Good, well. We have that in our favour. And the fact that Lucy has been included on the order.'

'Thank God for "cock-ups",' he says bitterly.

'What do we do now?' I ask.

'First thing in the morning, I'll get on to their solicitor to negotiate access. Then I'll brief counsel to draw up a replying affidavit in case the negotiations don't go in our favour.' She sees my confused face. 'It just means that if they don't agree to access, we'll be able to argue it out at the court hearing in three weeks' time. And I can pretty much assure you that we will get access.'

'Could you let us know how the negotiations go as soon as you can?' Greg asks. 'We need to talk to the children.'

The thought of telling Rachel and Toby nearly chokes me.

'Yes, of course,' she says.

'When do we have to hand them over?' asks Greg.

'I'll find that out tomorrow.' She stands. 'Right, I'd better be off. It was good to meet you both.' She holds out her hand. 'Till the morning, then?'

~

We stand at the door until her car pulls away. Then we go inside.

'What do you think of her?' asks Greg.

'I don't know. What do you think?'

'I like her,' he says.

'You do?'

'She's straight. Says it as it is. No bull.'

'She doesn't seem to have much heart, though, does she?'

'We don't need heart, Lucy. We need balls.'

'Well, she certainly seems to have those.'

'Let's hope so. We're totally in her hands.'

'I still can't believe it.'

'I shouldn't have written that bloody book.'

'Don't blame the book. Blame fear. Millions of people are bipolar. It's not a licence to take their children away.'

'Not unless they're dumb enough to go on record saying how out of control they were. That driving thing is going to sink us, Lucy. I know it. I can convince anyone I'd never commit suicide so that the children would find me – not after my experience. But the driving thing – I can't argue with that.'

'Your condition is under control. You haven't had a relapse in almost two years. Your psychiatrist will vouch for you.'

'I know, but what about this bloody Section 47 Report? It's going to hammer us.'

'That's if they go for it.'

'You heard Freda. They'll go for it.'

'We need access. We need to be able to reassure the children. All I can think of is what Hilary might say to turn them against us, the lies she'll come up with. She had so much control over them once. We need to see them. We need to keep in touch.'

'I know.'

~

We watch Rachel sleep, safe and secure in her land of dreams, cheeks flushed, and features relaxed and trusting. There's no trace of the gutsy little girl who once declared war on me with a fury I later came to admire, only a softness that reminds me of how she came to my rescue after her grandmother's visit, how she's always looked out for her little brother, and how she did the same for her father as soon as he came home. She looks so peaceful. It kills me that there's nothing we can do to protect her from this.

Toby, in his room, looks so innocent. Vulnerable. This is the boy who has always made me smile, who likes Horrid Henry and Captain Underpants, and who says 'Hello, sir' to every dog he passes in the street. This is the boy I couldn't bear to lose.

It doesn't seem right for us to be sleeping apart. We should be herding together, practising safety in numbers. But there is safety in nothing. A process has been set in motion without our say to take the children from us. A person we've never met will decide our future as a family.

Neither Greg nor I sleep. Every few minutes, one of us sits up, flicks on a bedside lamp and scribbles something down – an argument in favour of us as parents, an argument against them as guardians, a word or phrase that might help explain all of this to Rachel and Toby. Rachel and Toby, the children I once wished away, but whom I've come to love as if they were my own.

40.

Greg takes Rachel and Toby to school as though it's a normal day. I wait by the phone.

When he returns, we wait together.

At eleven, just as we're trying to decide whether it's a good or bad sign that Freda hasn't called, she does.

It's bad. Access denied. The most they'll do is let us talk to the children over the phone, twice a day, at allocated times.

Greg, who has been so patient, loses it. 'Who gave them the right to make the rules?' He looks at me. 'This means war, Lucy. This means fucking war. If they want to play the bully, let's see how tough they are. Let's see how fit they are to be parents, how mentally stable?'

'What'll we tell the children?' It's all I can think of.

'Well, I don't know about you, but I haven't a clue what to fucking tell them. "Sorry, guys, but we don't make the decisions any more. Out of our hands. Don't look at us."'

'Greg, they're coming at three. We have to think of something. We have to pack.'

'I can't believe this. I can't fucking believe it.'

We pack, in the hope that it'll clear our heads. It only makes us worse, putting away all their things in cases and bags – games, books, sewing things, drawing stuff, pillows, clothes, uniforms, togs, hurley stick, hockey gear, skateboard, helmet and protective pads. It makes it all real. Definite.

We discuss and argue, and argue and discuss what we should or shouldn't say. There's no way they should learn how out of control things are. Still, we can't lie, invent some three-week holiday they're not invited on. Even if we wanted to, it wouldn't work. If a Section 47 Report is requested, a strange man will come asking Rachel and Toby questions. God knows what Hilary will say. And what will we tell the kids if, after the three weeks, we don't get them back? They'll never trust us again. Somehow, we have to give them as much of the truth as we can, without the accompanying worry. Impossible, considering *we* know the truth and *we're* terrified.

~

We hear Rachel's quick footsteps echoing in the school corridor. She rounds a corner, shoving her second arm into her coat, her school bag slung over one shoulder. She beams when she sees us, looking delighted to be let out early. Then she sees our faces.

'What is it, Dad?' she asks as soon as we reach her.

He hugs her tightly. I pick up her bag, which has fallen to the floor.

'Is Toby OK? What is it?' She looks from Greg to me, to Greg.

'Toby's fine,' Greg says. 'He's still in class.' He rubs her cheek. 'We wanted to talk to you about something.' His voice is so gentle.

'What?'

'Wait till we get outside, pet,' he says.

She looks at me.

I force a smile. *How are we going to do this?*

There's a park, opposite. We sit on the edge of a fountain, Rachel in between us. All around, spring is adding optimistic touches. Bluebells spreading out under trees, daffodils in cheery clumps, crocuses and snowdrops. A red balloon floats high over the buildings on the other side of the park. In the distance, a mother lifts her toddler out of a safety swing. Beyond the railings, people run for a bus.

'Rachel, sweetheart,' starts Greg. 'We've something to tell you.'

'I know,' she says. 'Is it bad?'

'You know Gran and Granddad Franklin?'

'Are they OK?'

'Yes. Yes, they're fine. It's just that they want you to stay with them for a while.'

She's surprised. 'For a sleepover?'

'Well' – he looks at me, then back at Rachel – 'for a bit longer than that.'

'How long?'

'About three weeks.'

'Three weeks? But that's ages. What about school?'

'You'll still be able to go to school.'

'But why do they want me to stay for three weeks?'

'Not just you, honey. Toby, too.'

'But why, Dad?'

'It's a long story, Rache. And kind of hard to explain . . .'

'Try.'

He nods, then takes a deep breath. 'Remember when I was sick?' She nods. 'Well, Gran and Granddad don't really understand about bipolar disorder very well, and they think I can't be a proper dad if I have it. So, they want to mind you for a while.'

'But you're better now, Dad. Just tell them.'

'They won't listen.'

'I'll tell them. They always listen to me.'

'Sweetheart, there's something else I have to tell you.'

'What?'

'For those three weeks, Lucy and I won't be able to see you. We'll talk on the phone, twice every day, but we can't go see you, and you can't come home.'

She looks very wary. 'What's going on, Dad? This doesn't sound right.'

'Well,' Greg struggles. 'It's just that Gran and Granddad want you to live with them for good . . .'

'*What?*' She stands suddenly, turning to face her father. 'No way.'

He stands, too. 'Now, Rachel, that's the last thing Lucy and I want. We want you with us . . .'

'Good. Then just tell them.'

'Rachel, the thing is,' Greg says, with obvious difficulty. 'Actually, honey, could you sit down for a sec? I'm trying to tell you something.'

She leans back against the fountain.

Greg does the same. 'You see, Gran and Granddad have asked a judge to decide who you should live with.'

'A judge? Why? This is crazy.'

'Rachel, remember the time in France when we were driving down that mountain?'

She nods.

'Well, that was because of the illness. You know that. You understand. But Gran and Granddad don't. They're worried that I might do it again, and they think they're protecting you by having you live with them. They don't understand that I'm taking my medication now, and that I'm fine. Lucy and I have to explain all that to the judge. A very clever lady is going to help us do that. She's a solicitor and she really knows her stuff. Together, we're going to convince that judge that we're the best people to look after you.'

'What if you don't?'

'We will.'

'How do you know?'

'I just do.'

'Dad. This doesn't sound good.'

'It's OK, Rachel. I promise, you'll only have to stay with them for three weeks.'

Don't promise, Greg; we said we wouldn't.

'But I don't want to,' says Rachel. 'What if I tell the judge that? He'll listen to me, won't he? It should be up to me who I live with, shouldn't it?'

'It should, pet. But it isn't.'

'But I'm twelve. I'm almost a teenager. I know what I want. And I want to be with you. I want to stay at home.' She begins to cry.

'Rachel. Rachel, sweetheart. Please. Come on. You have to trust me. We'll sort this out. You just have to be patient. And do this one thing. Just go there for three weeks. Remember when I had to go into hospital? That was for longer. And we managed then, didn't we? It was tough for a while, but we managed. And you looked after Toby so well for me, didn't you?' He lifts her chin. 'Remember? You were great. I need you to do that again, pet. He's too young to understand. We can't tell him as much as we've told you, Rachel. He'd be too afraid, poor little fellow.'

'I'm afraid.'

'I know. But you have to trust us that we are going to convince that judge that your home is with us. We will. It might take a while, but we *will* do it.'

'Promise?'

'Promise.'

She looks at him for a long time. Then she sighs deeply. 'All right. I'll do it.'

That she thinks she has a choice breaks my heart.

We discuss what we should say to Toby. This gives Rachel a focus outside of herself. Toby's a pretty copped-on seven-year-old, she reminds us. We should be honest with him.

~

And so, to the boy with the brown eyes, we offer a simplistic, optimistic, watered-down version of what we've told his sister.

'I'll be with you all the time,' Rachel reassures. 'It'll be like a holiday. Wait till you see. I'm going to bring my pocket money and buy you a treat every day.'

'Really?'

'Yeah.'

'Even chewing gum?'

'Yeah. And when we get home, Lucy and Dad will get you loads of treats. They might even get you a new app.' She looks at us hopefully.

'Absolutely,' Greg says.

'Can I *bring* the iPad?' he asks.

'You can bring anything you want,' says his father.

'And I'll still be able to go to school?'

'Yep,' says Rachel.

'And hurley?'

'Yep.'

'But what if my tooth falls out?' he says, wobbling one of his bottom set.

'The tooth fairy will find you.'

I hope Greg's right. I look at Rachel, and she understands. She'll take care of it.

'What time will you be ringing?' he asks.

'Before you leave for school. And just before bedtime. OK?'

'OK. And when the judge decides, we're *definitely* coming home?'

'Definitely,' lies Greg.

And I don't blame him. I'd dare anyone to look into those brown eyes and admit the truth.

~

The doorbell goes at three, on the button. The children shrink back, looking suddenly smaller, younger.

'I don't want to go,' says Toby.

Greg bends down to him, puts a hand on his shoulder. 'You have to be a big boy now, Tobes,' he says, gently. I imagine similar words being said to Greg many years ago.

'Come on, Toby,' says Rachel. 'The sooner we go, the sooner we'll be back.'

How I wish it was true.

We open the door to a surprise.

'Hilary!' four voices exclaim, two angry, two happy, all surprised.

'What are you doing here?' Rachel asks.

'I'm going to help your grandparents mind you,' she says with a warm, warm smile. She looks more like her old self, her eyes bright and focused, her posture confident. She is back in the driving seat. Plan A, executed. Now on to Plan B.

I look at Rachel. Her face is alight. 'How did you know Gran and Granddad would be minding us?'

'They told me,' she says cheerfully. 'They asked me to help them. And, of course, I said yes.'

'Of course,' says Greg, voice laced with sarcasm.

She smiles at him.

'The children's grandparents have been granted custody,' Greg says. 'And *that* is who will get it.'

'They're just in the car,' she says, standing her ground.

'Well, you'd better get them, hadn't you?'

'Whatever,' she says in a tone that implies it's all the same. She turns and walks down the steps to the car.

Rachel looks up at Greg. 'What's wrong, Dad?'

'Nothing, pet.' His voice softens. 'It's OK. It's just that if your grandparents want to mind you, then they should come to collect you. That's all.'

In the car, they're staring straight ahead, no doubt thinking they're the good guys, saving their grandchildren from a deranged parent. Hilary bends down as they lower the window. After a brief discussion, SuperBen steps out of the car. He walks tall and proud, Hilary right behind.

'Hello, Greg,' he says curtly. 'What seems to be the problem?'

'Don't start me off, Ben, or so help me . . . You wanted the children? Have the decency to come for them in person.'

'Children!' their grandfather calls. He swivels and starts down the steps, expecting them to follow. Far from the Pied Piper . . .

'Come on, guys,' says Hilary, cheerfully. 'Wait till you see what Gran and Granddad have got you. A hamster, a PlayStation . . .'

'A hamster?' asks Toby. 'Deadly.'

They chat together on their way to the car. We are right behind.

'You can pick a name for him, and feed him, and look after him,' Hilary enthuses.

'Really?' he asks.

'Yeah.'

'Deadly.'

'It's really good to see you, Hilary,' says Rachel. 'Why didn't you ring us?'

Hilary makes a point of looking at me, then says to Rachel, 'I'll tell you later.'

~

Greg loads the suitcases into the boot, his face tight. Rachel and Toby stand obediently by the car as Hilary opens the back door. I hug each of them, not wanting to let go. But their arms slip away. Greg lowers himself to one knee and draws them to him, eyes closed.

'I love you, OK? Just remember that. I love you. You'll be back soon. I promise.'

Slowly, reluctantly, they climb into the car. Greg stoops down at the back window. Toby, closest to him, stares out, his hand on the glass, fingers splayed. I will him to lower the window, but he doesn't. Hilary sits between the children. I want to punch that triumphant look right down her throat. Rachel, at the far side, leans forward to look at Greg. As the car pulls away, she stretches out and, resting her hand on his leg, she tries to comfort her brother, who is now crying, and calling for his dad.

I bite my lip as they disappear up the avenue. I put my arm around Greg and he pulls me into such a tight hug, I know it's for him as much as me. For a long time, it's all we can do. There is nowhere we want to go, nothing we want to do, except be with them.

41.

Greg heads for the punchbag. I make for the phone.

'Surely there's *something* we can do,' I say to Freda.

'Keep in touch with the children. Keep every pre-arranged phone call. And . . . try to be positive.'

'But can't we be doing anything to strengthen our case?'

'I'm working on it, Lucy. We've already lodged the replying affidavit. We've contacted Professor Power's office to request a report. And we're tracking down a suitable psychiatrist for the Section 47 Report. At this stage, all you can do is wait.'

'If only we could see them. Two phone calls a day . . . It's just not enough. Even if we could write to them, send them little things, just to let them know we're thinking of them . . .'

'I'll talk to their solicitor.'

'Thanks, Freda.'

'You just have to be patient now, Lucy.'

~

We can't stay in. Everything reminds us of them. Their favourite foods are in the fridge. Rachel's pink Groovy Chick mug peeps out from the cupboard. Toby's frog wellington boots lie abandoned in the cloakroom. Their clothes are entwined with ours in the washing machine. We have to get out. Get air. Keep moving.

There is only one thing we can talk about, think about; only one thing that matters. We can't eat, sleep, work. We can't do anything, except regret. And that's too easy. Writing the book was a mistake, according to Greg. But I think our only mistake was not explaining to Ben and Ruth about the illness once Greg was better. And so, rather than argue, we regret in private.

Stunned questions are repeated over and over by my parents, Grace, Rob, Fint. Answering them is exhausting, depressing, humiliating and many other things, none of them good. Their fury is appreciated, but doesn't help.

I think I must be Freda Patterson's most annoying client, ringing her constantly.

'Has Professor Power's report come in yet?' I ask, going through the checklist I drew up at three this morning.

'Not yet, no. If nothing's arrived by the end of the week, I'll chase it up. These things take time. Psychiatrists are busy people. To them, it's just paperwork.'

'Have you had any luck finding a psychiatrist for the Section 47 Report?'

'We're on to it, Lucy. If I've any news, you'll be the first to know.'

'Thanks, Freda.' I know she thinks me neurotic. But maybe she's used to this. Maybe everyone acts out of character when their family is under threat.

As soon as I hang up, I call Professor Power myself – just so he knows how much more than paperwork this is.

~

We live for the short, awkward telephone conversations that are all we have to keep close to Rachel and Toby. As the minutes edge closer, we perch by the phone, silent and tense, hoping it will go well, that we won't say anything to upset them or make them more homesick than they already are.

'So, how are you?' Greg asks Toby. 'Did you have a good day?' Pause. 'Did you have a good day at school?'

It's so unnatural. Question after question just to get him to talk. It makes us sound hyper. And probably makes the children nervous. If only we could see them, be with them, we'd know what to say, what they'd need to hear. We'd sense it. We mightn't have to talk at all. But on the phone, every word counts; every word has to be chosen carefully. And it isn't just the words. It's the tone. Too happy and they'll think we're fine without them. Too low: they'll worry.

'Hi, Rachel,' Greg says. As he listens, his smile disappears and he looks at me. 'It's a long story, Rachel . . . We had our reasons, pet . . . I can't talk about them now, OK? You have to trust us on this, Rache.'

When he finishes the call, I ask what she said.

'She wanted to know why we stopped Hilary from seeing them.'

'Didn't waste much time, did she?'

~

Night-time calls are the worst, when Toby is tired and wants to come home. It makes me want to march over there, bang on the door and demand them back.

One night, Toby is upset because Greg's not with him to read a story.

'I can still read you a story, Tobes. Just hang on a minute till I get a book.' Greg hands me the phone and runs upstairs.

'Hey, Tobes,' I say. 'How's Hammy?' The one thing guaranteed to excite Toby is his hamster.

'Great. He ackshilly yawned today. Like a baby. I could see all his teeth.'

'Wow.'

'Yeah, and he jumped off the first level of his cage and landed on the sawdust.'

'On purpose?'

'Yeah, 'cause he did it again. He keeps doing it. He's mad.'

I'm glad he has something to distract him, even though it is another notch in their belt.

Greg arrives back with a book, and begins a story about owl babies who miss their mummy. Halfway through, he stops and looks at me. 'He hung up.'

'Ring them back.'

'Can I do that? The agreement is two phone calls. I don't want to risk it. You know what Ben's like.'

'You were cut off.'

'Still. I'm not sure I should risk it.'

'Why did he hang up?'

'I don't know.'

'He was probably tired.'

'Or upset. I hadn't got to the bit where the mummy comes back.'

'He knows the story. He knows she comes back.'

'Well, then, maybe he was bored.'

'Or needed a pee. Who the hell knows? This is impossible.'

'Maybe Rachel will call us back.'

The phone stays silent for the rest of the night.

~

Waiting for news from Freda is like waiting for a Dublin bus. Nothing, nothing, nothing. Then, ten days after the children have been taken, we receive three pieces of news together. One: Ben and Ruth have agreed to us posting things to the children. Two: Freda has found a suitable psychiatrist, available at short notice to do a Section 47 Report. Three: Professor Power's report has arrived. She's emailing it over.

We sit at Greg's laptop, refreshing his email over and over. In fairness, the report arrives in minutes. And we read together in hungry silence.

To Whom It Concerns

Greg Millar has been a patient of mine for twenty months, initially as an in-patient at St Martha's Hospital, where he was diagnosed with bipolar disorder, subsequently as an outpatient, regularly and consistently attending my clinics. Mr Millar's condition is extremely well-controlled on lithium, the standard treatment for bipolar disorder.

Prior to admission and treatment, Mr Millar experienced one episode of mania (which led to the dangerous-driving incident outlined in the legal documentation) and one bout of severe depression, which was accompanied by suicidal urges. He was admitted to St Martha's Hospital at that point and commenced treatment. Since then, for a period of almost two years, Mr Millar has been entirely free from episodes of either mania or depression. This bodes very well for the future.

Mr Millar has an excellent understanding of his condition and the need to comply with his medication. He has returned to an excellent quality of life and is very well supported by his wife. He has published a well-respected and, I would say, widely helpful autobiographical account of living with bipolar disorder. The extent and demands of such a project are indicative of his return to good health.

It is my professional opinion that Mr Millar is a highly responsible and loving father who does not present any danger whatsoever to the children he has brought up single-handedly since the death of his first wife, seven years ago. I recommend that Mr Millar be reunited with his children immediately. I am happy to give evidence to this effect.

Yours sincerely, Professor Con Power

'Oh my God. It's great!' I say.

'Only if they don't call for a Section 47 Report. But they will, Lucy. Ben will have hired the biggest and best legal firm in the country. You can count on it.' His tone is defeatist.

I look at him, hoping he isn't heading for a low. 'Come on. Let's go buy things for the kids,' I say brightly. 'I want to get a package out to them today by SwiftPost.' For the first time since that yellow envelope arrived, there's something we can do.

We buy a calendar of The Simpsons for marking off the days. We buy a new game for Toby featuring one of his favourite cartoon characters, Spongebob Square Pants – an appropriate nickname for his grandfather, I think. We buy the remaining five books in the Lemony Snicket series. Rachel can read them to Toby. We get the Charlie Chaplin and *Home Alone* box sets for Toby. We're back in the car before I notice the theme – vulnerable characters coping in adversity.

~

With every day that passes, we send a surprise to the children. We don't expect much from it. But it has a surprising consequence. It starts conversations flowing. Every day, there's something new to talk about. They love the fact that when they get in from school there's a package waiting, personally addressed to each of them. They've never received anything by post before. Now, with every day comes something new to look forward to. It reminds them that we're thinking of them, that we care and that we know them better than anyone else.

Meanwhile, we do what we can to help our case. This means preparing for a court hearing that is, more than likely, going to be postponed. Freda sets up a meeting at her office. She introduces us to our 'counsel'. Jonathan Keane is in his forties and already completely grey. He looks so sure of himself that, even if he were buck-naked, you'd probably guess his profession. He smells of cigarettes and mints. I wish Freda was representing us in court, but a barrister it has to be.

The meeting is to build an affidavit – a sworn, written statement putting forward our case. It's Jonathan Keane's job to write it. He grills us. When did Greg become high? Was I there then? Did I do anything to prevent the dangerous drive down the mountain? Did I know of the suicide plan? When was Greg diagnosed? How has he been since? Career-wise, what has he achieved since? Did Greg, *in any way*, ever hurt the children?

I have to remind myself that Jonathan Keane is on our side.

From all the questions, we learn a few things. Some judges are more sympathetic than others. It's pot luck who we get. There won't be a jury; just a judge.

'Less intimidating,' says Freda.

'Depending on the judge,' Greg replies.

I'm not sure what Greg's social standing and career success have to do with anything, but Jonathan points out that they should impress a judge. I will be sold as the 'stabilising influence'. I worry how this must make Greg feel.

Ultimately, what this affidavit must show is that Greg's condition is well-controlled, and that we, as a couple, are not only responsible and capable of looking after the children, but also the best people to do so. Going by the questions Jonathan Keane has asked, it will take a small miracle to prove that.

The meeting lasts an hour, but so much is covered, it feels longer. Just as we're finishing up, I remember the media and how interested they are in Greg's life. I can see the headlines and the pressure that that would put on Greg and the children.

'That won't happen,' reassures Freda. 'The parties in family law cases cannot be identified in order to protect the children.'

Thank God for that.

42.

The morning of the hearing finally arrives. I dress in the clothes I laid out the night before – a formal suit, like a criminal going to trial. In the mirror, I seem faded, as though I've lost substance; not just weight, but bulk. Is it possible to lose height?

I think of the children, who will be at school, Toby not completely aware of the day's significance, Rachel knowing only too well. I pray for one outcome: the children returned, case dismissed. I close my eyes and will it.

On the way to court, I have to ask Greg to pull over. I open the door and empty the contents of my stomach onto the wet tarmac. Then I tuck my embarrassed head back into the car. In silence, he hands me a tissue.

We meet Freda on the steps of the High Court.

'Couldn't be more prepared,' she says.

I've never been in the Four Courts before. I've never been in any court before.

The place is buzzing. Important-looking people rush, here and there, black capes flapping in their slipstream. Others are huddled together in urgent discussion. Some wear wigs, many do not. All look confident, at home. Then there are people like us. All, regardless of status, reduced to the same level here – at sea, nervous. To the lawyers, we're today's business. Just another case. X versus Y. Soon to be replaced by more of the same.

In court, we sit through case after case. As each one ends, groups of people leave, until, finally, the lines of mahogany benches have emptied but for our legal teams. Ours is the last case.

'Where are Ben and Ruth?' I whisper to Greg. 'They have to be here, don't they?'

He looks as unsure as I feel.

I look at their barrister to see if he's concerned. The man doesn't look as if he ever gets concerned about anything.

Maybe they don't have to come. Maybe they're outside. Maybe they'll arrive any minute now. I look back at the door. Then at their barrister again. I slip my hand into Greg's and give it a squeeze.

The judge sits at his elevated mahogany bench, towering over us, Peter at the Gates of Heaven.

When their barrister stands, he calls for a postponement, pending a Section 47 Report.

All becomes clear. They didn't show up because they knew it would be postponed. They have been in control from the beginning.

How can they do this?

Tears blur my vision. Rachel and Toby won't be coming home. We said three weeks. We promised. My stomach heaves. And I have to run from the court.

I make it to the toilet in time to retch over its not-so-clean bowl.

How is this justice?

~

When I get back to the courtroom, Greg and Freda are waiting for me at the entrance. It's over.

'Are you OK?' they ask together.

'Fine. I'm so sorry. What happened?'

'Jonathan sends his apologies,' Freda says. 'He had to dash off. Well, that went as well as it could have.'

'But they called for a Section 47 Report,' I say. 'Rachel and Toby won't be coming home.'

'That was a given, Lucy,' says Freda.

'I'd just hoped that maybe . . .'

'We have to be realistic. What we expected to happen has happened. On the upside, our psychiatrist will be doing the report.'

'Well done on that,' Greg says.

'That's what you're paying me for.'

'And you did well on the access,' he continues. 'Daily access for two hours, starting today.'

'Thank God,' I say.

'I wanted to punch the air when the judge scolded them for denying access,' Freda says. She looks at me. 'You realise that was, ever so slightly, good for us.'

The downside, I discover, is that the court case has been postponed for another seven weeks to allow for the completion of the report. We'll have been apart, in total, two and a half months by the time of the court case.

I walk down the steps of the High Court, my legs weak, my knees shaking. *What will we tell them? How will they ever trust us again?*

~

'They were always going to ask for that report,' says Greg, walking back to the car. 'At least we controlled who does it. And we have daily access.'

'I know. But seven weeks. *Seven weeks!*'

'We'll see them every day. And, by God, we'll make the most of it.'

'What if Hilary uses this to tell them we lied, that they can't trust us? Who knows what she's already said?'

'We'll have them for two hours every day, away from that environment. We have to use that. If you're negative, they'll pick up on it. We have to be positive. They have to believe it's just a matter of time.'

'But it isn't. We've no guarantee we'll get them back. If that report goes against us, we'll never get them back.'

'Thinking like that won't get us anywhere. Lucy, you have to help me here: back me up, not bring me down.'

I see it then, the one positive in all of this: adversity has made him determined. I can't take that from him. 'I'm sorry. You're right. I'm sorry.'

But as we drive home in a car that smells of vomit, and I take stock of our situation after five minutes in court, I can't ignore the fact that everything hinges on a single report by someone we don't know, someone who has access to all of Greg's medical records. If that one report goes against us, the children are gone. Regardless of how determined we are.

~

Visits are to take place at Rob's apartment – neutral territory – with Rob as supervisor. Ben and Ruth are to drive the children there for six o'clock and collect them at eight.

We get to the apartment for five. Rob's already there. Bang on six, they arrive. We rush to the door. Open it. They seem to have grown. They're wearing new clothes.

Toby runs in, straight to his father, hugging him.

'Dad! Dad!'

Greg lifts him up and hugs him tightly. He looks so happy. 'How's my man?'

'Where's Robert?' asks Ben.

'I'm here,' says Rob, behind us, his voice protective.

'Hi, Rob,' shouts Toby.

'Well, I'd better go,' says Ben.

'You do that,' Greg says.

'Hi, Rachel,' I say.

'Hi.' Her voice is flat.

'Honey,' says Greg. 'Come here, give your old man a hug.'

She walks to him obediently. She lets him hug her.

'How're you doing?' he asks.

'Fine.'

He pulls back, holds her out from him. 'Look at you. You're getting so grown up.'

She looks down.

'Have you eaten? We've got in pizza and Coke.'

'A margherita?' asks Toby.

'Of course. Come on, let's go to the kitchen.'

Rob has already begun to serve up. He hands Rachel a plate.

'I'm not hungry,' she says.

Greg looks at me.

'Why don't we all sit down, anyway?' I suggest.

At the table, Rachel stares into her Coke as if it holds a key to the future.

Greg and I have a slice to keep Toby company, though I haven't been able to eat anything in three weeks and worry that it will come back up.

Rob makes himself scarce, which is lovely.

'Why didn't we go home?' asks Toby, matter-of-factly, mouth full. 'Why did we come to Rob's?'

'Ah, well, we thought you'd like to see him, too,' says Greg.

'That's not true,' snaps Rachel. 'We're here so Rob can watch you. Hilary told me.'

Greg and I exchange looks.

'What?' asks Toby, confused.

'Gran and Granddad just wanted Rob to be around, that's all,' Greg says.

Rachel sighs loudly and looks out of the window.

Silence.

She glares at Greg. 'So, what's the story? When are we coming home? The three weeks are up.'

'I'm sorry, Rachel, but this is the best we can do for the moment,' says her father.

Toby is eyeing him very carefully now.

'It'll be another few weeks . . .' Greg starts.

'Seven,' she says.

Toby puts down his triangle of pizza. 'Seven weeks? I thought you said three weeks.'

'Come here, Tobes.'

Toby slides off his chair and goes to his father. Greg lifts him up onto his lap.

'The three weeks was until we got to see each other. The three weeks are up, and here we are.'

'For two hours,' snaps Rachel.

'I thought we were coming home today,' Toby says, looking bewildered.

Has Hilary told Toby one thing and his sister another? Or maybe she's told Rachel the truth and kept it from Toby.

'I'm sorry, guys,' says Greg. 'I should have explained better.' He pauses. 'Today, the judge was supposed to make his decision. But, instead, he picked out a doctor to do it, because he thinks the doctor would do a better job. The doctor wants to meet all of us, so he'll take a few weeks to make up his mind. That's why you have to stay where you are for the moment. But, we explained to the judge that it would be unfair if you couldn't see Lucy and me until the doctor made his decision. The judge agreed. So every single day until the decision is made, we can all get together for two whole hours, here at Rob's.'

'Two hours isn't much,' says Rachel.

'I know, but when you think about it, it's pretty good. By the time you come home from school, do your homework and have dinner, it'll be time to come here.'

'I don't want to go back to Gran and Granddad. I don't want to. I want to go home.' Toby starts crying.

'I know, sweetheart,' Greg says, kissing the top of his head, 'I know.' He holds him close and rocks him. When, at last, Toby's tears have stopped, Greg says, 'From now on, we're going to see each other every single day. And then, when this is all over, you can come home for good.'

'When?'

'As soon as we can. But we'll see you every day. And you'll still get the surprises in the post. And we'll still ring you every morning before you go to school and every night before you go to bed.'

'I know how hard this is,' I say. 'But, things went well for us in court today. The judge picked a very good doctor to do the report. So, we all just have to be patient and make the most of our time together, until you're home. OK?'

'OK,' they both say.

'And don't always believe everything Hilary says,' says Greg.

Rachel looks at him. Says nothing.

'Now, let's go out and have some fun.'

43.

We make a discovery: there isn't a lot you can do with children in the space of two hours, at six in the evening. There isn't enough time for a movie, once you travel there and back. We would take them for something to eat if they didn't always arrive just after their dinner. They're too tired to do anything energetic. And, anyway, though it's almost May, there's still a chill in the air.

Staying in brings its own problems. It reminds us of what's happening. Access visits. Conversations. Pressure to talk. We want to have fun for the time we're together, to relax, enjoy ourselves and forget that we'll be separating in two hours.

Soon, we find a solution. Rob invites visitors. Nobody said he can't have guests while the access visits are taking place. First to come are my parents, who are so ecstatic to see the children that they almost suffocate them. Mum brings new stitching things for Rachel and gives her a tapestry lesson. Dad brings a few bits and pieces that need fixing. Wouldn't surprise me if he broke them deliberately. The children finally manage to lose themselves for two hours.

Grace and the children visit next. So happy is Toby to see Shane and Jason that he calls them his cousins: 'Look, my cousins are here.'

Within a week, we receive a call from Freda. She wants to make an appointment with the psychiatrist responsible for the Section 47 Report. He wants to interview the two of us separately. We opt for the earliest possible date. The psychiatrist, a Dr Bowman, also wants to attend one of the access visits. We delay that by a week, hoping that the children will be more comfortable with the visits by then. Rachel still has difficult moments.

~

There's nothing fancy about Dr Bowman's waiting room. Straight-back chairs line the walls. A table displays a few outdated magazines. The curtains are faded. Greg and I sit side by side. His appointment is first. The psychiatrist sticks his head around the door and calls Greg's name. I squeeze his hand to wish him luck.

Alone in the waiting room, I switch off my phone. I pick up a magazine. I look at the pictures, nothing registering. I get up and walk to the window.

I tell the secretary I'm popping out for a few minutes.

I walk the length of the street, trying to prepare answers to imaginary questions. I vomit. In public. Again.

~

I'm back in the waiting room, standing by the window, when the door opens and Greg emerges. I can't ask how it went, because Dr Bowman is right behind him. He introduces himself and leads me into his office.

Two armchairs face each other. There's a notepad and pen resting on one. He offers me the other.

I sit. Then become aware of my arms. I unfold them in case he thinks me defensive.

'This must be a difficult time for you,' he says.

I nod.

'Well, I'll try to make this as painless as possible.' He smiles.

I can't seem to manage one. 'Thank you.'

'So, it must have been quite a shock when you realised that the children's grandparents wanted custody?'

'Yes.'

'How did you feel about it?'

'Initially, I couldn't believe it. I thought it must have been a mistake.'

'Why?'

'Greg's an amazing father. He'd never do anything to hurt Rachel or Toby. Never. It seemed incredible that just because he had a medical condition, that gave them the right to take his children from him. I didn't think something like that could happen in this country. Not today.'

'So, he didn't drive down the side of a mountain and put your lives in danger?'

I gather myself. 'Yes, he did. I'm not denying that. But that happened before Greg was diagnosed, before he was on medication. That was almost two years ago. He takes his lithium. His condition is well-controlled now. We lead a normal, healthy life. He has never had a relapse. Not once. He is a good father, a great father.'

'So, how do you think he ended up in this situation?'

Painless, my arse. 'Greg wrote a book that he believed would help people. He spoke publicly about his experience to encourage others to get help and to stress how important it is to stay on lithium. He didn't go on record as saying he was dangerous. He put it in context. He said, "This is what happened to me. And this is what I'm doing about it. And everything's OK now." He was open and honest about being bipolar, and some people are just too naturally fearful to try to understand what that means.'

'Do you think that writing the book was a mistake?'

'No. I don't. It would be so easy to blame the book. But that book needed to be written. For so many reasons. So Greg could stop hiding, so he could move on and start writing again, so I could understand. It wasn't meant for publication. But I thought it would help other people. I thought it would ease the stigma of mental illness. Greg's mother, who'd personally gained a lot from it, also urged him to publish it. He did it against his better judgement. He regrets it. I don't. Writing that book was good for us, and I'm sure it was good for a lot of people who read it. We just should have explained to Ben and Ruth about Greg's condition before it was published. That was our mistake.'

'Do you think it would have made a difference?'

That makes me stop. 'I don't know. I've always assumed it would have. But maybe it wouldn't. Maybe they'd never have understood.'

'Do you think they're narrow-minded?'

'I'm not saying that. Just that they haven't tried to understand. They could have called us up. We could have talked about it. But they didn't. They just came in, all guns blazing.'

'But, surely, they must have a genuine belief that the children are in danger? What about Greg's suicide plans?'

'Plan, singular. One plan. No attempt. And now just a bad memory of a time before medication. Not a good enough reason to take his children from him.'

'Did Greg tell you he was planning suicide?'

'No.'

He writes something. I'm losing this. What can I say to convince him that the problem is with them, not Greg? 'Look, Greg's never been good enough for them, bipolar or not.'

'I'm sorry?' He looks up.

'He's never been good enough for Ben. He didn't have the right background, didn't go to the right school.' I hesitate before saying, 'They blame him for killing their daughter.'

'Could you explain that last comment?'

'Catherine, Greg's wife, died when she was having Toby. They blame Greg for her becoming pregnant.'

'They said that?'

'Well, no.' *Shit.* 'But they can't look him in the face. Rachel and Toby are their only link to their daughter, and nothing Greg does will ever be good enough for them.'

He raises his eyebrows.

'They have unrealistic expectations, that's all I'm saying.'

'I see.'

'Greg would never do anything to hurt Rachel or Toby. If you knew him, you'd know that. He would never plan a suicide that would expose the children to it. When he was ten, his father killed himself. Greg found him. Believe me, there is no way he would do that to his children. No way. You have no idea how much he loves his kids.'

His pen is racing across the page. I wish I could take the words back, words that have just confirmed that he had suicidal tendencies despite witnessing his father's suicide. I wish I hadn't been included in that court order. In trying to save Greg, I'm sinking him.

'Look. I know I'm making a mess of this. I don't know what to say, here. Greg's a great father. Being bipolar doesn't change that. He loves his children, and they love him. He's a better parent than I'll ever be. You're a psychiatrist. You know. It's just an illness. Greg takes his medication. He is totally committed to staying healthy. He loves his family. The children mean everything to him. They lost their mother. Please, don't let them lose their father.' *Oh God, don't make me cry.*

'Would you like to stop for a while?' he asks, offering me a hankie from a box on his desk.

'I'm sorry. This is so hard, so stressful. I'm not myself.'

'I understand,' he says, but adds, 'It must be difficult coping with bipolar disorder and children from another marriage.'

'They might not be my children, but I love Rachel and Toby as if they were. You know,' I say, my voice high, 'everything was going so well. Everything had settled. We'd just become a proper family. Then this.'

I say nothing about Hilary. I can't see how it would help. It would just sound like some mad conspiracy theory. And, anyway, talking about her would only make her more important. He might interview her. And who knows what she'd say?

Finally, the session ends. I feel like crawling out. But there's no time for crawling – or anything else. We have to be at Rob's in forty minutes. If we're late, Ben could use it against us.

~

In the car, I let my head fall into my hands. 'Oh, Greg. I've blown it. I was too honest.'

We go through what I said.

'Lucy, that was fine. The only thing I wouldn't have mentioned was Ben not liking me because of my background. His background and Ben's are probably the same.'

I groan.

'Doesn't matter.'

'No, you're right. I sounded paranoid. When I told him they blame you for Catherine's death, he asked me if they ever said anything. I had to say no.'

'Don't beat yourself up, Lucy. He has access to all my medical records. Whatever isn't in the book or the recording of the radio interview is in the records. He has access to anything he wants. He knows everything anyway. If you'd wanted to hide anything, you couldn't have.'

'This is all my fault. I should never have encouraged you to write that stupid book.'

'No.' He puts a hand on my leg. 'You loved me enough to get me to write it. And I wrote it out of love for you. It's a pure thing. I've stopped blaming it. We'll get Rachel and Toby back. We will. That's all there is to it.'

44.

Days pass, but it feels like a whole season. Daisies, dandelions, buttercups and clover erupt from long, lush grass. The horse chestnut tree outside the house bursts into leaf as though someone has waved a magic wand. New ivy leaves on the back of the house are soft and glossy.

Grace calls round one evening and says to my husband, 'I'm taking her out.'

'Good,' Greg says. 'She could do with it.'

She takes my hand and pulls me away from the new game I'm stuffing into an envelope for Toby.

'Greg, can you finish this, please?' she asks.

'Yep. Go. Go, go, go.'

~

'What's going on?' I ask, in the car.

'We're going to have a chat. And a walk.'

She drives to Killiney Hill. The evening is stretching out, heralding long days ahead.

'Right, let's go,' she says. 'Nothing like a bit of fresh air to clear the cobwebs.'

'Slow down. What's your hurry?'

She stops and waits. 'Sorry.'

We fall into step. Sunlight dapples the forest floor where ferns are beginning to unfurl. I love the way they tend this place, nurturing nature, taming it in places, but mostly letting it be. I breathe it in, logging the memory for later. I circle my shoulders, stretch my arms. Everything feels so stiff. But it's good to be out.

'You OK?'

'Yeah, just stressed.'

'You should eat, you know.'

'No point. Nothing stays down.'

'Why not?'

'I don't know. Stress? The slightest thing has me throwing up. This is killing us, Grace.'

'Lucy, you shouldn't be vomiting. No matter how stressed. Loss of appetite? Yes. Diarrhoea? Yes. But not vomiting. How long has this been going on?'

'Since the court case.'

'But that's, what, three weeks ago? You must be exhausted.'

'Tell me about it.'

'You're out of breath. Do you want to sit down?'

'Yeah.' We've reached a bench on the side of the hill where the trees fall away below us, down to the sea. The water sparkles and the waves roll onto Killiney Beach.

'When was your last period?' she asks.

'Do you have to be so direct?'

'Yes. So, when?'

'I don't know. It hasn't exactly been top of my agenda.'

'Think back.'

I sigh. Shrug. All I know is that it hasn't been another thing to worry about since this all began. Then, I look at her, with sudden realisation. 'It's been over six weeks.'

'You're pregnant, Lucy.'

'You can tell by looking at me, can you?' I don't need this. Not now. Not in the middle of a custody battle. 'Stress can make your periods stop, can't it? Weight loss can. I'm about as stressed as a person can be, and I've lost tons of weight. I'm not pregnant.'

'What's the big deal if you are?'

'Are you kidding? It would be disastrous. To announce that a baby's on the way, now of all times, when Greg's children have been taken from us. What would they think? That we're replacing them? That we planned it? That we're getting on with life without them? I mean, having a baby at any time would be difficult, given that it would be our first child together and Rachel and Toby might feel left out. And it's not just the children. It's Greg. Childbirth killed Catherine. Like he'd really want to hear I was pregnant now. It would be a disaster. You're wrong, Grace. I'm not pregnant. I'm stressed.'

'Stress doesn't lead to vomiting. And look at you, you're as white as a sheet.'

'I'm tired.'

'You're probably anaemic.'

~

As usual, Grace is right. After a week of denial, I finally take the test she insisted on buying in a late-night pharmacy on the way home from Killiney. I should be happy. I should be ecstatic. A new life. A little person Greg and I have created together. Instead, I'm terrified. I can't tell him. Not now. When I place my palm against my stomach it feels the same. I'll take another test.

~

Dr Bowman arrives at Rob's before the children. We offer tea, coffee. He declines. I'm about to comment on the weather, but everyone knows I couldn't care less. He asks Greg where he gets the plots for his Cooper books.

The doorbell rings. Greg and I both jump up. I laugh and go to sit back down, but Greg takes my hand, and we go to the door together.

On his way in, Toby trips. He comes down hard on his knees and starts to cry. We rush to comfort him. He wants Rachel.

Dr Bowman has come into the hall. He's standing quietly, observing the scene.

Rob and I go in search of plasters. Good old Rob, making his presence felt, careful to ensure that his role as supervisor can't be questioned.

The incident sets the tone for the visit: Toby sniffling, bad form; Rachel comforting; Greg and I trying too hard to distract Toby. We sound unnatural, on edge. So much depends on this. Everything.

'Where are Joe and Eileen?' asks Toby. My parents.

'They couldn't come today because Dr Bowman's here.'

Toby frowns at Dr Bowman.

'What about Shane and Jase?' Toby asks me.

'Not today, Tobes. Tomorrow, OK?'

'Who's he looking for?' Dr Bowman quietly asks Greg.

'Lucy's family. They're close.'

He nods. Says nothing. Then he asks, 'Do you often have other people attend the access visits?'

Shit.

'Just Lucy's parents, her sister and her kids, occasionally. The distraction helps Rachel and Toby relax and forget that they'll have to go back in two hours.'

Dr Bowman takes notes.

I imagine them: 'Parents uncomfortable being alone with children.'

The weeks crawl by. Finally, there are only days to go. And still there's no sign of the report.

'It *is* unusual,' Freda admits when I call her. 'I'll contact his office.'

It turns out that Dr Bowman is off sick. And has been for two weeks.

'Oh God. They're not going to postpone it again, are they?' I ask.

'His secretary insists that the report will be ready on time.'

'But what if she's wrong?'

'Let's sit tight for now.'

On the eve of the court date, we're still 'sitting tight'. I'm in Get Smart trying to distract myself with work. It's no good. I go in to Fint. He hands me *another* granola bar, the only thing I seem to be able to keep down.

'If you lose any more weight, I'll have to start force feeding you.'

I smile. 'You already are.'

He grows serious. 'How's Greg holding up?'

'Honestly? I'm afraid to look at him.'

He points at me. 'If that psychiatrist says anything other than that Rachel and Toby should come home, he's the one who needs his head examined.'

I circle his office chewing my fingers instead of granola.

He opens his box of juggling balls. 'Here. Have these.'

'I can't juggle.'

'Learn.'

~

And then it's tomorrow and we're heading into court. Knowing that it's going to be postponed. Twenty minutes into the drive, Greg has to stop as, once again, I make my mark on the streets of Dublin.

'Lucy, you need a doctor. This can't go on. You have to get this checked out.'

'I'm fine. It's just nerves. Have we time to stop for mints?'

'Of course, but maybe a pharmacy—'

'I'm going to call Freda.'

'OK.'

Freda is also en route. 'I'm expecting it to arrive by courier at the courthouse,' she says. It's the first time I've ever heard her sounding frazzled.

Does this, albeit sick, man know what he's doing to us?

~

Outside the courtroom, our barrister, Jonathan Keane, looks impatiently at Freda.

She shakes her head. 'I thought it would be here.'

'Feck,' he says.

All I can think is, *What will we tell the children?*

And then we have to go in. Our case is almost up.

I sit beside Greg on a hard, wooden bench, trying not to look at Ben and Ruth with their raised chins and stiff upper lips. Instead, I focus on the judge who sits up there, day after day, deciding people's lives. He does it without blinking, without – apparently – feeling. And that is probably the only way to do it without losing your sanity.

I'm cold and sick and on my last mint when our turn comes up.

Jonathan Keane makes his way to the stand. Slowly. He looks at Freda, one last time. She shrugs hopelessly.

'Your Honour—' he starts.

Then, bursting into the courtroom is Freda's assistant, carrying a yellow envelope. She glances about, sees Freda then hurries the envelope to her. Greg and I exchange a hopeful glance and fumble for each other's hands. Freda rips open the envelope. Then she stands and delivers its contents straight to Jonathan Keane, nodding as she does so.

'We have the Section 47 Report, Your Honour!' he says, just in time.

The opposing counsel stands. 'We've not seen this report, Your Honour,' he barks.

'It's just – literally – arrived. Dr Bowman has been ill. Your Honour, the children in this case have been separated from their parents for ten weeks now. They are suffering—'

The judge raises his hand in an 'Enough!' gesture. 'I'll allow it. Please read the report to the court.'

Jonathan Keane frowns down at the words, words that will save us, or sink us.

'To Whom It May Concern,' he reads. 'I have been asked to consult on the case of Franklin versus Millar and Arigho. To this effect, I have consulted Greg Millar's medical notes and spoken in detail with his psychiatrist, Professor Con Power. I have interviewed the applicants, the respondents and Rachel Millar, aged twelve, who requested a hearing in a letter I enclose with this report.'

Greg and I exchange a surprised glance. Greg looks so proud I could cry.

Jonathan Keane continues to read. 'I have attended an access visit between the children, Rachel and Toby Millar, and their father, Greg Millar, and stepmother, Lucy Arigho. I have witnessed the children interact with their grandparents, Benjamin and Ruth Franklin. I have also spoken to the principal of the children's school. These are my findings.'

Breathe, Lucy. Breathe.

'Firstly, it is clear to me that the children's primary bond is with their father.' Keane looks up, pausing for effect. 'He has been a guardian to Rachel for twelve years and a sole guardian to both children for seven. It has been suggested that he is a danger to his children on the basis of past episodes relating to dangerous driving and suicidal urges. I have taken this claim very seriously in my evaluation of this case.'

Is this good or bad? I thought it was good, but now . . .

'Having gone through Mr Millar's notes and consulted with Professor Power, I am in no doubt that these episodes were the direct result of bipolar disorder, a condition with which Mr Millar was diagnosed shortly after the events took place. This is important as it explains his behaviour. The crucial fact, however, in evaluating this case is not whether or not Mr Millar was a danger two years ago, prior to diagnosis, but whether or not he is a danger to his children now.'

I squeeze Greg's hand.

'Mr Millar has, from the time of diagnosis, responded well to treatment. His improvement has been steady and lasting. He has had no relapses of either mania or depression. He has an excellent understanding of his condition and the need to adhere to medical treatment. When this treatment began to interfere with his writing, though tempted, he did not discontinue it, appreciating, as he did, the importance of compliance. He worked with his physician at securing an alternative solution. This is very encouraging. Mr Millar has never missed a doctor's or outpatient appointment and has regularly attended anxiety management classes. He has a healthy lifestyle, and was happy and fulfilled prior to the removal of his children. He had taken up his career again, writing a book on his experience of bipolar disorder that has proven helpful, not only to Mr Millar himself and his family, but to many people who suffer from this, often stigmatised, condition. As Professor Power's report for this court indicates, the completion of such a work is indicative of Mr Millar's sound mental health.'

I'm still waiting for the 'but'.

'Mr Millar has the support of a wife who has helped him through the hugely challenging times pre and post diagnosis. She has been, and continues to be, a solid support both generally and specifically with the children, whom she looked after while Mr Millar was in hospital. The environment from which Rachel and Toby have been removed was a healthy, caring and supportive one.

'Given Greg Millar's medical history since diagnosis, in particular his compliance with treatment and his lack of relapse, his outlook is eminently positive. He has done and continues to do exceptionally well. I am confident that he does not, in any way, pose a threat to his children.' Keane looks up and pauses – for what seems like ages. Then he's off again.

'The enforced separation of the children from their father, *rather*, has proven detrimental to their mental health. Rachel and Toby Millar experienced traumatic and sudden separation following the death of their mother. To be so suddenly taken from their father, their stepmother, their home and routine has proven a further unnecessary trauma. Toby, aged seven, began bed-wetting as soon as he was removed from the home.'

Oh God. I touch my heart. Tears well. *Little pet.*

'At school, he has become withdrawn.'

I sniff and root in my bag for a tissue. Greg gets to me first with one of his. And I see that his eyes, too, are tear-filled.

'Rachel, aged twelve, has reacted with anger. Her behaviour has become uncooperative and troublesome at school. It is clear to me that both children are displaying signs of emotional distress.'

We need them home. I swear to God, if we don't get them home, I'll take them myself, kidnap them if I have to . . .

'Greg Millar has an eminently treatable psychiatric condition. It is my view that the very fact that it *is* psychiatric has worked against him. While the children's grandparents do not appear to bear Mr Millar any direct malice, it is hard to comprehend how they could initially deny him access to his children. This was most upsetting and unfortunate. I do not believe that the current living environment is best suited to the children's welfare. Rather, it is my view that continued separation would result in ongoing distress and psychological trauma.' Keane's voice grows louder as he says, 'I *strongly* recommend that the court returns Rachel and Toby Millar to the care of their father and stepmother immediately. Yours sincerely, Dr Vincent Bowman.' Our barrister looks up in an 'I rest my case' manner.

And I am full-on crying now, and Greg is putting an arm around me and pulling me to him.

But that's not the end.

Our barrister addresses the judge.

'Dr Bowman has included a letter written by Rachel Millar to support his report.'

The judge nods. 'Yes. Read it, please.' He tips his head back in concentration.

'Dear Dr Bowman,' Keane reads. 'I want to tell you how much Toby and me love our dad and our stepmum, Lucy. We love them so, so much. More than anything. We want to be together because we belong together. Gran and Granddad don't understand. I've told them that Dad has bipolar disorder and he's fine now because he takes his tablets. But they won't listen to me. No matter how many times I tell them. Dad is still a good dad. No, he's a great dad. He's our dad. And we should be with him. Not over here. I hate Hilary.' Keane looks at the judge. 'Hilary is the children's former childminder, now working for their grandparents.'

'I see. Thank you.' He gestures with a quick wave to continue.

'It's all her fault. I thought she was my friend. But she told Granddad lies about Dad. I heard her. She said Dad was dangerous. She made stuff up about him. She made Gran and Granddad afraid. I don't know why she did that. But she did. She said that Lucy lies. But Lucy doesn't. Hilary does. All the time. We love our dad and Lucy, and they love us. You're a doctor. You know about Dad's sickness. You know he's better now. And he's just as good at being a dad as he always was. And we are a family. And families should be together, especially if they want to be. Please, Dr Bowman, make them send us back to Dad and Lucy. Some day, when you're not too busy, maybe you could come and talk to me, because I want to tell you all of this so you'll believe me. Please, Dr Bowman. Children should have rights too. Love, Rachel Millar.'

'Wow,' I whisper. 'Just wow.'

And then the judge is speaking. 'I rule that Rachel and Toby Millar be returned to the custody of their father and stepmother – from which they should never have been removed in the first place.'

Greg and I cling to each other, not believing it's over. It's finally over.

Greg pulls back, gripping my arms. 'We're going to the school, now. Right now.'

I'm out of the bench before him.

We hurry past Ben and Ruth who look like they've been slapped across the face – hard. They gape at each other in silent shock. Ruth's mouth opens and closes like a fish, but no sound comes out. They don't even see us.

~

Outside the courtroom, we thank Freda and Jonathan Keane – repeatedly.

'Can we keep Rachel's letter?' I ask.

Freda smiles. 'Absolutely. I'll just get a copy for our files then send it on.'

'Thank you. For everything.' I throw my arms around her – whether she likes it or not.

'I'm so happy for you,' she says, patting my back.

And I love her suddenly. I love the entire world. Bar two people. Three, including Hilary.

~

Out on the street, I jump up and down. I punch Greg's arm. We run to the car. And, as we race to the school, my thoughts turn to Rachel and how she must have felt when she realised that Hilary wasn't her friend; alone and separated from us. She's such a strong kid. A heroic kid. A warrior.

I open the car window. It seems like centuries since we were in that oppressive, hopeless situation, driving to the courthouse, preparing for the worst.

We're almost at the school when Greg's phone starts to ring. By the time he's pulled over, it's stopped. He looks at the screen, then at me.

'Missed call from Freda.'

We stare at each other.

'It couldn't be bad news. Not now. It's over. *Isn't* it?'

Greg calls her back. There are a lot of 'OKs' before he finally hangs up. Then he turns to me.

'Ben and Ruth want to meet us. They want to talk.'

'Well, they can bloody well wait.'

'I love you,' he says.

~

Rachel is let out first. When she sees our grinning, emotional faces she runs to us. Greg scoops her up in his arms. He hugs her then raises her up.

'I am *so proud* of you. Your brilliant letter was read out in court.'

When I finally get a hug, I add, 'You're my hero, d'you know that?'

She pulls back and smiles shyly.

'That letter was *hugely* influential, Rachel. *Never* forget that,' I add.

She looks hopeful. 'Was it?'

'Ye-es.'

'Even though I'm only a kid?'

'Especially because you're a kid. A very smart, eloquent, tough-as-nails kid. You helped *so much*.' And then I say it, for the very first time. 'I love you.'

Her face lights up. 'Me too.'

'You love yourself, or you love me?' I tease.

She laughs. 'You.'

'About bloody time.' I squeeze her so tightly.

Then a little boy comes running up the corridor. Fast.

We'll make him OK again. We'll fill him with love and security. He'll be fine. He'll be fine.

And then he's in his father's arms, and everyone's laughing. Except for me. I'm crying – again. *Bloody hormones.* I look at our little family, back together, and, for the first time since this whole thing began, I want to go home.

~

Ben and Ruth arrive the following day when the kids are at school. There's no sign of Hilary. I sincerely hope this means that we never see her again.

We show them into the sitting room, in silence.

'We had to talk to you.' Ben clears his throat. 'To apologise.' He looks at his wife, but Ruth hasn't raised her eyes since she sat down. 'It seems that we've made a mistake,' he adds.

I feel like shouting, *A mistake? Have you any idea what you've done?*

'As soon as we heard that report being read out in court, we were most distressed. We believed, we *genuinely* believed that the children were in danger.'

'You could have picked up the phone,' Greg says. 'You could have called to discuss it. That would have been the decent thing to do.'

'With all due respect, you hadn't been entirely straight with us in the past.'

'And why might that be? You'd put anyone on the defensive, Ben, tearing over to France, questioning me as if I was on trial.'

'We were worried.'

'You were aggressive. There's always this underlying threat with you. You don't exactly get the best from people.'

'That may be. Still, at the time, we took your word over Hilary's. Imagine our shock, then, when we heard you on the radio confirming much of what she'd said. We assumed that there were other things you couldn't speak about publicly, other aspects . . . Well, things Hilary relayed to us.'

'Like what, exactly?'

He pauses. 'Well, you never hurt the children, did you, Greg?'

'What do you mean, *hit* them?'

'Well, yes.'

'No, Ben, I did not.' He is simmering with rage.

'But why would Hilary have lied to us?'

For the first time, Ruth looks up, her eyes searching Greg's.

'The fact that we fired her may have had something to do with it,' Greg says. 'If you doubted me, why didn't you ask the children?'

It is Ruth who speaks now. 'We felt that they had been damaged enough.'

I know, right there and then, that she is the one behind all of this. She is the one who believed Hilary, who worried for the children, who nagged her husband to act.

'We are so sorry, Greg, Lucy,' she rushes. 'We should have come to you. But we were afraid for the children. We felt we should act quickly. We truly believed they were in danger. And when they came to stay, they seemed so unhappy. We thought it was because they'd been damaged. Toby wetting his bed, Rachel so rebellious . . .'

'They had been damaged,' Greg says. 'By being taken away from their family, their security.'

Tears fill her eyes, and she roots in her handbag for a tissue.

Ben takes over. 'We know, now, that we were wrong. That's why we came to apologise. We cannot apologise enough. We should have had more faith.'

Suddenly, I can't stop myself. 'Yes, Ben. *And* Ruth, actually. You should have had more faith in Greg, a man who, from the age of ten, raised his kid brother almost single-handedly. Who didn't have to rely on posh schools and cosy networks to make his way. Whose wife broke his heart when she gambled with her life and lost, but who kept going because of his children. Greg Millar is a writer who is read by millions of people all over the world and who has managed not only to cope with bipolar disorder, but to be open about it as well, to risk his own career, his own happiness, to help others. If you can't see that, then I feel sorry for you. I really do.' I realise that, at some point, I've stood up, and that now I'm getting teary. 'Anyway, I've said enough.' I sit down, surprised by my outburst almost as much as my smiling husband seems to be.

'I hope you won't punish us,' Ruth says. 'I hope we can continue to see them.'

Ah!

'You're their grandparents,' Greg says. 'And, much as I'm tempted, I'd never deny them access to you. It might be a while, though, before they're ready to visit. Especially Rachel.'

Ruth bows her head. 'We understand.'

When they're gone, Greg hugs me. 'Thank you for making me sound amazing.'

I kiss him. 'You *are* amazing.'

'When you sum me up like that I *do* sound pretty amazing.' He smiles. 'Damn. I should have recorded you.'

45.

What I hadn't realised was that, while my imperfect family was falling back into place, a perfect one was falling apart.

'I'm leaving Kevin,' Grace announces to me, a week after Rachel and Toby have come home.

I look at her, thinking of the boys. 'Grace, I know things have been difficult between you, but your relationship is so normal, so stable . . .'

'Too normal. Too stable. I can't breathe.'

'But you're the perfect couple . . .'

'That's the whole point. Nothing's perfect enough for Kevin. Not me. Not the kids. Not the house. I'm suffocating. Dying.'

I don't know what to say.

'He's so controlling. I've spent my life striving for perfection. I'm just so tired.' She looks it, shoulders slumped, face drawn.

But I can't let her give up. 'I thought you liked things perfect.'

'I thought I did, too. Until I had kids. I don't want them to be like me, living up to other people's expectations. I want them to be kids, just plain, ordinary kids who're allowed to get grubby, messy, be crabby, noisy. But that's not what Kevin wants. Oh no. He wants them seen, not heard, in bed before he gets home, squeaky clean. I want real live boys with jam on their faces, scuffed shoes, mismatched socks, long hair. I want them to breathe. *I* want to breathe. Do what I want, when I want. Go out at night instead of staying in listening to him moan about other people so he can feel better about himself. I want to work. I want my life back. I'm tired of being held up to the light and checked for smudges. Have you any idea how hard it is to live with someone who always expects more?'

'Yes.' We grew up with the same mother – a mother who has changed, but who Grace substituted with Kevin.

'You know the funny thing?' Grace asks. 'You always envied me, but I envy you. You've always done your own thing. Gone to art college. Married a man you loved despite the challenges; challenges you've got through together. You're so lucky.'

I smile, still bruised by all that has happened.

'And what did I do? Married a man who was perfect on paper.'

'A lot of people would think that I made a mistake.'

'Well, they'd be wrong. Look how it's worked out. And do you know why it has? Because you married for the right reason, the only reason to marry – love.'

'I'm sure there are millions of people who married for love and it didn't work out. I'm sure there are millions of people who would advise against marrying for love.'

'Well, I'll tell you what I'd advise against – marrying for logic. If I was to do it all again, I'd go for passion, risk, adventure.'

'It's not all it's cracked up to be.'

'If I stay in this marriage, I'll die. I will. I'm not going to let it happen. I'm too young. The first time I saw you with Greg, I knew I'd made a mistake. I've never had that passion. There's no way Kevin and I would have got through what you have. We're together, but we're not a couple. He does his thing, and we fit around that. I need to be with a man who notices I'm there – for the right reasons. I need passion in my life. I need a life.'

I'm coming round.

'I've learned so much from what you've been through. When you asked for my help with Greg, I realised just how much I missed being a doctor. It's what I've always wanted to do. And I'm not doing it. How could I have given that up? I wanted to be the perfect wife, the perfect mother. But I've only made myself unhappy. I can't hide it any more. I'm too tired. I'm thirty-three, but I feel eighty-three. And that won't change unless I change it.' She takes a deep breath. 'I'm going to ask Kevin for a separation.'

'What about Shane and Jason?'

She looks heartbroken. Her voice wobbles. 'My little men.' Her eyes well, and she looks up and blinks to try to clear her tears. 'Shane and Jase are the only reason I've kept going so long. I don't want their mum to be separated from their dad. But their mum is me. And their dad is Kevin. And I can't do that any more. I want to be as fair as I can, to sit down and talk it through with Kevin. I want him to see them any time he likes. We can even live close to each other, if he wants. I'll keep them in the same school, keep as much the same as I can . . .'

'What about counselling?'

'Can counselling make you love a person you never did? Can counselling do anything when you've married the wrong man? I have to do this, Lucy.'

I nod, take her hand and squeeze it. 'Well, then, I'm here. Round the clock. You know that.'

'I know.'

I wait until Saturday, when everyone's sitting down to breakfast. I stand at the head of the table. Clear my throat. 'I've an announcement to make.'

They all look up, stop chewing, cereal bulging in Toby's cheeks.

'Well, I've two.'

Greg looks astonished.

'Firstly, I just want to say how great it is for us all to be back together.' I close my eyes. 'So, so great.' Already, I'm getting emotional.

'Hear, hear,' says Greg. I can tell he's wondering what the second announcement is.

'The second announcement is also a family announcement, which is why I'm telling everyone together. Because . . . We're going to have an addition to the family.' I raise my eyebrows and smile.

Greg pales.

Rachel says, 'Oh my God.'

Toby asks, 'Are we getting a dog?'

Greg is suddenly standing. 'Are you sure?'

I nod, and am so, so relieved when he smiles, comes over and takes me in his arms.

'What is it? What's going on?' asks Toby.

We turn back to the children.

'Lucy's having a baby,' says Rachel.

Toby's mouth drops open, as if to say, 'How did *that* happen?'

I smile at him. 'A baby brother or sister for you.'

I wait for someone to qualify that with the word 'half'.

Instead, Toby puts in a request. 'I want a brother.'

'And I want a sister,' says Rachel.

A minor battle breaks out.

I turn to Greg. 'Are you OK with this?' I ask quietly.

He slips his arms around my waist. 'More than OK,' he says softly. 'Much more than OK.' He kisses my forehead and draws me into a hug. And as I lean into him and let my body relax, over his shoulder I see, fluttering in through the open window, a bright blue butterfly. It makes its way towards us as though dancing on air, and I smile, because it feels like a blessing: I have been given another future.

AUTHOR'S NOTE

If you enjoyed this book – and I really hope you did – you might consider writing a review on amazon.com. It's a wonderful way for me to connect with readers. Feedback is always welcome and very much appreciated.

ABOUT THE AUTHOR

Aimee Alexander is the pen name of bestselling Irish author Denise Deegan. She writes modern family sagas about ordinary people who become extraordinary in a crisis. Aimee lives with her family in Dublin, where she regularly dreams of sunshine, a life without cooking, and her novels being made into movies. She has a master's degree in public relations and has been a college lecturer, nurse, china restorer, pharmaceutical sales rep, public relations executive and entrepreneur. Visit Aimee's website at: www.aimeealexanderbooks.com.

Printed in Great Britain
by Amazon